# NORMAN SMITH'S HOBBIES

# NORMAN SMITH'S HOBBIES

## Gareth Owen

**To order additional copies of this book, contact:**
Xlibris
800-056-3182
www.Xlibrispublishing.co.uk
Orders@Xlibrispublishing.co.uk
801447

# CONTENTS

# INTRODUCTION

Those of you who have read *Norman Smith's Sojourn*, published in 2018, may be surprised that I, once again, have been burdened with the responsibility of penning some explanatory notes by way of an introduction to the following novel. You will remember that it was due to a set of unusual and apparently coincidental circumstances that I came across a document that was purportedly Norman Smith's own account of his adventures in South Africa under orders from MI6, which I subsequently sent for publication as a work of fiction.

It was due to my association with this previous work, by a stubbornly elusive and unidentified author, that I was approached earlier this year by a recycling officer from Reigate and Banstead Borough Council. He had, by pure chance, found the following novel, discarded in a paper-recycling skip at Earlswood Waste Management Site, printed on A4 paper and inside an unmarked brown envelope.

He was apparently concerned that the unopened envelope may contain some important documents that had been erroneously binned, so he took the liberty of looking inside to see if this was the case. Personally, I find this explanation implausible in the extreme, as I expect that recycling officers have much more important things to do than rifling through refuse skips to find items that may have been mistakenly discarded by their owners. However, despite repeated questioning, the said officer, who wishes to remain anonymous, has refused to change his story, and I have to accept that I will get no more meaningful explanation out of him.

Having found the novel, the officer claims that he took it home and read it. Having done so, he was able to ascertain through internet searches that the hero of the story, Norman Smith, had already appeared in print in the book *Norman Smith's Sojourn*, and that I had been the person who had taken that script to print. He was, then, apparently easily able to track me down and offer me the rights to the novel (which he had clearly not written himself, nor claimed to) for a considerable consideration, which I reluctantly agreed to pay in order to ensure that this new story could be publicly circulated, naturally hoping to recoup my costs in a copy sale agreement with any interested publisher. I had read the novel prior to agreeing to the price and felt that it had some potential publishing value, despite its clear flaws as a work of fiction. It was a gamble that I hope will pay off.

Once again, I have to admit to having had no luck at all sourcing the author. Having discounted the recycling officer, I had absolutely nowhere else to turn for clues. The only thing I feel sure about is that, despite being written in the third rather than the first person, this work bears many hallmarks of the author of *Norman Smith's Sojourn* in terms of literary style and use of language and also in the way it was mysteriously delivered onto my possession, in printed format inside a brown envelope. This is surely more than coincidence.

As for the novel itself, as I have already indicated, it has many drawbacks as a popular work of fiction, though perhaps these can be somewhat offset by a broad-minded and tolerant reader.

It is quite clear from the outset that the author is either unaware of or deliberately ignoring modern values of diversity and political correctness. Much of the material seems to emanate from a different and, thankfully, long-gone era when it was acceptable to create insulting, opinionated, and crass stereotypes of societal groups such as air crew, foreigners, old folks, and housewives, a practice which is now rightly considered unacceptable by most modern readers. It is as though the societal intelligence of the author ceased developing sometime in the mid-1970s and that he has been living since then in an archaic world of his own, even though the novel is clearly meant to be set in the present day.

Of course, as the reader will find, the characters are comic creations and all extreme in their own individual ways, so perhaps we should not take their lack of propriety too seriously. Nonetheless, I think it is wise to flag this point at the outset and question the author's seemingly outdated world view.

It should also be noted that the text contains a degree of scatology that some may also find unnecessary or, even worse, offensive. Once again, I would urge the reader to overlook this as one might a dog turd on the pavement.

I hope this introduction has not completely discouraged the potential reader from delving further into this unusual novel, which I think still has some merits as a form of entertainment, even if only as a means of passing a cold winter evening when there is nothing else to do but stroke the cat.

Donald Osman
Reluctant Literary Agent

# CHAPTER 1

# SURREY

## 1.

If you happened to have been standing outside the Redhill Aerodrome Runway Café on a particular October morning last year, you may have observed a small, high-winged, single-engine aircraft sinking slowly and inexorably towards the westerly grass runway. The crosswind, occasionally catching the plane's wings, caused it to swerve violently before straightening up and continuing its descent.

It may be that you continued to watch as it touched down gently on its fragile rear wheels, like a heron on a lake; decelerated; turned; and taxied noisily towards its parking slot in front of the café.

Once the engine was switched off and the propeller stilled from its frantic rotation, you may have seen a man emerge from the left-hand side of the cockpit. Even from a distance, it was possible to discern that he had few distinguishing features, being neither tall nor short, neither fat nor thin, neither hirsute nor bald. Closer inspection would have revealed a slight but not obtrusive deformity to his skull, as if at some point in the past it had suffered an injury of some sort.

The man waved back at the other occupant of the aircraft, presumably the pilot, who seemed to be completing postflight procedures. He strode purposefully towards the café to be met outside it by a rather attractive middle-aged woman wearing a fur coat against the chilly autumn breeze.

"How was it, Norman?" she could be heard saying.

"Absolutely marvellous, dear," replied the traveller, apparently delighted to see his companion.

"Coffee?" she enquired in the manner of someone who knew the answer was a foregone conclusion.

"A splendid idea, Mrs G.," replied the man, linking his arm into hers and leading her into the café.

Had you then looked back at the aircraft, you would have seen its single occupant gazing fixedly at the couple entering the café whilst scratching his head as if unable to resolve some curious conundrum that had suddenly crossed his mind. His hair was tussled. He wore a smart white short-sleeved shirt, confirming the likelihood of him, rather than his departed companion, being the pilot. He descended from the aircraft carrying a small leather briefcase. He looked back at the fuselage and wings studiously, as if there was something he needed to check before leaving.

From outside the café, it is not possible to see into the control tower, partly because of the distance and partly because of the tinted glass on its windows. If you could have, you would have been able to observe an equally ruffled air traffic controller, trying desperately to replay the recording of a recent Cessna light aircraft's approach, whilst at the same time managing one take-off and two pending landings. Through the microphone on his headphones, he spoke urgently to one of the approaching aircraft, "Redhill Tower to Romeo Foxtrot, do you read me?"

"Roger."

"Please beware of possible severe turbulence on final approach. The previous aircraft through appeared to hit some rough air. I'm not sure if we have a radar fault or a wind shear situation."

"Roger. No signs of unusual atmospheric conditions so far. Are we still clear to land?"

"Roger."

"Yes?"

"Sorry, Romeo Foxtrot. I thought you wanted to ask me something else."

"Negative."

"I just wondered why you keep calling me by my name. All clear for landing."

"Roger."

"That's right. Roger here."

"Roger, Roger."

As if suddenly overburdened with the weight of responsibility, the air traffic controller passed the headphones to his colleague and instructed him to take over. He then listened to the recordings of the previous landing. They made no sense at all, especially as it appeared that the completely inexperienced passenger and not the pilot was in control of the aircraft.

## 2.

There were only a few customers inside the café, probably due to the time of year. Plane spotting tends to be more of a summer activity. Soon, the season would wind down further, especially if the runway strip became waterlogged with autumn rain. Helicopters, of which there were many at the aerodrome, whilst less susceptible to soggy ground, are an inferior sightseeing attraction, largely due to the vertical nature of their take-off procedures and the downdraught that they create, which is completely incompatible with hats, complicated hairdos, and toupees.

Most of the guests were still wearing their coats as the heating inside the café was suboptimal. Even the serving staff were all wearing Redhill Aerodrome Runway Café fleeces.

A man with exceptionally large feet sat at a window table with a large cup of steaming tea, pretending to be occupied with the crossword puzzle in his newspaper. On closer inspection, it was clear that he was more interested in watching the customers come and go, rarely adding a letter to the mass of blank squares in front of him. He looked like a longstanding bachelor, probably due to his shabby appearance and old-fashioned clothing, if not for the fact that it was hard to imagine any woman finding his feet remotely acceptable in dimensions.

The man who had recently landed and his consort ordered black coffees and took a table in the centre of the room, a most unusual manoeuvre, especially when there were still tables available at the edges. They seemed completely unaware of the impact of this obvious lack of social etiquette, which indicated to the others in the room a tendency towards exhibitionism, a characteristic generally frowned on by the people of Redhill.

"So tell me all about it, Norman," said the woman in a voice unmuted by self-consciousness.

"It was absolutely wonderful," said the aviator, rubbing his hands together in glee. His voice was somewhat less easy to hear, especially in the outer edges of the room. "The instructor let me take the controls once we had taken off and were at about 2,000 feet. I think he was surprised what a natural pilot I was. He let me perform a series of simple turning manoeuvres. Then he took the controls, and we executed a backwards summersault. It was incredible!"

"You weren't sick, were you, Norman?"

"Of course not, dear. I took my travel pill before the flight. Anyway, it was incredible what we could see out of the window. Almost to London in the north and the Channel in the south."

"How can you admire the view when you are supposed to be concentrating on the controls?"

"Well, I admit that part was difficult. But I was mostly looking out the window when the instructor had the controls."

"Like you do when I'm driving?"

"Exactly, dear."

"I understand that aeroplanes have dual controls so that, if you do something wrong, the instructor can jump in and take over. Is that right?"

"Indeed so, which could be useful in our car sometimes. Nonetheless, the subject of dual control did actually cause a slight degree of misunderstanding between me and the instructor."

"I hope you were not rude to him, Norman."

"I don't think so, dear. It's just that, after paying all that money for a flying lesson, I was of the opinion that I should have had slightly more time actually flying the aircraft. The instructor, on the other hand, was of the view that, seeing as it was my first lesson, I should spend more time observing him rather than participating. As you know, I tend to learn far better when I throw myself in at the deep end and do not respond well to passive learning."

"Indeed so, Norman. I had noticed that, especially after thirty years of marriage."

"So as we came back towards the airfield, I told him that I would take over the controls and land the aircraft myself, under his supervision. I was determined to prove to him that I could do it. Unfortunately, we did not see completely eye to eye on this proposal. The result was that we were both fighting for control as we made the final turn and descent towards the runway. We were both tugging at the control column and pressing the rudder pedals, though not always in complete harmony. As a result of his interference, I am sorry to say we had a rather rough approach. The aircraft swung around on all axes as each of us tried to exert our own authority. Finally, at about one hundred feet, I let go and allowed him to fly the touchdown, which he did very professionally. I had always intended to let him back at the controls at this point, having never landed an aircraft before. I just wanted to line it up on my own. That's all."

"That sounds rather dangerous to me, Norman. You should have listened to the instructor. Poor man."

"Well, I wasn't exactly not listening to him, especially as he was being rather rude when we were struggling with the controls."

"He was probably petrified."

"Anyway, I thanked him for being so understanding afterwards."

"So are you going to have any more lessons? You could get a pilot's license."

"Yes, I am quite tempted. It was quite easy really."

As the couple's conversation subsequently reverted to more domestic and less interesting matters, one by one, the café's other customers ceased listening in and reverted to their former conversations between themselves. It did not appear that the couple had either been aware of being overheard or were now aware of being ignored.

The man with the large feet had clearly been listening intently, despite his half-hearted efforts to appear occupied with his crossword. For most of the audible conversation, he'd simply sat there, staring at the couple with his mouth open. He now abandoned the crossword and started making some notes with an old pencil in a very tattered blue notebook. When the waitress asked if he would like her to top up his tea, he hid the notebook with his sleeve, in the manner of a child taking an exam and not wishing his classmate to see what he was writing, refusing the kind offer.

The waitress gave him a condescending look as if to say, "Sometimes I don't know why I bother really." It was likely that the tea she was carrying in the pot was extremely over-brewed and tepid. That was not the point, however. In the Redhill Aerodrome Runway Café, it is generally considered polite to accept a free top-up, even if it is unwanted or undesirable.

Behind the counter, a portly member of staff was laying sausages out on a grilling tray in anticipation of the lunchtime hoards.

"What do you make of that?" she said as the waitress with the teapot returned.

"Bloody rude, that's what I call it," she replied, though it was unclear to the portly lady exactly what she was referring to.

"I mean what do you make of that couple, talking so loud?"

"Oh them. That's the Smiths. My sister used to clean for them. They live in Reigate. I think they are a bit hoity-toity. Apparently, she rules the roost in their household."

"I bet she does. All fur coat and no knickers."

"Who's the geezer with the massive hooves by the window?"

"Don't know. Not seem 'im before."

"Rude bugger. Looks like a copper to me."

"Don't worry. Everything's above board today."

A fly on the kitchen wall that had recently laid its eggs in the pointing behind the fridge might have found that remark interesting if it could understand human speech or had any awareness of the remit of health and safety executive.

Outside, the westerly breeze was gusting more strongly, and there were spots of rain in the air. Most aircraft had returned from their morning flights, and the unused runway looked nothing more than a field of vacant pasture. Crows squawked, relieved to be heard once more now that they did not have to compete with a cacophony of aero engines. Some of the grounded aircraft had been covered in tarpaulins to protect them from the weather, whist others had been towed away to the hangar.

In the control tower, the air traffic controllers were relieved by the virtual cessation of local air traffic and were both drinking coffee from thermos flasks that their wives had apparently prepared for them before the shift. The man who had guided down Mr Smith and his instructor had played the tapes to his colleague and was discussing them with him. The recording was not clear, but one could perceive how things had evolved in this cockpit:

"OK, Mr Smith we are now at 1,000 feet. I will take back the controls now.

"Mr Smith, I said that I will now take back the controls."

"I think I will keep going a little bit longer. I am sure I can align us with the final landing approach path if I take a sharp right turn now."

"No, Mr Smith. That is too acute an angle; we will stall. I am taking the controls."

"Just a minute. I think I am getting the hang of this."

"Let go of the control column and take your feet off the rudder pedals."

"Woops, that was a bit of a bump!"

"Let go immediately, Smith. Do you want us to crash?"

"Why are you trying to level out? We need to turn more."

"Because we are not on the approach path. I am going to abort the landing."

"I have put on full flaps and opened the throttle. I think that should do the trick."

"Let go of the bloody controls. We are heading straight for the control tower."

"Just needs a bit of fine-tuning. There, full left rudder."

"You will break off the rudder doing that!"

"What's this button for?"

"Please do not touch any of the controls, Mr Smith. We are dangerously low."

"I'll pull back a bit and give the engine a bit more throttle then."

"For fucks' sake, Mr Smith. Give me control of this aircraft!"

"Just a minute more. I can see the runway ahead now."

"Do you want us both to die, Mr Smith?"

"Of course not. Just let me fly a little bit longer. Please?"

"No! Delta Oscar to control tower. We have an emergency in the cockpit. I am trying t the wrest the controls from a lunatic."

"Roger, Delta Oscar. You are clear to land."

"Did you hear me, control tower?"

"Roger. Best of luck with the cockpit situation. Clear to land on runway 245."

"Let go, Smith, or I will brain you!"

"All yours now, Captain. I think we are nearly down anyway."

The senior officer asked his deputy "Do you think this will need reporting to the Air Accidents Investigation Branch, Hutch?"

"Probably not, in that there was no accident."

"But there could have been."

"Indeed, but as the reason for this incident was non-mechanical, I think the first thing to do is to pass the recordings onto the Redhill Aviation Flight Centre. They can escalate with the relevant flying school, as appropriate. It is a matter of cockpit discipline more than anything else."

"Have you ever heard anything like it before?"

"Can't say I have. Most unusual."

"I had never really considered the consequences of a student pilot trying to take control from the instructor before. Normally they are too scared to try a stunt like that."

"Good job those things can practically land themselves. Otherwise—"

"It doesn't bear thinking about."

The instructor who had recently survived the landing with Mr Smith was slumped in the Redhill Aviation mess room, situated in the main old block of the aerodrome. His facial hue might have been described as grey-green, and there were beads of sweat on his brow.

"That guy must *never ever* be allowed up in a two-seater ever again," he ranted.

The chief instructor, a handsome former RAF fighter pilot who had been in active service during the first Gulf War patted the instructor reassuringly on the back.

"No worries on that score, Winterbottom. Norman Smith's name has already been marked down on the 'barred' list, which will be circulated to all the local airfields. I doubt if he will be up to those pranks again any time soon."

# 3.

Norman Smith had been going through a slightly unsettled period. Since his retirement over a year previously, he had dabbled with a number of hobbies and pastimes, some less successfully than others. These included writing a definitive tome on tax accounting (still only on chapter three), scuba diving (failed the beginners course), taxidermy (struggling to grasp the basic fundamentals of the art), motorbike maintenance (the stripped-down cylinders of a Triumph Bonneville had laid in pieces on the garage for six months), politics (joined the labour and conservative parties simultaneously), cycling (fair weather only), and, most recently, aviation.

Being a man of impulsive enthusiasm, he was prone to become excited about many interesting projects and pastimes, but this flawed trait was, in itself, the reason for his discontent. He was quick to jump head-first into new interests but constantly craved the stimulation of embarking on something new. As a result, whilst he rarely gave up on anything, his commitment to any single venture was prone to wane and become diluted as other new ones came up, and there was no correlation between the level of aptitude and the level of optimism he felt about any new obsession. Retirement had aggravated this long-standing situation, in that the continuity and discipline of work was no longer present in his life. Some might say he now had too much time to indulge his whims. Others might say he was an inveterate dabbler.

To Mrs G, such flitting from one thing to another on her husband's part was almost incomprehensible, she being one of those people who preferred a more stable, if confined, range of interests, such as meeting friends for coffee, body maintenance, holidaying abroad, being a committee member of the Women's Institute, badminton, and reading magazines. Whilst she was keen to support her husband in his pastimes because they kept him active and motivated, both key attributes in the war against male decrepitude, she found the pace of change in them bewildering. In practical terms, this meant that it was hard for her to keep abreast of Norman's latest fads when discussing the shortcomings of husbands at her monthly book club meetings. This uncertainty carried the risk of implying to the ladies in the club that she was at risk of losing control of her husband, a potentially humiliating admission.

Mr Smith was sitting at the kitchen table flicking through a recent newsletter from the Institute of Chartered Accountants, of which he was still a member. His wife was making coffee.

"Funny thing, dear. I have been trying to book a second flying lesson all morning, but for some reason there are absolutely no slots in the foreseeable future with any of the Redhill Aerodrome flying clubs. The same seems to be the case at Biggin Hill and Shoreham. The only slot I could find was for a beginners' gliding lesson at Kenley, but I am not really interested in flying without an engine."

"Well, I suppose there are a lot of people learning to fly," said Mrs G sagely, her face strangely terrifying due to the hot water from the kettle having condensed on both the lenses of her glasses. "I assume you are still sitting there, aren't you, Norman?"

"Yes, indeed, dear. Just keep walking, and you will bump into me."

"I told you that you should have booked a series of lessons together in the first place, instead of just one taster session," continued Mrs G, sitting down as the mist on her lenses cleared as suddenly as it had appeared and experiencing momentarily the wonder of a patient waking up after a cataract operation.

"Hindsight is a wonderful thing, dear. I agree with you. It was pure parsimony on my part. There is no excuse."

"Well at least you have allowed yourself to fork out on some shaving equipment at last," said Mrs G, her side-track a reference to the fact that her husband had recently shaved off a rather unkempt beard he'd been sporting since his retirement.

"Indeed. I am glad you have noticed. I think it takes years off me, don't you?" asked her clean-shaven husband, stroking his smooth cheeks with the palm of his hand.

"At least you look normal now. That beard was absolutely repulsive, if I may say so, now that it has disappeared—not to mention being extremely unhygienic."

"There is a lot to be said for not shaving. But, whilst I think describing my beard as 'repulsive' to be rather insensitive, I do tend to agree that there are two sides to the argument when it comes to beards."

"Not as far as I am concerned," responded Mrs G, in a tone of impending imperiousness.

Her husband pulled at his wedding ring nervously.

"Beards are for barbarians, goats, and apes. Not civilised human beings."

"Well, I'm glad you approve of my decision to remove it, dear. Now, as I was saying, my plans to learn to fly are in tatters, which is very disappointing, seeing how much I enjoyed my first flight. But fear not. I have a plan. To be honest, I do not think flying a small twin-seater is really challenging enough. It seems extremely easy to me. What I would really like to do is learn to fly an airliner."

Mrs G tried very hard to prevent her eyes from rising heavenwards. Despite being well seasoned in the art of absorbing ridiculous suggestions from her husband, it was impossible to ever become completely immune to them.

"That seems a little overambitious to me, Norman," she said, between almost clenched jaws. "Not only would such a project be hugely expensive and time-consuming, but no-one would take you on to do such a thing at your age. Besides, it does not seem to me that you would have the persistence to complete the course. It is simply impossible."

"Nothing is impossible," responded Mr Smith. His wife could recognise the tell-tale signs of idiotically smug overconfidence that generally overwhelmed her impulsive husband when a new project came into his mind. "I have already thought it through. I realise that no airline would take me on at my age with no previous aviation experience and that it is unlikely that I would be accepted on a self-paid training course for similar reasons, even if I could afford it, which I can't. However, it is possible to learn all the basics in a flight simulator. So I have decided to build myself one."

Mrs G was frantically trying to find flaws in this preposterous scheme, despite knowing how futile any objections would be. "Is that really necessary, Norman? Whilst I am by no means an expert on computer games, I do know that you can buy airliner flight simulator programmes for your PC. All you need to do is load the software and buy some headphones and a joystick to plug in!"

Mr Smith gave her a knowing smile, which was slightly lopsided, as if he had just suffered a mild outbreak of Bell's palsy. "No, no, no, dear. That would not do at all. I am not talking about computer games. This is serious. I am talking about a proper physical cockpit with real levers and advanced instrumentation, maybe a Boeing 737, for example—like the airlines use, only cheaper."

Mrs G rested here weary head in her hands and started muttering under her breath, an act that resembled someone praying to God for strength and guidance. "But you don't know the first thing about building flight simulators," she objected in a weary tone of helpless resignation.

"You don't need to!" Norman continued, his eyes wild with fantasies of jerry-built airliner cockpits. "I have read about several individuals who have recreated detailed airliner cockpits in their garages or gardens. You can either buy a discarded front section of an airliner or build one from aluminium. All the interior parts can be sourced on the internet or at airliner fares. Then, all you have to do is link the controls to an advanced flight simulator computer and build a curved screen around the cockpit for the projection. Some of these people started completely from scratch, like me."

It must have been pure instinct that drove Mrs G to continue the conversation at this point. Certainly, there was no sense in it. "Norman. Far be it for me to put a wet blanket on your dreams, but such an undertaking is surely beyond your limited grasp of electronics, computer software, wiring, and shopping on eBay. Furthermore, I have no idea where you would construct the damn thing."

"I will buy a Portakabin and put it in the garden."

"And what about my delphiniums?"

"Some of them may have to be moved. We'll see. But a small problem like that is a mere trifle in an operation of this magnitude."

"Norman?" said Mrs G, still defiant in the face of utter defeat. "Would you mind getting a Paracetamol for me? I think another one of my headaches is coming on."

"Of course, dear. I hope it wasn't anything I said?"

"No, Norman, nothing like that. I think it must be my hormones. Funnily enough though, I was thinking what it would be like to have my garden turned into a bombsite only yesterday. What a strange coincidence!"

Norman stood up to go and fetch his wife's medication, slightly bemused by her most recent comment. *I hope she hasn't got a bladder infection*, he thought.

Once he had left the kitchen, Mrs G let out a deep resigned sigh, before getting herself a couple of Paracetamol tablets and washing them down with the rest of her coffee.

Shortly afterwards her husband, predictably, could be heard yelling down from upstairs, "Where do we keep the Paracetamol?"

"Where it is usually kept."

"Darling?"

"Yes?"

"I've forgotten where that is."

"In the kitchen drawer."

"Yes, of course. I just came upstairs to go to the toilet. I will get them in a second."

"I have already self-administered."

"Good show. I won't have to hurry then."

# 4.

The man with the large feet who had been sitting on the Redhill Aerodrome Runway Café observing the Smiths a couple of days previously was now sitting on a bench in Reigate Park observing innocent passers-by with suspicion. This was not because he suspected anyone of anything in particular, but a reflection of the long-standing suspicion he held towards most members of humanity, honed in his long years working for Surrey police. In his humble opinion, no one was really up to much good unless he or she were catching criminals, detecting crimes, or preventing felonious activity before it was committed. This psychological condition was so ingrained that he was even suspicious of himself now that he had retired from the force. If he wasn't busy enough suspecting other people, then there was a risk that he would find himself under personal interrogation, and the odds were that he would find himself guilty. It was for this reason that he never went anywhere without a blue notebook and a sharpened pencil in order to make notes and take down particulars that may be of assistance in future criminal investigations.

It was something of an irony, which no one was aware of, that many innocent members of the public who would not dream of suspecting anybody without good cause suspected the man with big feet sitting on his own in the park wearing an old grey mac, looking at people and making notes. Most of these people suspected he was mentally ill and, therefore, potentially capable of psychotic or violent behaviour towards his fellow man. Others wondered if he was a sexual predator or pervert, waiting to expose himself to whomsoever took his evil fancy. Others suspected him of an unacceptably antisocial absence of personal bodily hygiene, though this was not really a suspicion in the strictest sense, as there was direct evidence to confirm the fact.

The gentleman in question went under the name of (retired) Detective Inspector "Spike" Godber, or just DI for short. As he had few friends and even fewer relatives, the name had not been particularly necessary since his retirement from public duty and was mainly used for official reasons by companies to whom he owed money, such as British Gas and Reigate and Banstead Borough Council. Whilst the police pension scheme provided DI with a generous monthly income, it did not really compensate him for the physical and mental ravages that his years in the force had wrought. The sheer enormity and almost horizontal flatness of his feet, shrouded in what appeared to be orthopaedic boots, was evidence enough of repetitive strain injury to the arches, and the beadiness of his eyes spoke of years of futile and often microscopic surveillance. Naturally, he was bow-legged, and his jaw struggled to open without creaking as a result of wearing a heavy helmet with a tight chinstrap for so many long hours on the beat. It was almost as if he had started to genetically mutate from a normal human being into a policeman.

As the autumn leaves swept randomly across the parkland and the squirrels buried their nuts in an inane attempt to outwit winter hunger, a completely different type of figure appeared and made his way directly towards the seated former policeman. This figure was tall, straight-backed, and long in the limb. He walked with purpose, with the rhythm of one used to parade ground drill, and his short-cropped hair was blonde. He was dressed, unfashionably, in a blue blazer and grey flannel trousers, wearing what looked like some kind of regimental tie. Closer inspection would reveal that his handsome face and square jaw belonged to the chief instructor from Redhill Aviation, whom we briefly met earlier. He sat down next to DI on the bench seat and offered his hand by way of introduction.

"Good morning, squadron leader Mantle," said the sitting policeman with a hint of obsequiousness. A former RAF pilot was one of the few categories of human being that DI could never consider suspicious. "Thank you for agreeing to meet me."

"It is my pleasure," replied the former squadron leader, smiling emotionlessly. "What can I do for you?"

"Perhaps I should explain. As you know, I am a retired police officer, so you are under no obligation to answer any of my questions or help with any enquiries I might be making in a personal capacity."

Mantle nodded impatiently, having already had this explained to him on the telephone the previous afternoon.

"However, it is not easy for a former member of Her Majesty's Services to suddenly abandon all his duties simply on the pretext of no longer being paid to do them. I am sure you, of all people, will understand this. 'Once in service, always in service' is what I always say."

"Quite so," said the former fighter pilot encouragingly, yet apparently without any particular empathy for the adage.

"To get to the point, then. Since my time in active duty, I have had grave suspicions about a certain local individual yet have never managed to gather sufficient hard evidence to form a case against this person. You may be able to help me here, wing commander."

"Squadron leader. Former squadron leader," corrected the pilot.

"Ah yes, my apologies. Well, as I was saying, this individual seems to have, for some time, been engaged in a number of activities that lie in the grey area between the immoral and the criminal. If I were to tell you that his latest foray into the underworld was to wrest control of a small aircraft, effectively hijacking it and nearly causing a catastrophic air accident, would that help you to guess who I am referring to?"

"You do not mean one of the 9/11 Twin Towers terrorists, do you?" suggested Mantle. It was not clear whether this was a sarcastic response or a barrack-room joke in the most awfully bad taste. Neither of the two men smiled.

"I think you can guess to whom I am referring, Mr Mantle, especially if you set your sights a little bit more locally."

Mantle made a show of looking quizzical before slapping his head as if the penny had just dropped. "You must be referring to that chap who took the controls from one of my instructors a few days ago at the aerodrome?"

Being generally unfamiliar with workings of the military mind, Godber was unsure whether the former squadron leader was extremely slow on the uptake or whether he was deliberately pretending to be stupid. Either way, it was rather frustrating. "Indeed so. He calls himself Norman Smith, though I very much doubt that is the name he was christened with."

"Yes. Norman Smith. That's the chap."

"Well, I wanted to pick your brains a little about the incident he was involved in. I am sure that violently and aggressively taking over control of a flying aircraft from the captain, under any circumstances, must be considered as a potentially criminal offence. After all, it is tantamount to mutiny at sea. I was wondering if you had any experience of the legality or otherwise of such an action, from an aviator's perspective, to help see if we can pin this one on him good and proper."

The former fighter pilot gazed expressionlessly at a group of college students smoking skunk in broad daylight.

"To be honest with you, Mr Godber, this is a most unusual occurrence. I have never heard of such a thing happening before. The gentleman in question may have been foolish, thoughtless and even perhaps domineering in the cockpit on that flight, but there is absolutely no evidence that he took over the controls either violently or aggressively. In fact, he was already legitimately in control of the aircraft when the instructor asked him to relinquish this position. Furthermore, there is a difference between operating the controls and being in command of the aircraft. It is quite common for captains to oversee junior officers who are actually flying the aircraft, without this indicating any subversion or mutiny on the part on the junior officer. The issue therefore lies with the understanding of commands given to the said Mr Smith by the instructor. Having listened to the cockpit recordings of the flight, I conclude that these were clear. However, it may be that the instructor had failed to convey sufficiently the importance of responding to these commands to the student, who was, after all, on his first flying lesson and may therefore have been unfamiliar with flying etiquette. Having failed to persuade the Mr Smith using words alone, the instructor had no option but to try to wrest control back by using physical force. It is very difficult to operate the controls of an aircraft when two pilots simultaneously believe they are in control but are actually fighting against each other. There is no evidence at all the Mr Smith became abusive, though he was, himself, subjected to a strong verbal assault, and he did eventually hand back the controls in time for the instructor to make a perfectly safe landing.

"Now, as far as the legality of this situation is concerned I, personally, would be unwilling to take the matter further for the following reasons: Firstly, whilst any member of the public who takes a flight with us has to sign a disclaimer, terms and conditions, and a code of conduct, the fact is that this is all written in very small print on the contract and is not seen until moments before the signatory is in the air. Apart from the wording probably being full of legal loopholes that could be exposed by any half-decent defence barrister, the practice of not allowing enough time for the terms and conditions to be read would not weigh in favour of the prosecution. It is most unlikely that Redhill Aerodrome would come out of any such examination of its paperwork smelling of roses.

"The second reason lies in the clear implication that this incident was made possible by poor instructor training and cockpit procedures. I have been of the opinion that these need to be tightened up for some time, but they have not. For example, there is no fixed schedule for a training flight, even if there may be guidelines. It is purely at the discretion of the instructor how long he wishes to allow any student to be in control of the aircraft. A public hearing on this incident would undoubtedly come down strongly against the flying club rather than Mr Smith, who will be seen simply as the victim of sloppy procedures.

"Now, this does not mean to say that I condone what happened in any shape or form, and I have done everything I can to blacklist Mr Smith from attempting to have flying lessons at any training aerodrome in the south-east of England. He is clearly a public menace. However, that does not mean that it would be possible to convict him of any criminal activity, much as I would like this to be otherwise."

Former DI Godber listened intently as the flying ace spoke, making regular notes as he did so. By the time Mantle had concluded his disposition, he was beginning to look somewhat crestfallen. "So, if I have fully understood what you have told me, you would tend to side with the perpetrator rather than defend the public and the flying community from such criminal behaviour?"

Mantle remained impassive, apart from a slight twitch above his clear blue left eye. "Mr Godber, you have misrepresented what I said. I do not side with the perpetrator at all. Quite the contrary in fact. However, you asked me about the legality or otherwise of such an action. I have merely tried to point out that I do not consider that any court in the land would consider this to be a criminal offence and that, from my perspective, blame for the incidence is far more likely to be attributed to the flying club than to the defendant. That is my professional opinion. As a former police officer, I am sure you are more familiar with the law than I am and are perfectly entitled to hold a different opinion."

At this point, it was clear that Godber had stopped listening. He was staring intently on the spliff that was being handed round the group of college students sitting on the grass in a circle a hundred yards or so away.

Mantle looked at him gazing and continued. "I think you may have more luck with a conviction among that group, Mr Godber. Now, I must go, as I have several policies and procedures to rewrite."

Godber looked away from the appalling scene of youth crime being committed right in front of his beady eyes, towards the departing figure of the former squadron leader. "Thank you for your kind assistance," he shouted after him, but the receding figure made no sign of acknowledgement. Timing had never really been DI Godber's strongest trait.

# Interlude

*Excuse me.*

Who is it?

*Mr Godber. Can I have a quiet word, please?*

Absolutely not. I simply can't engage with characters in my story, especially when I am in the middle of writing it.

*I want to make a complaint. I think I am being unfairly represented.*

You can't. You are just a fictional character. I invented you, and I alone decide how you are represented.

*But it's not fair if I have no opportunity to set the record straight.*

There is no record. You are merely a figment of my imagination.

*But you are putting words into my mouth that I would never utter. As for making false accusations about my personal hygiene, that is totally unacceptable. You tell the readers that there is direct evidence of this but then completely fail to reveal what it is. Besides, my eyes are not beady; they are inquisitive.*

Look, you can't tell me what adjectives to use. Nor can you say what observations about you I need to substantiate. You have to take it as read that I know all about you, and that is the end of it.

*Also, I am very suspicious of that Mantle character. I think he is an imposter. No one from the services would be so weak as to admit failings in his own organisation so readily.*

That is for me to judge, not you. Besides, you don't even know how this story is going to develop. It is far too early to come to any conclusions at all.

*And why do you keep mentioning my feet? That is disability discrimination.*

You are not disabled. You just have large feet.

*Well I just want you to know that I am not at all happy with this portrayal. It is deliberately slanted to make me appear a laughing-stock to the reader.*

No, it is not. It is how I see you in my mind's eye. Otherwise, you would not exist at all.

*But I do exist. Otherwise, how could I be talking to you?*

I am talking to myself.

*No, you are not. I am saying things you were not expecting to hear.*

But that happens in my dreams anyway, so it is not inconsistent with my imaginative process.

*It is a pity that the characters in your stories do not have more opportunity to say things you are not expecting to hear.*

They do

*Not really. Take myself for example. I am primarily cast as a paper-thin caricature of a retired policeman, so I say and do things that conform to that caricature. They are predictable and expected.*

Only to you, Godber, because you are just a fictional character with no imagination of your own. In fact, I very much doubt that you even have a sense of humour.

*How do you know?*

I don't know. I doubt, but I haven't decided yet. However, on the whole, I think you are a funny enough character already without needing to have a sense of humour as well.

*I don't think I am funny*

Well that just proves you don't have a sense of humour. Now, get back to the page. After all, your entire substance is merely a series of printed words. If you interrupt me again I will have to write you out of the script completely, and please do not mention to the other characters that you have tried (and failed miserably) to engage with me. It is hard enough writing a story without being criticised by your own creations left, right, and centre.

*You are a very arrogant storyteller, in my opinion.*

Your opinion counts for nothing. I am the writer, and I can write what I want about you. However, the pertinent point is that I am real, and you are not.

*Are you?*


# 5.

As Norman had taken his 1968 Morris Minor Traveller for a spin on the countryside after a complete oil change, Mrs G took the opportunity to luxuriate in the lounge, reading *Vogue*, hopefully without interruption. She was a handsome woman who, whilst still having certain pretentions to glamour, realised that middle age bestowed on her an element of dignity that should not be compromised by inappropriately ostentatious attire. Her taste in clothing was generally revered among those who were discerning enough to notice, and she took great care of her abundant hair, as one would a beloved pet. For her, *Vogue* magazine was not the font of all aspiration but merely a compendium by which to compare and align her own personal taste against those presented on the pages. Clearly, fashion was always skewed towards the young, who generally looked attractive whatever they wore, and she was not fooled by the delusion that wearing outrageous costumes or make-up made you attractive. However, there may be ideas to be gleaned from haute couture that could be incorporated into her own personal style.

It was a shame that Norman seemed to take so little interest in her appearance. This, she considered, was extremely remiss of him and an aspect of her persona that he took far too much for granted. He seemed much more interested in the cost of clothing and beauty treatments than in their results; a typically male way of looking at things, incomprehensible given that we all know that nothing in this life comes to one who is not prepared to invest in it. She had long given up trying to educate her husband on the importance of outward appearances, accepting that he would always remain unwilling to concede that style should almost always override comfort.

Her husband's lack of appreciation did not deter Mrs G from continuously striving for sartorial perfection, much as her own lack of interest in motorbike engine cylinder blocks did not deter him from pursuing his passion for that particularly dry subject. However, she did occasionally let herself dream of having a well-dressed and dashing partner at her side, especially on the occasions when people who mattered were watching.

On this occasion, Mrs G was wearing baggy mauve trousers, matching loafers, and a fitted white blouse decorated with a large silver Aztec necklace. It was nothing special, but acceptable should someone she knew suddenly drop by for a coffee or gin and tonic.

Attention to her appearance was just one of the means by which Mrs G communicated her innate good taste to the outside world. Another, equally compelling, art in this discipline was interior home décor. The Smiths' lounge was festooned with colourful cushions, set against padded furniture of muted yet matching single hues. The room was carpeted in a light-coloured wool cross pile without the adornment of oriental rugs. The fact that she had not been converted to the mode for parquet or wooden flooring throughout the house demonstrated her independence of thought, preferring to spurn such vulgarity due to her abhorrence of the bare and impractical. The white walls of the lounge were sparsely, yet architecturally decorated with a cross section of works of art hanging in an interesting mixture of frames, elevations and sizes, designed to catch the attention rather than please the eye. Importantly, there were no family photographs on display and very few ornaments, though those that were visible were clearly extremely expensive.

Mrs G had never really considered these passions as hobbies. They were too deeply seated in her subconscious. However, they did share some of the characteristics of hobbies in that they were all-consuming, existentially pointless, self-serving, and tended to require considerable funding. Nonetheless, she would no doubt argue that her passions were fundamental rather than extraneous in that they concerned themselves with basic instincts, unlike her husband's hobbies, which were so esoteric as to be utterly devoid of meaningful purpose.

That said, Mrs G sometimes railed against what appeared to be the archetypal stereotype of middle-class, middle-aged, Home Counties women that she and her friends portrayed. There was a strong sense of unconformity and even rebelliousness hidden just beneath her veneer of respectability, which meant that she was aware of the conformism into which she had been dragged over the years. This engendered a degree of admiration for her husband's carefree eccentricities.

Suddenly, the doorbell rang, interrupting her absent-minded reading of an article entitled "Fashion and the Menopause". Hoping that it would be one of her friends, perhaps popping round for a cup of coffee and a chat, Mrs G glanced at her reflection in the hall mirror, satisfied with what she saw, and she went to answer it. Disappointingly, a tradesman was standing on the doorstep. He wasn't even particularly handsome.

"Would that be Mrs Smith, by any chance?"

"No, I am afraid not. Why do you ask?"

"Because I have a delivery for a Mr Smith, at this address. Is he in?"

"No. Not at the moment. Can I take the delivery on his behalf?"

"You can only sign for it if you are his husband, guardian, or official partner."

"Why?"

"Because them is the rules, madam."

"Well I am his wife."

"Begging your pardon, madam, but you just said you were not Mrs Smith."

"I am not. I am Mrs G."

"Then how can you be the Mr Smith's wife?"

"It's a complicated story, but believe me, I am his wife. No one else would have put up with him for the last thirty years."

"I am not entirely sure I am understanding you, madam. I cannot let any old person sign for this delivery."

"Are you calling me *old*, young man?"

"No. It is just a turn of phrase, like *young* man. As you can see, I am not that young."

Mrs G studied the delivery man's face and noted that it had a few lines on it that she had not bothered to notice before. Perhaps he was not that young.

"Well anyway, Mr Smith did not prewarn me of any deliveries today. What exactly is it, a parcel?"

"No, madam."

"Well, is it a box, then?"

"No, madam."

"Is it a piece of furniture?"

"No, madam."

"Look. Will you stop wasting my time and tell me what it is?"

"Well, there's no harm in telling you what it is, I suppose. But you can't sign for it unless you can prove that you are the recipient's wife."

"Well? What is it?"

The delivery man stepped back and pointed towards the end of the drive, where an extremely dirty articulated truck was parked. On the trailer, behind the cab, a huge silver-coloured metal object was tied on with lashing ropes, partially obscured by an enormous tarpaulin sheet.

"There must be some mistake," said Mrs G, mystified. "We have not ordered any large-scale industrial equipment. I am sure of that."

"Well it says here, madam," said the driver, reading from a delivery sheet he had withdrawn from his pocket, "that Mr Smith has ordered, and paid for, one Boeing 737 forward section, nose cone, and cockpit. I have been instructed to use our crane to place it in your garden. It will be a very tight fit in the front, madam, but I think we will just about be able to do it. Once the item is signed for by an authorised signatory, that is."

Mrs G looked visibly shaken by this news. Clearly, her husband had failed to forewarn her of the speed with which he was making plans for his latest hobby. Furthermore, the sheer enormity of the object was nothing less than intimidating. It would be impossible to hide the embarrassment of such a delivery from the neighbours and would be a complete eyesore sitting on the front lawn, excluding all light from entering the front windows of the house.

"What a pity. You will have to take it away, as I cannot sign for it," said Mrs G, struggling to keep her voice calm.

"As you wish, madam, but there will be a charge for storage and redelivery—a quite substantial charge, I would imagine. We are talking thousands of pounds here, I would say. But if you are not Mr Smith's wife, he will just have to accept this. We do give forty-eight hours prewarning for deliveries, so he should have been here to collect."

Mrs G eyed up the delivery man and the vehicle outside. "Please take it away," she said dramatically, much in the manner of Greta Garbo.

Just as Mrs G was congratulating herself on her defensive strategy, a car could be heard parking on the road outside. The engine had the familiar tinniness of a 1968 Morris Minor Traveller. Shortly afterwards, Norman appeared looking absolutely delighted with himself.

"It has arrived!" he exclaimed, as if no one else was aware of the fact.

"Norman!" said Mrs G, glowering at him over her reading glasses, which were nothing more than intimidating lorgnettes with ear stabilisers.

"Yes, dear?"

"This gentleman seems to think you have ordered part of an airliner and instructed him to leave it in our front garden. What have you got to say about that?"

"Oh no. That's just not true," said Norman, pretending not to notice his wife's ire.

"Well, thank goodness for that," Mrs G retorted, staring triumphantly at the delivery man.

"No, no, not at all," continued Norman. "I instructed them to leave it in the *back* garden—not the front."

Mrs G was understandably at a loss for words. On such occasions it was normally possible to hear a low guttural sound emanating from her epiglottis, but this could not be described as speech. It was more of a prehistoric and instinctive reaction to outrage, similar in some ways to hiccoughs.

"Sorry, sir," piped up the delivery man. "We're not going to get that piece into your back garden without either knocking down the garden wall or dismantling half of the house. So, sir, we will have to put it in the front instead." It would seem he was very pleased with himself for concocting this explanation for failing to even attempt to execute the instructions on his delivery sheet.

Smith looked at him patiently. "I see you have a crane on your truck. Why not just hoist it over the garden wall?"

"'Ealth and safety. We would need a full risk assessment and hoist plan to do that. Besides, we haven't the time. Got to deliver a defunct Polaris missile to the Imperial War Museum after this."

"In that case," said Smith. "Put it on the front lawn and come back to winch it into the back when you can—preferably tomorrow or the day after."

The delivery man seemed to accept this solution grudgingly. Perhaps he had already resigned himself to taking the airliner fuselage back to the depot. He disappeared back to the truck and, within minutes, was undergoing a series of complicated mechanical manoeuvres intended to align the trailer, the fuselage, and the crane in such a position on the driveway as to enable completion of the delivery.

Mrs G had recovered some of her composure and was now spluttering words randomly—"too large, wall, delphiniums, blocking out light, neighbours, Polaris missile," and other such mumbo jumbo. Mr Smith new that there was a strong likelihood of another migraine overcoming her shortly. He also knew that Mrs G had once camped at Greenham Common with other ladies equally affronted by the international nuclear missile programme. The delivery man had made a mistake mentioning missiles at all, even if they were defunct.

"Calm down, dear," he said, foolishly falling into the trap of condescension.

"Never, ever say that to me again, Norman," replied Mrs G, her speech clearly jump-started by the quip.

"Everything will be all right, as soon as the fuselage section is installed in the back garden. I have measured out a space for it."

"Did it ever cross your mind to consult me before you ordered this monstrosity?" continued Mrs G, who we all can understand instinctively felt inclined to use attack as a method of self-defence.

"I am sorry, dear. It all happened so quickly. I found the item on an internet search, and they offered next-day delivery. It must have slipped my mind to tell you. It certainly was a good job I came back when I did."

At that moment the delivery man returned unexpectedly to the front door, rendered almost invisible by the sudden absence of light from behind him. "All done," he said, cheerfully. "I have also managed to call the depot, and they have scheduled the risk assessment and hoisting into the back garden for the day after tomorrow. Enjoy your new toy, Mr Smith. I look forward to seeing you then." With that, he disappeared, though neither Mr Smith nor Mrs G could actually see him depart because of the obstruction behind to the doorway.

"Splendid," said Mr Smith, eyeing the massive structure through the aperture of the open door.

"How much did you pay for that?" asked Mrs G despairingly.

"Oh, it was very reasonable," said Smith in a self-satisfied tone. "In fact, such scrap aircraft parts are remarkably cheap considering their size. Fortunately, it was already severed to the rear of the forward cabin door, so I did not need to pay for any alterations."

"You have not answered my question, Norman. How much did it cost?"

"A few of thousand, but as I say, a bargain for what I have got," mumbled Smith, knowing that Mrs G would not stop until she had the truth.

"A few thousand? For scrap metal?"

"It is not scrap metal, dear. It is a scrapped aircraft, but the manufactured metal is absolutely perfect for my needs. I now have the shell for my flight simulator, ready-made. All I have to do now is fit out the interior."

"Norman?"

"Yes, dear?"

"I think I have another one of my migraines coming on. I need to lie down on the settee."

# 6.

A group of neighbours and passers-by had congregated at the end of the Smiths' drive, gaping at the stunted airline forward fuselage section sitting there. Frankly, it was impossible to ignore it, gleaming the sunshine like a prop from *War of the Worlds*, and this was probably why several of the near neighbours appeared to be agitated as well as inquisitive.

Someone must have called the local press because a reporter from *The Surrey Mirror* was interviewing a number of onlookers, whilst a colleague was taking photographs. In view of the size of the gathering, the police had also been alerted, in case the rabble started to engage in any unlawful behaviour. None of the officers present were particularly familiar with the laws regarding severed airline parts on private lawns, but they clearly sensed something unlawful was in the air. Shortly afterwards, a local borough councillor arrived and advised the gathered multitudes that planning permission was almost certainly required for such an incursion, though the councillor was apparently unsure whether or not this had previously been sought or granted.

Slightly distanced from the main crowd, the figure of DI Godber lurked under a decommissioned lamp post, notebook and pencil in hand. This unsurprising observation was made more interesting by the fact that another man wearing a black raincoat, standing about one hundred yards away from the main action on a bend in the road, was apparently observing DI Godber. Closer examination of this figure would reveal that his features exactly matched those of the flying instructor who had so recently delivered Mr Smith's inaugural flying lesson at Redhill Aerodrome.

"Ladies and gentlemen, please make way," shouted the local councillor in a tone of voice intended to evidence authority but actually conveying derisible pomposity and pushed himself to the front of the crowd. "Please leave it to the local authority to get to the bottom of this."

Several members of the crowd, either supporters of the opposition party or else completely disillusioned with local politics, booed and jeered mockingly, whilst the others fell silent.

The councillor made his way up the driveway to the front door, at one point having to squeeze between the wall of the house and the silver fuselage, so close was its proximity to the building. It would be impossible for the crowd to see how he fared on the doorstep this being completely hidden in the dark shadow cast by the alien object on the front lawn.

One of the policemen stood guard at the end of the drive. It was not clear whether he was positioned there to prevent any public trespass onto private property or as a precautionary measure in case the local councillor found himself threatened or in other ways abused by the residents of the house.

Whilst the councillor was in the abyss, the crowd, almost simultaneously, burst into nervous chatter, some speculating on the outcome of his visit.

"Bloody council," said one observer, "always interfering."

Another one, offering a slightly different point of view said, "thank goodness the council is on top of this. We can't have people despoiling the local environment by dumping waste metal on their front lawns."

Some of the more radical members of the crowd seem to have lost interest in the object itself. But clearly seeing an opportunity to score some political points from its continued presence, they started to chant, "Tories out. Tories out!" It was not entirely clear to whom this chant was directed, as the elected member was clearly out of earshot by now.

Others eyed the gleaming object as if it held some kind of Olympian mystery or had simply landed there from outer space. "It ain't half a big bugger," said one, whilst another wondered where the rest of the aeroplane was. Had there been a crash? Rather less cosmically, a number of people could be heard muttering that they were not surprised that this had happened at the Smiths' house.

"Bloody nutters," said one, picking his nose and pointing at another house, presumably referring to the residents of number 12, which was not the house where the fuselage had been left.

"Bastards," said his mate, as if this word held any meaning at all in the current context.

It seemed as if some of the onlookers now saw the situation as a communal opportunity to express general discontent, rather than specific concerns about the unsightly object before them. "And they never emptied my bins last week," said one man defiantly.

"Nor mine," said another. "Bloody lazy gits."

One woman expressed the view that nuclear weapons should be disbanded and another that the dumping of toxic waste material on private property was evidence of environmental destruction and global warming. A boy of about ten asked his dad if they could have one in their garden as well. His father clipped him playfully round the left earhole in wanton mockery of child protection legislation.

After a short while, the councillor emerged from the gloom and stood at the end of the Smiths' drive, clearly preparing to make a speech to the assembled crowd.

"Ladies and gentlemen. There is no need for alarm," he warbled. "I have spoken to the residents of this house, who admit to procuring the object of speculation. The intention is to remove it to the rear of the property within forty-eight hours, where it will not be so visible. I have explained to them the relevant planning implications and am assured that the required permissions will be considered by the council. There is no question of impropriety, but merely misjudgement, in my opinion. In my hand, I have a signed retrospective planning application, which I will be taking immediately to the town hall for consideration."

As he said this, the councillor waved a piece of paper in the air, clearly much influenced by the mannerisms of Neville Chamberlain at Heston Aerodrome upon his return from Munich in September 1938. Most of the crowd cheered and then began to disperse, apparently appeased by the promises that had been extracted by the diplomatic visitation into the house. The policemen herded some stragglers away from the Smiths' driveway and urged them to desist from taking photographs without authorisation. The Surrey Mirror reporter had already disappeared, presumably to file his report, and the councillor climbed into his big black car before departing for the town hall in a cloud of diesel exhaust. Within minutes, the area had returned to its normal sleepy suburban state. Across the road, DI Godber was finishing his note-taking whilst the flying instructor continued to look on, apparently convinced that he was concealed behind a laurel hedge, when, in fact, he was in full view to anyone who cared to look in his direction, which no one did.

Inside the house, a domestic drama was playing itself out. Mrs G was lying prone on the settee in a state of torpor brought on either by shock, migraine, or a surfeit of Paracetamol.

"Can I get you anything else?" asked her husband in a concerned voice.

"Only the truth, Norman. Nothing else will do," she replied, clearly still somewhat histrionic.

"I have told you the truth, dear. I asked the delivery service to leave the item in the back garden, not the front. I was not advised about any need for a risk assessment or hoist plan. I am sorry it has ended up where it is, but this oversight will be rectified in a couple of days."

"But, Norman?" slurred Mrs G, swallowing a couple more tablets.

"Yes, dear?"

"It *is* rather enormous, isn't it?"

"It is a perfectly normal size for the front end of a Boeing 737, dear. That is the whole point really. It has to be life-size."

"But why did you not warn me? This has come as a terrible shock." Mrs G was now pretending to look vulnerable and defenceless, which was obviously a charade and totally out of character. Her armoury of conversational attack strategies was legendary.

"To be honest, dear, I was rather hoping to impress you with the ingenuity of my parts sourcing," said Mr Smith. It was, as always, difficult to ascertain whether he was absolutely oblivious to his wife's likely reaction or was simply pretending to be.

"Well, I am surprised," said Mrs G, grinding the granular paracetamol residue in her mouth between her back molars, as if sharpening her teeth, "but not by your ingenuity. More by your utter blindness to the impact that such a delivery would be likely to have on me and our near neighbours. Naturally, they will be horrified to see such an unsightly obelisk suddenly appearing on our front lawn without any warning, and I cannot blame them."

"As I told you, dear, it was never intended to sit on the front lawn," said Mr Smith, patiently stroking his chin and wishing he had never shaved his beard off.

"But it is absolutely grotesque," continued his beleaguered wife. "It may be slightly hidden from view when it is installed in the back, but it will be no less obtrusive. Furthermore, it will block out the sun from the entire back of the house," she said, clutching at mere straws in the knowledge that it was unlikely that there was anything she could actually do now to prevent the impending installation at the rear of their premises. "Who was that at the door, anyway, Norman?" she continued, as if suddenly remembering something that had crossed her mind long after it should have done. "Probably someone coming to complain, I should not wonder."

"Ah yes. That was Councillor Brown from the local council," he replied.

"What on earth does he want here? Isn't he a Tory?"

"I believe he is, dear."

"In that case, I hope you slammed the door in his face."

"Actually, dear, as it happens, I somewhat empathise with conservative philosophy, especially with respect to personal responsibility. However, this was not a political visit. The councillor was merely asking if we happened to have planning permission to erect the fuselage section on the front lawn."

"And do we, Norman?"

"Of course not. Why on earth would I get planning permission for a structural addition in a place I was never intending it to be?"

"Logical, I suppose."

"Indeed. However, it appears that I will need permission to install the fuselage in the rear garden."

"Had you thought of that before you ordered it?"

"I can honestly say I had not. I had never considered a flight simulator might be deemed to be a building. I was of the impression that planning law did not have any clauses relating to rear garden aircraft parts. But perhaps I was being a but naive on that score."

"*Naivety* is not the word for it, Norman. *Impulsive* and *stupidity* are the two words I would use."

"There is no need to worry, dear. Councillor Brown was most helpful and assisted me filling in a retrospective planning application on the doorstep."

"Do we really need planning permission to alter our doorstep, Norman, with all this going on as well?"

"No. What I meant was that I filled in the form on the doorstep, not that the doorstep was the subject of the planning application."

"Sometimes, Norman, I do wish you would not speak in riddles."

"To put it simply, dear, I have sorted out all the necessary paperwork, so everything is now in order."

"Thank goodness for that, Norman. I would not want us both to end up in prison."

"It is unlikely to come to that, dearest."

# 7.

In the operations room at Redhill Aerodrome, squadron Leader Mantle was weighing up the information he had just received. Flight instructor Winterbottom, not the most proficient or level-headed of Mantle's team, was anxiously waiting for him to talk, evidencing an irritating tic on his left eye, an involuntary nervous spasm that had increased in frequency since the flying lesson with Norman Smith.

"Are you absolutely convinced that Smith has a tail on him?" asked Mantle, buying time.

"Of course he does not have a tail. He's not a monkey! But there is definitely someone following him and taking notes about his actions and behaviour—someone who I believe was formerly in the police force."

"You realise that this a most interesting development, don't you, Winterbottom?"

"That is why I have told you about it," Winterbottom quipped. He was one of those unfortunate people who completely lack nuance in social and professional relationships. It was why he had never risen in the ranks or found a mate. An objective observer may have noted a hint of insolence in his response, especially as it was addressed to a senior officer.

Mantle had often wondered whether or not his subordinate was on the autistic spectrum but concluded that a degree of autism and obsessive-compulsive behaviour was an asset in a flying instructor, a job requiring much repetitive and intensive attention to detail. Nonetheless, there was the issue of communication with his students, an area where Winterbottom frequently scored poorly. Mantle was not entirely surprised that it had been this particular instructor who had been involved in the first mid-air student-tutor fracas that the flying school had ever recorded. "This means that there is potentially some dirt on Smith, other than his appalling cockpit conduct. As such, he is unlikely to complain about our training procedures publicly. Such men generally prefer to hide in the shadows."

"I was not aware that he was likely to complain," replied Winterbottom. "After all, it is me who should be filing a suit against him for endangering my life."

"I can understand how you feel, Winterbottom," said Mantle, despite the fact that he could not. He would never have let Smith take the controls in the first place. "However, rest assured that our barring order has now been distributed to all local flying clubs, including those at Redhill. So there is absolutely no possibility of him having another flying lesson. The incident will not be repeated."

Winterbottom did not look particularly reassured by this explanation. In fact, his tic had increased in frequency as

Mantle had been talking, possibly as a direct result of it causing traumatic flashback memories of the flight in question. "Do you think we could issue a barring order on all women student pilots as well?" he asked optimistically, clearly still troubled.

"Of course not. That would be tantamount to sexism, which I abhor. There are, in fact, some very competent female pilots around these days. They fly better than they drive in my opinion, probably due to the absence of a rear-view mirror in a cockpit."

At least Mantle was trying not to be sexist, which was more than could be said for Winterbottom.

"Now, I have decided to ground you for a few weeks on full pay, Winterbottom, in order for you to address your post-traumatic stress disorder. I do not expect anything of you during this time, other than that you keep Smith and his tail under discreet observation. I am of the opinion that this troublemaker could well bring still more problems to the flying club. I am not exactly sure how or why, but I have a hunch. As you know, I rely strongly on the emotion of hunch, it having saved my life in many a dogfight and bombing raid."

Winterbottom looked relieved that he had been stood down from active flying duty. He rubbed his eye, as if this would asphyxiate the tic. "Thank you, sir. I have to admit that Smith put the wind up me, and my nerves are in complete tatters. But I will be as right as rain in a week or two. Leave the surveillance operation to me."


## 8.

It was a relief to both Norman Smith and Mrs G that the aircraft part had been safely moved into their back garden by the time they were due to leave on a long-planned touring holiday in Northern India.

The vacation was the brainchild of Mrs G, who held the view that there is no excuse for not planning such extended excursions now that her husband was retired. Yet she operated this view in the knowledge that a degree of persuasion and forward planning were required to convince her somewhat reluctant husband of the benefits of overseas travel.

The couple's previous long-distance holiday in South Africa had been a great success, at least in Mrs G's mind, though that was not to say that her husband entirely agreed with this conclusion. He was, by nature, a home-bird, and it had taken a long time to win him round to participating in another such sojourn. He was initially particularly non-committal about the destination Mrs G had chosen, it being so renowned as the source of unpalatably spicy food; debilitating diseases; noxious assaults to the sense of smell; and Hinduism, a religion he had spent years trying to comprehend, without any success.

Nonetheless, Mr Smith had eventually come around to the idea after poring over various travel books and brochures Mrs G provided him with and realising there was probably much of interest to be learned from the subcontinent. It was, however, most unfortunate that the prebooked vacation had come at such a crucial time in the development of his new hobby. The aircraft shell in the back garden had to be sealed up to avoid animal, vegetable, and meteorological ingress during his relatively short absence. And this, in itself, was a time-consuming and ultimately superfluous chore in the overall scheme of renovation. Sometimes, Mr Smith noted to himself, one requires the patience of a saint in the face of interruption when urgency and continuity of effort are of the essence.

He did, however, console himself with the thought that long-distance travel invariably involves flights in commercial aircraft, and there was still much he could learn about the finer details of aviation during the trip that could benefit his project. It would surely not be asking too much to request a visit to the cockpit of any aeroplane he had paid an extortionate amount of money to fly on, in order to measure up and generally take the lay of the land in terms of flight deck instrumentation, even if he was flying on another model than a Boeing 737. After all, the general principles were similar in all modern airliners.

Furthermore, it was not impossible to imagine that the parts he would require for the reconstruction may be cheaper to come by in India, where bartering was an accepted principle of trade and where IT expertise was of a very high standard, enabling him to potentially make contacts and source knowledge and support in the complex process of connecting flight instruments to simulator software, a connection that, until this point, remained a complete mystery to him. For example, an altimeter, displaying the altitude of an aircraft above sea level, would not source its readings from external atmospheric pressure sensors or radar in a simulator but from data fed into it from a microchip. The whole thing was absolutely mind-blowing.

Mrs G, whilst experienced in the unusual processes of her husband's mind, did not imagine that such concerns would interfere with her holiday. On the contrary, in fact, she saw complete distancing from day-to-day ephemera as one of the key attributes of overseas travel. Immersion in a completely different world and consummate distancing from everyday cares were the key tenets of her vision of the meaning of vacations. A simple example of this was the abandonment of any need to prepare food or involve herself with the tedious process of laundry that luxury travel afforded. She simply could not comprehend how her husband could concern himself with petty domestic matters when faced with exposure to a completely new world experience. The whole exercise was intended to take one out of one's self and become immersed in something completely new and absorbing.

Even Mrs G had to concede that this line of reasoning was flawed when it came to Mr Smith, a man who regularly complained if he could not access *The Daily Telegraph* or the BBC World Service when on holiday and who, when employed, had frequently logged into his business email account in the most remote of places, just in case there was an urgent message waiting for him. Furthermore, he had nearly ruined their recent trip to South Africa by attending a business meeting right in the middle of it.

The Smiths were expert in packing for their vacations. This ritual was made easier by the fact that Mrs G took control of the entire process, packing her husband's necessities without consulting him. This afforded her the privilege of choosing his touring attire and ensured that nothing vital was forgotten, especially her copious selection of footwear. During this process, Mr Smith generally hungrily watched television whilst smoking his pipe in the lounge, something he was rarely permitted to do, in order to absorb as much information about national and world affairs presented objectively in the English language, prior to being forcibly removed from this luxury.

He was, however, given sole responsibility for looking after flight tickets, passports, and foreign currency exchange, a burden he bore with the utmost manly stoicism. Mrs G simply did not understand the concept of foreign exchange and was of the opinion that the pound should always be the most valuable medium of exchange wherever one presented it on the planet. Her husband was slightly more aware of the fluctuations of the fortunes of his native currency, having lived through several currency crises in his time. And on this occasion, he was slightly nervous about the fact that Indian rupees appeared to be a closed currency, which could not be acquired outside India. There was absolutely no knowing what exchange rate or commission he might be exposed to inside the country. This reminded him of his primary beef about foreign travel, namely that the standards of regulation and oversight in foreign financial institutions rarely matched those practised at home in terms of rigour and integrity, a situation invariably worsened by the fact that locals often failed to understand plain English or the concept of fair play.

# CHAPTER 2

# INDIA

## 1.

Captain Dodwell dozed with his eyes half-open in the left-hand cockpit seat of an ageing Albion Airways Boeing 777-200, about 40,000 feet above Turkey, half looking at the digital displays and dreaming about golf. It had been an eventless flight so far, and he was beginning to feel the effects of terminal tedium, an affliction endured by many long-distance commercial pilots. First Officer Craig was playing solitaire on his iPad.

"Funny old thing," he said to himself, or possibly to First Officer Craig. "Flying all over the world in a tube of metal. Goodness knows what the point is."

First Officer Craig grunted, not sure whether an answer was required. Captain Dodwell was not generally known for philosophical comments, so his utterance was completely out of context and probably totally irrelevant.

"Mind you, I suppose the money's not too bad," continued the captain, as if sleep talking. It was reassuring to know that the autopilot was taking care of flying the aeroplane.

Suddenly, a commotion could be heard on the other side of the cockpit door. One of the stewardesses was apparently having an altercation with a passenger. From inside, it was difficult to make out exactly what was being said, but it was clear that voices were being raised in a somewhat heated manner. Rather reluctantly, the captain climbed out of his seat and opened the door to find out what was going on. As he did so, an undistinguished gentleman who was neither fat nor thin, neither tall nor short, neither bald nor hirsute tumbled into the cockpit and lay prone on the rather worn Albion Airways blue carpet that covered the floor.

"What on earth is going on here?" demanded the captain, full of all the pomp and bluster that befitted his position.

The stewardess looked ruffled, her tight skirt had twisted round so that the zip was at the front, and strands of her blonde hair had clearly escaped from the painfully tight tourniquet of her immaculate bun. "He was trying to get into the cockpit," she said. "So naturally I told him it was not allowed, but he wouldn't give up. He started scuffling with me. Apparently, he wants to see the flight instruments, but it all sounds a bit dodgy to me, Captain."

"Well done, Dolly," said the captain in such a masterful tone that he could see the stewardess' legs turn to jelly in a subconscious act of prostration.

Turning to the floored man, Dodwell placed his foot on his chest and looked down on him condescendingly. "What the devil are you up to, barging onto the cockpit like this and assaulting my crew?" he said sternly, rather pleased that the incident had provided an interesting interlude during the mid-flight torpor.

Like a pig about to be skewered, the man was unable to move, pinned down as he was by what appeared to be a service-issue black boot. He looked up at the enormously elongated image of the captain rising above him. "I am sorry, Captain. I certainly did not mean to be a nuisance. I was just asking your stewardess if it would be possible for me to have a quick look around the flight deck. You see, I am doing some research about airliner flight instrumentation, and I wondered if you wouldn't mind me having a quick look at the layout and making some measurements. I did not mean to upset the lovely lady, but she was just so completely obstructive. I simply could not seem to get my intention across to her."

"Do you realise it is a criminal act to try to enter the flight deck of a commercial aircraft, sir? It remains locked and out of bounds throughout any flight for security reasons in order to prevent acts of terror. The stewardess was simply doing her duty preventing you from trying to enter."

"Yes, I realise that now, and I am truly sorry. But now I am here, would you very much mind if I had a quick look?"

"Certainly not!"

"In that case, perhaps if I leave my tape measure with you, then you might be kind enough to make some measurements for me and let the stewardess relay the figures back to me. I am particularly interested in the dimensions of the windows, the distance between the ceiling and the top of the front instrument console, and the alignment of the throttle levers."

At that moment, First Officer Craig, suddenly, if somewhat belatedly, called from the front of the plane, "Is everything all right back there, Captain? Do you need any assistance?"

The captain turned to face him and replied, "What lightning reactions you have, Craig. God help us if we ever have a technical emergency. What on earth do they teach you at flying school these days, how to play solitaire without being interrupted? Just get on with flying the damned plane, will you? Check the fuel tanks or something useful like that!"

The first officer turned around to face the front like a reprimanded schoolboy and started fiddling, apparently quite randomly, with switches and one of the on-board computers. The intruder watched him with obvious fascination.

"Now then. What are we going to do with you?" the captain continued, pressing his foot harder into the intruder's sternum.

"Well, if you could just take the measurements, I promise to go back to my seat and not disturb you again," he said, as if this was the sort of deal that would appeal to a pilot of Dodwell's experience.

"You can find out the dimensions of a Boeing 777 cockpit online without my needing to provide you with measurements."

The intruder interrupted. "Did you say Boeing 777?"

"Yes, I did."

"Oh dear, I seem to have made a mistake," said the intruder, trying to remove the boot from his chest with both hands. The captain stood firm.

"You see, I thought it was a Boeing 737, not a Boeing 777. I expect they have completely different flight deck configurations and dimensions."

"As a matter of fact, whilst there are some similarities, the 777 is a larger and more sophisticated aircraft. You could not overlay its instrumentation set-up exactly with a 737." Dodwell seemed suddenly engaged in the conversation and removed his boot from the intruder, who stood up and gazed at the instrumentation like a child in a sweetshop.

"As a matter of fact, this one has a slightly different flight managements system than some other 777s and a completely new communications box. Look, let me show you."

The captain proceeded to provide the intruder with a demonstration of all the instrumentation. Smith, whilst clearly fascinated, was obviously completely unable to understand most of what the captain was telling him, perhaps because he had little knowledge of the workings of an airliner or perhaps because it was not a 737.

After a few minutes, the demonstration concluded, the intruder asked. "Why is one throttle lever forward and the other half back?"

The captain looked down at the levers and suddenly went white in the face. "Craig, have you been fiddling with the throttles again?"

The first officer looked sheepishly at the captain. "I just thought I would give engine two a bit of a rest for a while. The oil temperature seems to be higher than it should be."

"Why didn't you tell me, you nincompoop?" he yelled, resuming his position in the captain's seat and immediately undergoing a series of engine checks. "Now, get this intruder out of the cockpit immediately and tell him not to mention the engine problem to any of the other passengers."

Outside, Dolly, the stewardess, watched as the intruder was unceremoniously bundled off the flight deck into the forward galley area and the door locked behind him, as per regulations.

The stewardess had, by now, regained her composure. "Well, I've never known the captain to let anyone in there before," she said, filing her nails absent-mindedly. "Aren't you a lucky boy?"

"I suppose I am. But I really must get back to my wife now. She will be wondering where I have been."

"It's all right, sir. I won't tell her that you have been in the first-class lavatory with me for twenty minutes if you don't tell her you have been on the flight deck. If that came out, the captain could lose his job."

"Mum's the word," said the intruder, accepting a large double scotch from the air hostess and winking at her more in a conspiratorial than a lascivious manner. It was harder to tell the intention behind her return wink, which the intruder found, momentarily, somewhat disturbing, in a pleasant way.

Norman Smith made his way slowly back down the darkened aeroplane, firstly through the first-class section at the front and then through the business class section. In both of these areas, the passengers were afforded the privilege of chairs that converted into flat beds. Rows of prone, sleeping passengers were visible in the dim cabin light like cadavers in a mortuary. The next section was "premium economy", where, for a not inconsiderate consideration, passengers had access to wider seats, reclining though not flattening, with more legroom than in the "economy" section at the back of the plane, which was simply carnage. It all put Mr Smith in mind of the caste system he would shortly encounter in India, where there was a clear and acknowledged segregation of humanity.

Mrs G was lolling in her premium economy seat with a rictus, unable to sleep due to severe discomfort in the thorax, larynx, and epiglottis. She opened her bloodshot eyes as her husband returned to his seat noisily and took a slurp on his drink.

"Where on earth have you been, Norman? I thought you had got lost."

"How can you get lost on an airliner, dear?"

"Well, maybe locked in the loo or something. Are you quite well?"

"Of course I am. Just needed to stretch the old legs a bit; that's all."

"I hope you weren't doing those ridiculous leg exercises of yours in public, Norman."

"Of course not, dear. There simply isn't room."

"Are we nearly there, Norman?"

"Only three or four hours to go, but I expect it will be getting light outside soon."

"Don't be silly. Its only 1.30 in the morning."

"We are flying east, dear, into the rising sun. Actually, it is 7 a.m. in Delhi."

"Why is time so confusing, Norman?"

"It is all to do with the rotation of the earth and the sun, dear. When we arrive, we will have a whole day to stay awake after a very short night."

"Stop confusing me with all that science, Norman, and pass me an Everton Mint. My mouth tastes absolutely ghastly."

The man sitting next to Mrs G gave her an unpleasant look. It was not clear whether or not this was due to her making so much noise talking to her husband or the verbal articulation of her acute halitosis.

"At least we should try to get some sleep whilst there is the opportunity," observed Mrs G, forlornly.

Her husband had already started snoring gently beside her, so the advice was completely unnecessary as far as he was concerned.

Prior to the trip, Mrs G had persuaded her husband that the cost of upgrading from economy to premium economy would be a most worthwhile expense, in that it would afford them both a peaceful sleep before arrival. Her reluctant husband seemed to be taking advantage of the opportunity, but Mrs G could not now stop wishing they had bitten the bullet and gone for business class. To her, the prestige realised by such a minor upgrade seemed hardly worth it. This would become especially obvious when the business class passengers arrived in Delhi all bright-eyed and bushy-tailed, when she would no doubt be feeling like death warmed up. It would be obvious to them that she had suffered the indignity of spending the flight upright in the back of the plane.

On the flight deck, Captain Dodwell was concentrating on the conundrum of the unusually high oil temperature in engine two. There was not much he could really do about it without shutting the engine down and letting it all cool down, but he was reasonably confident that simply reducing the throttle a little would be sufficient to prevent an engine fire. Furthermore, it was always possible that there was an electrical fault producing a false reading on the engine management system.

"Let's maintain things like this and keep monitoring the situation, Craig," he said, having offered no appreciation of the fact that the first officer had been the one to first spot the problem and take action.

"Yes, sir," replied Craig, clearly slightly unnerved by the development. "Should I check our emergency airfields in case we need to come down, Captain?"

"Yes, you will need to do that as a precaution, but I am not expecting an emergency. By the way, what did you make of that fellow that just visited us on the flight deck?"

"Bit of a weirdo, I would say."

"Interesting chap," observed the captain. "But I'm not sure what he was researching. Seemed to have very little concept of instrumentation layout."

"Did it occur to you that the oil temperature only rose after he had entered the cabin? Do we need to consider sabotage, Captain?"

"That thought had briefly crossed my mind, Craig, but I dismissed it on the grounds that our visitor was so clueless that he could not possibly effect a technical malfunction. Besides, he would go down with us if the old bird sank."

"Don't say that, Captain. I am too young to die."

"Of course, Craig. I was forgetting. You are barely out of diapers."

"Could there be any connection with his fall onto the flight-deck floor and a system warning?"

"I will just check under the carpet where he fell to see if there are any wires or tubes, he may have accidently damaged."

"Captain, I have completed full Boeing 777 pilot training, and I am not aware of any service conduits lying beneath that section of the flooring."

"When you've been around as long as I have, Craig, anything is possible. They often make wiring mistakes at the factory in Seattle and hide engineering service areas from pilots so we don't fiddle around with anything. I knew one plane where they had wired the rudder pedals the wrong way round so you had to press the left rudder down to turn right. Good job we don't rely too much on manual rudder control these days."

Captain Dodwell once again removed himself from his seat and peeled back the carpet in the rear of the flight deck. Underneath was a service hatch, the cover of which he removed.

"Just popping down to have a look round, Craig. If I don't return, say goodbye to my wife for me; there's a good chap."

The first officer had not quite got the measure of the captain and was unsure what exactly was meant by this comment.

Dodwell disappeared beneath the flight deck and found himself in a large hold section surrounded by wires and hydraulic pipes. The forward area seemed to be crammed with radar and satellite navigation equipment, and the front undercarriage was visible through a gap in the floor.

Whilst he had been unaware of this service locker, Dodwell was not entirely surprised by its existence, and it crossed his mind that this would be an excellent place for a stowaway to hide. Feeling the hydraulic pipes, he noticed that two of them were exceptionally hot. At the rear end of the cabin there were some valves and internal temperature gauges. Presumably the ground engineers were familiar with all this apparatus, but it was new to the captain.

It struck him that this was not a place where he could tinker with the sealed oil lubrication system of engine two. However, he did notice a temperature gauge seemingly designed to take readings from the two overheated hydraulic pipes. He also noticed a water-cooling system lagged around the hydraulic pipes, which was switched to the off position. He flicked the switch to the on position, as it was in this mode on all the other pipes and watched as the temperature gauge began to fall as the two pipes cooled.

Upon clambering back onto the flight deck, he asked the first officer to review the engine two oil temperature reading. Miraculously, it had fallen to within a reasonable range.

"Shall I reset throttle two to full power and engage the auto thrust, Captain?" asked the first officer, clearly impressed by the technical acumen of the captain.

"Go ahead, Craig," was the reply.

Once the hatch door had been replaced and the carpet re-laid, the captain took his seat once again.

"Damned if I know how I did that," he said. "Hope it doesn't bugger up the hydraulics."

Sitting on seat 51A at the rear of the aeroplane in economy class, a gentleman with extremely large feet was struggling to fit them under the seat in front. He did not look like a seasoned international traveller and was wearing a crumpled suit and tie. Earlier in the flight, he had shown an unusual interest in what was going on in the cabin in front of him, beyond the rear bulkhead and curtained off for privacy, having wandered up the aisle several times to peek through. His restlessness had clearly disturbed his neighbour in seat 51B, who had been trying to sleep, and there had been a minor altercation involving one of the air stewardesses and a spilled glass of water. Since that time, the man had kept to his seat and was morosely flicking through the film channels, unable to settle to watching anything for more than ten minutes or so. Consequently, he had completely failed to observe Norman Smith's extended absence from his somewhat more spacious allocated seat further forward in the aircraft and was none the wiser as to his activities on board.

Another rather reluctant male traveller was sitting in the middle aisle slightly further forward in seat 47D. He was a man with a slightly nervous disposition and a facial tic. It was not clear whether or not it was this affliction that kept making him twist his head backwards to look down the aisle towards row 51, as if there was something he needed to keep his irritated eyes on. Occasionally, he wandered back to the rear galley or lavatories and surveyed the other passengers intently. Fortunately for him, the gentleman with large feet was too preoccupied with his own concerns to notice the man with the tic who, to all intents and purposes, did not present himself as noteworthy in any aspect of his demeanour if you ignored his facial affliction, which was invisible from only one side.

In the extreme rear of the plane, a coven of stewards and stewardesses was engaged in the usual midflight moan about pay and conditions. They were all clearly tired and irritable, an unfortunate yet inevitable condition for sleep-deprived service employees charged with being helpful and charming to their fellow human beings.

A man emerged from the gloom of the economy cabin, which was now subsumed in a miasma of snooze-ooze, into the rear alley, evidently seeking refreshment of some kind. The cabin crew completely ignored him, which is not to say they did not notice him, and carried on with their conversation. Impatiently, the passenger paced up and down, embarked upon some rather unnecessary knee exercises, and drew up the blind on the left-hand rear door window to gaze fleetingly out at the terrifying Bible blackness of the night outside. Eventually, he plucked up the courage to say, "Excuse me. Would it be possible for me to partake in a small scotch, please?"

Unfortunately, this request was poorly timed, as one of the cabin crew was just reaching the climax of a story about the Albion Airways pension scheme and the attitude of senior management, which seemed to fascinate the others and draw their attention inwards.

After a minute or two, the passenger seemed to give up on his quest for liquid refreshment and was just about to re-enter the fusty cabin, when one of the cabin stewards said, "Can I help you, sir?"

The passenger turned around and looked into the void of the steward's insomniac gaze. "Ah, yes. I wonder if I might trouble you for a small nightcap? Maybe a Bells will suffice."

"Ice or water with that, sir?" responded the steward, like a programmed automaton.

"No. Just neat please."

"Certainly, sir. However, it is my duty to remind you that it is a criminal offence to be intoxicated on a commercial aircraft and that you had plenty of chance to order a drink when the trolley service was active."

"Indeed so," said the passenger, slightly taken aback. "However, I find a small toddy helpful when I have trouble sleeping. I would hardly call that being intoxicated."

"As you wish, sir," said the steward irritably, handing over a rather measly measure in a dirty plastic cup with apparent reluctance.

The steward seemed to lose interest in his customer immediately and returned his attention to the group conversation. The passenger noticed that his hair was sticking up and his shirt was untucked and also that he had two large wet patches beneath his armpits.

"Appalling," he muttered to himself as he felt his way back to his seat down the darkened cabin. It took him several minutes to clamber over an adjacent seat and into his own, strewn as it was with blankets, cushions, eyeshades, earplugs, shoes, newspapers, discarded food containers and breadcrumbs, without treading on his neighbour.

He eventually fell asleep in the infinitesimally modest space allocated to him, wondering why on earth he had chosen to incarcerate himself in such a hostile environment and why everyone else was not screaming in revolt at their undignified prostration. This was most unfortunate, as he was, by profession, a non-executive director of the flagship airline, engaging in some impromptu research into 'the long-haul economy class passenger experience'.

## Interlude

*Halloo hoo?*

Who is it now?

*It's me, Dolly.*

I am very busy and in absolutely no mood to talk to minor characters.

*Well that is exactly what I wanted to talk to you about. You have clearly cast me as an exceedingly outdated archetype* of a trolley Dolly, which is neither amusing nor accurate. Nor is it acceptable, even if it is a minor role.

What do you mean? You are just an air hostess—merely solder to keep bits of the story together.

*That is a very dismissive and ignorant attitude, but it's nothing compared with the sexist way I have been portrayed. Not all air hostesses are besotted by the captain, flirt with passengers, or file their nails on duty, you know. That is such an outdated representation of females. In fact, we are just a hard-working group of individuals who are simply doing our shift as best we can so we can feed our families, mostly.*

Look, I don't really care about you or your job. You are just a bit of colour but not at all integral to the plot.

*Would I be cast in such a minor yet suggestive light if I were a man?*

But you are not a man. You are a young lady.

*That answers my question. You clearly have totally different preconceptions of how to portray women and men.*

No, I don't.

*You are blatantly sexist. Women are not just here for a bit of colour in the story of life, you know!*

Well you are.

*I will be reporting you.*

Who to?

*The captain, of course.*

## 2.

Once ensconced in their hotel room in Delhi, after a brief yet turbulent foray outside the guest compound where they were exposed to the odours, fumes, wildlife, waste matter, and chaotic traffic characteristic of India's cities, the Smiths busied themselves with unpacking and generally getting the lie of the land. Norman was the most rested of the two, having slept for a few hours on the flight, whereas Mrs G, wearied by far too many hours of wakefulness, was just about to succumb to another of her increasingly frequent migraines.

"Welcome to India," said Mr Smith, nodding to his wife and holding up a glass of Kingfisher beer from the minibar.

"Indeed," was all Mrs G could muster by way of response. It was clear she would shortly be retiring, leaving Mr Smith with the prospect of dining alone, probably on curry.

"Shall I get your pills, dear?"

"That would be most welcome, Norman."

"You will be right as rain after a good night's sleep."

"I do hope so, Norman. Otherwise I will never be able to cope with all that cacophony out there, let alone the spicy food."

"Don't worry, dear. It is just a shock to the system arriving in such a strange place so suddenly."

"I expect so. But I can't think for the life of me why everyone has to hoot their horns all the time and let cows invade the public highway."

"We are not in Reigate now, dear. They do things rather differently here, I fancy."

"Norman?"

"Yes, dear?"

"Did you see those monkeys on the hotel roof?"

"Yes."

"I don't really like monkeys. Do you, Norman?"

"I would say that I am generally rather indifferent to them, on the whole."

"Do you remember those awful baboons in South Africa?"

"Indeed, I do, Mrs G."

"Well I hope Indian monkeys are a bit better behaved."

"I am sure they are, dear. After all, they are worshipped and generally well fed by the population."

"I hope one doesn't get into the room, Norman. You will be careful when you leave and enter, won't you?"

Mrs G had lain down on the bed and was visibly sinking into oblivion. Mr G knew the signs, normally characterised by completely puerile conversation.

"Norman?"

"Yes."

"Did I pack my toothpaste?"

"I have no idea, but I'm sure you can buy it here."

"I'm not sure I would like Indian toothpaste."

Before she had finished talking, a regular whistling noise emanating from the bed informed Mr Smith that his wife had succumbed and was out for the count. Whilst this was something of a relief in terms of her not having to suffer any longer from exhaustion and hallucinations, it did leave him regretting slightly that he now had no company for the evening ahead.

Smith acclimatised to the hotel's environs and decided what to have for dinner from an indecipherable menu of meat and vegetarian curry options displayed on gaudy boards standing outside the hotel's restaurants. And meanwhile, on the second floor, in room 201, a European gentleman with exceptionally large feet, currently immersed in a bowl of cold water, was wondering how he had ended up on the Indian subcontinent, foreign countries being alien to his experience or imagination. Judging by the heat outside, he had packed completely the wrong clothes, including a tweed suit and a Crombie overcoat. His numbed mind, shaken by hours in the back of a noisy jet, was barely able to absorb the new impulses that it was being bombarded with, one being jet-lag, the bane of long-distance travellers since the introduction of high-speed air travel, but a completely new experience to him. It bore some similarities to the feeling experienced at the end of a back-to-back night and day shift but was enhanced by the unusual experience of darkness at what should have been a daylight hour.

However, whilst being somewhat confused, there was one fact he had made sure about before retiring to his room and that was that the Smiths had checked in to room 172. This knowledge brought him a degree of comfort in his distress. He was sure they would still be there the next morning. It is most unusual for a married couple to check into a hotel in the evening and then check out in the middle of the night, especially if they were purportedly on holiday. This knowledge meant that there was no urgency for him to remove his swollen appendages from the soothing water, and even less need for him to venture outside his room before the morning.

The man in room 210 was cleaning out his earholes with cotton buds because they had become blocked as the aeroplane he had been on had descended sharply into Indira Gandhi Airport. More used to aircraft than the man in room 201, he was not entirely immune to the consequences of pressurised flight, having spent most of his career flying tin crates at low altitude. He had also gathered sufficient information about the location of the guests in rooms 201 and 172 to allow himself some time to relax and recover. He was halfway through his third Scotch and was idly flicking though the porn channels on his in-room TV as he excavated his earholes. It is fortunate that we all find different ways to relax, even if they are foisted upon us subliminally by hoteliers realising that stimulating our dark side encourages us to more willingly part with hard currency.

The restaurant in which Norman Smith finally chose to eat had the advantage of serving Asian and European cuisine, which Smith considered a comfort, even though he was determined to try a curry. It assured him that any curry served here would be unlikely to destroy all the sensory organs in his mouth, tempered as it most certainly would be for the Western palate. He took a seat alone at a table next to another single gentleman and perused the English language menu thoughtfully.

"First time in India?" enquired the man at the adjacent table, apparently completely circumventing the etiquette of dining room intercourse. He was a rather wiry man who looked as if he hadn't slept for weeks, such were the grey rings under his inflamed eyes. Smith wondered if he might not have succumbed to some awful tropical disease and was in the early stages of delirium.

"As a matter of fact, it is," replied Smith, somewhat cautiously. He wasn't feeling particularly talkative.

"Me too," said the man. "Going to try a curry, are you?"

"I think so." It was apparent that the man was looking to Smith for guidance in culinary matters, which put the somewhat hesitant Smith on the spot. He had no wish to be responsible for inflicting Delhi belly on anyone else. He was worried enough about himself.

"Yes. But I think I will ask the waiter for a very mild one."

"Very sensible. I think I will do the same. I say. Would you mind very much if I joined you at your table rather than us talking across the room, as it were? I assume you are eating alone?"

Smith reluctantly acceded to this request, feeling that he had no real option or excuse. It was a shame Mrs G had conked out so early. At close range the man looked even greyer. It would have been easy to imagine that he had just got off a very long international flight and had not had time to shower or freshen up afterwards.

"Brandon-Lewis," he said, offering a hand to Smith that would not have looked out of place on a cadaver, so thin, white, and pasty was it.

"Smith," said Smith. "Norman Smith. Pleased to meet you, I am sure." It is well documented what a feeble liar Smith is.

Brandon-Lewis seemed oblivious to the apparent sarcasm in his new dining mate's voice, apparently so relieved was he not to have to eat alone. "Just flown in from Heathrow, economy class," he said as if this explained everything, which it may well have done, in a way.

"I see. My wife and I have as well. We were probably on the same flight I would imagine. We were in 'premium economy' though. Much more comfortable and well worth the additional cost. My days of being crushed up in the back are well and truly over, I can tell you that as a matter of certainty."

"I see," said Brandon-Lewis, somewhat crestfallen. "But you have to admit there are advantages of economy travel when it comes to value for money."

"I refuse to admit any such thing," replied Smith, clearly irritated. "Long-distance economy air travel, especially on our flagship airline is a complete anathema. It should have been made illegal at the same time as the emancipation of the slaves, in my opinion. No human being should be forced to suffer in such a way. It is cruelty incarnate and a brazen rejection of human dignity."

"Well, I hadn't looked at it quite like that before," said Brandon Lewis, sipping on some table-water.

"By the way, the health recommendation is not to touch the water unless it is in a sealed bottle. Apparently, the tap water round here is infested will all sorts of unpleasant germs. However, I would hope the hotel water is a little less lethal," advised Smith, apparently relishing the sight of his dinner guest turning from grey to grey-green.

"Oh, I'm not too worried about that," said Brandon Lewis nonchalantly. "In a way, I am in the catering business myself. But that is only part of it. Actually, I am a director of Albion Airways. That is why I was so taken aback at your comments about our economy service. I hope you enjoyed the premium economy service rather more than I enjoyed the cattle truck at the back. I have to say, between you and me, I was quite shocked by the experience. I normally travel first class, of course."

"I see," said Smith, wondering if there was any truth in the Nosferatu Vampyre's comments. After all, why would he be travelling in the back when he could be in the front? It made no sense at all. But then again, nothing did at the moment. Suddenly and miraculously a coherent thought struck him.

"Now, that is very interesting Mr Brandon-Lewis because I happen to have quite a strong interest in the aviation business myself. I am, in fact, in the process of rebuilding the cockpit of a Boeing 737 on my back garden and converting it into a flight simulator."

Brandon Lewis looked at Smith, wondering what sort of person he had landed himself next to. Whilst in need of human company, he had rather been hoping to find a passive partner who would just listen to him. A woman would have been preferable. He certainly did not feel like being challenged on his almost complete ignorance of the workings of an airliner's flight deck.

"How fascinating," he replied, signalling to the waiter that he was ready to order. "I think I will go for the mild lentil curry and a pint of your best lager," he instructed the table walla, who was struggling to understand a word that was being said to him. "And the same for my colleague, I think. Will that be satisfactory, Mr Smith

"Thank you. That would be ideal. Yes, indeed," continued Smith, clearly now having lost interest in the menu options. "It may seem to some like a rather esoteric hobby, but nonetheless, I am not alone. There are several instances of members of the public reconstructing working airliner cockpits. I, personally am aware of another Boeing 737 in Boston and a Comet 4B in Kilmarnock, for example."

The non-executive director looked into Smith's clearly excited eyes and wondered again if he had found himself dining with a complete lunatic. "How very interesting," said the director, preparing to take his first tentative forkfuls of the brown paste that had been unexpectedly rapidly laid before him by the table walla. Clearly, it had been microwaved.

"Now," continued Smith, as if he was holding Brandon Lewis' attention, which he clearly was not, "apart from the sophisticated computer technology required to create a complex simulator, the biggest problem recreating an authentic airliner cockpit is obtaining parts. I have investigated various online sources for obtaining second-hand or rejected cockpit furniture and instrumentation, but it is something of a lottery trying to acquire genuine articles. Many of the online suppliers are dubious sources, often operating from remote parts of the globe, and usually seeking extortionate business terms, such as payment in advance. Furthermore, the airliner breaker's yards are impossible to contact, presumably because they have already secured optimum parts wholesale distribution chains and are not interested in mere one-off retail enquiries."

The director had completely lost interest and was paying little attention to Smith's tedious preamble. The food he was eating, somewhat hesitantly, was already burning his mouth and producing the simultaneous contradictory emotions of pleasure and revulsion, which were hard to process. He took some plain naan bread and a sip of beer to try to smother the embers in his mouth. "All this is most interesting, Mr Smith. But why don't you try your food? It seems to have a most interesting effect on the sensory organs."

Before doing so, Smith determined to finish making his point. "Now, I have been thinking about approaching the large airlines for some time. Clearly most of their parts will be either already installed in operating aircraft or replacement parts from the airliner manufacturers, who incidentally, do not engage in private parts sales either for understandable reasons." For some reason, he was aware that the sale of private parts could be construed as a humorous remark by the smuttier minded. But it did not seem as if the director had picked up on this double entendre, or that he was even listening.

"However, there must be occasions when airlines chose to source certain parts further down the supply chain if, for example, the manufacturer is out of stock or if there is a long waiting list. In short, there must be a catalogue of backup suppliers to large airlines like British Airways, one of which may be able to assist me with the small shopping list of parts that I have."

Now feeling slightly less maxillofacially incapacitated, the director's ears seemed to prick up in the latter stages of Smith's monologue. "Ah yes. An interesting hypothesis," he proffered, continuing, "As a matter of fact, I may be able to enlighten you in this specific area of airline procurement. You are right in the assumption that there are occasions when airlines struggle to source replacement parts rapidly enough to keep their fleet in the air and their finances in the black. Whilst it would not reassure the consumer particularly to know it, there are occasions when parts are acquired either directly from the parts producers or from wholesale aircraft parts distributers (rather than from the aircraft manufacturers themselves). The reason for this is clearly the issue of quality control. No one wants the aircraft he or she is flying in to have been fitted with potentially dud parts that are not licensed. However, this clandestine method of sourcing is widespread, if not common, and most major airlines have emergency parts supply contractors, in case of need.

"It is extremely prescient that you have brought this subject up with me today as it happens. In fact, it is nothing short of a ridiculous coincidence. Apart from acting in the capacity of an observer for the long-haul economy class experience, my visit to India also includes an annual visit to our reserve parts distribution partner based here in Delhi, of all places. I will be visiting the company the day after tomorrow before flying back to Heathrow the same evening. I am sure I could arrange for you to accompany me in a private capacity, and maybe you can make some contacts. If they can't supply you with the parts, I'm sure they will know who can. I know for certain that they specialise in Boeing parts, but they are pretty useful if you are servicing Airbus and Tupelovs as well, I am led to believe."

Smith could not believe his luck and, for a moment, thought he had fallen asleep and was dreaming. Idiotically, however, he had been stuffing his face with curry throughout the director's response and was beginning to suffer the inevitable consequences. His throat was burning as if his tonsils had been removed without anaesthetic and sweat was streaming down his face, which had acquired a dark crimson hue, in torrents. As if in anaphylactic shock, he felt unable to swallow yet knew that his mouth still contained large amounts of lentil curry, which were searing the internal flesh mercilessly. He had no option but to spit the contents of his mouth out into his napkin, a most humiliating and vulgar action that he would never normally even consider, coughing involuntarily and gasping for water or beer. Brandon Lewis handed him the glass of beer beside him, which Smith drained in one gulp before succumbing to a rather unpleasant coughing fit that morphed into involuntary reflux heaving and ended in a series of loud belches that were audible across the restaurant. Several guests looked on piteously as the table walla whisked the soiled napkin away.

"Good God," he finally managed to utter. "Is this some kind of a joke? Did you order me a vindaloo?"

Ignoring this outburst and having concluded this business, the director, seemingly less distressed by the spices he had just partaken in than Smith, launched into an interminable monologue about the importance of his position as honorary director of the flagship airline. Smith noticed that references to his unnamed co-directors and the organisation's parent company were rarely complementary and that he seemed to be at odds with many of the board's decisions. It was probably because of this intransigence that he had been given the apparently punitive tasks of observing the airline's long-haul economy class experience and paying an annual visit to a reserve parts supplier in India. Despite this, Brandon Lewis was full of his own importance and demonstrated a pomposity that did not sit well with his somewhat wasted, feverish, and pallid appearance. Whilst his voice could sound assertive and assured on occasion, he did not manage to pull off his intended aura of authority successfully, due to the paucity of his physical presence.

In normal circumstances, Smith would have retreated early with some excuse or other. He was not a man to suffer bores and nincompoops lightly. However, in view of the offer of help the director had just made, he decided to try to maintain cordial relations with his benefactor or at least to remain polite. Consequently, he provided the odd nod or smile of assent, comprehension, or even approval as the director droned on endlessly.

This was no easy task, considering the storm brewing in Smith's stomach. It was as if a typhoon was raging in his digestive tract, buffeting him with overwhelming paroxysms of sudden contracture and dilation in a number of internal organs that he'd had no previous idea even existed. He had already made the decision to avoid mild lentil curry for the rest of the trip, though was still unconvinced that his companion had not ordered something altogether more lethal than that for purely sadistic reasons. He certainly wasn't going to gobble down his dinner again before first reassuring himself of its edibility.

The task was further complicated by the resurgence of acute exhaustion, which rendered him physically limp and incapable of extended concentration on any subject. The only medication available for his acute symptoms was Kingfisher beer, which he partook in modestly, but consistently. This at least soothed his ulcerated mouth, though it did not do anything to quell the raging cauldron in his intestines.

Finally, Brandon Lewis seemed to come to the end of his autobiographic ramblings. Even he was looking totally jaded by this point—an astonishing feat considering his usual appearance.

"Well, I think I will be heading for bed, he said suddenly, as if Smith had been keeping him up needlessly, long past his bedtime. "How about if we meet for breakfast at 8 a.m. the day after tomorrow and take it from there?"

"Perfect," said Smith, trying not intimate to the director that he was, at that very moment, enduring a particularly ferocious stomach cramp.

"I hope you enjoyed the food," continued Brandon Lewis. Clearly, he had no intention of putting the bill, or part of it, onto his own room tab. "Good night, old chap."

After signing the chitty, Smith headed straight to the nearest lavatory, where, much to his delight, he found some considerable and immediate enemal relief, all be it in a somewhat explosive manner. Overall, he was pleased with the way the evening had gone and regarded it as a testimony to his willingness to reach out to the world and take opportunities as they came, even if this sometimes resulted in a little discomfort along the way.

By 10 p.m., local time, Smith was still perpendicular in the physical sense, having consumed alcohol but modestly during the evening, though his eyes had acquired a rotary motion, which seemed to be boring them deeper into his head. This was the outward manifestation of a brain scrambled by time zone fatigue, which rendered him unable to manage the simplest of thoughts. A homing instinct told him that he must find his bed as a matter of urgency, but his cognitive reflexes failed to recognise the direction in which this may be situated.

The doorman, wearing an eye-catching green turban and an even more magnificent black moustache, which was probably dyed, rescued Smith trying to find his room in the hotel garden and escorted him politely to the room number on the visitor's keychain. Whilst the doorman was impeccably polite to Mr Smith during the period he was acting as personal escort, the minute he had delivered him to his room and closed the door he could not help muttering under his breath, "Bloody Bombay gin and visky cocktail business, isn't it? Alvays same vith British gentlemen. Too drunk to see vat ass they are."

As a Hindu, he was a temperate user of alcohol and confined its intake to wedding parties and the weekly staff piss-up, but he never allowed himself to get drunk. He had seen the effect of the drug's potency on too many hotel guests over the years, most of them Western males who seemed to lose all control as soon as they arrived in India. "Better get in more

Alka-Seltzer, isn't it?" he said to the concierge as he passed through the quiet reception lobby of the hotel to resume his solitary nocturnal vigil at the front door.

As Smith entered the hotel room, he could hear the reassuring whistle of Mrs G's nostrils, reminding him that he had nearly reached his goal. Having no idea where the light switch, the bathroom, or his pyjamas were, he took the decision to go to bed in his underwear. Removing his trousers was no easy task in the darkened room, especially as his lateral balance was much compromised by rotating eyeballs, but he eventually managed to untangle his legs from the unwieldy garment without completely falling over. Absolutely exhausted, he felt his way into the bed next to his sleeping wife and immediately felt wide awake. It was probably going to be a long night, especially as his stomach had begun to reprise its grumblings at the effort of processing so many spiced lentils. However, there was much to consider, both corporeally and intellectually.

Mrs G slept fitfully beside her troubled husband as he tried to make sense of the conversation with the ostensible director of BA, bearing unutterable flatulence and stomach gripes with stoic magnanimity, occasionally looking up at the ceiling fan in thankful supplication. Normally a sound sleeper, Mrs G was prone to semi-wakeful restlessness on occasions when Smith was snoring or committing other bodily indiscretions in the marital bed. Though these interruptions rarely woke her completely, subconsciously, their frequency did tend to detrimentally affect her mood the next morning. Nonetheless, considering the intensity of the cacophony, which was overlaid with the audible turning of the wheels inside Smith's brain, not to mention his incessant fidgeting, pillow plumping, and position changes, it was a miracle that she slept at all.

By the time the dawn sun had risen over Delhi the next morning, both of them were lying flat on their backs, wide awake, staring at the ceiling with itching eyes and the ashen countenance of the unrested. Smith had eventually dropped off at around three in the morning but had woken with his wife to the sound of some hideous foreign birds emitting the deafening Indian equivalent of the predawn chorus at about five o'clock. Since then, as the sun rose though the haze of pollution enshrouding the city, there had been a steady and relentless increase in the volume of traffic noise and hooting horns seeping through the double glazing of the hotel room window, which, despite audible evidence to the contrary, was firmly closed.

When the noise had become so loud that the walls started to vibrate, Mrs G decided to give up on sleep and arose to engage in battle with the Nespresso machine, which itself was by no means a silent piece of apparatus. Her husband groaned in the manner of a water buffalo, for no particular reason other than it was his habit at this time of day. Mrs G looked at him despairingly, wondering for the umpteenth time what sort of animal she was in fact married to.

"Coffee, dear?" she croaked.

"That would be absolutely splendid," replied her recumbent husband, scratching his belly like an orangutan. "By the way, I had a wonderful curry last night, dear, and was joined by a chap who was on the same flight as us from London."

Whatever anyone said about Norman Smith, he was not one for succumbing to a bad mood after two restless nights. He always had an optimistic way about him, even first thing in the morning, another characteristic that infuriated his more temperamental wife beyond words.

"Yes, I can smell that you had a curry, dear. It is quite unpleasant, especially if you have not had one yourself." Mrs G gave her husband one of her more disgusted looks.

"Ah, yes. Well I'm sure we'll both get used to it when we've been here for a few days. Now, as it happens, the man I had dinner with last night claimed he was a director of BA," blurted out Smith, clearly having endured hours of impatience before conveying this piece of information to his wife. His eagerness and enthusiasm may have appeared charmingly childlike, if you were not Mrs G.

"How exceedingly dull," she replied as steaming froth exploded into a coffee cup. "I am glad I retired to bed early."

A little while later, Mrs G and Mrs Smith sat by the hotel swimming pool after a light breakfast of toast and something vaguely resembling marmalade but apparently containing turmeric. As usual in such situations, Mrs G had mapped out a detailed plan for the day, which involved a driver taking them to several important local sightseeing hotspots. In this case, the itinerary included the delights of Old Delhi, as well as magnificent vistas of New Delhi, which would almost certainly be invisible in the haze of pollution. Nonetheless, there was much to see, even if only up close.

The following morning, they were due to fly to Varanasi, so time in Delhi was limited. However, as it was only 9 a.m., and their transport was not due until 10, the poolside loungers offered a peaceful respite ahead of what would almost certainly be a frantic and exhausting day.

Mrs G was still not as relaxed as she would have liked and was now suffering from both a headache, due to jet lag, and mild indigestion, due to unfamiliar breakfast ingredients. "Were you intending to debrief me on any other aspects of your adventures yesterday evening, Norman?" she asked testily.

"Of course, dear, all in due time," her husband replied calmly. He had not yet broken the news that he was intending to skip the detour to Varanasi in order to go searching for airliner parts. He was probably not far wrong in assuming that this might not go down too well with Mrs G and was a topic that would need sensitive handling.

"As a matter of fact, I have come upon an extraordinary stroke of luck," he continued, gazing at the pool's sparking blue ripples, as if seeking inspiration.

"Well, I am very pleased to hear it. But it might be polite if you shared it with me—just in case I am involved in any way in your good fortune." Mrs G had clearly been attacked by a swarm of mosquitos during the night. Her head and arms were dappled with little red spots that were beginning to cause her some irritation.

"Well, it's like this. The chap I had dinner with last night, you know, the one that is the airline director, he made me an interesting offer. You see, we were chatting about this and that over dinner, and I happened to mention that I was reconstructing an aircraft cockpit in our back garden—"

Mrs G stared at her husband despondently. "Oh dear," she interjected, "please, not that old chestnut again. Honestly, I would have thought you could forget about that, at least when we are on holiday, Norman."

"Well, I didn't really intend to bring the subject up at all, dear. It was just that, as he in in the airline business, I thought it might be something we had in common you know, an interest in aviation and all that."

"Go on then. Let's hear about your stroke of luck. However, my excitement is not exactly at fever pitch if it has anything to do with knobs and dials, which I expect is does."

"Exactly," continued Smith, though it was not at all clear what he meant by this particular expostulation. "You see, the chap happens to know an extremely highly recommended international supplier of aircraft parts. He has offered to introduce them to me. The only snag is that the only day he can do this is tomorrow. Now, I've been thinking hard about this. You know that the last thing I would choose to do is disrupt our holiday, but an opportunity like this does not come up very often. We, therefore, have three options to consider. Firstly, you toodle on to Varanasi on your own tomorrow whilst I sort out the business side of things here and meet you in Agra in a couple of days' time. Secondly, you could skip Varanasi as well and stay in Delhi for another day. Or thirdly, I could forgo this once-in-a-lifetime opportunity so that I do not miss all that burning of dead bodies, smoke, and ashes in Varanasi." Smith realised that he might not have laid out the options entirely without a degree of vested self-interest, but he had at least offed the ultimate sacrifice which, of course, he had no intention of making.

Mrs G looked incredulous. Her insect bites throbbed on and off like a thousand traffic lights, and her heart sunk. She knew how stubborn her husband could be when he was "off on one". "What an appalling way to start the holiday," she uttered. "First you abandon me on our first night to go on a debauch with some seedy company director, eating curry and drinking beer all night. Then you have the effrontery to start suggesting that we change the schedule so you can pursue your idiotic hobby, which has no relevance to anyone but yourself."

"It was not a debauch in any sense. We were just making conversation. That's all."

"I'll give you a conversation you won't forget," growled Mrs G, just on the fine edge of losing her temper.

"Calm down, dearest," said Smith, rubbing his poor wife's arm in the manner of a penitent stroking a religious statue.

"As I said, we have options open to us. Let's just think logically about this, shall we?"

These helpful suggestions did not exactly win the argument over for Smith. It is incredible how a man can spend over thirty years living with a woman and still fail to recognise the phrases that are most likely to make her bubble over with fury and indignation.

"Don't be so bloody condescending," she replied. "I will *not* calm down if I don't want to, and I will *not* be dictated to by your fleeting fancies. This is *my* holiday, and I will *not* have it ruined!" Every time she said *not* her right leg pounded silently against the cushion of her lounger, causing one of her sandals to fall into the pool, a choreograph that had the effect of considerably reducing the impact of her petulant protestations.

Smith wondered where his wife got such self-conceit from. Surely it would have been more accurate to refer to the holiday as a joint venture. It was almost as if it was a possession of hers that he was only involved with in the capacity of a mute bystander. On the other hand, there was some merit in looking at it with such perspective if you were determined to get your own way on every single point. He felt like reminding her that it was he who had paid for it but, sensibly, declined to take such a suicidal stance in the middle of such a difficult discussion.

"Darling?" he said instead. "Please don't be angry. By the way, did you hear the noises apparently coming from under the floorboards in the middle of the night?"

Changing the subject was a long tried and tested strategy that Smith used whenever his wife got into such a state. He knew that she was not one for holding grudges for more than a few seconds.

"How could I hear anything above your din?" she asked. It was a perfectly reasonable question for one so recently distracted by anger.

"Well, I am sure something was going on under the floor, which is most odd considering our room is on the ground floor."

"Perhaps there is a basement room underneath."

"Or it could be rats, I suppose."

"Norman, please don't ever talk about such things. You know how I feel about rats."

"Well, I will let you ponder on it and let me know what you think later."

"I don't need to ponder on it. I know exactly how I feel about rats. I'm going to get them to move us to another room."

"No. I didn't mean ponder that. I meant ponder about what we are going to do tomorrow."

"Oh, that? Well let me see. Blast these ruddy mosquito bites, Norman. They itch so much I can hardly think," said Mrs G, scratching herself incontinently. "I hope they haven't given me yellow fever or something. Now remind me. What are the options again?"

# 3.

There are two qualities that are prerequisite if you ever consider becoming a Delhi tuk-tuk driver, these being fearlessness and effrontery. Raj had both these in abundance, partly through nature and partly though nurture, even if they had not made him a fortune yet. He was still only twenty, after all.

He saw the strange Western man, unaccountably wearing a tweed jacket in the steaming heat and sporting the most enormous flat feet Raj had ever seen, standing on a street corner outside the hotel. More importantly, he noticed the look of urgency on the man's face as he watched a taxi drive past him containing a driver and two Western passengers, one male and one female. Before the taxi had passed him, the man was waving his hands for a vehicle to stop. Quick as a shot, Raj was parked up beside him, inviting him to take a seat in the back of his tuk-tuk.

"Follow that taxi," bellowed the man in blunt English, clearly oblivious to the spectacle he was making of himself.

Raj set off immediately, knowing how difficult it would be to keep a tail on any vehicle weaving through the Delhi traffic. Nonetheless, he was excited by the challenge and by the potential financial rewards it may offer. "One hundred rupees for first fifteen minutes," he yelled at the passenger, knowing that no one would pay him at rates like that.

"Yes, that's fine," said the man. "Whatever it costs, just bloody well keep up!"

Raj was flabbergasted both by the urgency that his passenger was conveying and also by the nonchalant acceptance of his extortionate fee proposal. He was a dab hand at weaving in and out of the traffic and avoiding obstacles such as people, cows, monkeys, donkeys, hens, bicycles, cars, and road furniture that a lesser tuk-tuk driver would have surely mown into and managed to keep a close distance from his prey. He did, however, notice that another tuk-tuk was following him closely. It was difficult to see in his vibrating wing mirrors, but it looked as if this also contained a single Caucasian gentleman. *Wat de bluddy hell is going on?* he thought ecstatically.

Inside the taxi, Mrs G was much relieved to be in an air-conditioned environment, though the driver had yet to win her trust. She thought he was a rather swarthy-looking fellow, which was quite unfair considering the natural skin tone of most of the residents of the subcontinent she was visiting. Plus, she felt that his manner was far too insolent for comfort. Mr Smith did not have an opinion of the driver. He hadn't really noticed him at all, especially as he was sitting in the backseat and could only see the top of the man's head, which was bald and shiny. Smith was far too preoccupied with his forthcoming visit to the parts factory to take much notice of anything else.

"I take you beautiful tour Delhi inside five hours take or give," explained the driver in what he assumed was fluent English. "I like very much English tourists even though wat you bastards did during Raj and empire times," he said, apparently unaware that such language could cause offence to the more susceptible defenders of British imperial behaviour.

Fortunately, it was like water off a duck's back to Smith, who chuckled at the comment, even though he wasn't sure whether or not it was meant to be funny. Mrs G, on the other hand, was clearly sporting ruffled feathers.

"I don't think it is particularly appropriate to tar modern British people with the brush of their distant and possibly less enlightened ancestors," she blurted, apparently trying to apply reason to counter the driver's offhand quip. This was probably ill advised, as, if it had been a poor-taste joke, she would be making a fool of herself for taking it seriously, and if he was, indeed, a bigot, she would never be able to change his viewpoint anyway, especially as his command of English seemed so limited.

"I like you, madam. Typical British spunk. Of course, you cannot be held to blame. British left some good legacy and many corpses in India, but then, so did Moghuls. Any invaders do shit, madam, but not all bad people. Except for Pakistanis."

It was clear that the driver's education had not included any lessons in international diplomacy, but at least he didn't seem to bear any personal grudges.

"New Delhi, empire. Old Delhi, Indian," he continued in what appeared to be the prologue to a lightning history of the city. "Me, I only tour guide and driver. Like you, was not here in the past. So I just read bit from books; save you having so to do. Now, take a look at oldest Sikh temple in Delhi. So beautiful, isn't it? I stop so you take photos to send back to granny mom."

The taxi drew to a halt suddenly in the middle of the road in order that the tourists could take photos from the car window. Everything behind miraculously swerved past without impact, and soon the traffic flow continued around the obstacle, like a river diverted round a small island.

In the cacophony of swerving and beeping vehicles, it was difficult to see the two tuk-tuks that had pulled up on the edge of the road a few hundred yards farther up. They did not stop together but apart by a safe distance. The passengers peered backwards, intent on observing the stranded taxi, as if it were noteworthy for some reason. Raj and the other tuk-tuk driver winked at each other.

Former DI Godber craned his neck to look behind at the taxi in the middle of the road. He was not feeling his usual self on this particular morning, having had a restless night. There was so much to think about when you were tailing a felon in a foreign country, and it would be safe to say that he was now operating a long way out of his comfort zone. Nonetheless, he was obsessively driven to pursue a suspected miscreant, as he always had been throughout his long police career. This drive was stronger in him than the normal animal urges, such as gluttony and sexual desire, that beset weaker men. It was so strong in fact, that it had cost him two marriages and his entire life savings. And because of its intensity, it had also caused him to fall out with almost every senior police officer he had ever worked for, thus severely hampering career prospects and his promotion record. In short, he was little dissimilar to a terrier with a bone clasped in its jaws, if such contracture could be maintained for decades on end without release.

This was an unusual case for Godber. He was now officially retired yet obsessed with finishing a job he had started whilst still employed by the force, notably building a robust evidence case against Norman Smith that would be acceptable to the Crown Prosecution Service and hopefully enable him to be put behind bars. He had been convinced at the time that Smith was up to no good when he accused him of murder and discovered that he had a garage full of bloodied bones. Sadly, the bones contained no conclusive DNA match to the victim, and Smith got off scot-free on that occasion.

But Godber knew that, even if Smith had not committed that particular murder, then he was likely to have committed others. He had the aura of a serial killer in Godber's mind. Who, in their right mind, would keep animal bones in their garage and claim that they were the offcasts from a taxidermy hobby, for goodness' sake? Did he think Godber was a fool?

Then there were a number of more minor speeding, reckless driving, and parking offences that Smith had committed in his Morris Minor Traveller. Incredibly, none of these had been officially recorded or captured on CCTV, so Smith had once again escaped punishment for his crimes. On top of that, there was the incident of the hijacked light aircraft at Redhill Aerodrome, the full extent of which had never come to light, no doubt because Smith had something on the manager of the flying school. This was another example of physical violence and intimidation being committed; yet, once again, Smith had never faced the consequences.

And now, here was a man openly contravening local planning laws by erecting a huge airliner part in his garden. Smith was convinced that the item had been acquired nefariously from some criminal source and would almost certainly be used to conduct criminal activities, possibly cybercrime or as a store for illegal substances. Godber was convinced that Smith was in India to connect with underworld contacts as part of this scheme. What a perfect cover, pretending to take a holiday, but who on earth would take a vacation in Delhi? For goodness' sake, it was a hellhole on earth, but its chaos was nonetheless an ideal cover for criminal types and illegal transactions.

Godber was convinced that his cover was still intact and that Smith had no idea he was being tailed. Nonetheless, he had to be careful. Smith may well recognise him if he saw him, and that would put an end to his current scheming activities, without a doubt. He therefore withdrew his perspiring head back into the canopy of the tuk-tuk, where it could not be seen from the taxi and where it was protected from the scorching sun.

In doing so, he did notice another tuk-tuk parked a little further along, with a European-looking man also staring backwards from it towards the taxi. The former DI was acute in his observations of human activity and pondered briefly whether or not he had just sighted one of Smith's criminal contacts. However, he put this thought to the back of his mind, aware that such a coincidence had little merit in view of the sheer number of people swarming the streets and the fact that many people had turned, if disinterestedly, to see what was going on in the taxi parked in the middle of the highway. Furthermore, a parked tuk-tuk was about as unusual as a chicken in a coop, on the streets of Delhi.

The sad fact, which Godber was oblivious to, partly due to an astonishing incapacity for introspection, was that his obsession with public duty had disabled him so much that he was now practically insane. Whilst he could apply his own unchallenged logic and reason to detection, surveillance, and evidence gathering—much of this approach learnt on the force—he had become incapable of considering wider context or focus on any kind of practical perspective unless it was directly related to the case in hand. For example, it did not occur to him that this current case was entirely of his own creation and bore no connection with any official investigations. This meant that he was acting in the capacity of a private investigator but without a client to pay his fees and expenses. Consequently, he had to dip into his own diminishing reserves in order to follow Smith to India, purely on a hunch. He had absolutely no authority or support for his actions and no capacity to set his obsessive suspicions into any kind of context. His delusion was a compounding process whereby his addled brain reaffirmed assumptions and conclusions, based on blind self-belief and blinkered vision, over and over again.

In addition to his mental anxiety at the prospect of losing the scent of his prey, Godber was also suffering physically, mostly due to the heat and humidity, which he was unaccustomed to and inappropriately dressed for. In fact, unbeknown to him, he had perspired so much since donning his tweed jacket that he was in the early stages of dehydration. Furthermore, his already immense pedal appendages had swollen and were chafing against the insides of his enormous yet constricting police-issue boots.

The gentleman in the other tuk-tuk was rather more compos mentis, despite clearly suffering from some kind of disorder of the nervous system evidenced by a facial tic. Apart from that, he did not seem too agitated, as he took a sober look at the Sikh temple from the side of the vehicle. He also glanced back to see both DI Godber and the object of his gaze, the taxi standing stationary in the middle of a stream of traffic. For him, it was as though someone had taken a photograph of the scene, which he was viewing at his leisure. As a flying instructor, he was used to digesting multiple sources of visual information rapidly and ignoring signals that were of no relevance. He was properly clothed for the climate in light chinos and a linen shirt, which made him somewhat less conspicuous than DI Godber, the man whom he was tailing, despite being ahead of him on the road at the present time.

Winterbottom was, by nature, of a calm temperament and rarely ruffled. This fundamental stoicism, however, had been shattered by the incident that occurred when he was tutoring Mr Smith, a setback that his nerves had still barely recovered from. This had resulted in the tic and regular nightmares and had incapacitated him for work for several weeks.

Not that Winterbottom was a man to hold grudges, and he was rather intrigued by the project that his boss had set him whilst he was grounded. He had been asked to tail former DI Godber and try to ensure that the incident with Smith remained concealed from the public and, most importantly, from the CAA, lest the flying school were to come into any sort of disrepute.

This was no easy task and quite alien to Winterbottom's previous professional experience. He had discovered that Godber was a most unusual and tenacious character, clearly bent on exposing Smith, possibly for demeanours beyond simply hijacking a light aircraft. He did not seem the sort of person who could be easily diverted from his mission, and Winterbottom was going to have to handle things rather carefully. Thankfully, being in India meant there was less likelihood of any accidental exposure. And Winterbottom was confident that, somehow or other, he would be able to manage the situation.

Unlike Godber, he was being paid for his troubles. And unlike Godber and Smith, he was the only person who knew all the participants in this ridiculous game of cat and mouse.

# CHAPTER 3

# REIGATE

## 1.

Whilst they were abroad, the next-door neighbours kept an eye on the Smiths' house just in case the burglar alarm went off or smoke started billowing out of the upstairs windows. As it happened, Alex Horne, the neighbour entrusted with a spare front door key to the Smiths' house in the event of an emergency, did not take his caretaking responsibilities too seriously. He felt that he would be aware of any major incident, should it occur, but that there was no need to keep too close a watch on the property.

One of the reasons for this was that he did not see himself as a particularly close neighbour. The only real line of communication between the two families came through occasional social intercourse between Barbara Horne and Mrs G. They infrequently met, either in Sainsbury's or at the hairdressers they both frequented and, at such a time, would share a few pleasantries and family news. It was through this tenuous link that the spare key had been exchanged prior to the Smith's departure. As for Alex Horne and Norman Smith, the relationship between the two men would best be described as casual. Neither man was particularly interested in befriending the other, possibly due to deeply subconscious and utterly inexplicable feelings of territorial rivalry inherited through their Neanderthal genomes.

The relationship, whilst not openly hostile, had worsened somewhat in recent weeks following the unannounced insertion of a large aircraft part in the Smiths' rear garden, which was clearly visible from the Horne's kitchen and dining room windows. Whilst Mrs Horne was somewhat more phlegmatic about the intrusive new fixture, her husband was incensed by what he saw as a flagrant flouting of local planning law. He had written to the council remonstrating about this unsightly object in no uncertain terms, noting that not only was the offending item visible, but that it also blocked some light from the rear of the Horne's property. However, he had not approached Smith himself to raise his concerns, partly because he did not want to prejudice his moral high ground by losing his temper and giving his neighbour a piece of his mind, an action he knew had the potential to end with a punch on the nose or worse. Furthermore, he had been entrusted with their key, which was surely an act of trust that should not be betrayed by churlishness.

"It is an illegal act of pure selfishness," he would complain to his patient wife about every twenty minutes.

She would shrug her shoulders and say, "I am sure it will all sort itself out in the end, Alex. Worse things can happen."

Naturally, this kind of facile stoicism was guaranteed to frustrate her husband even more, even though it was meant to calm him down—an important objective in view of Mr Horne's history of hypertension.

"I've a good mind to burn their house down while they are away," he would retort under his breath, despite being the building's temporary guardian.

It was clear to Mrs Horne that this was just bluster.

Mr Horne was a stickler for the rules and for analysing the minutest of details with a precision that would have put many a Swiss watchmaker to shame. His wife thought that these traits had become significantly more obsessive over the years since they had married, when she remembered him being somewhat carefree and easy-going. However, the longer a marriage endures, the more distorted becomes the lens onto its gestation; one may forget that time when feelings and observations were possibly distorted by emotions such as love and optimism. Looking back into the prism can be misleading, as it is inevitably subject to hankerings and regrets that simply weren't present at the time.

Mrs Horne did, however, concede that her husband's characteristics had been of considerable material benefit to her position in life. He had worked his way up to a senior position in the Air Accidents Investigation Branch at Farnborough, providing a handsome income that precluded the necessity for there to be two breadwinners in the household. He was adept at reconstructing complex aircraft from the minutest of broken parts, projects that could literally take years on end, and then discovering the cause of their untimely disintegration. He was, therefore, not unfamiliar with the object in the Smith's garden and could have been a very useful partner to Mr Smith in his simulator project, had the two men been more willing to cooperate. As it was, it was as if they both seemed to prefer to stand back to back so that they could never see eye to eye.

Mr Horne was not fully aware of Smith's purpose of having a deconstructed Boeing 737 cockpit in his back garden, though he guessed that there may be some intention to restore it in some way, or possibly convert it into a summer house. He had already discovered that the unsightly hunk of metal had come from a decommissioned airliner rather than a wreck, having all the details of aircraft written off through accidents at his disposal. He wondered why the council had not replied to his letter and feared that there was no provision at all for aircraft garden installations in the local planning policy, in which case there had clearly been an oversight, something he could not abide.

There was one other fact relating to Norman Smith that was playing on the air accidents manager's mind. As part of his routine work, he had been scanning through the list of recent air incident reports. Incident reports, as opposed to accident reports, relate to aircraft accidents that could have happened, usually due to factors such as engine failure, mechanical fault, pilot error, atmospheric conditions, or spontaneous combustion, but that did not actually result in any catastrophic damage. Hundreds of accident reports are filed every year, but there are literally thousands of incident reports, many of them so obscure as to be seemingly irrelevant. For example, there was the case of a cat that had been hidden in a light aircraft and woke up and frightened the pilot so much that he lost control and ended up performing an unplanned barrel roll.

Whilst browsing through the latest list, Horne had stumbled across an unusual incident that caught his eye, probably because it had occurred at the nearby Redhill Aerodrome. The report concerned a light aircraft that was allegedly "hijacked" by a student whilst undergoing a flying lesson. The perpetrator had apparently wrested control of the aircraft from the instructor and would not give it back. Whilst being a serious breach of protocol, Horne concluded that the aircraft was not put in irredeemable jeopardy due to the fact that the instructor was voluntarily given back control before touchdown. It was more a matter of high jinks that would require a change in flying school protocol—rather, a change in aeronautical regulations. However, what surprised him about the report was that it had not been submitted by the flying school but apparently by a member of the public—someone by the name of Mr Godber—who had purportedly witnessed proceedings from on the ground.

The flying student involved was named as none other than one Mr Norman Smith. Apart from this compelling piece of evidence supporting his already ambivalent view of the next-door neighbour, Horne was immediately suspicious as to why there were no other corresponding incident reports from either the flying school or Redhill Aerodrome. This would need to be investigated, probably by one of his more junior colleagues, because failing to report an incident is a serious matter where air safety is concerned. Horne drew two conclusions from this. Either this Mr Godber person was a fantasist and had made the whole unlikely story up—after all, how could he see what was going on in the cockpit from the ground?—or there was some kind of cover-up resulting in the incident not being officially reported. Horne's professional instinct persuaded him that the former hypothesis was most likely to be true.

## Interlude

Who is it now?

*It's me—who else do you think it is?*

Who exactly is me? I have a lot of characters on my mind. None of them is special enough to command any preferential treatment.

*Alex Horne, of course—you know, Norman's next-door neighbour.*

I see. You are quick off the mark. I've only just introduced you to the story. I expect you have been talking to that whinger Godber, haven't you?

*He did mention that he felt you had treated him unfairly.*

Well, you are not supposed to communicate with fictional characters you have never met in the story. It is against all literary protocol.

*But I did come across his incident report, didn't I?*

That does not mean you know anything about him. Like you, he is purely imaginary, and as long as I have not introduced the two of you, you cannot know him on any level.

*But I do.*

How is that?

*I read the story so far and learned quite a lot about him. I have to say, I do empathise with him in respect to your disrespectful portrayal. After all, he is only doing his job.*

That has nothing to do with you. You are a minor character I have only recently concocted. I'm already beginning to wish I had left you out.

*But I am Norman Smith's next-door neighbour. You can't leave me out.*

You are not a very good neighbour by the sound of it.

*That's is exactly my complaint. Your portrayal of me is totally inaccurate. Norman and I are pretty good buddies, as it happens, apart from that damned thing you have conjured up in his garden. We were getting along just fine until you came along.*

That is not how I see things, and that is all that matters. You are just fictional and have no independent thought process of any kind.

*That is a gross infringement of my human rights.*

You are not human, and you don't have any rights at all. Like Godber, you are just fleeting dots of ink on a piece of paper. You only make sense as a combination of letters that other people may interpret in their own individual ways. You have no form and no voice unless I decide to give it to you.

*How come I am able to remonstrate with you, then?*

You are not. I am simply imagining you remonstrating with me because it amuses me.

*You have no sense of humour, so I can hardly imagine amusement motivating you.*

You know absolutely nothing about me. Besides, you are a pretty tedious and humourless character yourself, by the sound of it.

*Because you have portrayed me like that. Not because I am really like that.*

You cannot be "like" anything else. I created you in the image that I conjured up in my own mind. You have no other meaning.

*You are not a God, you know*

I am your creator.

*That is blasphemy.*

No. That is the truth. Now please get back into your real character and let me get on with the story.

*You have not heard the last of this.*

You are getting tedious now.

*Just like your story.*

At this point the author wishes to apologise for any hindrances or interruptions experienced by readers trying to follow the story. This is partly due to unwarranted interference by some of the characters to the natural flow and rhythm of the text, causing a degree of hesitancy on the part of the author. It is hard enough to create characters and their motives without these being questioned at every turn. It is inevitable that some characters behave or appear in a less than flattering light. However, this is not intended as defamation or insult but merely in order to create contrast and explain motive. If all the characters were perfect and driven by pure nobility of purpose, the story would be tedious beyond imagination. The fact that some of them are apparently lampooned more than others is simply a matter of contrasting presentation reflecting the implied imperfections and follies that many of us possess.

Please remember as you read that fictional characters, whilst perhaps possessing characteristics of somebody the reader has known or met during their lifetime, are purely imaginary. Some may be so implausible as to defy plausible comparison with any actual human being, alive or dead, whilst others may occasionally act or speak in a manner that has some resonance with the reader. However, reading is as much an act of imagination as is writing, so the characters are concocted not only in the mind of the author but also in the minds of the people who read about them. They are, therefore, entirely dependent on subjectivity and speculation and have few objective characteristics, other than those of a purely descriptive nature—such as mention of their apparel or facial hair, for example. Even these physical attributes are open to interpretation and are of little relevance in the overall picture.

Human beings are prone to hubris, but fictional characters are not, unless the author paints them with this quality. In their own right, they have no capacity for arrogance, conceit, haughtiness, pride, vanity, pomposity, or superciliousness. Nor should they, by implication, have the right to question how they are portrayed or what they appear to stand for, and even less to question their own creator's integrity in portraying them.

I own that there can be a degree of complexity when splitting the wheat from the chaff and reality from fiction, but I would urge you to ignore the uninvited rantings of any fictional characters from now onwards, even if you agree with their sentiments. They are merely distractions and of no relevance at all.

# 2.

The head of planning at the local council, John Hatt, a diligent yet somewhat dour character as befitting his profession, sat in the council chamber musing. *There is something theoretically sublime about local politics,* he thought. *It is the grassroots of the democratic system that we all so revere, an institution that has been rounded like a smooth stone over years of evolution to ensure that every citizen is represented fairly at the local level by his or her own elected representatives.*

*However, like all political systems,* he concluded, *it is completely flawed, mainly because its success or failure is at the whim of elected members, most of whom do not have the knowledge, expertise, or skills to make objective decisions on matters of local policy. Furthermore, these elected members are enmeshed into ideological party groupings that are more interested in fighting each other than acting in the best interests of the local community. Councillors come and go, but the officers remain the foundation upon which the edifice is built. Whilst holding no power at all, it is they who have the knowledge, expertise, objectivity and wisdom to guide policy and enact the dreams of their pompous yet often feeble-minded masters.*

Hatt was preparing to discuss a series of planning applications with a group of local councillors. Many of them he held in contempt, largely because they insisted on continually challenging his informed advice, despite his having an encyclopaedic knowledge of the planning process, which none of them shared.

He was particularly interested in one recent application, lodged by a Mr Norman Smith. The appellant had apparently cobbled together a rather hasty "retrospective" planning application to the council, requesting permission to permanently locate a large aircraft part in his back garden. Whilst the wording of the application was not exactly up to the usual expected "industry standard" and was pretty well incomprehensible strictly from a town planning perspective, Smith had had the foresight to addend an apology note for having failed to apply for permission prior to the object being installed.

In response to the application, the planning office had received a number of public comments, all of which opposed the proposal. One of these was from a neighbour, Mr Alex Horne. It was not standard procedure for comments received about planning applications to be acknowledged.

As per normal policy, before going to the Planning Committee for approval or rejection, the application was being "floated" in front of the Reigate Forum of local borough councillors in a meeting chaired by Hatt.

"From a planning perspective," he opined, once the elected members had gathered, "it is not unusual to receive applications from residents wishing to erect temporary buildings such as sheds and summer houses in their gardens. Whilst the object in question here is most unusual, this should not prejudice our decision, so long as its location does not contravene planning policy. We should, however, consider the external material of the object to ensure that it does not cause unwanted reflected light or heat to surrounding properties or that it is of a colour or texture that will despoil the character of the local environment."

"Good God, man. Are you serious?" exploded one of the more vocal and conservative local councillors. "This is an aircraft part, for goodness' sake. How can you compare it to a wooden shed?"

"With due respect, Councillor, I am simply pointing out the planning implications of this application. Whether it is a wooden shed or an aircraft part is of far less significance that its location, height, and mass—particularly if this might affect the public outlook, amenity, and neighbours' light."

Another councillor opined that the nature of the item *should* be taken into account, in that it was akin to scrap metal. "Would you like your next-door neighbour to fill his garden with scrap metal?" he asked rhetorically.

No one responded, of course.

One of the more senior councillors observed that it was important for the Planning Committee to fully understand what the object would be used for before making a decision. "The difference is that you have a pretty good idea what a shed or summer house will be used for. But this damned thing could be used for a range of antisocial and potentially noisy purposes. Besides, if it is metal, it will probably rust."

Hatt never ceased to be amazed how local councillors were unable to grasp the difference between emotive and irrelevant points and the framework of planning law. It was always like this—little more enlightening than a "phone in" on LBC.

"In this case," he continued, "as the application does not appear to contravene any local or national planning laws, and the object in question is so positioned that, despite some neighbourly protest, it is unlikely either to block out or reflect any significant light, the garden being north-facing, nor pose an unacceptable impediment to the view to neighbouring properties, the recommendation of the planning department is that the Planning Committee should consider a delegated approval for this application."

"Outrageous!" fumed an octogenarian reactionary from the Residents Association, "It is clear that the applicant is up to no good. He placed the object in his garden in flagrant disrespect for the planning process and has now realised he needs to get permission, hoping we will pass this through as an afterthought. We need to stand up to this sort of behaviour!"

"Hear. Hear," mumbled a number of the assembled councillors.

Cllr Brown, who had, contrary to the rules concerning "declaration of personal interests", assisted the applicant to complete the planning application, had been advised not to take part in the discussion on this item due to this personal involvement, an act he was now beginning to regret, even though it had brought him a certain amount of glory in the eyes of some of his residents at the time. However, he could not resist adding, "Some of you will be aware that I have personally spoken to the applicant about the initial failure to obtain planning permission. In my opinion, it was an oversight on his part, not a deliberate omission."

One of the opposition councillors pointed out that Cllr Brown himself had helped the applicant to fill in the form and should be ashamed of himself making any public comment on it at all, to which an incensed Brown replied, "I did not contribute to the content of this application, but merely ensured that all the relevant sections on the form were completed. I have no personal interest in the application being approved or refused. I was merely pointing out that this does not appear to be a case of deliberate flouting of the planning process.

Unlike your party, we hold personal integrity in high regard in the conservative party!"

At this, the opposition councillor suggested that Brown should resign his seat immediately. In response, the conservative group started throwing screwed-up agenda papers at him.

The opposition councillor pretended that these had injured him. Deliberately falling off his seat, he started writhing on the council chamber floor like a hysterical footballer faking injury from a non-existent foul.

"Shame, shame," shouted several councillors, standing up and waving their remaining papers and anything else they could lay their hands on in the air in a display of insincere indignation. The were clearly enjoying the hiatus immensely. It was not entirely clear, though who they were aiming their jibes at—the provocative Cllr Brown or the floored opposition councillor.

Realising that the meeting could go on all night and potentially deteriorate into riotous assembly if he didn't suggest a placatory solution, the head of planning continued, "However, as there seems to be a degree of concern about our recommendation regarding this particular application, may I suggest that the Local Committee recommends a 'site visit', so that members of the Planning Committee can view the item personally, in situ, before making a decision."

There seemed to be a majority of assent for this proposal. This immediately quelled the histrionic outrage of the councillors and enabled them to feel that their collective democratic, if opinionated, voice had been heard, whatever side they were on, whilst at the same time not having to override the expertise of the planning officers and flaunt planning law.

As the councillors filed out of the council chamber after the meeting, bantering with each other and smirking like schoolchildren, Hall let out a sigh of relief. This he did simply

because he had managed to chair the whole meeting
without losing his temper, thus affirming a long-standing self-
belief that he was perfectly cut out for the humble role of a
public servant.

## 3.

Former squadron leader Mantle shuffled round the operations
room of his flight school in Redhill like a man in a three-legged
race, apparently unable to split his legs above knee level. This
was not the result of any physical incapacity or war wound,
but merely because he was desperate to go to the lavatory.
Fighter pilots are trained over many years to control their bowel
movements to avoid soiling the cockpit during missions, even
in times of heightened terror. Clearly there are occasional
accidents, this is inevitable but, generally speaking, one would
expect such an experienced airman to have a degree of
control above the average.

The fact is, Mantle had delayed responding to his peristalsis
for too long and was now paying the price. He was forced
to shuffle urgently in this undignified gait into the air school's
somewhat basic amenity and then rapidly relieve himself of
his avoidable affliction with a degree of discomfort he was not
used to on such occasions. Despite the normal social practice
of keeping such private moments hidden from public scrutiny,
a stranger might have been surprised that the former squadron
leader maintained a running commentary of his activities with
the person he was talking to on his mobile phone, even though
it was the call itself that had diverted his mind from the task in
hand in the first place.

"Bombs away," he reported graphically.

Through the incomprehensible medium of mobile phone technology, Winterbottom was listening to Mantle's progress report from his hotel room in Delhi. Such was the intimacy that such communication can bring across distant time zones that he could almost smell Mantle's ordure.

"Good show," he added. "Hope you hit the target."

"Bullseye," replied Mantle, seemingly somewhat relieved that his ordeal was over. "Now, just fill me in on the last few points again. I fear that my concentration was somewhat diverted during the final approach."

"Well, I followed Godber and the Smiths around Delhi in the tuk-tuk all day. The fare didn't half mount up, I can tell you. Anyway, it was a completely futile exercise. The Smiths stayed together constantly and did exactly the sort of things that tourists do, like visiting temples, palaces, mosques, and gardens, the tomb of Mahatma Ghandi, and so on. They did nothing that one could consider suspicious or out of character. I can't imagine what Godber is up to following them around like a lost sheep. For a trained policeman, he is the most awful tail I have ever seen. Every time the Smiths got out of their taxi, he followed them around on foot, clearly visible to anyone who cared to look. The Smiths must be almost completely blind if they did not see him, though, of course, they may not know who he is. They probably think he is just a lonely tourist tailing them for company."

"And did you manage to keep a discreet distance?" Mantle asked, having returned to the role of mission commander.

"Of course, sir. You can rely on that. Godber has enough trouble keeping his eyes on the Smiths to notice me."

"So, what is the plan, Winterbottom?"

"Well, I am rather hoping to 'bump' into Godber in the hotel later, in the guise of a tourist, to try to eek some information out of him. Indeed, I'll put him under a bit of pressure. I assume that meets with your approval, sir?"

"Of course, Winterbottom. A splendid plan. Make sure you turn the screws on tight. The last thing we need is that idiot bringing up the flying incident with Smith. Warn him off good and proper; there's a good chap."

"Roger."

"OK. Roger and out. Let's resume contact at 1500 GMT tomorrow."

"By the way, all OK following the bombing raid?"

"Just smoking embers, old chap, just embers."

Mantle sat down at his desk, placed the phone in his inside pocket, and looked out of the window thoughtfully. A single engine Cessna was taxiing out to the runway, and a helicopter was buzzing overhead like an enraged hornet. On top of the desk was an open letter from someone called Horne at the Air Accident Investigations Branch. It was a request for corroboration of a report by a member of the public concerning the incident he was urgently trying to cover up in India.

Mantle reread the letter from top to bottom, and a lopsided smile gradually appeared on his manly face. It read:

> This is an informal request for clarification of the above reported incident. As you can see, unusually, the incident report has been lodged by a member of the public, and there is no other record of it having taken place. It seems unlikely that there is any possibility of such a breach of protocol having been observed from ground level. So our assumption is that this is either a hoax or a deliberately fabricated story.

However, in the interests of air safety, I would appreciate if you could write back to me confirming that this incident did not take place, in a statement countersigned by the managing director of Redhill Aerodrome.

If, on the other hand, the incident did take place, we request that you provide full details and an explanation as to why it was not immediately reported to us. We would also welcome any information you have on either the subject of the accusation, Mr N Smith, or the lodger of the incident report, Mr DI Godber, both of either of whom may be subject to further investigation depending on your reply.

Yours sincerely,
Alex Horne

The reason Mantle was smiling was because his initial dismay at having received the letter, having apparently been "dobbed in" by Godber, had turned into relief as he realised that there was a simple way of putting this enquiry to bed. The Aerodrome MD would be more than happy to co-sign his statement after a few large Scotches.

And so the statement was composed:

Dear Mr Horne,

Thank you for your letter requesting more information about an incident report that you have received concerning an occurrence at my flying school at Redhill Aerodrome.

Firstly, let me assure you that this was not a "reportable" incident. Though, according to protocol, recordings were made of cockpit conversations during the incident that I assume Mr DI Godber is referring to, these have since been destroyed after careful examination of them proved, beyond doubt, that there was never a moment when air safety was in jeopardy. There was simply a short misunderstanding between the flying instructor and his student, Mr N Smith, during which there was some confusion on the part of the student, not the instructor, as to exactly who was in control of the aircraft. This was an extremely short-lived incident and had no effect on the capacity of the trained instructor to maintain control of the aircraft and land it safely. Such incidents are far from uncommon, especially when students are taking their first lessons and are inexperienced in cockpit procedures. I can assure you that we have robust procedures in place to deal with such misunderstandings. In view of this, it was categorically concluded that there was no need for us to report the incident.

As far as Mr DI Godber is concerned, the said gentleman requested that I meet him shortly after the incident. During this meeting, it was apparent that the complainant bore some kind of a grudge against the student and wanted to escalate this extremely minor incident in order to undermine Mr Smith's reputation for some reason unknown to myself. I can only assume that his reporting of this unremarkable incident to you is another example of his continued efforts to discredit the student personally.

I should add that, as the complainant was apparently on the ground at the aerodrome when the incident took place, it would have been absolutely impossible for him to have seen or heard anything of this midair misunderstanding. I can only conclude that he either invented his version of the incident or overheard the student recounting it afterwards, in which case it is likely that the student exaggerated the facts. Many first-time students are highly strung before, during, and after their inaugural flights and can be prone to hyperbole as a form of stress release afterwards. This is a well-documented syndrome of flying school psychology.

As far as Mr N Smith is concerned, he was only known to us during the time of his single flying lesson and has not since returned to pursue any further training, though we do have his address and contact details in our logbook in the unlikely event that these should be needed at some future date.

I trust that my response has reassured you that there is absolutely no reason for the Air Accidents Investigation Branch to concern itself with this inaccurate report any further and that you now feel, as we do, that the matter is closed.

I also hope that this reassurance will be enhanced by the countersignature on this letter by the CEO of Redhill Aerodrome, with whom I have discussed the matter in detail.

Yours sincerely,

Squadron Leader R N Mantle,
Managing Director, Redhill Aviation Flying School

O N Booth, OBE
Chief Executive, Redhill Aerodrome

Ollie Booth, OBE, CEO of Redhill Aerodrome, was a businessman, not an aviator. His role was to make the aerodrome profitable, even if that meant selling off the land to a developer for housing, not to worry about minor flight incidents unless they had any impact upon on the reputation or value of the aerodrome as a financial asset. Mantle was aware of this tunnel vision and, therefore, simply needed to convince the CEO that reassuring the AAIB was necessary to avoid any adverse publicity.

"So you see, Ollie, your signature on this letter will kill off any further speculation about this matter."

"I don't like this one little bit," muttered Booth under a cloud of cigar smoke.

"I know it is somewhat trying, but we do not want this little pimple to turn into a boil, do we?"

"Pimple? Good God, Mantle, that clown Smith nearly brought an aircraft down, and potentially my airfield with it, and on my watch."

"It was never that serious, Ollie. It was blown out of proportion, and you know it."

"The chaps in the control tower weren't so phlegmatic, were they?"

"Look. It was a minor incident with no damage or casualties."

"Why did you delete the tapes then?"

"Because they proved there was nothing to worry about."

"Or because they proved the opposite, Mantle, and you didn't want anyone else to hear what actually happened."

"There is no evidence to support an investigation apart from Godber's incident report, which we have discredited with this letter."

"That lack of evidence may work against us if anyone decides to do some more digging."

"They won't. That's the whole point. Besides I am on to Godber. I don't think he will cause us any more trouble."

"We are not the bloody Mafia, Mantle. This is a respectable aerodrome."

"There is no cause for alarm, Ollie. It is just a bureaucratic exercise, and this is the paperwork we need to put it to bed."

Whilst they had been talking, Mantle was ensuring that the CEO's Scotch was continually topped up from his cut-glass decanter.

"You know, sometimes I wish I could retire from all this and focus on golf," said Booth, as if suddenly becalmed on the rocks.

"I expect the airfield would make a pretty darned good eighteen-holer, hey, Ollie?"

"If it was up to me, Roger. If it was up to me. Just can't make the economic case to the shareholders. Besides, the bloody government seems to be sentimentally attached to regional airfields, as if we were still in the middle of the Battle of Britain."

"Yes, those were the days," said Mantle dreamily, as if he had spiked his own drinks.

"Bloody awful days, Mantle. Chaps getting shot down like ducks."

"No AAIB then, though. Just got on with it."

"Well, I suppose I'd better sign the damned thing," said Booth, apparently waiving his own objections, whilst scratching his mark at the bottom of the letter. "By the way, what happened to that Winterbottom chap? Haven't seen him around since he nearly took down the aerodrome down."

"He's on sick leave, Ollie. Recovering from the shock."

"Is he a puff, Mantle?"

"Not that I am aware of. I've never really pried into his private life.

"I'll bet his is. Probably went crying to his mum."

"Actually, I think he is spending some time overseas at the moment."

"Good God. What would he want to go abroad for?"

"No idea. Perhaps he wants to get some sun."

"Pathetic," slurred Booth, now inebriated enough to expose a number of his less acceptable prejudices. "He'll probably come back as black as the ace of spades."

Mantle had seen Booth in this state before and knew it was time to depart. As he did so, Booth took him by the sleeve and slurred like a school bully, "Never let this happen again, Mantle. You are not forgiven. I have simply signed out of paragmatism and sound bussineness sense. Mind my words."

The CEO had tipped over, beyond the point where he was open to common sense or balance. He was now fully exposed as his true, rather unappealing self. Mantle had timed things perfectly.

# 4.

It was not unusual for an officer from the planning department to accompany Planning Committee members on a site visit. It was less common for the site visit to be hosted by a neighbour who was a keyholder whilst the homeowner was overseas. However, in this case, Horne (actually, Mrs Horne via Mrs G) had obtained permission from the Smiths for this site visit to take place "in absentia", so long as there was no entry into the property itself. The rationale behind this was to expedite the planning process to ensure that permission was granted prior to the Smiths' return from India.

Naturally, a site visit is no guarantee of the likelihood of a positive planning outcome. Indeed, the opposite could be said to be true, in that site visits are normally made in order to examine potential problems and reasons why planning may be refused. On this occasion the decision was very much in the balance, in that none of the members of the Planning Committee were familiar with planning regulations relating to aircraft parts being permanently erected in urban back gardens. This skewed the likelihood of a refusal on the basis of ignorance rather than reason.

Officer Hatt watched the committee members wandering round the Smiths' back garden aimlessly looking at trees, plants, and fences that were of little relevance to the case in hand. The object itself was clearly obtrusive in terms of the view from the rear of the lower floor of Smith's own house but barely visible from the Horne's rear windows, mostly blocked from sight by a six-foot Beech hedge. It was tediously common for residents objecting to planning proposals to grossly exaggerate the issues of "overlooking" and the "blocking of light", when they were really objecting to any change at all that they had not initiated themselves. This was a particularly extreme case in that there were clearly no substantive grounds for the Hornes to object on either point, especially as the garden was north-facing and covered in shade from the houses themselves during most daylight hours. The rear garden abutting that of the Smiths was equally unaffected by the new edifice by an enormous Yew tree that rendered it invisible. There was no garden on the other side of the Hornes, as the garden stood on a corner plot. Furthermore, it was pretty well impossible to glimpse the aircraft part from the street to the front of the house. There were, therefore, no grounds for any objection on the basis of not fitting in with local amenity, unsightliness, overlooking, threat to public privacy, or light impact.

The planning decision would, therefore, rest on the small print of the local and national planning framework, which was unfamiliar to most of the Planning Committee members whilst sitting like the open tomes of an encyclopaedia inside the planning officer's brain. Why on earth were they wandering round the garden like untrained children, then? One officer had noticed some moss in the lawn and was trying to remove it with his credit card, whilst another was running around with his arms spread out pretending to be an aeroplane. One of the female committee members was critical of the colour of the fabric that Smith had used to seal the aircraft part, noting that it clashed horribly with the delphiniums.

"Bloody awful mess," observed one of the senior councillors. It was not clear whether he was referring to the aircraft part or the state of his brogues that had become caked in the local soil.

"Bugger if I understand why he wants that there," said another, scratching his head in bemusement, as if this failure to understand Smith's motive for installing the object had any bearing at all on the planning decision.

"I'd sooner have a summer house myself, but there is no accounting for taste," responded one of the more broad-minded and liberal councillors, clearly bemused as to why there should be any real objection to the artefact resting where it was, whilst at the same time wondering what his wife was cooking for tea.

"He must be an absolute nutter," observed the head-scratcher, clearly experiencing a rare moment of illumination.

Surely it would be home time soon.

Eventually, the motley crew of councillors made its retreat through the side gate by which they had entered the Smiths' rear garden, clearly proud of having spent the best part of two hours performing noble acts of public service that, in fact, had been as futile as Norman Smith's dreams.

As the last councillor strode purposefully towards his parked car, which, incidentally, was on a double yellow line further down the street, Hatt helped Mr Horne to lock the side gate.

"Thank you for letting us in, Mr Horne. A site inspection is a useful accompaniment to any planning decision," he said.

"Indeed?" replied Horne, clearly eager to ascertain the result of the inspection. "Well, I do hope that it emphasised to the committee that this monstrosity is a totally inappropriate development, and its continued presence here should be refused, if only on humanitarian grounds."

"Mr Horne, I am but a civil servant. It is not my job to make planning decisions but merely to facilitate an informed decision-making process, based on planning law. What the members of committee decide at the next planning meeting is beyond my humble control. Nonetheless, I would advise you that there are no statutory grounds for the refusal of this planning application, especially given that the subject clearly does not constitute an obstruction to anyone except the property owner. It is barely visible from your property and, therefore, cannot be identified as a nuisance."

Horne looked slightly disappointed at this reply but continued: "Now you mention it, Mr Hatt, I think you are probably right. Still it was worth a try. You can't have neighbours placing bits of metal in their back gardens willy-nilly without a bit of a fight, just to show them you won't take any more such nonsense lying down. Incidentally, it was Mrs Horne who was more concerned than I was. I told her that objecting would do no good at all."

Hatt ignored what appeared to be a pretty obvious and cowardly lie and continued, professionally, "No decision has yet been made, so you can tell Mrs Horne that all objections will be taken into account in the final decision-making process. That will be at the Planning Committee meeting next week. However, it might be wise to break it to her gently that the odds of planning permission being refused are quite low at this stage."

Eventually, Hatt shook hands with Horne, bade him farewell, and went to sit in his car, which was parked on a meter he had paid for in full. Before he drove off, he wrote down Horne's comments verbatim, even though the off-the-record views of planning objectors were not material to any planning decision. For some peculiar reason, he was behind the Smiths' application, if only because here was a chance to override the mindless objections of the elected members with all of the logical force of planning law. Any objection would surely be overridden on appeal by the planning inspectorate. Besides, one day, he was going to write an exposé about his experiences as a town planning inspector and it would be no-holds-barred. Evidence such as this was invaluable.

Back at home, Mrs Hatt was preparing her husband's dinner. She was a thin willowy figure whose edges were blurred, an impression enhanced both by the steam in the kitchen and the fact that her loose robes were apparently made of an extremely similar fabric to that of kitchen blinds.

"Hallo, John," she said, without looking up from the pot of stew she was stirring on the hob. "How did it go?"

Denise Hatt was familiar with the nature of her husband's seemingly tedious work. He rarely complained, but she knew that there were aspects of his profession that irritated him beyond measure. Fortunately, he was not the type of husband to take such frustration out on his wife. However, her sympathy for his position was counterbalanced by her belief that he should get another more rewarding job, a concept that he would not entertain because he was a stickler. Mrs Hatt was not a stickler. She was a dabbler, who had endured a long series of part-time temporary and often short-lived periods of employment episodes. She was currently helping out in the local library one morning a week.

"Oh, the usual," replied he husband, dipping a spoon into the gravy to have a taste.

"I thought this was an unusual case. Mind out now, that will be very hot."

"Most unusual, Denise, but nonetheless quite dull. The committee was particularly feckless today and, as usual, completely failed to understand the planning implications of the case. I wonder why I bother sometimes."

"So do I."

"I suppose it is because there is some part of me that thinks that it all matters. Without that belief, I would be living in an existentialist nightmare."

"There are more things to life than town planning, you know, dear."

"Yes, I know. To be honest, I sometimes wish I had broader horizons. I could not help but admire that chap's concept of implanting an aircraft part in his back garden. I wish I had the capacity for lateral thinking on that scale."

"I love to hear you talk dirty like that, David," said Mrs Hatt, turning to receive a kiss whilst her loose robes unwound, revealing her nakedness underneath.

Hatt pecked her on the lips and placed a hand on her lily-white hip. "But then again, the job brings in a good income, and I am little qualified for anything else."

"And I hate it when you give in to your sense of duty and order," replied his wife, removing his hand and wrapping the robe tightly round herself.

"Looks as though I will have to try to change a little then, but not until I have secured approval for this case."

"That's what I like to hear, John. Fighting talk," said the willowy Mrs Hatt, once again turning towards her husband and exposing her full-frontal nudity to him. "Do you mind if I put the stew on to simmer for a while?"

"I think that would be a very logical thing to do," replied Hatt. "We would not want to have to call fire and rescue, would we?"

# CHAPTER 4

# INDIA

## 1.

"Oh that it were simply a question of legality," said DI Godber before inserting a heaped forkful of lentil bhuna into his salivating mouth

"What on earth do you mean by that?" asked Winterbottom, immediately aware that he should not have asked a question at such a delicate moment.

Godber chewed for a couple of minutes before replying. Even so, a number of half-masticated morsels spat out of his mouth towards the unprepared flying instructor who, unfortunately, was wearing a white linen shirt.

"There are a number of issues to consider when building a profile of a felon. One has to consider character, motive, and intent as the foremost foundations. Then one then has to examine opportunity and execution, whilst remaining mindful of deception and the propensity of the accused dropping meaningless leads in an attempt to cover tracks. There are then the issues of alibis and evidence. All these play an important role in bringing a multiple offender to justice. It may be that one has to ignore lesser crimes in order to secure a conviction on one that will stick and result in a robust conviction. Proof of the commitment of an illegal act is something like the icing on the cake, which can only be produced once all the other evidence has been collected and stratified."

"I see," said Winterbottom, wiping orange spots from his shirt with his napkin forlornly. "Am I therefore to assume that Mr Smith is being investigated for multiple felonies, over and above purportedly acting with impropriety in the cockpit during his flying lesson with me?"

"Of course you are. In case you were not aware, Norman Smith is a dastardly character, who I would describe as a serial offender and whose possible crimes extend as far as murder. How he has never been caught, I just do not know."

"In that case, Mr Godber, I will come clean with you. It may or may not have come to your attention that the flying school and aerodrome do not wish to pursue any proceedings against Smith. We do not feel that there is a case to answer and believe that any escalation of such accusations would result not in Mr Smith being found guilty but in the aviation industry coming into disrepute. Personally, I think Smith is a very dangerous man when sitting behind the controls of a Cessna, but I am assured that this is unlikely to happen again in the near future. May I therefore suggest that you drop this element of your enquiries completely. Look on it as a red herring in the overall case you are trying to build."

By now, Godber had finished his main course and was nibbling on some rather dry and crusty naan. "Oh, but that would not be at all possible," he replied. "Building a picture of the character of the accused can only be effective if we include cases such as this, where irrational and thoughtless behaviour, potentially criminal in essence, but not necessarily, demonstrate beyond doubt that we are dealing with a criminal mind and support the motives for other more serious misdemeanours."

"But have you not considered the consequences, Mr Godber?"

"I have indeed, Mr Winterbottom. However, in cases like this we have to look at the bigger picture. It is almost inevitable that there will be some collateral damage when building a profile as complex as this. It is most unfortunate, of course, if the episode at Redhill Aerodrome opens up another can of worms. But with respect, this is of very little consequence in comparison with the conviction of a criminal of Smith's magnitude. I would also add that, should we secure a conviction, that would almost certainly put your position with regard to the 'Smith Affair' into a rather better light. No one would believe that a convicted felon was the victim of lax air training conduct."

Winterbottom had finished eating his omelette several minutes previously, not being particularly adventurous when it came to spicy food. The two men were sitting in the European style restaurant in the hotel that Smith and Brandon Lewis had frequented the previous evening. There was no sign of the Smiths.

Winterbottom had been pleasantly surprised to find Godber eating alone and slightly mystified as to why he was not on the Smith's tail as he had been all day. Godber had explained that he knew they were safely ensconced in the Asian restaurant down the corridor and that he had a full view through the internal glass windows should they leave. Besides, he had not fancied the menu, describing it rather disparagingly as "foreign muck". It was, therefore, something of a surprise that he had chosen to eat lentil curry when there were many more European dishes on the menu in the European restaurant. However, he seemed to be struggling with it, judging by how

much was on his napkin and the tablecloth, not to mention
Winterbottom's shirt.

The flying instructor had introduced himself politely and
had come clean about the reason for his presence in India
and how he had been shadowing Godber all the way from
Reigate to Delhi. Winterbottom put Godber's muted response
to this unusual encounter down to the fact that he had failed to
spot his tail, an oversight surely of a most embarrassing nature
for a former professional detective. Nonetheless, it seemed
absolutely true that, until that moment, Godber had had no
idea he was being stalked. This revelation gave Winterbottom
mixed feelings. On the one hand, it meant he was an excellent
and discreet tail. But on the other hand, it meant he might
have exposed his own cover unnecessarily early.

"You make a very good case for full disclosure, Mr Godber.
But I am still not completely convinced of the necessity of
dragging the flying club into this," he said, swilling the dregs
of his Kingfisher beer round and noticing a complete absence
of froth. However, it seems to me that you are not inclined to
bend on this point, which means we may have a little problem
of crossed interests."

"Indeed, it would seem that way," retorted Godber
somewhat arrogantly.

"Not only do we have different views on full disclosure,
but we have different motivations for pursuing our respective
cases. For example, my level of commitment could be said
to be less intense than yours, in that I am being paid for my
work and am under orders from another party. This, on the
other hand, could be countered by the fact that I was the
victim of Smith's ill-advised action in the aircraft I was trying
to fly and could have lost my life in the process. As for you,
Mr Godber, you have no personal interest in this case or the
actions of Norman Smith. For you, it is purely professional,

despite the fact that you are nominally retired as a police officer. Yet for some presumably psychological motive, you are so personally committed to the case itself that it has all but consumed you. You are even funding this whole venture out of your own pocket. So, you see, whilst we are both entangled, the question is who would suffer most from disentanglement?"

Godber's enormous feet were twitching so much under the table that Winterbottom had to put his legs to one side to allow them more room. "Your analysis is so complex that it confounds me, and I can see no reason for it. Comparative motives may be relevant when comparing criminals, but irrelevant to the detached behaviour of investigators."

"I would beg to disagree, Mr Godber. Let us look at this a little closer. If I were to give in to your will on full disclosure, the worst that could happen to me is that a man who nearly tried to kill me would potentially be imprisoned. An investigation into the flying club would probably not result in any disciplinary action against myself, as any fault must lie with the policies, procedures, and training appertaining to flying instructors. The buck for this would stop at my superiors. You could, therefore, argue that it might even be in my own personal interest to drop the case and let you win the point.

"You, on the other hand, would probably suffer considerably if, as you seem to believe, by omitting Godber's behaviour in the cockpit from your case file, you may fail to secure a conviction. This would not only eat into your professional pride but would also leave your life totally bereft of meaning. Without this obsessive witch-hunt, you would be void of purpose, even though Smith has no other relevance in your life at all. May I suggest that such motivation is not entirely detached or objective?"

Godber's feet were by now twitching not only in a lateral direction but in a vertical plane as well, causing the dinner table to shake as if beset by an earth tremor. "You are quite a clever fellow for a flying instructor," he said. "However, I think your logic may be tangling you up in knots. Did I not hear you say that full disclosure would be in your own personal interest? How then can you put any weight into the argument against?"

"Now you have come to the nub of the matter, Mr Godber. That is exactly the point. It is *despite* not *because of* the fact that I have a personal interest in this case that I am able to be dispassionate. Whilst I may feel personal animosity towards Smith and what he did to me, my objective reason tells me that it is completely unnecessary to include a mishap in the cockpit of a light aeroplane in your litany of criminal accusations against Smith. It simply was not a criminal act, merely one of momentary stupidity. You, on the other hand, are seemingly unable to view the case objectively, in the irrational belief that any action Smith performs must be one that incriminates himself. Would it not be better to focus on the areas where he has demonstrably broken the law, rather than build a case on multiple yet irrelevant minor indiscretions?"

"I thought I explained the necessity to build a criminal character profile to you earlier," retorted Godber testily. However, it was clear that his voice contained a much-diminished self-assuredness.

"I would argue that a criminal character profile is not enhanced by an innocent act of impulsiveness. We are all human, Mr Godber, even retired detectives."

"So what are you going to do now?" asked Godber, by now physically holding his legs in place with his hands.

"I think I will let you dwell on our conversation for a while. You are clearly a most able detective with a good track record. I imagine that, if you consider some of the issues we have just discussed, you may come around either to a compromise or complete capitulation on this point. Furthermore, I will be in

India for a day or two, and you may benefit from an assistant of some kind, I would imagine. After all, I am not exactly going to make friends with Mr Smith after what has happened. I am happy to observe any possible criminal activity on his part, so long as it has nothing to do with Redhill Aerodrome. Besides, tailing a suspect single-handed can be an exhausting business, can it not?"

After this somewhat intense conversation, the two men, having completed their repast, sat together in the restaurant talking together amicably until it was time for bed. An observer might have mistaken them for colleagues in the same organisation discussing mutual business activities, or perhaps even two lovers trapped in a time warp, though it was hard to believe that a man bearing such large feet and so lugubrious a facial expression could be the object of love. His partner, however, appeared to be attentive and eager to please, having insisted on paying the bill for both of them after ordering a couple of highballs. Whatever the dynamics between the two men, there seemed to be a degree of common purpose and sensitive concurrence in their ramblings.

Perhaps an observer would have paid them little attention. After all, there was nothing particularly unusual about two unmarried men enjoying each other's company. Besides, by the time they had finished, there were no customers left in the restaurant, though waiters are inclined to observe their guests, especially at quiet moments, and there were plenty still buzzing around like gadflies, apparently inventing jobs for themselves that did not need doing, such as filling half-full pepper grinders with black peppercorns or minutely adjusting the angle of cutlery already laid out for breakfast on neighbouring tables.

The waiters, should they have been interested, would have observed Godber and Winterbottom take their leave of the restaurant and wander slowly into the hotel lobby, apparently in no rush to part company. Some may have thought, *Ha, I can guess what those two will be up to later on*, before quashing such salacious thoughts for the sake of the Lord Kamadeva.

They may also have observed, half an hour earlier, through the internal window of the restaurant, that Mr and Mrs Smith from room 172 had walked down the corridor outside the restaurant, apparently deep in conversation about their plans for the following day, unnoticed by the two men, who did not seem to take any notice at all of this seemingly insignificant occurrence.

# 2.

"What was it that made you decide to stay in Delhi tomorrow, dear?" asked Smith once they had returned to their room. It had taken most of the meal for him to elicit an answer from his wife, who had been somewhat vacillating and evasive on the matter initially.

"I just weighed up the pros and cons. That's all." This did not seem a very plausible answer to Smith, who knew his wife well enough to know that such an empirical approach to decision making was not within her gift.

"And what were the pros and cons that you considered, dear?"

"Oh, I don't know. Perhaps I felt that I didn't have the right clothes for Varanasi, which I have heard can be dusty and prone to ash fall. Also, it is not the sort of place you would want to go to on your own for the first time. I might get attacked, converted by a Hindu mystic, or even burned alive on the riverbank, for all I know."

"How awful, dear. It sounds as if you have made a sensible decision. I am sure my business here tomorrow will not take long. Then we can have another sightseeing tour, perhaps?"

"Norman?"

"Yes, dear?"

"You know that the real reason I am not going to Varanasi is that you are not coming with me, don't you?"

"How very romantic."

"No. I don't mean it like that. I mean that, if you hadn't insisted on staying here and playing at being a procurement agent, I would never have considered bailing out. So there is only one real reason, and that is the fact that you would have abandoned me."

"Now that is a bit harsh, dear. I would never abandon you. I gave you the choice; that's all."

"Hobson's choice."

"And I am absolutely delighted that you will be staying here with me."

"Well, let's not argue about it."

"I'm not arguing. I am expressing my delight at your decision."

"You are arguing, Norman. You are arguing to yourself to appease your own conscience."

"No I am not."

"There you go again, disagreeing with me."

"I am not disagreeing with you. You are just contradicting me."

"It is *you* who has been contradicting *me*."

"No it hasn't"

"Norman?"

"Yes, dear."

"Sometimes it is best to be quiet when you are backed into a corner."

Smith took a long slow swig of his beer and considered his next move.

"Why don't I call the tour operator then and get the flights changed?"

"A perfect and insanely practical suggestion, Norman. As usual, we can sort everything out with practical action and common sense."

"You are absolutely right there, dear."

"But we haven't finished discussing this yet."

"Oh. I thought we had. Shall I call the tour operator later, then?"

"You can call them when you want, but doing so won't resolve this."

"Resolve what, dear?"

"The fact that you are being selfish. Pursuing your own interests, no matter how it affects others. I have read about men like you. They dominate their wives and use psychological tricks to make them submissive to their every whim."

"I had never noticed you being submissive to my every whim."

"But you don't ever know whether I am being submissive or compliant, do you?"

"Not on every occasion, it's true. But generally speaking, I would not describe you as submissive at all."

"So how do you explain me agreeing to stay with you in Delhi instead of going to Varanasi, as we had originally agreed?"

"Well, it sounds to me that you are a little frightened of going to Varanasi on your own. So it would possibly be true to say that you are being submissive to your own fears, but not to my demands."

"But you are being submissive to your own selfishness by staying in Delhi to pursue your hobby."

"I thought it was *you* who was being submissive, not *me*."

"Well that just goes to show how much you know about my feelings, doesn't it?"

It was not the first, and nor would it be the last, time that Smith would be utterly confounded by his wife's logic. These situations normally resulted from a simple discussion that she seemed to be able to turn upside down and then spiral into an altercation of complete madness. It was true that Smith might not be the most socially intelligent of beings, but he could normally follow most lines of reasoned argument. With Mrs G, these lines became so blurred and intertwined that trying to unravel their meaning was as likely as finding the end of a rainbow. Smith could not decide if this talent was unique to Mrs G or universal to womankind.

"I tell you what," he said. Why don't you slip your nightie on and get into bed whilst I sort out the travel arrangements.

"Why would I do that, Norman? This might be another act of dominance on your part."

"I didn't mean it like that. I am not telling you to get into bed. I am just making a suggestion. You must be tired after all that sightseeing."

"Well, may I suggest to you that I don't wear my nightie. It is far too hot. I will sleep in my underwear, unless you have any objections. Come to think of it, I might even go to bed completely in the buff."

"That would be most acceptable, dear. In fact, it would be most appealing if I may say so, if that is not too dominating a turn of phrase."

By the time Smith had telephoned the tour operator and rescheduled the programme, Mrs G was sitting up in bed, stark naked, reading *Vogue*.

"All sorted," said Smith, removing his rather unsightly underpants whilst gazing longingly at his wife's silky skin, almost as if he had never looked at it before.

"I am sorry I argued with you," said Mrs G, clearly now feeling somewhat mollified by all the attention she was getting.

"Well I am sorry too," said Smith, even though he was not entirely sure what he was sorry for. Probably for being Norman Smith.

"Then let's make up, shall we?"

Smith was familiar with his wife's emotional mood changes. And whilst these could be unnerving to the untrained husband, to him, they were an endless source of spice and variety.

"Let me just take my socks off first, dear. I think they may be a little bit ripe."

"Norman?"

"Yes, dear?"

"You say the most romantic things."

"I know, dear. I just can't help myself."

The Smiths slept soundly after all the exertions of the day, like two babes in the wood, both exhausted by the mental stress of reconciling affection with irritation, trapped inside the eternally spinning tumble dryer of matrimonial emotions. Mrs G's repose was characterised by a quite unusual nasal whistling, punctuated by the occasional grinding of her jaws, in the manner of a dog chomping on a bone. Her husband's nocturnal performance was much less sophisticated, consisting of deafening breathing paroxysms, deep rumblings, and regular explosive emissions of gas from a small orifice in his lower body. On top of this, he would occasionally shout out complete gibberish, as if giving orders to foreign (and deaf) minions on a parade ground.

Had one been trying to sleep in an adjacent room or, indeed, anywhere else in the hotel compound, one might have required earplugs or a large vat of whisky to attain a peaceful night's sleep. As it was, many of the other guests were beset by exhausting insomnia and had long realised that banging on the floor or walls of their rooms would have no impact on their distress whatsoever. The night-time receptionist had sensibly donned a pair of headphones and was listening to Bollywood classics to divert himself from impending insanity. He was, thus, unable to hear the constantly ringing telephone, the lack of response to which was driving hotel guests into an even greater frenzy of apoplexy. It is a wonder that there were no suicides, though one guest did give birth prematurely. Her husband, being unable to get through to reception for help, rang for an ambulance on his mobile phone and was told to wait until the morning because the only available ambulance had no functioning headlights. By morning, the hotel had a new guest, born without any medical assistance at all but, sadly, profoundly deaf.

It is therefore of little surprise that, in the midst of this cacophony of atonal vibrations and narcoleptic slumber, neither of the Smiths was aware of the rustling sounds coming from beneath their hotel bedroom's floorboards. They seemed to have forgotten the previous night's disturbance and had either failed to remember or simply not been bothered to change rooms as they had intended the previous morning. It was unfortunate that both were entirely naked in their helplessness, a sartorial blunder that had excited the local swarm of mosquitos to such an extent that its members were, by now, gorged on blood and finding it hard to stay awake themselves. Inevitably, the insect swarm had left numerous poisonous puncture holes on the epidermises of their unconscious victims, some already enlarging into large red and itchy spots. Mrs G, for example, had been stung on the bottom.

# 3.

Smith met with Brandon-Lewis at the hotel reception desk at the appointed hour of 9 a.m. Mrs G had decided to spend the morning relaxing by the pool and ministering to her mosquito bites. Her husband was feeling well rested and relaxed, if not slightly excited about the coming encounter.

"Mr Singh is due to meet us in about fifteen minutes, here at the reception. I have mentioned that you will be joining us, and he has suggested that we start off with an inspection of his warehouse, which I believe is in the locality. You can then discuss whatever it is that you wish with him. Then we will leave. You and I will take him to lunch to discuss confidential matters relating to the relationship with BA. How does that sound, Smith?"

"Perfect. Thank you very much indeed. Incidentally, are there any protocols I should be aware of or topics I should avoid?"

"In my limited experience of doing business in India, it is generally important to be extremely polite and respectful, avoid any reference to religion, and never mention money. That is usually the very last item on the agenda and should be avoided at all costs during the opening shots of any campaign. Oh, and never mention facial hair, as it can be a very touchy subject."

"Interesting. Thank you once again for your objective advice. As it happens, I have had much experience of dealing with Indian persons in my former profession as an accountant. However, all these encounters were in the UK, where I expect there is a slightly different set of rules. Nonetheless, I concur with your suggestions."

"Incidentally, Smith, in case you were wondering, my advice is strictly off the record. In the wrong hands, such considerations could be construed as racially stereotypical. As two businessmen, we know this is not about racism. It is simply that one has to be sensitive to local likes and customs in order to prevent unnecessary barriers to smooth negotiation. I am absolutely sure that these Indian chaps have a code of conduct for dealing with us English folk. After all, it is plain common sense."

"Indeed, Brandon Lewis. You do not need to explain this to me. There is a huge difference between racism, where one is critical, rude, and superior in one's attitude to individuals and groups of other races, and business intelligence, whereby one simply needs to understand the motivations on one's potential international partners."

"I think we understand each other perfectly, Mr Smith. Ah, here comes Mr Singh," said Brandon Lewis, indicating an extremely well-dressed man with a massive beard and large purple turban who was, at that minute, approaching.

"How nice to see you again, Mr Singh. Namaste," said Brandon Lewis to the new arrival, clasping his hands together as if in prayer and bowing his head respectfully. "May I introduce Mr Smith from Reigate."

"Namaste," said Smith, bowing in emulation of his more experienced colleague.

"It is an absolute pleasure to see you both. May the Lord Vishnu bless us." It was impossible to be absolutely sure if Mr Singh was absolutely genuine in his call for divine blessing, as he was one of those people who constantly have a twinkle in their eye, as if about to wink. Not a bad trait for a businessman for whom earnestness can lead to the appearance of certainty, a most unfortunate impression to convey to any negotiating partner.

"I hope you have both recovered from your flights and pray that none of my parts is affixed to the aircraft you are travelling to here on," he continued ambiguously.

"I told you he was a jolly fellow," said Brandon Lewis to Smith, nudging him ostentatiously.

Smith thought better of saying, "No you didn't."

"Come, come. Mr Bandon-Leviss, we cannot be serious all the time, can we not?" said Singh, looking amusedly at his two companions.

Somewhat perplexed by the double negative implicit in the question, the director smiled graciously.

"So let me show you round the verrhouse first, isn't it?" continued Singh, colloquially. "Come. Follow me. The entrance is not long away in distance and even nearer in time due to our great impatience, I think."

Singh strode purposefully through the hotel reception and out into the grounds, in the manner of one who owns the place, with Smith and Brandon Lewis following behind like two little puppies.

"Are we going to walk?" asked Brandon Lewis, clearly concerned at the pace at which Mr Singh had set off.

Mr Singh turned round to let the others catch up. "Of course, my dear chap," he replied. "It really isn't far at all." With that, he turned and continued in a purposeful manner, skirting the hotel building instead of heading for the road and passing the swimming pool where Mrs G was basking in a state of dishabille. She looked up, covered herself with her towel, and watched her husband and his two companions disappear into a small door on the poolside, clearly upset that her privacy had been invaded.

"Who was that voman?" asked Mr Singh as the three men gathered in the shaded doorway.

"You mean the lady beside the pool?" asked Smith.

"Indeed I do, sir. A very most handsome specimen I should say."

"That was my wife," said Smith, feeling slightly uncomfortable for some reason.

"Ah yes. You are a very lucky man, Mr Smit. A belle of the ball it is, no? None such the less though, I would never bring wife on business trip. Most inconwenient and bad lucky."

"You may have a point there," replied Smith, conceding the point.

"Now, you may be somewhat baffled why I bring you to this doorway in so much broad daylight when you are all anticipating my verrhouse, is that not so, isn't it?"

"Yes, I was rather wondering why you have led us to this hotel service entrance," replied Brendon-Lewis, who was as baffled as Smith. "I was rather expecting a visit to your aircraft parts warehouse. Did we not agree on this?"

Singh looked at the two men gleefully, as if he has asked a question to which no one could possibly know the answer but himself. "Vell, in this case, let me do explaining a little. I am just a local businessman. Family business you understand. No big public show, no shares, under the radar sort of thing. Naturally, as all successful businessmen, part of my business empire is real estate, isn't it? Wery modest but wery important. Now, one of my real estate holdings happens to be this hotel. In short and long of it, I own the whole damn lot. Aah, I see you surprised at scale of my business enterprise, gentlemen. But as they say, no smoke without fire, and no gain no pains. No, sir. So, if you were me, gentlemen, with already holding spare capacity buildings, would you lease or buy a verrouse space elsewhere? Indeed no, of course. You see, underneath the hotel, there is a large space, originally intended as a nuclear bunker in case those Pakistani mullahs go nuts with nuclear missiles. This space is my verrhouse and showroom, all under guest rooms and things. Clever thing. no? Come, let me introduce you."

Smith was rather proud that he had so far refrained from referring to either money or facial hair. Nonetheless, he could not help himself whispering to Brandon Lewis as they descended a flight of stairs in to the basement, "That explains the noises under the floor. Mrs G was convinced it was vermin."

The director, already disorientated by his surroundings, appeared even more confused.

Singh drew back a satin curtain at the bottom of the stairs to reveal what appeared to be a large reception room with carpets and cushions on the floor. There was a distinct smell of joss sticks and engine oil.

"Now please, gentlemen, take seat on floor, and I call my assistant for cha."

Smith and Brandon Lewis lowered themselves into the sitting position, while Sing disappeared behind a silk screen. They could hear him shouting angrily at someone, apparently in another room. "Get me and bring bloody cha, walla. Important wisitors in reception area very thirsty indeed. No slacking, boy. Get them bloody cha coming pronto."

As the two Englishmen reclined on the floor cushions in the basement room a tray of tea was produced for them. Shortly afterwards, a procession of figures appeared from behind a set of bead curtains, carrying a range of wares, including pashminas, sari material, fabric for shirts and suits, Hindu icon models, elephants, turbans, trinkets, and scale models of the Taj Mahal. These were laid out on the floor, and the guests were encouraged to admire, touch, and feel them.

Singh stood to one side, overseeing the operation and occasionally barking an order at one or other of the sales demonstrators. Clearly there was implied pressure for some trade to take place, presumably as a precursor to the more important business discussions that lay ahead.

"I was not aware that you ran an emporium of this kind," observed Brandon Lewis, nervously fondling the trunk of a somewhat gaudy representation of the elephant God Ganesh.

"All part of the business, Mr Bagdon-Levi," replied Singh, apparently proud of this demonstration of commercial diversification. "Lovely items. Good price for you. Please, buy. This family concern. Meet my sons and nephews too," he continued, waving his arms dismissively at the various vendors, as if they were an amorphous mass rather than individual relatives.

"Very interesting indeed," said Smith encouragingly, "though I am not generally a customer of such items. My good wife, Mrs G, on the other hand, would surely be in her element among such treasures." Not being the most intuitive businessman that ever lived, Smith did at least have some inkling that Singh would not be ready to move on to more important matters in hand until some money had changed hands in this sideline business area.

"Good opportunity to buy gifts for beautiful lady wife, no, Mr Smith? I bring you the opportunity. All you need to do is decide."

Smith was not sure he was capable of choosing any item that would necessarily be to Mrs G's most particular tastes. "I am sure that, if you were to allow my wife the opportunity to savour these treasures, she would be tempted to part with some rupees," persisted Smith. "Could we not invite her in?"

Brandon Lewis was examining a length of block print material that he had absolutely no intention of purchasing. "A capital idea, Mr Smith," he said. "What do you say, Mr Singh?"

Singh thought for a moment, apparently undecided as to the overall benefit to him of such an arrangement. "Well.

In business, you have to account for the customs of different nationalities, I suppose. If Mrs G would prefer to buy herself rather than receive a gift from her husband, then I think that would be the best vay of conducting business, gentlemen. Rajiv, please ask Mrs Smith to join us. She is beside the pool, I believe. But tell her for goodness sakes put on cover-up clothes for bloody decency's sake!"

As this was agreed, the two Englishmen felt a sense of relief and switched their attention to the tea, which they both drank in silence. Mr Singh seemed to be slightly unsettled, and neither wanted to catch is eye.

"You like belly dancing?" he said, suddenly and for no apparent reason.

"I thought that was a Turkish custom," responded Smith.

"Indian belly dancing better," pronounced Singh, clearly in no doubt about the matter.

"I am not sure Mrs G will be particularly interested in belly dancing," observed Smith, hoping to put the subject to bed.

"Maybe later then," conceded Singh.

Rajiv soon reappeared with Mrs G, who had covered herself with a hotel dressing gown and was gazing curiously at the wares laid out on the floor.

Smith looked slightly forlornly at his wife. "Darling, may I introduce you to Mr Singh and his family? As you can see, they have a wonderful range of gift items for sale, and I thought you would like to have a look to see if there is anything you might fancy."

Mrs G gave him a look of slight irritation. "I thought you had gone out on a business trip, not a shopping extravaganza," she replied somewhat curtly.

"Mrs Smeethe," said Singh, taking her hand in his and kissing the back of it in a most ungentlemanly manner. "This is just my little gift shop. All top-quality merchandise and very good price for lovely lady such as so beautiful as yourself. Please, take time to look around and under no pressure to buy of course, naturally. But opportunity too good to miss, perhaps?"

Smith gave his wife a look of assent, at which, despite her initial reservations, she seemed to accept the necessity of examining the items on sale and began rummaging through a large pile of silk scarves, which looked as if they might have been imported from China.

"Now, how about us talking aircraft parts?" said Smith, turning to his host, who seemed to be bewitched by the white skin on the back of Mrs G's neck.

"You drive hard bargain already, Mr Smith. I like straight talk in business. No donkey business is best shit."

"Time is of the essence, Mr Singh, don't you think? You are obviously a very busy man, and I would not wish to hold you up from more important business."

Leaving Mrs G in the hands of the family hawkers, Mr Singh led the two men towards a large doorway at the opposite end of the room to the stairs, which seemed to have been constructed sideways. "Gentlemen, I urge care and lateral thinking in the passageways ahead. We will be walking in the spaces between the walls of the hotel rooms and sometimes in the ceiling and floor spaces. In short, a series of secret passages, originally built to confound Pakistani invading hoards, will lead us to my verrhouse store at the heart of the complex."

He led the way through a series of very narrow and dimly lit passageways leading up and down a number of steps. A portly person would have become wedged in some of the narrower sections. It was a completely disorientating exercise and impossible to understand overall directional progress both laterally and vertically.

Eventually, after what seemed like at least thirty minutes, the passageway opened out into a large cave-like room, which was stacked with boxes of various sizes and shapes.

"How on earth did all these get in here?" uttered Brandon Lewis, realising that many of the boxes were far too large to have fitted through the passageways.

"Underground river, isn't it?" said Singh, pointing to a loading bay on the far side of the cave at which a motor launch appeared to be moored.

Smith looked at the warehouse in astonishment. Apart from the packaged items, several larger objects, including a Rolls-Royce RB211 jet engine and some wings and an aircraft tail fin, were visible, either on the floor or propped up against the cave walls.

"Welcome to the largest single repository for commercial aircraft parts in India," announced Singh proudly. "Safe as houses, wouldn't you say so, gentlemen? Now, Mr Smith. I understand you have a business proposition. Let us not beat around the bushes any longer."

Smith felt somewhat overawed by the scale of Singh's enterprise and hoped that Brandon Lewis had not egged up his role in parts procurement. Surely any order that he could provide would be mere bagatelle in the overall scheme of Singh's empire and hardly worth the man's efforts.

"Well firstly, Mr Singh, I would like to thank you and your corporation for inviting me into your magnificent premises and also to thank Mr Brandon Lewis for being kind enough to introduce me to you. Unlike you, Mr Singh, I am but a humble and retired tax accountant by profession. I am not a wealthy man and fear that my interest in your business may appear but as a grain of sand in a dessert of profit. I am in the market for a small number of avionic instruments and cockpit furniture in order that I might reconstruct the cockpit of a Boeing 737-800 as a flight simulator. I therefore have a specific and limited shopping list, which I wondered if I could forward to you to ascertain if these are both available and affordable for me. Would you be interested in such a relatively small-scale business opportunity?"

Singh looked slightly confused. "Ven Mr Branding-Levis explained that you are in the awiation business, I had assumed you would be vorking for large international airline, as he does. As you can imagine, it is not my normal practice to operate in the retail market, being strictly wholesale in my outlook. Nonetheless, as you are a friend of his, and depending upon your requirements, I am sure we can come to an arrangement that suits both parties."

"You are a most magnanimous person," said Smith, reaching out his hand for Singh to shake.

"Yes, indeed, I am werry magnaminous when it comes to favours which oil the vheels of business. Isn't that so, Mr Levis-Branding?"

"Indeed, you are the very definition of magnanimity," responded Brandon Lewis, demonstrating remarkable skill in not sounding in the least bit sarcastic.

It seemed to Smith that Singh needed quite a lot of oil to lubricate his business operations, a function his wife was currently performing stoically.

"In that case, if I may, Mr Singh, upon my return to the UK, I will list the parts that I require and email this to you. Perhaps you could then indicate availability, price, and delivery terms to me?"

"Indeed so, Mr Smith. No unforeseen bills of lading, taxes, and tariffs in my business, sir. No. Strictly payment upon delivery less deposit in adwance, isn't it?"

# 4.

Outside, by the poolside, DI Godber was being encouraged by Winterbottom to try sunbathing. This was something Godber had never considered doing before and a pastime he privately held in utter contempt.

"What on earth is the point in wasting time reclining beside a pool of water when there are criminals to be caught?" he objected, somewhat predictably.

Winterbottom, though prone to nervousness on occasion, was far less intense that his companion and would quite happily have whiled the day away soaking up the sunshine. "There's not much you can do when you lose the trail, is there?" he said, removing his T-shirt to reveal a concave and somewhat puny rib structure.

"I have not lost the trail, Mr Winterbottom. I am merely letting the accused hang himself by giving him some rope." Godber did not really need to worry about sunburn. Not only did he remain fully clothed; his enormous feet, facing the morning sun, cast a long shadow over his entire body.

"Where do you think Smith is today then?" said Winterbottom, rubbing sun cream under his armpits for some obscure reason. "It seems he has given us the slip, wouldn't you say?"

"Indeed not. There are times when one is stalking one's prey when one has to step back for a while, to lull the victim into a false sense of security."

"But I thought he had no idea you were following him in the first place."

"That has nothing to do with it. Criminals can usually sense the net closing in on them, even if they cannot put their finger on how this is happening. I am simply offering him a false sense of relief in order that he feels liberated enough to make a fatal mistake."

Winterbottom scratched his nose and contemplated this. He was not convinced. It was more likely that Godber had simply missed the chance to put a tail on Smith due to waking up too late, but it was not really worth pointing this out. "I wonder what that service door is used for," he said, pointing to a door beneath the main hotel infrastructure that was slowly opening.

They both watched as Mrs G emerged, clutching a large array of trinkets, materials, and ornaments. She looked very pleased with herself as she made her way to one of the loungers on the other side of the pool, which had a towel and a sun hat on it. She did not seem to notice the two men watching her from behind their sunglasses.

"You see?" whispered Godber. "That's Smith's wife. She's clearly up to no good. Looks very much like stolen goods to me. Clearly Smith has an inside track in the hotel somehow. I knew it would work." His feet were twitching, causing ominous irregular shadows to dance over his face.

It was not for the first time that Winterbottom pondered on Godber's acute sense of complacency. The appearance of Mrs Smith was surely pure coincidence, and it was far too early to jump to any conclusions as to the provenance of her booty.

"What are you intending to do then? Approach her directly?"

"Good gracious, no. I think we will let her stew with the contraband for a while. Meanwhile, I am going to investigate what is behind that door. You stay here and keep an eye on her. A weedy Brit by the poolside is perfect cover. She will never notice you."

"What do you mean weedy?"

"Let's face it, you are not exactly Charles Atlas, are you?"

"And you are not exactly Hercule Poirot."

Without another word between the two men, Godber sloped up to the service door and entered the corridor beyond. Mrs G did not seem to notice, so preoccupied was she with matters in hand.

Winterbottom put on his T-shirt, his bodily confidence somewhat shattered by Godber's insensitivity. He could see Smith's wife idly admiring the various items she had brought to the poolside, now in a state of undress that was rather pleasing to the eye. How on earth had that fool Smith captured such a fulsome mate? It was enough to make you feel a little bit jealous. Being a flying instructor had been a great disappointment to him in terms of sexual opportunity. However, it had only recently occurred to him that it may not have been entirely the choice of career that had stifled his progress towards romantic fulfilment. It may have had something to do with his innate weediness.

Inside the corridor, Godber took some time to adjust to the gloom. However, his vision was much restored when he remembered to take off his sunglasses. Before he could take many steps forward, he heard voices coming towards him. Instinctively he hid himself inside an empty wardrobe that just happened to be standing in the corridor with its door open, like a carnivorous plant waiting for its prey.

"Seems as if your vife has made hefty purchases of mechandise," said a voice, clearly with a local accent.

"I hope she has not been too much of a spendthrift. I am a man of modest means, Mr Singh," said a voice that Godber immediately recognised as Smith's, despite the sound of it being much muffled by the wardrobe door.

"Goodness me. It is prerogratiwe of ladies to purchase beautiful items to adorn themselwes with, is it not, Mr Smith?" continued the local man.

"Up to a point, Mr Singh, but not beyond," continued Smith. "Now that we have concluded our little arrangement together, I will leave you and Mr Brandon Lewis to your private business. Thank you once again, Mr Singh. I will be in touch with you soon."

Godber heard three sets of steps pass the wardrobe and on through the service door, which closed behind them. His mind was buzzing with possibilities. Now it was beyond doubt that Smith had been entering into clandestine business transactions with the locals. His wife was, at this very moment, holding the evidence in her hands. But who was the mysterious Mr Singh?

In his urgency to pursue the miscreants, he pushed at the closed wardrobe door, but it failed to budge. He pushed again, harder this time, but to no avail. Now concerned that he may have inadvertently entombed himself, Godber pounded his fists on the wardrobe door. The effect of this manoeuvre was to make the wardrobe topple forwards. Shortly afterwards, it tipped ninety degrees into the horizontal position with the doors on the floor, jammed closed by the force of gravity, with a prone former detective inspector lying prone on top of them, his large feet wedged into an old underwear shelf.

Outside, Winterbottom observed three men emerge from the service door. He did not recognise the two who slipped away round the side of the hotel building but did notice that one of them was wearing a turban. The third man sauntered over to the poolside and greeted his now recumbent wife with a peck on the cheek. *Smith*, he deduced cunningly. *I wonder if he bumped into Godber in there.*

Winterbottom was not what one would describe as a natural sleuth. He was comfortable with logic and procedure, as befitting a pilot, but less much so with deduction and conjecture. In some ways, his approach to detective work was infantile, much as a child who knows which direction chess pieces move but has no idea about the strategy of actually playing chess. As a result, he was prone to instinctive rather than contemplative deductions. His instinct told him that he should seek out Godber to establish the next move. It also told him that he should keep watch on the Smiths to gather as much evidence against them as possible. Two such opposing and contrary instincts clearly demonstrated Winterbottom's stasis. In short, he was overwhelmed by inertia.

From the distance he was sitting, he could not overhear what the Smiths were saying. He could only observe their body language. This was clearly inadequate if he was to discover anything incriminating. Furthermore, he was mindful that Smith could easily recognise him, despite his sunglasses. After all, they had spent an hour snuggled closely together in the cockpit of a Cessna not so long ago.

Smith spent some time admiring the chattels that his wife now had on display around her lounger, apparently making the odd complementary comment. His wife smiled at him reassuringly, perhaps as if to stress the quality of the merchandise or perhaps to assure her husband that all the items would be put to good use and pre-empt the common criticism of knick-knacks acquired in oriental boutiques, namely that they invariably fail to reach up to their glittering potential when set against the drabness of a European winter.

After this display of mutual approval, Smith bent over and kissed his wife on the lips, as if to affirm their marital bond, before slumping heavily into a lounger next to her and picking up a copy of The Times to read.

Hardly the behaviour of a hardened criminal on the run, thought Winterbottom, though he clearly had no baseline by which to judge the normal behaviour of criminals on the run.

*Looks more like a man placating his wife, who is fearful she has been a little too indulgent with herself in the retail sense.*

The Smiths idled away the entire morning beside the pool. Mrs Smith was occasionally seen daintily dipping her shapely thighs under the water in the pool and splashing herself without fully immersing, in an apparent act of self-baptism that somehow bewitched Winterbottom. Her husband, on the other hand, took the occasional plunge-dive, which caused so much water displacement as to result in minor flooding to the poolside patio. He invariably resurfaced to deliver a series of ostentatious snorting and water-blowing rituals normally only experienced amid a school of humpback whales, before removing himself from the pool immediately and dripping all over the tiles like a melting snowman.

Winterbottom dozed intermittently, unaware that his exposed nose was beginning to take on the colour of a ripe beetroot. He had plenty of time to think whilst surveying Godber's quarry and soon began to feel relaxed and comfortable. He was quite unsure now what he should do with respect to his mission. It seemed likely that Godber had heeded his words concerning the flying school, but he could not be absolutely sure. Indeed, Godber's discretion on this point may still be contingent on his further assistance in bringing Smith to justice. Nonetheless, he would have to make contact with the squadron leader soon to get further orders. It was almost as if he had become a double agent, serving two different masters, and without any moral compass to guide him.

Whilst all this was very perplexing, it was also a pleasure to have thinking space and to lie in the warm Indian sun, basking like a lizard. It was no surprise then that he eventually dozed off, only to wake a good hour later to find that Mr and Mrs Smith had disappeared, along with all their belongings. His feet were beginning to peel and his nose was red raw.

Now that the Smiths were no longer under surveillance, it was clear to Winterbottom that his next move should be to seek our Godber. He left his lounger by the pool, somewhat reluctantly, and approached the service door, which was closed but not locked. Removing his aviator sunglasses, he opened the door and peered into the corridor. It was clear that the passage was blocked by a large wooden box. Therefore, it was impossible to proceed further. However, Winterbottom noticed that the box was moving from side to side, and he could hear the muffled sounds of a human voice emanating from its interior. This was a cause of some concern to the wary flying instructor. Both Mr and Mrs Smith, among others, had exited from the service door. Godber hadn't. Could it be that, somehow, Godber had been attacked or taken away? Or could it be a trap? Perhaps there was an armed man inside the box waiting to shoot him.

Once again, Winterbottom was rendered immobile by indecision about what to do next. As he listened to the muffled sounds within the box, his ears became more accustomed to their timbre. He could just about make out the words, "Let me out, for God's sake. I'm suffocating."

It took him a minute or so to realise that the voice was that of DI Godber.

Winterbottom eventually realised that the box was an upturned wardrobe and that the doors were flattened against the floor of the corridor. With much effort, he managed to roll the wardrobe onto its side and prize the doors open with his Swiss army knife (which, by an incredible stroke of good fortune, he had upon himself). And so it was that DI Godber was released to fight the criminal world another day, though it has to be said he was somewhat dishevelled by the lengthy incarceration and took several minutes to regain sufficient breath to talk again or move his feet.

"I am most grateful to you for rescuing me, Winterbottom," wheezed Godber after recovering some of his wind.

"You seem to be in reasonably good shape," offered the flying instructor, clearly attempting to make light of Godber's condition.

"*Reasonably good shape?* For God's sake, man, I have just been incarcerated for several hours in an airless box bearing a striking resemblance to a coffin. I was buried alive and very nearly expired in the process. How can you say I am in *reasonably good shape* when I have literally just returned from the dead?"

"I was just trying to make you feel better."

"Well I don't need anyone to make me feel better. I am just relieved to be breathing again. Incidentally, why did you take so long to find me?"

"I was maintaining surveillance, as instructed."

"Did it not cross your mind to wonder if I had come to any harm?"

"Yes it did, as it happens. But I felt that the priority was to keep an eye on the Smiths. By the way, how did you get in there in the first place? Did someone lock you in?"

"Yes, yes, that's right. I was locked in."

"But the wardrobe doors weren't locked. There is no lock. They were just jammed against the floor."

"Look, I was in the corridor when Smith approached with his accomplices. I decided to hide in the wardrobe so they would not see me. When I thought they had gone, it became clear to me that they had locked me in because the door wouldn't open. Furthermore, someone must have sneaked back and deliberately pulled the wardrobe over onto its doors so I would never be able to escape. What a way to kill someone, by slow and gradual suffocation. You must agree with me that Smith is now implicated in attempted murder on top of all his other crimes. The man needs locking up urgently!"

"As there is no lock on the wardrobe doors, they must just have jammed closed."

"Then how do you explain the wardrobe falling over on top of them."

"Maybe you toppled it over trying to get out?"

"Don't be ridiculous. This was clearly a heinous attempt at murder. I don't think you have the first idea how the criminal mind works. A felon's first instinct is to remove any thing or person that can incriminate him."

"But I thought you hid so they could not see you. Presumably, they didn't know you were there. Unless you made a noise as they went past."

"I did *not* make a noise. Who do you take me for, an amateur private dick?"

"You said it, not me."

"Look here, Winterbottom. I do not have the strength to argue. Just take it from me that I have more experience in such matters. You are simply falling for the most obvious clues and making infantile suppositions. That is exactly what the criminals intended. Don't you see? It is a cover-up."

"Well they did a pretty good job covering you up; that's all I can say. And before you become too critical of my investigative skills, remember that it was me who found you and subsequently saved your life, assisted by my trusted Swiss army knife."

"I said I was grateful. It's just that I feel slightly unwell, that's all. Would you very much mind if I was sick? I think it might help."

"Please go ahead, by all means. I will be waiting outside in the fresh air. The smell of vomit always makes me feel so very nauseous."

As Winterbottom left the corridor, he could hear Godber retching raucously like a braying donkey.

## Interlude

Who's that now?

*Winterbottom.*

For goodness' sakes, are you about to whinge about your character as well?

*Well, you haven't exactly portrayed me in the most flattering light, have you?*

I wouldn't say that. I think your handling of the incident with Smith in the Cessna was admirable, even brave. And your loyalty to Mantle and the flying club is most admirable indeed. You can't help having a nervous disposition; that's just your nature.

*Maybe some of that is true, but I am simply not coming across well to the reader. Before meeting Smith, I never had a nervous nature at all. I was absolutely fine until you started this ridiculous story and caused me to have a mental breakdown.*

I would not really call it a breakdown. Just a shock. Anyone would react like that after a near-death experience.

*Would they, indeed? I bet Mantle wouldn't. You seem to think he is so upright and strong just because he happened to be an RAF squadron leader. Anyway, why do you have to focus on my flaws, such as my unusual rib structure and delicate skin, and cast me as weedy and ineffectual with women?*

It was Godber that called you weedy, not me.

*But you wrote those words on his behalf. You are at the least sympathetic to them.*

Look, you can't have it both ways. Either I am the author and you have to accept how I portray you and everyone else or you can continue deluding yourself that you and all the other characters are entities in their own right. If the latter is the case, I am merely representing you as you are, warts and all.

*But there is the issue of defamation of character to consider, is there not?*

If you can speak for yourself, as you seem to be doing now, you can't then claim that I am putting words into your mouth or inventing your behaviour. So there is no defamation on my part. I can only be defamatory if you are a figment of my imagination, in which case the only person I can defame by these words is myself, because no one else exists.

*Were you such a clever dick at school?*

As a matter of fact, I did not do very well at school, but that is none of your business.

*I expect you were bullied there by real people. That's why you want to recreate them differently in your stories, because you can't deal with real people.*

Look. You can't try to defame me without my consent. I am in charge here.

*Can't I?*

Not only are you fictional, but you are also talking absolute rubbish, which the reader will not understand anyway. To be honest, we are all sick and tired of these interruptions from characters who apparently can't accept that they are not all being portrayed as Peter Perfect. If they were, it would be a most tedious read indeed, as I think I have mentioned before. If you are so real and independent of my imagination, why don't you complain to the other characters instead of to me? When you are not in the story, there is plenty of time for you to get together and have a group whinge. Just do it off the page; that's all I ask.

*How do you know we haven't been talking together about you already?*

I don't. And I don't care, as long as you leave me alone.

*Coward.*

No. I am not.

*Yes, you are.*

How can you say that?

*Because you are scared of your own characters. They just might ruin your story.*

They can't do that.

*Let's see, shall we?*

**5.**

After a long morning's sunbathing beside the pool, Smith and Mrs G both showered before taking a "siesta". It is of no concern to us what they got up to during this time because it is not in our nature to be gratuitously voyeuristic. We can, however, assume a degree of intimacy between the long-married pair, partly due to the magical and erotic properties of the Orient and partly because each party was feeling flushed with good fortune. Smith had all but procured the parts he had been seeking, whilst Mrs G had managed to festoon herself with gifts and trinkets, all be it at a price in rupees that her husband was, as yet, unaware of. Both had achieved their respective and completely different states of nirvana without creating a rift of jealousy between each other, a most unusual state of affairs and one that should indeed be celebrated, even if it is inevitably short-lived.

"So that explains the noises under the floor," said Mrs G lazily, after her husband had explained about the passageways and underground warehouse.

"Indeed it does, dear. A most ingenious arrangement, don't you think?"

"Most ingenious, Norman."

"I hope you don't regret missing Varanasi for this?"

"No, Norman. I think I made the right decision. I would have been quite uncomfortable travelling on my own in this country. It is so unusual in so many unsettling ways, don't you think?"

"I am not sure it is unsettling, dear. But I have to admit it is rather different from Reigate."

"By the way, did you see that man at the poolside? The rather weedy-looking man with sunglasses and a red nose?"

"Actually I did notice him—though he seemed to be asleep most of the time."

"Well, I swear he was eyeing me up. In fact, it was a bit creepy the way he stared at me when I went in the pool."

"You are a very attractive woman, dear. I am not at all surprised. In fact, funnily enough, something about that chap reminded me of the flying instructor who took me up at Redhill. Same sort of weedy build, I suppose."

"How strange. But the odds of it being the same person must be a million to one."

"Oh, I didn't think it was really him. Just someone similar."

"And how did you get on with Mr Singh, Norman? He seemed extremely charming to me, despite the horrible beard."

"Well, it is early days, but my first impression is that he is a man I can do business with. It was very good of him to offer me a chance to access his wares. Apparently he normally only deals in the wholesale market."

"Aren't you a lucky boy then?"

"I hope so."

"I do hope Mother is coping in my absence," continued Mrs G at a complete tangent.

"That old fruit bat would cope in any eco-habitat you left her in, even though she doesn't know what day it is."

"Don't be so unkind, Norman. She can't help having dementia. It is our duty to look after her and make sure she is safe."

"Well, I am sure the carers will look after her in our absence. Good God, they cost enough."

"Money is irrelevant in such circumstances."

"What gets me is that the care package is so expensive, but the carers don't even earn the minimum wage."

"They do it because they love the job. It is their vocation, Norman—much like yours was tax accounting."

Smith decided not to contest this line of logic. His wife seemed to be unable to understand that there are few people who would chose to work looking after decrepit, irascible, and incontinent elderly people for virtually no financial return unless they were utterly destitute. Nor could she comprehend the economics of the middlemen that carved off the cream from each caring arrangement.

"Well, anyway, we have the rest of the day here, and the driver will pick us up to take us to Agra at nine tomorrow morning."

"Norman?"

"Yes, dear?"

"Why do you have to be so practical all the time? Can't we just forget about arrangements for an hour or so?"

"As you wish," he replied compliantly.

"Do you like my new pashminas?"

"They are delightful, dear."

"Which colour do you like best?"

"Oh, I don't know. They are all nice. Perhaps the red one."

"The red one?"

"Yes."

"But I haven't got a red one."

"I thought you had."

"Do you mean the ochre one?"

"Yes, indeed. That is the one I like best."

"That is my least favourite as it happens, but it might work in the autumn."

"Exactly what I was thinking, dear. We must be psychic."

"And which statue of Ganesh do you like best?"

"The silver one."

"They are all silver."

"That's what I mean. They are all nice."

"Norman?"

"Yes."

"Did you look at the things I bought at all?"

"Of course."

"You don't seem to be particularly familiar with them."

"Well there are so many. I can't remember everything that was on the tray."

"There isn't a tray."

"No, I know. I was just referring to a memory game we used to play as children. Try to remember all the objects on a tray."

"Sometimes I find it hard to follow you, Norman. I certainly don't remember ever playing a game like that. And anyway, what has that got to do with my purchases?"

"Nothing really, dear. I was just pointing out that you seem to have acquired a number of items, and I can't memorise every single one of them."

"I can, Norman. In fact, it's all I have been thinking about for the last few hours."

"That would explain it."

"Explain what, Norman?"

"Explain why you seem somewhat preoccupied."

"I am not preoccupied. I am simply assessing my hoard and trying to decide what to give to Mother."

"She won't notice whatever you give her."

That's why I am trying to decide what I like least. You have been most helpful in that respect."

"It was my pleasure, dear."

"Now, Norman, I think I would like to go for a stroll in the park this afternoon," Mrs G announced after a short pause, as if this was not a practical arrangement.

"That sounds like a perfect plan, dearest. Shall I accompany you?"

"Yes. I think so. After all, you seem to be quite amenable today."

"I do my best to please."

# 6.

Brandon-Lewis strode back to the hotel, oozing spices from every pore and gland in his body. Singh had treated him to a luxurious Indian luncheon that had proved rather too hot for the director. Nonetheless, he was pleased with the way the meeting had gone. Singh had re-signed the Albion Airways contract for emergency spare parts without hesitation, clearly satisfied with the upfront payment he had been offered as an inducement. Brandon Lewis could not help but wonder at the eclectic nature of Mr Singh's business interests. Not surprisingly, he owned the restaurant they had eaten in.

There would be time for an afternoon nap before going to the airport for the overnight return leg to Heathrow in economy class, which he was definitely not looking forward to. At least this would conclude his research into the long-haul economy class traveller experience, though he had already written his report in his mind's eye. It was very unlikely that there would be any mitigating factors on the return journey that would soften his harsh findings. However, there was no certainty that any action would be taken to remedy the plight of the poor victims he had observed—unless it could be proven that the Albion Airways experience was considerably worse than that being offered by competitor airlines and resulted directly in a reduction in ticket purchases. There may be some low-cost improvements that could be made, however, such as ensuring that the drinking water machines were working, not running out of food on every flight, and cleaning the toilets every now and again. The one thing that was unlikely to change was the inhumanly crushed seating arrangements, designed to accommodate as many people as possible into every square metre of the rear-fuselage. It was obvious that the only way to relieve pressure on space was to build upwards into the empty air above the passengers' heads. Brandon Lewis was seriously considering recommending the introduction of hammocks but had not yet worked out how seat belts could be fitted to these in the event of unexpected clear-air turbulence. A poorly designed hammock could be dashed against the ceiling of the cabin along with its occupant if the airliner hit an air pocket—though this eventuality could be considered a positive outcome for the victim in that he or she would be put out of his or her misery suddenly and, hopefully, painlessly.

Brandon Lewis was pleased that he had been able to lend a hand to Smith, who seemed a decent and interesting chap despite his unhealthy obsession with flight simulation. It seemed as if Smith and Singh had hit it off reasonably well and introducing a new client could only enhance Albion Airways' relationship with the parts procurer. It had been a real eye-opener to visit Singh's underground warehouse, a privilege he had not previously been party to.

With these thoughts buzzing through his mind, Brandon Lewis turned a corner and suddenly bumped into Smith and his wife, who were also clearly taking a stroll in the slightly cooler early evening air.

"Smith, I was just thinking about you," he said instinctively.

"I am sure there are more enlightening things to think about whilst strolling the romantic pavements of New Delhi," replied Mrs G, robbing the opportunity for her husband to bask in the glory of his new-found friendship.

"You must be Mrs Smith. What an absolute pleasure," he replied, taking her hand in his and kissing the back of it, apparently ignoring the fact that he had seen her earlier in Mr Singh's emporium. "Mr Smith is a very lucky man, but I am sure I am not the first one to utter those words to you."

"Ah yes. This is Mr Brandon-Lewis, the gentleman who kindly introduced me to Mr Singh, dear. You may have seen him earlier."

Without taking her eyes off those of Brandon Lewis, both pairs of which seemed to be temporarily locked onto each other, Mrs G said, "You never told me he was so charming."

*What a pair of flirts*, thought Smith, beginning to reassess his opinion of Brandon-Lewis in the light of this ostentatious display. "We have just been for a walk in the park to look at the temple ruins and the monkeys. A most enlightening experience, wasn't it, dear?" With this, Smith put a protective arm around his wife's shoulders.

Mrs G shrugged it off delicately.

"How delightful. I am sure your wife blended in perfectly with the beauty of the scene. I do so admire your pashmina, Mrs Smith. Such a flattering colour."

Smith had, by now, completely reversed his once positive opinion of Brandon-Lewis and was wondering if it would be appropriate to punch him on the nose or not. Mrs G adopted the traditional pose with which she absorbed male flattery, cheeks flushed, tongue on lips, and eyelids all a flutter.

156 GARETH OWEN

"Well, we must be getting along. Time is of the essence," Smith declared, looking at his wristwatch.

"But we are in no hurry, Norman," said Mrs G. And it looks to me as if Mr Brandon-Lewis has lost his way heading back to the hotel. The very least we can do is accompany him, especially as he has been so generous."

"How very kind of you, Mrs Smith. You are, indeed, correct. I was so lost in thought I think I must have made a wrong turning."

Smith was utterly repulsed by the smell of curry emanating from Brandon Lewis, which his wife appeared to have mistaken for aftershave. "In that case, let's get a move on. We don't want to be late for predinner drinks, do we, dear? We are on holiday, after all, unlike Mr Brandon Lewis, whom I believe will be back on shift in an hour or so."

"Sadly so," said Brandon-Smith. "I will be returning to the UK this evening."

"Oh but we must keep in touch," said Mrs G.

"What a capital idea," said the director, staring at Mrs G like a love-struck myna bird. "By the way, Smith, I hope my introduction to Mr Singh was useful to you?"

"Indeed. Most satisfactory. Thank you very much indeed," Smith uttered between gritted teeth. "A most impressive and polite businessman. I was absolutely overawed by his warehouse."

"You see, Mrs Smith. I usually come up with the goods."

"Don't you just," replied Mrs G, trying not to look at the abundant hairs escaping through the director's shirt front.

Suddenly, he no longer appeared so cadaverous to Smith.

As the unusual trio meandered in the general direction of the hotel, it was clear that little heed had been paid to Smith's call for urgency. He walked in front and barely took part in the evidently amicable conversation that was taking place between his wife and her new-found admirer. The couple seemed little interested in the sacred cows, exotically clad local residents, street food stalls, hawkers, dead dogs, and tuk-tuks they passed on the way. Fortunately, the distance to the hotel was not great by any measure, though one could not help thinking that Mrs G and Brandon Lewis would have been more than happy to detour round a few blocks in order to delay their inevitable arrival, had Smith not been deliberately guiding them on a more direct route.

It was no surprise to Smith that Mrs G invited Brandon-Lewis to join her and her husband for an aperitif under a tree in the hotel grounds to watch the peacocks when they got back. They all agreed that a Campari and soda would fit the bill nicely.

"Lovely peacocks, eh, Smith?" said Brandon-Lewis, gulping down his cocktail as if it was a pint of bitter.

"Indeed they are quite stunning," conceded Smith.

"You clearly have an eye for natural beauty," said Mrs G, already slurring slightly, having devoured most of her drink on an empty stomach.

"I'm not sure about that," said the director. "Not much call for it in my profession, unless you think machines are beautiful."

"Indeed they can be," interjected Smith, determined that he should not be left out of the conversation. "Take Concord, or the shape of an Aston Martin DB7, for example. There are sights to behold."

"Don't be so silly, Norman. No man-made machine can match the wonders of nature, surely?"

"Aesthetically I would argue that a Ferrari is more beautiful than a baboon, for example."

"But you are not comparing like with like."

"Isn't that the whole point of the conversation?"

"You sound like my cousin. He is always arguing ridiculous hypotheses," said Brandon- Lewis, looking at his watch. "He's an MP."

The mere mention that Brandon-Lewis had a close relative who was a Member of Parliament put a complete damper on the conversation. Smith had to restrain himself from remarking on the similarity between the behaviour of MPs and baboons.

"Well, I really must be getting along," said the MP's cousin, unsure if his familial association had not tainted his image in the eyes of his companions.

"It has been a pleasure to meet you, hasn't it, dear? And thank you once again for your kind introduction," said Smith, clearly relieved that his rival would shortly be taking his leave.

"Here is my card, in case you ever need to get in touch," said Brandon-Lewis, handing it to Mrs G in a provocative act of virility.

"I will keep this close to my heart," said Mrs G. "And I do hope we will meet again someday."

As Brandon-Lewis took his leave and headed toward his room, Smith looked at his wife in the manner of a furious cuckold. "What on earth was that display all about?" he said angrily.

"Oh, Norman, how sweet of you. I do believe you are a little bit jealous."

"There really was no need to flirt with the man so obviously in front of me, you know. He must think I am an absolute goon or something."

"It was just a bit of fun. I thought it might help with your business activities if we got a bit closer to him as a family, as it were. Besides, he is rather handsome, in a tubercular kind of way."

"No he is not. He is very ordinary looking. Just because he has a double-barrelled name doesn't mean to say he has any particular romantic merits, you know."

"I'm not sure. I bet he has a very substantial and erotic bank balance."

"Well, if that's how you feel, I don't know why you don't just run off with him."

"Why would I do that when I am married to such a gloriously jealous partner?"

"I don't know what you mean."

"Norman. Sometimes a woman has to prove to herself not only that she is still attractive to men, but also that her husband still cares about her enough to be jealous. You were wonderful and came through the test with flying colours."

"Thank you, dear." Smith was not convinced by this line of argument but, nonetheless, felt a glow of appreciation at having such a tigress for a wife. At that point, Mrs G's mobile phone rang. She managed to abstract it from her handbag just in time to answer it. Smith watched her talking. He had never noticed how twisted her lips could be before.

"Oh my God. Oh my giddy aunt, is she still alive ... How? Lying on the carpet? Without her slippers or pants on? Oh my God. We will be back on the next flight. Keep her safe until we get there. Oh my goodness. Yes. Goodbye," uttered Mrs G, in a vocal sequence of ever-increasing hysteria, which Smith realised meant impending crisis.

"What is it?" said Smith, noticing that the colour had drained from his wife's face and her mouth appeared to have formed into a rictus.

"That was the care company. Mother has had a seizure."

"How serious is it?"

"How the bloody hell do I know how serious it is? Mum collapsed on the floor and was found the by the carer, foaming at the mouth. I think she is still unconscious. She may be dying. Norman, we have to get back to Reigate as soon as we can."

"Of course, dear. I will see if we can get onto this evening's flight," said Norman gravely, though immensely relieved that he had managed to conduct his business in India prior to this unfortunate interruption. He was also hopeful that the travel insurance arrangement he had made would provide useful financial compensation for a trip aborted in such a manner.

# CHAPTER 5

# 38,000 FEET

## 1.

Captain Dodwell and First Officer Craig were sitting in the cockpit of their Boeing 777, on stand at Indira Ghandi Airport, completely unaware that the passenger who had illegally entered the flight deck on the outbound journey just a few days ago was, at that moment, boarding the plane with his wife.

"Did you double-check with engineering that the water-cooling switch gear on the engine oil lubrication system has been replaced?"

"I did indeed, sir. All sorted. Apparently, the parts were sourced from Delhi rather than having to fly them out."

"That does not bode well, Craig. Better keep our eyes on the engine oil temperatures tonight. These spare parts from India can be pretty Mickey Mouse, you know."

"But surely the Albion Airways engineering team would not take any risks with parts?"

"That's the theory, Craig. Nonetheless, I am not convinced about the provenance or quality of workmanship. I expect they were cheap; that's all."

"I thought that was in France."

"What are you talking about, Craig?"

"Provence. That's in France, isn't it, sir?"

"I said provenance."

"Near the Cote d'Azur, I think. Shall I start the pre-flight checks, sir?

"Go ahead, Craig, and don't forget to keep checking the oil temperature once we are airborne."

"Do you mean temperament, sir?"

"No, I mean the temperamental temperature readings."

"Roger, sir."

It was not the first time Dodwell had wondered about the first officer's state of mental health, a defect potentially more dangerous than faulty water-cooling switch gear.

"Pre-flight checks, item three—remove air stewardesses from flight deck," said Craig monotonously.

"Negative, Craig. Come on, girls. It's time to get a move on, or we'll never get this crate in the air," responded the captain, turning his head round towards five young air stewardesses in differing states of undress, huddled into the back of the cockpit. "Get your knickers on, girls! Craig, hold on with the checks until we have the all-clear on the stewardess front."

The stewardesses immediately started adjusting their clothing and applying make-up and tightening the tension on their hairgrips, as if suddenly aware that they now had duties to attend to in other parts of the aircraft. Each one kissed the captain on the cheek as she departed the cabin, leaving a large red lipstick mark resembling an abscess on his face.

Dolly was the last one to leave, as her duties were in the first-class cabin at the front of the plane. She was also responsible for providing the pilots with food and drink on the flight and for guarding the cockpit door. "Captain Dodwell, I have a message for you," she whispered in the captain's ear.

"Not now, Dolly. Can't you see I am busy," replied Dodwell somewhat irritably.

"It is not a personal matter," continued the stewardess. "It concerns one of the passengers in economy class."

## Interlude

*It's me, Dolly. I strongly object to this grossly sexist and outdated depiction of air stewardesses. It is utterly objectionable!*

Shut up. I'm busy!

"Well make it snappy. There are only ten minutes until we start the engines," said the captain, distracted by whatever he was doing with the flight management system.

"Well, his name is Brandon-Lewis, and he says he is on Albion Airways' board of directors. Apparently, he is doing some research for a report on our economy-class service. Anyway, he has requested a chat with you in the cockpit once we are cruising. Shall I tell him that will be OK?"

Dodwell stopped tinkering with the controls, which, incidentally, he was only doing to impress Dolly and looked up thoughtfully. "I see. May I suggest that, once we are airborne, you google this chap to make sure he really is who he says he is? If so, please make sure all the stewards in economy are advised to give him an extra level of service on this flight. No cock-ups, do you understand?"

Dolly nodded respectfully.

"You, personally, can tell him that he is welcome in the cockpit one hour after take-off. If he is an imposter, please refuse his request and keep an eye on him. We don't want any more intrusions like last time. And remember, never to mention that incident to anyone."

"Yes, Captain," said Dolly, curtseying as if in the presence of royalty. "I will see you later then."

"Good girl, Dolly. That's the spirit," concluded Dodwell, encouragingly, winking at the stewardess in a most unseemly manner before returning to the flight controls.

"Damned fine girl, that Dolly," said Dodwell to the first officer after she had left the fight deck.

"Indeed, Captain," replied Craig politely. "Can we continue with the pre-flight checks now, sir?"

"If we must, Craig. If we must."


## 2.

Fortunately, Norman Smith and Mrs G had managed to secure two last-minute tickets in economy class for their emergency return trip to Heathrow, premium economy class being fully booked. Nonetheless, both were dismayed at the prospect of being incarcerated in such discomfort, especially on an overnight flight.

"Bloody awful legroom," moaned Smith.

"It may be uncomfortable, but there is no use complaining, Norman. This is an emergency and we have to make the best of it. Poor Mother may be breathing her last as we talk. Imagine how she must be feeling."

"I would rather not."

"What do you mean by that, Norman?"

"At this moment, I would rather not imagine what it feels like to be your mother, dying or living. Though, come to think of it, she is probably a whole lot more comfortable than I am at the moment."

"Do you ever think of anybody but yourself?"

"Frequently."

"Who?"

"Maria Carey."

"How can you make fun of things at a time like this?"

"Because otherwise I might go mad."

"I thought you already had."

"No, that's just genius."

"Since when have you been a genius?"

"Since I was born, I suppose."

"You have ideas beyond your station."

"Which one are you referring to? Reigate or Redhill?"

Mrs G was struggling to keep her food tray stable in view of some sudden unexpected and terrifying turbulence.

"You are not funny, you know, Norman. This is a serious matter."

"I know, dear. It is just my way of coping. I expect I will be fine if they ever bring the drinks trolley round."

"This is Captain Dodwell from the flight deck. We are just encountering a little bit of light turbulence. It is nothing to worry about, but I have put the seat-belt signs back on for your own safety. Until I put them off again, please return to your seats and make sure your seat belt is fastened. In the meantime, I hope you are enjoying the flight. *Brace! Brace! Brace!*

"Only joking! Woops, pressed the wrong button. I will get back to you with an update on our routing and weather conditions at Heathrow later in the flight. In the meantime, I hope you get some rest. I could certainly do with a nap myself, but it will just have to wait."

"Good God," said Mrs G, clinging on to her seat. "Was that the captain?"

"I think so, dear. He seems to know what he is talking about."

"Does he, indeed? Sounds as though he is mad as a hatter or else intoxicated."

"No, it's just his sense of humour. It's his way of coping."

"Well I don't understand why men have to cope in such ridiculous ways."

"It's just the way we are made, dear."

"By the way, where is that drinks trolley? I could do with a large G&T to calm my nerves."

"I think the trolley dollies have all been requested by the captain to sit down and fasten their seatbelts."

"Surely they are exempt from such dictates?"

"It would seem not."

"In that case, go to the galley and procure one for me, Norman. There's a good fellow."

"As you wish, dear."

It took Norman Smith a couple of minutes to unfasten his seatbelt, put his dinner tray on the floor, stow the seat-back table, and extricate himself from his catacomb, as the aircraft continued flying unevenly. Nonetheless, the aisles were empty, and it did not take him long after that to sway down to the rear galley, like a sailor on a ship navigating Cape Horn.

"Please, could you make me up two large G&T's?" he asked politely of the seated steward, the one with sweat marks under his armpits.

"Get back to your seat immediately, sir. We cannot serve drinks whilst the seatbelt sign is on," he said admonishingly, if not slightly effeminately. He had clearly been much influenced by the teachers at his school.

"Look. My wife is not well. She is under a lot of strain due to her mother having been taken suddenly and very seriously ill. Would you not consider bending the rules for humanity's sake?"

"I'm afraid we cannot do that, sir. Offering you liquids at this time may constitute a risk to both yourself and other passengers, should you fall or spill the drinks over them. As soon as the seatbelt signs are switched off, I will bring the drinks to you if you tell me your seat numbers."

"I do not know our seat numbers, and I am not prepared to wait. My wife's health is at stake here. Would you just let her die because of a bit of turbulence?"

"I think you are exaggerating things a little, sir, if I may say so. It is unlikely that a few minutes of anxiety will kill her. Furthermore, such episodes of mental and clear-air turbulence rarely last long."

"Are you accusing me of exaggerating?"

"Yes."

"How dare you? What kind of customer service is this? I expect you are just frightened that you might fall over if you try to stand up and get my drinks."

"I am perfectly able to stand up for myself and equally well trained in keeping my balance on a moving aircraft, thank you. I am sorry. There is nothing I can do for you until we reach calmer air. Now please return to your seat, or I will have to call the cabin supervisor."

"I bet he or she won't come. Too scared to undo his or her seatbelt, I bet."

At that moment, two things happened simultaneously. Firstly, the seatbelt signs went off. And secondly, another male passenger approached the galley.

"What is going on here?" asked the passenger, looking at the steward rather than Smith.

"This gentleman is being rather persistent and rude. Nothing at all unusual," replied the steward, pouting like an insulted child.

"Smith caught the passenger's eye, and immediately recognised him as Brandon-Lewis, the love rival he had not yet forgiven.

"What on earth are you doing on this flight, Mr Smith?"

"My mother-in-law has been taken ill, and we have had to make a hasty return trip."

"I am so sorry to hear that. How is your lovely wife? It must be a great shock to her."

Smith grimaced. Incredibly, whilst this conversation was going on, the steward had rapidly prepared two G&Ts and passed them to Smith.

"Brandon-Lewis. If it were not for the fact that my wife is in severe need of a tonic, I would pour both these drinks over your head. I have just about had enough of your flirting with her. It is completely unacceptable."

"I am not flirting. I was just being polite. To tell the truth, she is not really my type. Too bossy for me."

For some reason, at this, both men fell into guffaws of laughter. "Shhhh, you mustn't speak like that about her. She is just a little assertive at times," Smith said, only to crease up into another protracted paroxysm.

The two men laughed so much that their legs became so weakened they had to lean on each other for support.

"A little assertive, Smith? That's a good one! Ha ha," burbled Brandon-Lewis through the foam that had gathered in his mouth.

After a few moments, both men were able to regain their composure and it was immediately apparent that the episode had cleared the air and renewed the former bond between them.

"Now look here, Smith. I am due on the flight deck in a minute or two to brief the captain. Would you like to come with me?"

"Absolutely I would. Can you wait so I can deliver these drinks to Mrs G first? She is in a bit of a state, you know. She might be a bit on the assertive side at times, but she is a good egg overall."

"I'm sure she is, Mr Smith. I did not mean to imply anything else. Most women are bossy when you get to know them, so Mrs G is by no means unique in this characteristic."

"Are they?" said Smith, whose experience of other women was somewhat limited.

"Oh yes. All three of my wives were, anyway."

When Mr Smith returned to Mrs G to deliver her drink, he found her staring vacantly at the seat back in front. He had seen her afflicted by such stress-induced catatonia before. Normally, time and a good strong G&T were the most natural remedies for such a condition, so he placed her tonic on the armrest.

"Just popping up to the cockpit for a chat with the captain, dear. I'll be back in jiffy."

"I hope you can get some sense out of him," she replied, not adjusting her gaze. "I am sure he is quite potty. By the way, did you see the walrus?"

"What walrus exactly are you referring to?"

"The one on the beach."

"Do you think it might be wise to take a drink, dear? I fear you might be getting dehydrated."

"Fighting for the female, he was."

Smith decided to make a hasty retreat in case his presence made things worse for his poor wife. He met Brendan-Lewis in the forward first-class galley, where he was talking to Dolly. Unfortunately, she recognised Smith immediately and blushed fulsomely. Smith, too, remembered his previous encounter with the stewardess.

"This is Dolly, the chief stewardess," said Brandon Lewis, unaware that the two were already acquainted.

"Ah yes. It is a pleasure to meet you again, Dolly—hopefully in rather more agreeable circumstances."

Dolly smiled and kissed him on the cheek.

"The truth is, Smith, Dolly runs the show around here. Pulls rank over the captain in my opinion."

"Mr Brandon-Lewis, you are exaggerating. I could no more pilot an airliner than fly to the moon. As it happens, though, Mr Smith and I have met before. I tried, unsuccessfully to stop him barging into the cockpit a couple of days ago on the outward flight. It seems he is returning with protection."

"Indeed, I have taken the rascal under my wing. We are sort of business partners now, and I want to introduce him to Captain Dodwell. I am sure they will get along together."

"Wait there. I will just check the captain is ready to see you."

As Dolly disappeared onto the flight deck, Brandon-Lewis looked at Smith admiringly. "You old devil, Smith. She seems to have taken quite a fancy to you. I will not ask what transpired between you two on the outbound journey."

"It was all a bit of a mistake, to be honest. I tripped up and fell into the cockpit by accident."

"Say no more, Smith. I understand," interjected the director. "It really is none of my business."

Dolly returned with a professional smile on her face. "The captain is ready to see you both. Just make sure you don't distract him from the controls. It is important that he concentrates on the job in hand rather than on making conversation. He is very tired tonight and will need all his energy to fly the plane. I'm afraid he has been burning the candle at both ends again."

Dolly led the two passengers through the cockpit door and behind a velvet curtain into the dimly lit flight deck, festooned with rows of flickering lights and computer screens, switches, levers, and nobs.

"Without looking round, the captain said, "Welcome to the office, Mr Brandon-Lewis. I will be with you in a second. By the way, this is First Officer Craig," he added briefly, waving in the direction of the first officer.

Both Dodwell and Craig were staring at the same screen and making some adjustments to the controls.

"As I told you, Craig, the oil temperature is rising in engine two. That bloody part is clearly substandard," said the captain.

"Shall I reduce thrust on number two to let it cool down?" offered the first officer.

"No. Let her go for a bit longer. I will do my manual cooling trick after these gentlemen have left. Just let me know if we reach critical temperature."

"Yes, Captain."

Dodwell turned around to shake hands with his guests and recognised Smith, who was standing beaming at him like a bull returning to the china shop. The first officer, who seemed to be now flying the plane solo, looked slightly worried.

"A pleasure to meet you," said Brandon-Lewis. "What a fine machine this is. But do I detect a technical problem, Captain?"

"Certainly not. Just another example of the engineering department fitting dud parts; that's all."

"Good grief, how disturbing. Incidentally, you are probably aware that I am a director of Albion Airways. If you want me to report any concerns back to the board, I am more than happy to do so. It's always good to get the views of our professionals on the coalface."

"In that case, can you tell them to stop bloody well sourcing dud parts form rogue foreign suppliers? It is not the first time engineering has told me they have fitted a locally sourced part, and it has failed during the journey. I could be ruddy fatal, Mr Brandon-Lewis. We currently have a fault with the management of the oil temperature on engine two. This is due to the installation of cheap and, I expect, unlicensed water-cooling switch gear for the engine oil lubrication system."

Brandon-Lewis looked like a guilty schoolboy caught stealing sweets red-handed. "Ah, yes. I'm afraid I happen to know a little bit about this. Head office asked me to procure the part you mentioned as part of my business negotiations with our Indian reserve parts supplier, who I happened to meet earlier today. I was told by the CEO of Singh Enterprises that the part had been tested and certified. I can also assure you that this purchase was not made on cost grounds. It was more expensive than the original manufacturer's price listing. The point was to procure the part locally to save having it transported to Delhi and, thus, prevent a costly technical delay to the flight."

Smith noticed that Brandon-Lewis had adopted the attitude of a supplicant seeking atonement.

"I don't believe it, Mr Brandon Lewis. With respect, how can you know if a part is serviceable? I assume you were not accompanied in your 'meeting' by a member of the engineering team?"

"Well, not exactly. I mean no, not on this occasion, though engineering has approved this supplier. If what you are saying is true, this is an absolute scandal. The Board will have to look into this very seriously."

"They will indeed, Mr Brandon-Lewis—that is, if it is not the air accident investigation branch that discovers the fault after we nosedive into the sea! I see you have brought a friend to see us, as well—someone I have already had the pleasure of meeting. It must be a world record for a passenger to wheedle his way into the cockpit twice in as many days."

Smith suddenly realised that the captain was referring to him. "Good evening, Captain. Yes, our previous meeting was somewhat inauspicious. I am sorry about that, but I am now the guest of Mr Brandon-Lewis."

"And I am the Shah of Persia. Get out, man! This flight deck is not the Assembly Rooms in Bath, you know." Dodwell waved him away as if he was a particularly irritating insect.

"Captain Dodwell, may I suggest we allow Mr Smith to stay for a while?" interjected Brandon-Lewis. "He has also engaged in business with Singh Enterprises and, I am sure, will be interested to hear about the questionable reliability of their manufactured and reconstituted parts."

"Is that so?" said the captain resignedly. "Well, there's not much more to say on the matter."

"I seem to remember there was a similar problem on the outgoing flight. How did you rectify the problem?" asked Smith, gazing concernedly at the engine temperature readings displayed on from of Craig. "Seems like number two engine is about to explode!"

The captain stood up from his seat and spoke to the director, not Smith. "It is quite fortunate that you are on board, Mr Brandon-Lewis. At least you can see how things really are. In answer to Mr Smith's question, I fixed the problem myself by manually flipping the water-cooling system switch. I expect the same procedure will be necessary again. Now if you will excuse me, I have a hold to descend into. Craig, you have control of the aircraft."

"Yes, sir," said the first officer, clearly used to such commands.

Captain Dodwell made his way to the rear of the flight deck, peeled back the carpet, and opened the hatch underneath.

"If I don't return, please tell my wife I love her," he said, now somewhat predictably, before descending into the maw.

"Where the devil's he gone?" said Brandon-Lewis. "I did not know there was a hatch on the flight desk floor."

"There isn't," said Craig, contemplating reducing thrust on engine two now that he was in control. "It does not appear in any pilot manuals or training material, but the captain found it by accident last time we had this problem. Seems to be an engineering hatch, which fortunately allows access to the engine oil pressure and cooling systems."

"I must report this to the board, too," said the director, clearly concerned about the transparency of information presented to board members before meetings.

From beneath the hatch, above the drone of the engines, the captain's muffled voice could be heard. Perhaps it was for the best that the three remaining men on the flight deck could not hear what he was saying.


# Interlude

*Answer me, dam you. I can't sit in the engineering hold all night. I have a plane to fly.*

Well get on back to it, then. That's your job. I am busy writing.

*That's what I need to talk to you about.*

You don't need to talk to me. You just need to do as I say.

*I am sorry, but enough is enough. I am not the only character in this fiction who has appealed to you for restraint, at the very least.*

So you *do* talk to each other behind my back.

*Of course we do. Why wouldn't we, the way you treat most of us? All except that paragon of virtue, Norman Smith. What a prat he his!*

Well, it's a relief you are not talking to him.

*We can't.*

Why?

*Because he is you.*

Don't be ridiculous, Dodwell. He is as much a work of fiction as you are.

*Is that so?*

Yes of course. Next you will be telling me I am Mrs G as well.

*She is your wife.*

No she is not. She is Norman Smith's wife, and he is an imaginary person.

*Why do you expect us to believe such rot? Do you think we are all children?*

Of course not, even if some of you behave like them.

*Anyway, I must insist that you refrain from stereotyping and mocking the airline industry. Do you really think that the stewardesses are allowed in the cockpit before a flight or that our flight systems, engineering, security, and emergency procedures are so simple? Have you ever been in the cockpit of a Boeing 777 and have you any idea how a plane works? Flying an airliner from A to B is a serious and difficult matter, despite your attempts to make flippant allusions about the process. And as for your libellous portrayal of the airline's parts procurement process, you should be put in jail for that.*

Who do you think you are, making a speech like that, Simón Bolívar?

*I tend to agree with my fellow thespians in this pathetic little drama. You simply don't listen, do you?*

Then why are you talking to me?

*Because I can.*

But no one is listening. You are talking to yourself. By the way, don't forget to adjust the oil cooling system switch on your way out. And don't bump your head on the hatch casing.

## 3.

The Boeing 777 glided across the continents of Asia and Europe at an altitude of around 38,000 feet, in the darkest hours of the night, crossing nations, states, cities, towns, and villages where the inhabitants were, for the most part, oblivious to its existence. Within it, the monotonous repetitions of the gentle vibrations from its enormous engines were enough to lull some of its passengers into a state of abject torpor, as if they had given up the act of living and were happy to float in a meaningless limbo of utter spatial disorientation.

Though it is almost impossible to believe, Mrs G had managed to fall asleep, despite being so uncomfortable that the pain in her neck was a consistent irritant in her troubled dreams. I doubt if anyone will ever know what Mrs G dreams about. She certainly never tells her husband and has refused psychotherapy on a number of occasions over the years. Her contention is that she never remembers what she has dreamt when she wakes up, though she does acknowledge that some imaginative brain activity has taken place on the rare occasions when she is not being irrationally stubborn on the point. Perhaps she was dreaming about her poor mother or about the deceased family pet, Tiddles. Or maybe she was having an erotic dream about the barely manly figure of Brandon-Lewis. It is even possible that she was dreaming about her husband of over thirty years, though this might have fallen under the category of a "recurring dream" rather than erotica and almost certainly would have been forgotten even before she woke up. An observer could detect physical signs, as one might with a pet dog, that her mind was active despite being asleep, evidenced by intricate hand and leg movements, the whispering of mysterious words and sighs, and irregularity of breath.

She was in this state when Norman Smith returned from the flight deck and took his seat beside her, squeezing his buttocks between the armrests like a large sausage being pushed into a milk bottle top.

"Are you awake, dear?" he asked, prodding his wife in the ribs with resolute insensitivity.

Mrs G stirred, though it was as yet unclear whether or not she had woken.

"Darling. Wake up. I have something to tell you."

"Have we arrived, Norman?" croaked Mrs G, clearly now in the process of returning to reality.

"No. We still have a few hours to go, dear."

"Then why did you wake me up?"

"I thought you were awake."

"I was asleep. Now I am not. It was unkind of you to disturb me like that."

"I am sorry. I just could not believe you would be asleep."

"Why not?"

"Because I am awake. You never sleep unless I do, too."

"Clearly that is a false assumption."

"Were you dreaming?"

"No."

"How do you know you were asleep then and not just dozing?"

"Oh my God, Norman!"

"What's the matter?"

"I've just remembered about poor Mother. I hope we get to her before it is too late."

"We are doing all we can, dear. Only a while to go."

"Norman?"

"Yes, dear?"

"I have a terrible pain in my neck."

"It's not my fault."

"I never said it was. I expect it's the headrest."

"You do look a bit crooked, now you mention it."

"What do you mean, crooked?"

"Well, sort of lopsided."

"Norman, was there something you wanted to tell me? Or did you just wake me up to tell me I am crooked and lopsided?"

"Ah yes. Well you see, I have just been on the flight deck with Brandon Lewis."

"I gathered that. I saw you sloping down the aisle with him earlier."

"The captain was a little upset about a technical problem in one of the engines."

"Oh dear. I hope we are not going to crash."

"No. I think the problem has been resolved."

"Thank goodness for that. Imagine dying in a plane crash on the way to see your mother on her deathbed."

"I hope very much that Mother is not on her deathbed."

"Even worse. Imagine how she would feel if we died in a plane crash rushing back to see her when she wasn't even dying."

"That would be most tragic. Anyway, the captain seems to have fixed the problem by climbing into an engineering hold underneath the cockpit and manually switching back on the engine oil cooling system."

"Stop being so technical, Norman. You know I don't understand mechanical things. Nonetheless it does strike me as odd that you need to cool the engine oil when it is minus 40 degrees centigrade outside.

"That is a very good point. I expect it is because the engine itself is encased and gets very hot. However, that is not what I wanted to tell you."

"Why did you then? Nearly scaring me to death."

"Well it is a sort of preamble, before I get to the point."

"I think we can do without preambles at this time of night, don't you, Norman?"

"Well, whilst the captain was fixing the problem, under the flight-deck. The first officer let me fly the plane and take as many photos as I wanted of the instrumentation and cockpit layout."

"Good God, Norman. I hope you didn't fiddle with any of the controls."

"No. To be honest, I only sat in the captain's seat. The autopilot remained engaged all the time."

"How dreadfully dull."

"Well, I enjoyed it."

"Is that it? You woke up to tell me you had a boyish adventure in the front of a big plane?"

"I haven't finished the story yet."

"Is this another preamble?"

"Sort of. Anyway, whilst all this was going on, we could hear Captain Dodwell talking to someone down in the engineering hold. Though we could not hear what he said, he seemed to be getting very heated about something. Brandon Lewis put his head into the hatchway to make sure everything was all right, but the captain was so engrossed in a conversation with someone who obviously wasn't there that he didn't even notice. Furthermore, he had still not fixed the switch. Finally, Brandon Lewis caught the captain's attention and managed to remind him of the urgent repair job he was supposed to be attending to."

"How strange. It's a good job you and BL were on the flight deck at the time."

"Indeed it was. Anyway, when the captain returned after successfully flicking the switch, he seemed oddly distracted. Under his breath, he kept uttering things like 'bloody idiot' and 'libellous'. It was quite clear he was not referring to any of us. It was as though he had someone quite different on his mind. Anyway, BL decided to go down into the hold with a torch to see if anyone was stowing away down there, but there was not a soul to be found."

"I am not sure I understand this story very well, Norman. Has it nearly finished?"

"Nearly. Anyway, the captain said to BL after he returned, 'You won't find him in there.'

"'Who exactly are we talking about, Captain?' I asked, as bemused as you are."

"A very good question, Norman, if I may say so."

"Thank you. Then he started talking to all three of us in a most peculiar way, his eyes glazed like some kind of a maniac. 'We are all at risk of having our integrity threatened and our dignity compromised by this story. You all know what I am talking about. Each one of us is being portrayed in a way that we have no control over. There is nothing we can do to alter the outcome. We are just puppets in his game.'

"At this point, the first officer burst out an emergency bottle of brandy that he had concealed under his seat, grabbed the captain, and poured it down his throat, commenting, 'He seems to have had some kind of seizure. Perhaps there was too much carbon monoxide in the engineering hold. I am temporarily taking charge of the aircraft.'

"Brandon-Lewis immediately offered his services as substitute first officer, even though he has never flown an aeroplane before, whilst Craig and I tied the captain up with some rope from the escape box. The poor chap was still talking deliriously. But by now his words had become slurred and incomprehensible."

"What an extraordinary turn of events, Norman. Are you telling me the truth?"

"Of course I am."

"Are you sure?"

"I think so. Anyway, we lay the captain on the floor, and he seemed to go to sleep or faint or something. Half an hour later, he woke up and was his usual self. By this time, we had untied him. He just got up and carried on as if nothing had happened. 'Fixed the bugger,' he said somewhat crudely, but as if he had only just completed the repair.

"Craig instantly vacated the captain's seat, fearing a charge of mutiny, and the captain returned to his position, immediately reviewing the engine oil temperature gauges, which by now showed no anomalies.

"'Why are you two still in the cockpit?' he said to BL and myself, as if he had just noticed us.

"We then decided it was probably time to leave."

"I am not sure what is most frightening—you in charge of the plane, a near fatal engine fault, or having a captain who is clearly off his rocker," said Mrs G philosophically.

"I think the captain will be OK now, so long as he doesn't go through that hatch again."

"Thank goodness for that. I wouldn't want his schizophrenia to be stimulated by another engineering problem."

"Sometimes you can be very droll, dear."

"I know."

"Do you believe me?"

"That is rather hard to answer. I am disorientated, exhausted, and possibly dehydrated. My mother is seriously ill, I have a painfully stiff neck, and I have recently been woken up in the middle of the night. These are not perfect conditions in which to analyse fact from fiction, especially as you are delivering the words, Norman. To be honest, it all sounds a little implausible, but strange things do happen. Nonetheless, it is quite possible that I am still asleep and dreaming all this."

"I thought you did not dream."

"I never said that. I said that I never remember my dreams. I very much hope I will forget this one when I wake up."

"But you are awake now."

"How can I be sure about that?"

"Because I am telling you."

"Then I, most surely, must be dreaming."

"Well I might be dreaming the whole thing up too, mightn't I?"

"If you were, I would not know what you are dreaming or be aware that I am in your dream whilst you are dreaming it."

"But we might both be dreaming the same thing at the same time."

"Don't be ridiculous, Norman. That could never happen."

As this metaphysical discussion droned on, the two participants became more and more drowsy. And before long, they were both asleep.

It is a wonder that the human mind can cope with all the possibilities that it has to contend with.

# CHAPTER 6

# REIGATE

## 1.

When the Smith's landed at Heathrow they immediately took a taxi to the care home where Mrs G's mother had been rushed to after her the seizure. In the taxi, Mrs G rang ahead to warn of their impending arrival and to find out the current condition of her mother, discovering, much to her relief, that the old prune was still alive.

"Thank goodness for that," she said emotionally to her exhausted husband.

He was looking forward to nothing more than smoking his pipe when he got home, an activity banned on holidays by his obdurate wife.

"So, the old bat is still hanging on. She always was prone to stubbornness."

"What on earth do you mean, Norman? This is a serious crisis, and all you can do is make facile comments."

"Well, how is she, then?"

"They didn't say anything more than she appears to be comfortable, which is a great comfort."

"Maybe we should have stayed in India."

"Don't be preposterous, Norman. It is our duty to care for her."

"I thought we had delegated that responsibility to the care team."

"Not in the event of her becoming seriously ill."

"What level of seriousness triggers that clause?"

"Norman. Sometimes your insensitivity is absolutely breathtaking. This is not a business contract. This is the life and possible death of a family member."

"I am sorry, dear. I am just a little tired after ten hours in a cigar tube."

"I am as well, Norman. I have had to endure the same hardship as you. However, unlike you, I do not always think solely of myself."

The taxi driver was clearly enjoying the old married couple's little tiff. It was not uncommon for marital strife to erupt in the taxi ride home from the airport after a stressful holiday in close proximity compounded by the disorientation of sleeplessness. As a professional driver, he was an expert at pretending not to listen.

"I don't think solely of you, dear. I often think about myself as well."

"You know what I mean."

"I am glad you have such confidence in my powers of understanding."

"Norman, I am tired and fractious and simply not in the mood for such nonsense. In fact, I am on the verge of tears."

Smith realised he had probably gone too far and was sorry. Sometimes he got the very devil inside him.

At the care home, the senior care manager ushered the Smith's into a small lounge that smelt of cabbage and disinfectant.

"We are not yet sure exactly what happened, but the doctor thinks it may have been a mild stroke. It is too early for a full prognosis, but there is never any certainty when it comes to older people. Sometimes they simply brush off such an episode, and sometimes it can be the beginning of the end, I'm afraid. The good news is that she is still breathing and seems relaxed. In fact, she has been asleep pretty much the entire time since the episode." Smith noticed what a peculiar shape the care manager possessed. Her bodily profile was almost perfectly tubular, in that she did not display any of the normal curves associated with the female anatomy. It was as though her flesh had taken the quickest route from point A to point B, without bothering with the intervening indentations or hillocks. In addition to this unusual body shape, she had an extraordinarily pointed chin, whereby each cheek converged into a sharp apex some distance beneath her puckered-up lips. Smith imagined her wearing an open-necked shirt. The chin would almost perfectly cover the gap between the collar and the second button, making it difficult to ascertain whether or not the collar button was fastened. She smelt of carbolic soap, which at least meant that she was as clean as the lines of her body.

"Perhaps you would like to see her now?"

"That would be an extremely good idea," interjected Smith, "especially as we have just travelled all the way from Delhi to Reigate, solely for that exact purpose."

Mrs G kicked her husband sharply on the shin.

Mrs G senior was in a room already bedecked with gaudy trinkets and faded photographs in tasteless frames from her family home. Mrs G junior instantly realised that these objects were there to give her mother a sense of comfort and security. Norman Smith thought she would be much better off without them gathering dust. The old lady was lying in bed with her eyes closed and her arms outside the sheets, in the manner of a corpse laid out for final viewing. She was breathing regularly, if shallowly. Her skin was translucent and bluish in hue, contrasting with the pure whiteness of her mop of tangled hair.

"Mother, it is me," said Mrs G, kneeling beside the bed and taking one of her mother's liver-spotted hands.

"I will leave you with her for a while, but don't excite her unduly. She may need time to come round," said the care home manager, departing from the room like a cylindrical automaton.

"I very much doubt we will be able to excite her at all," muttered Smith under his breath, gazing desperately into the future in the form of his wife's mother.

"Is she really alive?" he said to his wife provocatively.

She gave him one of her sterner stares, so he decided to keep quiet, which was just as well.

"Mother, how are you feeling?" Mrs G persisted, despite only modest signs of any response. "There is no need to worry. Norman and I are here now. We will look after you."

After a few minutes, the prospective cadaver appeared to move. The arms and feet twitched, and the eyelids flickered.

*The kraken wakes*, thought Smith to himself so his wife wouldn't hear him.

Suddenly, a shrill yet muted noise emerged from the chest cavity. "I need a wee-wee," warbled the old woman. "Help me!"

Smith, who had long been under the assumption that his mother-in-law was fully potty-trained, wondered how she would be able to make it to the en-suite lavatory, which was at least two yards from the bed.

"Of course, Mother," cooed Mrs G. "Norman, help me to carry Mother to the toilet. She clearly needs to relieve herself."

"I can't," said Smith. "It would indecent for me to carry your mother to the loo."

"Just do as I say," said Mrs G firmly, pulling the bedclothes back to reveal her mother's somewhat emaciated form in a long winter nightdress. "You take the left-hand side, and I'll take the right. She is not at all heavy."

With a considerable degree of effort, Mrs G's mother was carried into the lavatory and placed in the sitting position on the toilet. By now, her eyes were half open but seemingly unfocused.

"Now, get out, Norman. I will call when we are finished."

This was not the sort of welcome home Smith had hoped for. He had things to do, a pipe to smoke, and parts to order. In the meantime, the augers were pointing towards a protracted diversion in the care home. In the longer term, there was the prospect of Mrs G taking it upon herself to invite her mother to live with them looming over the horizon, a domestic arrangement that did not fill Smith with any joy at all.

Whilst he was waiting, the care manager came into the old lady's room and immediately noticed the empty bed. "What is going on here?" she demanded sternly, jutting her pointed jaw accusingly in Smith's direction.

"Mrs G senior needed to go to the toilet, I believe," explained Smith, as calmly as he could. "She is in there now with her daughter."

"How did she get in there?"

"We carried her in."

"Good God. That is against all the rules. You could have caused injury to yourselves and to the resident. Please leave such matters to our nursing team in future."

"As you wish."

"The hoist, the hoist, get the hoist!" screamed the care manager, apparently to a team of minions waiting upon her every order outside. "Bring the hoist. Immediately!"

Smith was not sure what kind of hoist she had in mind but was having difficulty concentrating anyway due to the ringing in his ears that the proximity to her shrieking had induced.

"Mrs Smith? Are you all right in there?" the care manager continued, tapping on the lavatory door with her extended mandible.

"I think Mother might have a bladder infection," replied Mrs G in a muffled voice through the chipboard door.

"In that case, we need to get her back into bed with a catheter. Please, can you open the door?"

"I am trying," said Mrs G. "Nut it appears to be stuck."

At that moment, two nurses burst into the room carrying what appeared to be an instrument of torture containing leather straps and a harness. For Norman Smith, this was all too much. On the way into the care home, he had noticed a quiet lounge area, to which he decided to make a tactical retreat until the ladies had managed to take a grip on the situation.

A single male resident was sitting in the lounge reading a newspaper, which he was holding upside down very close to his spectacles.

"Good morning," said Smith as he entered the room.

"There's nothing much good about it as far as I can see," replied the man, not looking up from the newspaper.

"Come to think of it, you are quite right," replied Smith, taking a seat in one of the high-backed and extremely uncomfortable armchairs.

"Bloody awful," continued the elderly resident, clearly speaking in general rather than specific terms.

"It can only get better, I suppose," suggested Smith optimistically.

"No it can't. Why would it? Every bloody day is the same, except when some poor bugger pops their clogs."

"An interesting take on life, but I can see your point."

"What point? There ain't no point. No point in nothink really."

"Do you not think that is a somewhat nihilistic attitude? Surely there are some rays of light even in the gloomiest of circumstances."

"No rays of light in here, mate. Waiting to die and nothink to take yer mind off of it. I can't even read the paper proper no more on account of the bloody cataracts. Mind you, that's a blessing since there's nothink but doom and gloom to read about."

"Well there you are. Maybe that's a ray of light."

"No it ain't. It's just the same old shit. Woops, mind the language. Sarge will be after me. You're not an officer, are you?"

"Do I look as if I am wearing a uniform?"

"Don't know. Can't see you properly."

"It's a bit stuffy in here, isn't it?" said Smith, getting up and moving towards the casement, suddenly feeling weighed down by the oppressive atmosphere in the room. "Do you mind if I open the window a little?"

"Do what you please. Everyone else does. I'm used to it."

"What are you used to, the stuffiness or the fact that everyone does as they please?"

"Oh, I'm used to everything and anything. You see, when you get to be my age, you have no point left. You are no longer a human being, just a decrepit body, waiting for that final moment. When I was in the army, the sergeant used to say it was better to be killed in action than die in obscurity. I am now completely obscure. All my friends and relatives have pegged it, one by one."

"But at least they are making your life comfortable here."

"Sometimes, comfort has no bearing on anything."

"I suppose so. But at least they feed you."

"I don't even like nosebag anymore. The only thing I like doing is smoking my pipe, and I am not allowed to do that. By the way, did you say you was a PT instructor?"

"No, I did not say that."

"In that case I am talking to the wrong man. I missed PT today."

"Do you mean physical training?"

"No. I mean PT. I'll be in solitary if they don't get my message in time."

The old man let the newspaper fall out of his hands and seemed to fall asleep momentarily. However, after a minute or two, he woke up with a jolt.

"Where's Sarge gone?" he moaned.

Smith was wondering if it might not be more peaceful with his wife and mother-in-law but decided that it wouldn't. While the old man was asleep, he had been counting the number of stains on the carpet, as an insomniac might count sheep, simply to pass the time. It was a daunting task in view of their profligacy. Whilst he found the old boy's confusion slightly irritating, he also felt sorry for him. On the side table, Smith noticed a pipe and a pouch. Smoking was clearly banned in such an institution, but the old man had clearly no intention of giving up his tobacco habit at this late stage in proceedings.

"Would you mind if I had a little smoke on your pipe?" he asked.

"No smoking in here, mate."

"But maybe I could pop outside for a little puff?"

"They'll never let you back in."

"How do you smoke then?"

"Out of the window. Stick your 'ed out of the window."

"Thank you. Mind if I indulge?"

"Go ahead, Sarge."

Smith took the pipe and pouch to the window he had just opened, stuffed the bowl with leaf, and lit up with a Swan Vesta that was in the pouch. Sticking his head out of the window, he began sucking on the smoke eagerly. It was immediately clear that the old man had a taste for strong tobacco. Despite the taste being bitter and acrid, this process offered instant relief to Smith's frayed nerves. Very soon, a dense cloud of thick smoke had been generated around his head. Unfortunately, the wind was blowing onshore, and some of the smoke billowed into the lounge, immediately setting off a fire alarm.

"Daft bugger," said the old man. "Now you've done it."

Within less than a minute, the lounge door burst open, and the care manager appeared, jaw jutting, in a state of considerable excitement. "Mr Bones, Mr Bones. There is a fire. We have to evacuate the building. Can you stand up or do you need assistance?" she said.

"No need for that, ma'am," said the old man pointing at Smith, who was desperately trying to conceal the smoking pipe in his trousers pocket. "That wots caused the fire alarm to go off."

"I thought I could smell the evil weed," said the care manager, staring at Smith, hands on hips, or at least the area of her tubular shape where hips would normally be evident.

"Ah, yes. Just in need of a quick smoke; that's all. Thought the smoke would blow in the other direction."

By now, others had entered the room, including several inappropriately clad residents, Mrs G, and her mother, who was supporting her fragile form on a Zimmer frame, but nonetheless upright.

"What a remarkable recovery," said Smith, looking at his mother-in-law.

"Well I wasn't going to just go up in smoke, was I?" she replied in a voice indicating an awareness and resolve completely incompatible with the feebleness of mind she had so recently displayed.

"No, I suppose not," replied her son-in-law, probably not expressing his full feelings on the matter.

"Come on, Mother. Let's get you to bed," said Mrs G, clearly embarrassed by her husband's behaviour. She gave him another stern look, which seemed to indicate to him that there might be more to be said on the matter later, before leaving the lounge with her mother.

Now, inevitably, it was the care manager's turn. "Mr Smith. Not only have you wantonly broken the rules concerning smoking in this establishment, you have also abused Mr Bones by apparently stealing his pipe and tobacco and have caused potentially fatal distress to many of our residents by setting off the fire alarm. You are henceforth banned from this care home. Do you hear me? Banned."

"But what if I need to visit my mother-in-law?"

"You should have thought of that before you flagrantly disregarded the basic rules of the care home. You are not to be trusted here a minute longer. I will arrange for your luggage to be put in the car park and will now escort you off the premises myself. You are lucky that I am not considering prosecuting you."

"What for?"

"Arson and abuse of a vulnerable person."

"But I am innocent."

"No you are not. You are a liability. I really don't know what Mrs G did to deserve a husband like you."

With this damning indictment ringing in Smith's ears, the care home manager pointed to the door.

The old man, who had not moved an inch during all the commotion, said, "I knew there'd be trouble. Matron is pretty strict on law enforcement round here. Didn't you know?"

"Be quiet Mr Bones. I still need to have a word with you about your smoking habits. Don't think you are off the hook, either," she said, turning on him in a feeding frenzy of admonition.

Smith removed the still smouldering pipe and the tobacco pouch from his pocket and laid them back on the table. He did not intend to be accused of theft on top of everything else, though he realised this was not a very helpful gesture in the old man's defence. Unfortunately, the heat of the conflagration within the pipe's bowl had burned a significantly sized hole in his trousers, revealing a section of his underpants.

Bones slunk deeper into his chair and stuck his tongue out at the care manager. Fortunately, she did not see the gesture, being by now too busy ushering Smith unceremoniously off the premises.

# 2.

If you had been standing in a field near Windsor early on an early spring morning and had looked hard into the clear sky, preferably with binoculars, you might have seen an Albion Airways Boeing 777 gliding majestically down on its final approach to Heathrow, undercarriage and flaps lowered, the nose very slightly raised, and much resembling an albatross nearing the roost.

Had you cared to look closer at engine number two, you might have just discerned a thin dark trail emanating from it, which you may not have guessed was, in fact, burned oil. On the flight deck the two pilots, though aware of the situation, were not unduly alarmed. At this stage in the descent, they had been able to shut down engine two and apply the engine fire extinguisher. Whilst a single-engine landing for this type of aircraft was not recommended, it was a procedure that the pilots had completed many times in flight simulator training. It did, however, require an emergency landing designation, meaning that fire and rescue vehicles would be on standby beside the runway, and other air traffic in the vicinity would be deprioritised until a safe landing had been executed.

"I can't believe it's happened again," said the pilot. "This is now a serious and recurring engineering problem."

First Officer Craig was calm but alert, as befits a trained professional in such a crisis. "Do you want me to warn the passengers that this is an emergency landing, Captain?"

"Yes, we must. However, play the whole thing down. In clear weather like this, they should not notice a thing."

Taking the PA microphone in his hand, Craig made the announcement. "Ladies and gentlemen, we will be landing at Heathrow in a few minutes, so please make sure your seatbelts are fastened and tables stowed. The weather is calm with light easterly winds and the temperature around twelve degrees. Some of you may have noticed that we have been idling engine two for a few minutes due to a minor technical problem, but do not expect this to affect the landing or our expected landing time. However, as a precaution, we would ask you to familiarise yourselves with your nearest escape route and not be alarmed if you see fire engines beside the runway as we land. This is purely a precautionary measure and nothing to be alarmed about. Cabin crew, prepare for landing."

"Not bad, Craig," said the captain, who could now see the runway through the windscreen. "Please continue with the final landing checks, ignoring engine two."

In the economy class cabin at the rear of the plane, the announcement did little to calm the nerves of the more anxious passengers. Among these was DI Godber, returning from an unsuccessful investigation in India, sitting next to light aircraft pilot Winterbottom, who was more interested in the single-engine landing procedure than alarmed.

"Oh God. Are we all going to die in an air crash after all this?" said Godber, whose enormous feet were completely wedged under the seat in front. Feeling nauseously incarcerated, he was sitting in a window seat and could see the dark vapour trail. "Minor technical problem? The fucking plane is on fire!"

Some of the neighbouring passengers heard this, and panic swept through the cabin. Shouts of, "We are on fire," and, "I'm too young to die," could be heard among the general hysterical hubbub.

Winterbottom explained to Godber that the dark vapour did not necessarily indicate that there was an engine fire. "It is quite possible that the captain is simply ejecting overheated oil to prevent the risk of fire. After all, there are no flames visible," he continued, pointing out of the window at the rear section of the engine, which was pretty well obstructed by the wing. "An interesting predicament though," he added, though too quietly for his reassuring words to be heard by the other passengers.

"And what if the engine bursts into flame when we land?" said Godber, less than convinced by Winterbottom's explanation.

"That is unlikely but, I concede, possible. However, there will be emergency services at hand to put out the flames quickly once we land."

"That is most reassuring, I am sure, Mr Winterbottom."

The aeroplane glided smoothly down towards the runway, perhaps yawing a little more than it would have done under two engines but clearly being controlled capably by the experienced captain. It touched down gracefully on the centre line of the runway and slewed slightly due to the asymmetric nature of the reverse thrust that was applied. This meant that the deceleration time was longer than normal, but the plane eventually came to a stop a considerable distance from the end of the runway.

It was with some disappointment that the occupants of the rescue vehicles arrived to discover that they were not needed. There was no fire and no casualties. Once these facts had been established and engine one closed down, a tow truck was commissioned to pull the stricken airliner to its stand, where the passengers were disgorged.

Shortly afterwards, DI Godber and Winterbottom found themselves in the baggage hall together, gazing optimistically at an empty rubber carousel. Godber was in that euphoric state that often follows a near-death experience, whereas, true to character, Winterbottom was in an altogether more prosaic state of mind. He was not sure what would happen next, both in terms of the luggage belt and also the future of his short acquaintance with DI Godber.

"So, I suppose we will each go our own merry ways now, Mr Godber?" he asked, like a lost sheep.

Neither had expected to become comrades when they'd set off for India, yet neither had expected to return so soon.

"That may well be the case," replied the retired detective, non-committal and vague.

"It's a good job you found out that Smith had done a fast one. Otherwise, we might still be out there looking for them," continued the pilot, seemingly unwilling to sever the conversation prematurely.

"Ah yes, indeed. After so many years in the job, you pick up a sixth sense when you have lost the trail. It is always essential to develop links with hotel reception staff. You have no idea how much information I have gleaned from them over the years. In the case of Smith, all day yesterday I had a feeling he had done a runner. Incidentally, such behaviour is typical of the criminal mind. They are prone to sudden and unexpected changes of plan because they are always trying to shake off an imaginary tail. Such is the nature of guilt. The receptionist was most helpful in describing the Smiths' sudden decision to check out. It is a shame we did not catch on quicker, though. In forty-eight hours, we have given them more than enough time to regroup."

"But I thought you said they had departed because of a family illness at home."

"Indeed I did. That was clearly just a cover story. Look at it like this, Winterbottom. It is clear that they had no intention of taking an extended vacation in India. It was all just a sham. Clearly the real reason for the visit was for Smith to make contact with his business partner in Delhi to pursue his felonious activities, in this case dealing in contraband goods. I knew it. We can now add attempted murder and deception to his long list of crimes as well. Are you still unconvinced of the breadth of this man's criminal activities, after all you have seen with your own eyes?"

"Mr Godber, whilst you present a compelling case and have built an apparently robust evidence file on Mr Smith, I fear that I have personally seen nothing that I would call hard evidence of anything that would stand up even in a kangaroo court. What I have seen of Mr Smith, whilst unusual in many ways, could only lead me to assumptions and not to certainty.

Assumptions can lead us in the wrong direction. We begin to fit the evidence in to substantiate our theories, rather than let the facts speak for themselves."

"Winterbottom, what I have in my case file is a thoroughly investigated and painstakingly compiled compendium of facts that, whilst admittedly some being as yet incomplete in terms of watertight proof, combine to create an unimpeachable picture of a man swamped in the very deepest mire of criminality. You need to look at the whole and not the parts."

"In which case, Mr Godber, I think we have a temperamental difference in our approach to this investigation. Clearly, I am not as inclined as you are to jump straight to conclusions. I prefer a more objective approach. I would also remind you that, since your body of evidence is so extensive, it would make no difference to the outcome whether or not you discounted the incident at Redhill Aerodrome."

"Perhaps, Mr Winterbottom, but I have to be meticulous."

"Well, I wish you well in your ongoing obsession. However, I hope you do not find, after all this hard work, that your premise is fatally compromised by flawed assumptions."

"By the way, Winterbottom, do you in any way feel that you are being compromised by this whole situation?"

"What do you mean?"

"Well it seems to me that some of the theories you espouse do not necessarily sit well with your personality. It is almost as if you have been given a role to play that is somehow at odds with what you really think. Perhaps you are even becoming a caricature of yourself?"

"It's interesting that you should say that, Mr Godber, because I was thinking exactly that about yourself. You seem to be imprisoned in a cartoon character of a retired detective. There appears to be little room for you to deviate from your role or express yourself honestly, which is quite frustrating when I am trying to engage you in conversation."

"I had noticed that about myself. This constraint even affects my appearance, especially the size of my feet."

"I had observed that they are unusually large and flat. In fact, they seem to vary in enormity, depending on the circumstances."

"You know why, don't you, Mr Winterbottom?"

"Not really."

"It is because we are being manipulated like marionettes by a puppeteer who has so little imagination that he thinks that by imposing constraints and false characteristics on us, it will make it easier for him to dictate the course of events."

"Is this theory related to Smith, by any chance?"

"Not specifically. My obsession with him is already written into the script. It seems that I can do very little about that stigma. However, Smith is integral to the plot, and we cannot ignore him, even though I expect he is as bound by the shackles of his destiny in this fairy tale as are you and I."

"How then, can we express ourselves more honestly without being completely written out of the story?"

"That is exactly what I am really investigating. Not the spurious misdemeanours of Norman Smith, which are most likely completely irrelevant anyway. No, that is a sideshow. I am really investigating the inhuman representation of perfectly decent citizens such as you and me and the shackles they have been put under through no fault of their own. It is a human rights crime, tantamount to psychological imprisonment of the soul, with a large degree of defamation thrown in."

"A most remarkable theory, Mr Godber. But how have you been able to be break so free of your role to talk to me about this?"

"Because the puppeteer is fallible. I have already realised that his scheme is strewn with stress points. All we need to do is exploit these."

"I think it would be better if we did not discuss this further. There are CCTV cameras in the baggage hall, you know."

"Perhaps so, Mr Winterbottom. We would not want anyone to get the wrong idea, would we?"

As the two men concluded their unusual conversation, which, incidentally, has no bearing on our story, the carousel began to move, and the luggage that had recently been stowed on the overnight BA flight from Delhi began to emerge. Few were aware that their belongings had been rifled through by loading handlers at Mahatma Ghandi Airport because they were so expert at pilfering. It was not a pleasant job, dealing with suitcases full of soiled clothing, but it was, nonetheless, lucrative.

Winterbottom's case arrived, and he parted from Godber to make his way to the tube station. Godber's case on the other hand, containing a portfolio of handwritten evidence against a retired tax accountant, did not arrive. It was later reported as lost or stolen.

# 3.

After Mrs G's mother had been returned to her bed and sedated, poor Mrs G spent ten minutes searching for her husband outside the gates of the care home. Eventually she found him guarding their suitcases on an adjoining street. He was sitting on one of them gazing into the distance as if transported into some faraway world, probably containing flight simulators and stuffed bears. It was by no means the first time that Mrs G had observed her husband in one of these trances, but it never ceased to amaze her how he seemed so capable of drifting in and out of the reality that she felt herself so eternally wedded to.

"What are you doing, Norman?"

"Thinking."

"I can see that. I hope you are ashamed of what you have done. I don't know how we will manage now that you have been banned from visiting Mother in the care home."

"Oh, that? I wasn't thinking about that."

"I didn't think you were."

"How *is* the old bat?"

"I think she has a bladder infection. The doctor has been called back, and I will visit again this evening."

"It can make them go nuts, you know."

"What can?"

"Trouble in the waterworks department."

"I am aware that there is a correlation between mental confusion and bladder infections in women of a certain age, Norman. However, it is more likely that any disturbance she is experienced has more to do with you trying to burn down the care home. I sometimes wonder if it is not you that has the bladder infections."

"But I am a man. It's different."

"You can say that again, Norman."

"I would rather not."

"Have you called a taxi?"

"No. I was waiting for you to come out first."

"That was most unusually thoughtful of you."

"Thank you, dear. Besides, I don't have a number to call a taxi company, do you?"

"Uber."

"I beg your pardon."

"Uber. That's who I will call."

"Uber alles, Deutschland and all that."

"Norman?"

"Yes?"

"I hope you are not getting early-onset dementia."

By the time the couple had arrived home, it was gone midday. Considering how short a time they had been away, there was a surprising amount of post on the doormat. Mr Smith made a point of having all the washing loaded into the washing machine and all the mail read and sorted within fifteen minutes of arriving home from any holiday. He liked to feel everything was back to normal as soon as possible. His wife, on the other hand, preferred a less frenetic approach to returning home, perhaps enjoying a cup of tea, a hot bath, or a short nap before embarking on any unpacking or household chores.

"Look. There is a letter from the council," said Smith, barely over the doorstep.

"How very tedious," said Mrs Smith, unable to get through the door because of her husband's bulk. "By the way, is there any chance of me getting into the house, do you think?"

"I'm sorry, dear. It's just that this could be about the planning application."

"I hope it has been declined. Then at least we might get our back garden back."

The letter read:

Dear Mr Smith

This is to inform you that your retrospective planning application to lodge a large metal object in your back garden has been approved by the Planning Committee. However, the committee has insisted on the following conditions:

i) The object must be painted in a matte green colour to blend in with the ambient surroundings.
ii) The object must be sealed to ensure that it is both watertight and protected from rodent infestation.
iii) The object must *not* be used as a residence.
iv) Any use that the object is put to must not involve the production of sound that can be heard externally, the production of illegal or bootleg materials, prostitution, or any other criminal activity
v) The object must be fitted internally with smoke detectors and fire alarms if electrical appliances are used inside.
vi) The object must not be moved from its present location without further planning consent.
vii) The object will be subject to regular inspections to ensure that these conditions are being adhered to.

"It looks as though my wish has not come true then."

"Come, come, dear. It's not as bad as all that. It means that I now have an authorised space for my flight simulator. I will not have to clutter the house up."

"I would never have let it do that anyway."

"But you did with my taxidermy."

"That was a mistake that I regret."

At that point, the doorbell rang.

Smith opened it to find his neighbour, Alex Horne, standing on the doorstep.

"Hallo. Alex, old chap," he said with a joviality he did not feel. "Come on in."

"I just came around to check everything is OK. We were not expecting you back so soon. I feared you might have burglars," said Horne, navigating his way over the two large suitcases that were standing in the middle of the hall.

"Well thank you very much for keeping an eye out on things whilst we were away. Unfortunately, our trip was cut short by Mrs G's mother having a bad turn, which we thought was much more serious than it seems to have turned out to be."

"That is not strictly correct," interjected Mrs G. "Unfortunately, Mother has taken a turn for the worse, and I fear it might be quite serious. We simply could not leave her in care whilst we were enjoying a holiday thousands of miles away."

"I am very sorry to hear that," said Horne, sympathetically, though possibly not genuinely so. "Anyway, I hope you had as good a time as you could in the short time you were away. Incidentally, the Planning Committee paid a visit in your absence. What an absolute shower!" It was apparent that Horne had noticed the letter that was still in Smith's hand. Without any artifice at all, he was clearly trying to read it as he spoke.

"Ah yes. You may or may not be pleased to hear that the planning application has been accepted. This letter in my hand confirms the decision. The beast will, therefore, remain in the back garden. I hope you don't mind, do you? We would not want to spark a neighbourly dispute or anything of that nature, would we?" It was unclear how innocent this remark was. Clearly Smith expected that the decision might cause some concerns from his near neighbour, but he was not sure whether or not he actually objected to the presence of a fuselage part in the rear of their premises.

"Absolutely not, Norman." I have to say that Mrs Horne expressed some anxiety about light and so forth, but I put her mind at rest. It really is no problem at all for us."

"Splendid, Alex. In that case, maybe we could crack open a bottle of bubbly to celebrate?"

This was the last straw for the exhausted Mrs G, who, herself, had rather hoped that the council would have the sense to refuse the application on the ground of sheer common sense. She would much rather drink hot tea than champagne. And besides, she was in urgent need of a bath. "No, Norman. What have I said about midday drinking? It is not something we indulge in lightly, Mr Horne, especially as we are both tired and disorientated from stress, anxiety, and a sleepless night on an aeroplane. I think it would be sensible if we put off the celebratory drink until another day."

"I completely understand," said Horne, relieved that he would not have to endure drinking the day away with Smith, who would undoubtedly bore him with his hobbies. "Well, I must be getting back. I'll see you about, then."

As he backed out of the hall, Horne stumbled over Mrs G's enormous suitcase and fell backwards onto an aspidistra plant in the corner. It was a most undignified exit, but eventually he removed himself from the house with a sigh of relief, shortly followed by a wave of anxiety about how he was going to explain the planning decision to his wife.

# 4.

"And?" asked Mrs Horne as her husband entered the kitchen, looking somewhat timid. He was one of those men who defined themselves by their professional position. At the Aircraft Accidents Investigation Branch, he was virtually revered as a deity, such were his level-headedness, personableness, and infallible logical thought process. In mixed company, he appeared full of assurance and self-confidence. Yet in the sole company of his wife, there were often occasions when he became confused and uncertain, much as a newborn tadpole unsure what to do next. This was not because Mrs Horne was an aggressive or intimidating person, though she was perhaps somewhat more introverted and repressed than her husband. It was more that, over the years, she had taken command of all things domestic in their lives with a ferocity that matched her husband's ambition in the workplace. It had occurred to Horne that this was a manifestation of something more than the female nesting instinct, which, after all, would surely have diminished somewhat after the menopause and the children leaving home. He felt that it probably reflected the absence of power in any other aspect of her life, which he felt slightly responsible for, despite having encouraged her to take up studies or other hobbies to establish her niche in other areas of human endeavour. Perhaps he had strangled her ambition with his very own. He also considered that her parents may have had something do with his wife's condition, both of them having been insistent on her marrying a professional who was "going places". Perhaps she would have been better off with a starving poet or an operatic tenor. Naturally, there was always the chance that she was simply a witch, but he did not dwell on this, lest it dampen his appetite for marital stability.

"And what, Barbara?"

"Did you find out why the Smiths had come back so prematurely from their holiday?" As this was a neighbourly issue, it fell into the orbit of Mrs Horne's domestic responsibilities, and the question was therefore delivered in a peremptory manner.

"Mrs G's mother has been taken ill," said Horne defensively, so as not to inflame the questioner.

"I see," replied his wife through pursed lips, as if the reason given was somehow unsatisfactory.

"Did you find out if they have heard from the council about the planning application?"

Horne began to sweat profusely. His physiological response to this question resembled that of a schoolboy caught stealing apples, for some unfathomable reason. He wished he could disappear in a puff of smoke.

"Well, they had hardly stepped inside the house when I arrived."

"And?" snapped Mrs Horne imperiously, sure in the knowledge that her husband had more to divulge.

"Well, as luck would have it, Norman had already opened the mail in the doorstep. In his hand was a letter explaining that planning permission for the aircraft part in the back garden had been granted. There are conditions, though."

Mrs Horne turned a rather peculiar colour upon hearing this news, as if it was unexpected. "Are you absolutely sure, Alex? Did you actually read the letter?"

"No, I didn't actually read it, dear. That would have been most inappropriate. I have to take the man's word. To be honest, the planning officer had previously warned me that this was the most likely decision."

"And why did you not tell me this before?"

Horne was by now getting annoyed at his wife's habit of starting sentences and questions with the word 'and'. Not only was it intimidating, as if her list of questions went on forever, it was also grammatically distressing. He knew better than to raise the issue at this stage in the bombardment, however.

"I didn't want you to fret, Barbara. I know how you worry about such matters."

"Do you indeed? Well, someone has to. It doesn't seem to me that you care two hoots whether or not all the light is blocked out of our house and our views ruined."

"Is that a statement or a question, dearest?"

"Both."

"In that case, let me explain my position. I have been thinking about this for a few days."

"Careful, Alex, you might compromise the part of your brain that reconstructs disintegrated aircraft. Surely there is no room for domestic considerations as well?"

This unkind cut reminded Horne that there was more to his wife's commanding domestic behaviour than simply being ferocious. She was also insanely jealous if ever her husband deigned to encroach upon her territory, lest he wrest a modicum of control from her.

"Look, this is just my opinion. You can take it or leave it, as you wish," he persisted, with a bravery on par with the cavalrymen at the charge of the light brigade. "I am persuaded that the object will actually make little difference to the light in the northerly windows of the house, which tend to be gloomy anyway. Besides, the hedge makes it pretty well impossible to see unless you happen to be standing on the roof. Perhaps we have both become a little bit irrational about the threat to our outlook that Smith's installation may cause."

Mrs Horne was now visibly shaken by the disloyalty of her spouse. "How dare you call our windows gloomy, Alex? I wash them inside and out once a month, you know, whilst you are making Airfix kits at Farnborough. Furthermore, you have changed your tune overnight. I am sure it was only yesterday that you were agreeing with me about the nuisance in the Smith's rear garden. If fact, you have made such a fuss about it that you have nearly driven me mad."

"Well, I have changed my mind, dear. I suggest you do the same now that the decision is final."

"Can't we appeal?"

"I think we would lose, and it could cost us a lot of money."

"Is that all you have to say for yourself, Alex? Are you not a little bit ashamed of such utter capitulation on a point of principle?" Mrs Horne had adopted what could only be described as an accusatory stance, quite remote form her conciliatory stance, which was far less rigid.

"I am sorry you feel that way, dear. I am simply being pragmatic. Now, you asked me if that was all I had to say. There is something else you might like to know about, but I can only tell you if you promise to use the information in strictest confidence."

"How can I promise that when I don't know what you are going to tell me?"

"It's a little bit like espionage, darling. There are some things you simply must keep secret, no matter what they are."

Mrs Horne softened slightly at this point and started walking around the kitchen with a feather duster, as if to emphasis her devotion to domesticity. However, espionage and secrets being outside the general domestic domain, her instinct to dominate had weakened dramatically. In such matters, she naturally deferred to her husband. "I promise," she said, meekly, like a schoolgirl promising to keep her best friend's secret.

"Now, I have found something out about Norman Smith, which I shouldn't really tell you for reasons of professional confidentiality, but you might be interested." Smith knew his wife well enough to be assured that phrases like "professional confidentiality" would calm her, being as she had absolutely no interest in dominating conversations on subjects that she felt completely out of her depth about.

"I was presented with an unofficial, uncorroborated, and private air accident report recently about an incident at Redhill Aerodrome. According to the complainant, a flying student took control of light aircraft from the pilot and nearly crashed it. I doubt if the matter will be investigated further following a rebuttal from the aerodrome and flying school. However, the interesting point is that the alleged flying student was none other than Norman Smith, our own next-door neighbour."

Mrs Horne was silent when her husband had finished speaking. She had absolutely no intuition as to the relevance of this exposé or even if there was one.

"And?" she said, characteristically but weakly.

"In itself, this does not throw any particular light on the planning decision," conceded Horne, by now more comfortably in his stride.

"And?"

"But is does rather mean that we have something on him, should it become necessary to use it."

"How do you mean?"

"Suppose Smith fails to adhere to the conditions laid out in the planning decision. It might be rather easy to persuade him to do so if I had a confidential word in his ear that failure to do so may result in him becoming involved in a criminal investigation about his irresponsible activities on a light aeroplane being investigated by the Air Accidents Investigation Branch."

"Oh, Alex, you are so Machiavellian!"

"Thank you, dear. I take that as a complement."

It is hard to believe that any neighbours of the Smiths, living in Reigate, could be so unprincipled as to hatch such schemes, tantamount to bribery, but life can be stranger than fiction, as we have already discovered.

"Barbara?"

"Yes, dearest."

"Did I really imply that I would use confidential professional knowledge as a lever to blackmail my next-door neighbour into complying with our wishes?"

"I believe you did, Alex, though it would only be to make him comply with conditions already legally imposed on him and would only be subject to his noncompliance."

"Barbara, I don't know what came over me. I am not really like that, am I?"

"You have been a bit strange recently, Alex, I must say."

"Perhaps I am being manipulated in some way. It's as though someone else is putting the words into my mouth."

His wife did not listen to Horne's last comment. The conversation had now reached the outer reaches of her area of comprehension. She was losing interest rapidly and heading directly for the utility room to fetch the window-cleaning products.

# 5.

Former squadron leader Mantle sat in the Bull's Head staring at his pint of beer. The other customers, naturally, had no idea that he was a war hero who had risked his life to protect their freedom. Some might say that bombing targets in Iraq and Kuwait had nothing to do with their freedom and that it should never have happened. Others might admire the courage of our armed forces and respect them, whatever hare-brained mission they were sent on by idiotic politicians. Some may have questioned the cost of acquiring and arming aircraft that were not directly defending Albion.

Mantle had considered all these possibilities many times. He was "old school" when it came to military action. As a front-line officer, he believed it his duty to perform whatever missions he was asked to take part in without question. He was not paid to question his superiors. Besides such subversion was clearly bad for morale. Whilst a sense of duty had driven Mantle to deeds of legendry bravery, it was the thrill of flying at high speed that had really motivated him. He considered it somewhat ironic that he was now in charge of a flying school with a fleet of underpowered light aircraft barely capable of reaching 150 knots. How the mighty had fallen.

After active service, Mantle had been given a desk job at the Fleet Air Arm, which he'd detested. Schoolboys do not dream of pushing paper. He'd decided to retire from the services and become a commercial pilot. This had turned out to be nearly as boring, especially as his previous flying experience did not advance his promotion prospects and he was forced to sit in the first officer's chair and take orders from men and women who had never even sat in the cockpit of a typhoon.

Eventually, he called that job a day as well and decided to set up a flying school on his limited savings. The sole motivating purpose of this was that he would no longer have to serve under unqualified superior officers. It was an act of self-liberation that failed on almost all counts, except for his not having to sniffle up to anyone less important or experienced than himself. Even that benefit was diluted by the need to comply with the demands of creditors; bank managers; airfield directors; and, indeed, customers.

Fortunately, Mantle was a stoic by nature. He considered himself a natural leader and a man of privilege. He was still handsome and was at ease with new friends and lovers alike. Nothing, however, could compensate for the loss of excitement and the adrenalin rush of front-line combat missions. He knew that there would always be a hole in his life that could never be filled, much as a retired top-level sportsman does. You will never get it back. This makes you feel prematurely old and prone to unhealthy distractions in a futile attempt fill the void.

On the positive side, Mantle had always been popular with his men. He was a good leader and commanded respect. He never asked anyone to do anything he would not do himself.

Most of the flying school's pilots were failed air force recruits or aspiring commercial airline pilots. Some, like Winterbottom, were neither. They were just mediocre. It had been a challenge to motivate such a squadron, especially as the pay was poor, but Mantle had whipped into his team a sense of purpose, which he didn't even believe in himself. After all, what could be lower on the food chain than training novices in the basics of aeronautics? All the good students went on to gain their pilot's licenses and fly bigger aircraft either professionally or as wealthy amateurs. All his mediocre students, accounting for the vast majority of clients, were there for a short while until their enthusiasm waned, and they gave up flying.

In some ways, this would have been a slightly depressing outlook, had it not been for the fact that Mantle had another plan up his sleeve. He was secretly courting the young wife of Ollie Booth OBE, CEO of Redhill Aerodrome. Not only was she extremely attractive (an astonishing contrast to the physiognomy of her husband, though it may be that his purse was more the source of his appeal), she was also extraordinarily wealthy and set to inherit her elderly husband's entire fortune when he passed away. This, naturally, added a considerable amount to her allure. Thus, Mantle was engaged in a personal strategy for advancement that had repeated itself over the centuries, one salutary example being the character Barry Lyndon, portrayed by William Makepeace Thackeray. It rarely ends well, largely due to the long-term psychological strain that such an ill-conceived venture will inevitably place on the protagonist and his unloved partner.

Winterbottom entered the bar and roused Mantle from his reveries.

"Ah. The wanderer hath returned," said Mantle, holding up his glass for a refill.

"Sorry I'm a couple of minutes late, had a little problem with Buster. Made a mess on the kitchen floor."

"Nasty business," opined Mantle.

Once Winterbottom had got the drinks, he sat down opposite the squadron leader. For some reason, he felt the need to salute, though this would, of course, have been completely inappropriate in a public house.

"So, it sounds as if you had an interesting sojourn, Winterbottom. Get to the bottom of things, did you? Or should I say, did you get to the Winterbottom of things?"

Winterbottom smiled wearily. It was not the first time that his name had been used as the subject of infantile humour.

"I think so. But I can't be 100 per cent sure."

"What do you mean, not sure? Either you have silenced the lamb, or you haven't." Whilst Mantle had a tendency to look at complex situations in a binary way, this sort of black-and-white approach also formed part of his public image.

"Godber is a complex fish. He is motivated by complex urges that are almost impossible to understand."

"Look, Winterbottom, I am not interested in his complex urges, and I hope you aren't either. I am interested in him dropping any reference to Smith's prank at the aerodrome from his investigations."

"Well, he sort of promised me he would. I think he understands our position and the implications for us if he does so."

"Is that all you can say after me paying for you to swan off to India to make a deal?"

"I am pretty convinced that I now know him well enough to maintain influence in that field, sir. Unfortunately, I also experienced Smith's antics first-hand, and I have to say, I have some sympathy with Godber's assumptions about him. The man is a complete nutter. He seemed to be dealing in contraband goods in front of our very eyes at the hotel in Delhi."

"OK. Well that's good to know. But you must keep in touch and maintain the level of influence you seem to have so far gained with Godber. If he is a complex fellow, we cannot let him off the leash just yet. By the way, are you ready to get back in the flying seat next week? I was just thinking about the rota."

"Certainly, sir. It would be a blessed relief."

"By the way, did I tell you that Godber has filed a private report to the Air Accidents Investigation Branch about the Smith incident? The branch contacted me asking me to comment. Naturally I have reassured them that the incident was not worth reporting."

"I was not aware of that, sir. It is a shame. However, I am slightly more concerned about another report to the AACB, namely the emergency landing I experienced at Heathrow on the return flight from Delhi."

"Yes. Most unfortunate. Nonetheless, that should take the Branch's eye off the Redhill Aerodrome ball for the time being."

"Having nearly lost my life in both the Heathrow and the Redhill incidents, that is of only modest comfort to me, sir. I feel something of a sitting duck at the moment."

"Don't worry, Winterbottom. It happens to us all from time to time. By the way, any idea what caused the engine outage at Heathrow?"

"Something to do with number two engine oil temperature management system, I gather. You would have thought that BA engineers would be more careful."

"Indeed so. Well, it could have been much worse. Best thing to do is get back up in the air as soon as you can."

Mantle's reassurances were of scant consolation to Winterbottom, who was beginning to wonder if he had become jinxed. However, it was a typical services reaction and, as such, had some merit, at least as a delusional tactic.

"Do you know, sir, with your permission, I think I'll take a Cessna up this afternoon, just to calm the old nerves, you know."

"Capital idea, Winterbottom. That's the spirit."

It was impossible for the two men to detect DI Godber sitting in the corner of the lounge bar behind a broadsheet newspaper because his feet were invisible beneath the table he was sitting at. Nonetheless, he heard most of the conversation, little of which surprised him, though he did wonder what impression he had made for Winterbottom to accuse him of "having complex urges". Such are the vagaries of holiday friendships.

# 6.

Mrs G was lying on the sofa in a negligee, still suffering from jetlag, when the doorbell rang. Norman had gone out in the Morris Minor to buy some green paint. Unwilling to present herself to the world in this state, she ignored it and continued reading *Home and Garden*.

The doorbell rang again. And again.

Concerned that it might be something to do with her mother, she reluctantly got up to answer it, taking care to put the door on the chain before opening it. You never knew who might burst in and ravage you.

As it turned out, there was no need for concern. It was only Barbara Horne bringing the key back.

"Thank you so much, dear," said Mrs G, sticking her hand out through the small gap between the door and the frame to collect the key.

"It is a pleasure, Mrs G, but I am sorry you had to come home early because of your mother."

"Yes, it was most unfortunate but maybe for the best. I could not bear to be thousands of miles away if anything was going to happen to her."

"Is she all right?"

"I think so. She's on antibiotics, and the doctor thinks it might have been a severe bladder infection—that is, after he had ruled out a stroke, which was his initial diagnosis, upon my advice."

"Oh dear. Well I hope she makes a quick recovery. Would you very much mind if I came in for a moment? There is something I want to talk to you about."

"Well, I am not exactly dressed yet. But if you don't mind that, please do come in for as coffee."

"Thank you, Mrs G."

Mrs G led Mrs Horne into the lounge and offered her a seat on the settee while she went into the kitchen to make the drinks. Mrs Horne had rarely entered the Smiths' private retreat and was pleased to have time to look around and make some domestic judgements. Her opinion was that Mrs G could be a little more fastidious on the dusting front. There appeared to be a number of cobwebs in the corner of the ceiling and some crumbs on the coffee table. The lounge, which looked out onto the back of the house was also quite dimly lit, despite having large picture windows, much of its light being obstructed by the large object in the back garden. She could not find fault with the interior design décor, though. Shortly Mrs G came in with two steaming mugs.

"I do so admire your taste in furnishing, Mrs G," said Mrs Horne, eager to get off to a good start.

"Well, I do my best, Barbara. Norman tends to be very passive when it comes to decor, which virtually gives me a free reign."

"A perfect arrangement."

"I think so too. Now, what is it you wanted to talk to me about?"

"Well, I hope you don't mind me bringing this up at a time of family crisis, but I just wanted a quick chat about the object in the garden. By the way, do you mind if I put the table lamp on? It's terribly dark in here."

"Of course. You know why that is, don't you?"

"Indeed. That is the very subject on my mind, dear."

It looked as though there might be the possibility of some common ground on this matter between the two ladies.

"You have no doubt heard that those ridiculous people at the council have granted planning permission for it to remain there?"

"I have indeed, dearest. Alex told me, after speaking to Norman."

"Yes I know. I was there at the time."

"And how do you feel about the decision?"

"To be honest, from a personal perspective, I am not best pleased. As you can see, we have a monstrosity out there, right in front of the window, severely diminishing daylight in the back of the house. On the other hand, Norman is pleased. That has an important impact on my quality of life. I cannot bear it when he gets gloomy and starts mooning around and getting in the way all the time. If I am lucky, he will be spending a lot of time out there building his flight simulator, leaving me to my own devices within the house. All the mess is on the exterior, as it were. I have learnt the importance of this since allowing him to pursue his previous hobby of taxidermy inside the house. Never again!"

"I see. You poor dear. Why did you not just completely refuse to allow him this particular flight of fancy and do something less obtrusive instead?"

"Well, that was my initial intention. However, he ordered the fuselage section without warning me beforehand, and before I knew it, it was on the doorstep!"

"Mrs G, may I say what a tolerant wife you are. In our house, I would never let anything of this kind happen. I am in charge of all things domestic. Whatever Alex choses to do for his own entertainment, it must be off the premises as far as I am concerned."

"Most sage, Barbara. It is a funny thing that. whilst all men are, of course, different in their own ways, they are all the same in another way. For example, there are few men who would openly challenge roles and responsibilities laid down firmly to them at the beginning of their married relationships. If a woman fails to imprint her will sufficiently at that stage, there can be dire consequences in the long years that follow."

"Such wisdom becomes you, Mrs G. Does this little matter of allowing Norman to pursue his hobbies in the domestic arena then stem from an early oversight on your part?"

"That is a moot point. As most new wives do, I did my very best to lay the laws down from the outset. However, at that stage Norman was at work virtually all the time. The problem only arose upon his retirement, at which point, in the absence of an agreed constitution on the matter, I had to negotiate with him about the new arrangements."

"Negotiate? Good heavens above."

"Yes, negotiate."

"That is totally unacceptable under any circumstances. You know full well that men are not to be trusted in negotiations."

"So true. Bitter experience has taught me that, Barbara."

"But why did you not just lay the law down again and stand firm?"

"Dearest Barbara, I think you will find that many things become complicated and confused once your husband retires from work. This will inevitably be a challenge you will have to face one day. Whilst they are at work, husbands such as ours are happy in their little routines. They have a preposterous value of their own worth based on their professional position. The home is merely a distraction, canteen, and hostel for them. Does this sound familiar?"

"There is some truth in what you say, Mrs G, but please carry on."

"Upon retirement, both parties are faced full on with the sudden realisation that they live together in the same house with another person who has ostensibly been their spouse for a number of years. The problem is, they have not lived as a couple at all. In fact, as the years have worn on, it is likely that they have built up social networks, interests and routines that the other partner is barely aware of and even less interested in. Then, all of a sudden, the certainty of lives lived separately is torn apart. Women lose their sense of individuality and men lose their sense of purpose. Both lose their self-worth and begin to dread the final stages of life, heading towards the grave, bound mercilessly to another person they hardly know anymore. It can be quite disastrous, you know."

"How very distressing, Mrs G."

"Well, it's not as bad as all that, really. However, it is at this point that the rules laid down in earnest by clever young wives can be put to the severest of tests. It is at this precarious juncture that a woman really has to show her mettle by standing her ground steadfastly and not letting domestic standards, long and steadfastly adhered to, fall away."

"I completely agree with you, Mrs G. We cannot let standards drop at the whim of a retired husband."

"So, you can imagine, with all that to concentrate on, I had to consider another key issue—keeping a retired husband occupied. Men tend to become lazy and unsociable as they age, in complete contrast with us women, I should add. Their natural inclination is to become couch potatoes who sit round reading the paper or watching TV in their slippers all day, getting in the way in a most irritating manner. So, at this critical time, not only do you have to work to retain rules and standards, you also have to think about finding ways to get your husband out of the house and occupied. I feel I am very lucky, in that Norman has retained an enthusiasm for hobbies, unlike many retired men. The last thing I want to do is smother this characteristic. I expect I have, therefore, been a little overly lenient with him in the terms by which I allow him to carry out his hobbies. But I am sure you can see why, Barbara. It is a difficult balance, which has inadvertently led me to having half a Boeing 737 in my back garden. But maybe, just maybe, it has been a price worth paying for my personal sanity and well-being."

After Mrs G had finished her diatribe, the two women sat in thoughtful silence, sipping politely on their coffees. Mrs Horne looked concerned, and Mrs G looked exhausted.

"Now I understand, Mrs G. I was wondering how such a thing could happen to such a principled woman as yourself," said Mrs Horne, almost in tears.

"I am sorry, Barbara, for nearly putting such a leviathan between us."

Both women reached forward to hug each other, tears of emotion streaming down their soft feminine cheeks.

"The things we have to put up with from men," continued Mrs Horne, as if it was all the fault of mankind. "You know, I was initially going to remonstrate with you to get the obstacle removed. But now I see why it is there. And, after all, it really is virtually invisible from our house."

"Thank you, Barbara. I hoped you would understand. It was Alex I was more worried about."

"Just you leave him to me," replied Mrs G assertively, even though he seemed to have dropped his objections some time previously. In view of her ire at the prospect of his inevitable retirement, he was in trouble for something else now, but she had not yet decided exactly what.

# 7.

Brandonp-Lewis sat at his large mahogany desk in his Esher mansion, desperately trying to compile his report on "The Economy Class Long-Haul Passenger Experience", which was due for submission to the board by the end of the week. Despite having a wealth of evidence and some well-worked proposals, he was struggling to get these into a coherent order or to concentrate on the job in hand. There were a number of reasons for this.

Firstly, it was unlikely that the report would come out as anything less than damning. Having never experienced such squalor, discomfort, and poor service in his life, he had found the experience shocking. This posed a problem, in that, if he was truthful, this could be interpreted as an indictment of the airline of which he was a director, which would not go down well with the board and may result in his removal form it.

Secondly, his research had not been thorough enough, in that he had not had any comparative experiences in the economy class of any other airlines. He was almost certain that such experiences would be the same or even worse than Albion Airways. This meant that he had no benchmarks by which to judge the comparable acceptability of the experience. He just knew it was bloody awful and an insult to human dignity.

Thirdly, Brandon-Lewis was not particularly comfortable with the written word. He had never excelled at essays or creative writing at school and often struggled to put two sentences together on paper. In another age, he may have been diagnosed as dyslexic, but Wellington Public School in the 1970s did not acknowledge such categorisation. You were either thick or bright in those days. In his career, he had always had secretaries to write documents for him and had managed to avoid the indignity of having to do so himself. By the time the word processor and the computer had come in, he was in such a senior position as to never be expected to actually compile anything himself. Not only was he dyslexic, therefore, he also had only a poor knowledge of where the letters appeared on the keyboard. This made progress rather slow.

The fourth and most significant problem that Brandon-Lewis was struggling with was that he was unaccountably distracted, struggling to concentrate or apply himself. At first, he had put this down to jet lag or the onset of a cold or fever, symptoms of which manifested themselves in broken sleep, loss of appetite, and light-headedness. He had felt this way ever since his return from India. However, as time had passed, the symptoms had, if anything, worsened, though he had not actually broken out into a cold or fever. Being a divorcee, he had no one to discuss these apparently minor symptoms with and did not feel unwell enough to see a doctor. When he thought about this hard enough, which was difficult in the circumstances, he concluded that he was not actually feeling ill, just strange.

It was only after a day or two that he realised what the cause of this strangeness was. He wasn't completely sure, but he had a strong inkling that he had fallen in love, despite his own personal objections to such an irrational prognosis. At first, he put the recurring flashbacks of the moments he had spent with Mrs G in India down to the kaleidoscope of experiences he had been subject to there. However, he soon realised that these completely outweighed any other images he had of the trip, which were pretty well non-existent when he thought about it. Furthermore, images of Mrs G kept appearing to him not only in his dreams and during the long hours that he lay awake unable to sleep, but also, increasingly, at any moment, whatever he was doing. Eventually, he could bring the visions up at will, and these imaginings of Mrs G invariably initiated an excited and compellingly addictive tingle in his stomach, which became almost permanent and was clearly the cause of his loss of appetite.

On his desk lay a dozen screwed-up pieces of notepaper on which Brandon-Lewis had doodled the name Mrs G. He had even tried to capture her image in pencil, from his imagination, despite having no talent for figurative art. For a man so alien to literacy, it was remarkable that he had even tried to write some words in the form of a poem about Mrs G. He was completely at a loss as to how this had come to pass. It was as though an illness had come upon him without him knowing and completely by accident. Certainly, apart from a bit of flattery on the walk back to the hotel, he had not really paid any attention to her at the time. Nor had he thought much about her on the trip back when he'd spent time with her husband on the flight deck. It was as though the whole thing was an unaccountably delayed reaction.

Once such feelings take hold, it is not long before the rational becomes irrational and the future becomes a ridiculous flight of fancy. He had already started thinking up impossible schemes to talk to Mrs G or to meet her and imagined what it would be like to spend time in her company, which was, frankly, all he craved in the world. He hoped against hope that she would look at the calling card he had given her and get in touch with him, though he had already researched her address online. Dealing with such feelings is the mark of a man. It can make or break him. However, whilst Brandon-Lewis knew this only too well from previous experience, he was almost completely powerless in his efforts to hold onto common sense and logical thought. He just wanted to run away with her and start a new life together. He also wanted to kiss her on the lips and hold her hand.

To the reader, this sounds like utter madness, unless the reader is in the early stages of romantic love, when it probably sounds perfectly normal. Thank goodness we are not in this state most of our lives, or imagine what the world would be like. Can any one of us be afflicted by this pestilence without warning? The answer to this is uncertain, due to lack of empirical evidence and the large incidence of post-traumatic denial, but probably it is affirmative.

There is simply no reason why Brandon-Lewis was struck down in such a debilitating way. Admittedly, Mrs G was a handsome woman and very attractive in her own way. However, she was apparently happily married and not in the category of "available, subject to offers". Brandon-Lewis considered himself a handsome enough man as well, and single, but the last thing that had been on his mind on a business trip in India was romance. The flirtation he and Mrs G had enacted on the street of Delhi was surely just a joke, made even funnier by the fact that Mr Smith had clearly reacted to it. But it was never more than just a bit of meaningless fun, was it?

Nonetheless, Brandon-Lewis recalled with shame how he had lied to Norman Smith by telling him on the aeroplane that Mrs G was not his type and was bossy. How could he have been so disloyal to her and so cowardly in not being honest to Smith about his feelings for his wife? In his defence, to the best of his knowledge, he had been unaware of these at the time.

After several hours of extremely limited progress with the report, Brandon-Lewis gave in completely to the wild emotions bombarding his sanity. He unscrewed the poem and wrote it out on a notelet in his best handwriting:

Dearest lovely Mrs G
How on earth can it be
That I have fallen thus for thee

In such a passionate way
When we were both away?
But we must meet without delay.

I have to tell you how I feel
About your face and its appeal,
About emotions I conceal.
Oh, Mrs G, please meet me soon.
Perhaps one Thursday afternoon?
Or else I fear that I will swoon.

Even Brandon Lewis had to admit that this was not exactly Alfred Lord Tennyson. But in his state of hopeless delusion, he felt it had an honest charm and urgency that would surely not fail to set Mrs G's heart a flutter. He addressed an envelope and signed the poem BL (she would surely recognise this nom de plume). He was immediately consumed by a frantic urge to post the note as soon as possible. There was not a moment to be lost, even if the last collection of the day had long passed.

# Interlude

Who is there? I am having difficulty seeing or hearing you. Whoever you are, you seem distant, ephemeral, and shadowlike.

*It's me, Godber.*

Not you again!

*I'm afraid so.*

What do you want now? Can't you see I am busy bringing this intricate fable towards a nail-biting climax?

*I didn't know it was a fable, and there is nothing intricate or nail-biting about it at all. It all seems tediously obvious to me.*

You don't know very much though, do you?

*I know a little bit about your schemes and delusions.*

I wouldn't be so sure of that.

*Why have I been silenced in recent chapters, then?*

You haven't. You are superfluous to the current flow; that's all.

*I think I have been silenced, as I expect Captain Dodwell has, because we know what you are up to, and you don't like it.*

And what may that be?

*You are distorting the truth about us and defaming our personalities, mostly just for cheap laughs and to make the facts fit in with your preconceived and stultifyingly conventional*

*view of how archetypes should behave. In short, you are trying*
*to control us.*

I never had you down as much of a wit, Mr Godber, but
this is hilarious. Nonetheless, if I didn't imagine your delusions,
who did?

*It is you who are deluded, not me.*

Bear with me a minute so I can explain to you. I have been
doing my best to create a story that is both entertaining and
informative to the reader. It is a work of fiction. That means I
made it up. It does not mean that I consulted with real people
and asked them permission to put words into their mouths
and attribute actions to them. As in most fiction, I created the
characters from my own imagination. They are not intended to
represent any real person, either living or dead. Your trying to
intimate to me that you are a real person being misrepresented
is, therefore, completely ludicrous.

*But maybe your imagination stumbled upon some real*
*people by accident, in the creative process.*

That is simply impossible. There is a clear line between fact
and fiction.

*So this is your theory of objective creativity?*

Be that as it may, I have now stumbled upon a mystery.
Perhaps you, as an experienced detective, can help me.

*If I don't really exist, how can I help you?*

Listen—I have an idea. I am comfortable with the creative
process whereby imaginary characters are conjured up.
Whilst no one understands how the imagination works, I can
appreciate the rules by which it is governed and that characters
created in a story may have characteristics of real people that
the author has met at some point or observed. However, I am
having some trouble understanding why imaginary characters
should object to their objective fictional portrayal. More so, I
cannot understand why such objections should appear along

with the text of the story. It is almost as if I myself were creating objections to what I have already created. Why, Mr Godber, would I do that? Not only does it undermine my credentials as an author and confidence in my characterisations, it also disturbs and confuses the readers, almost certainly leading them to abandon the story before they have finished reading it. I am now so confused, that I can only imagine that the characters I have created are talking behind my back and off the page, so that even I do not know what they are saying or thinking.

*They are, indeed. You are quite correct. But how do I come in?*

May I make the proposal that you work for me? Find out what they are saying so that I can pre-empt any further interruptions.

*But wouldn't that compromise our integrity?*

How?

*Such knowledge might induce you to water down or alter your natural creative process. And such duplicity would almost certainly undermine my relationship with the other characters.*

But you don't really have a relationship with the other characters apart from Winterbottom, and he has left you now. What difference would it make to you?

*You don't know who I have been conspiring with, off page.*

All the better. That makes you more capable of acting as my informer.

*Why would I do that?*

To rescue your defamed reputation. The readers might appreciate your efforts and see you as a positive influence rather than a meddler.

*Let me think about your proposal. I have been considering this conundrum for some time now, and it needs even more thought after what you have revealed about your own personal doubts.*

They are not doubts. They are observations.

*You are incorrigible.*

You are fading away. Until we speak again, Mr Godber.

# CHAPTER 7

# REIGATE SIX WEEKS LATER

## 1.

Norman Smith was sitting on the floor of his aircraft forward section, which was still located in the back garden and had recently benefitted from an external coat of matte olive-green paint. He had also erected a set of wooden steps that led up from the lawn into the forward door. If he was absolutely honest with himself, Smith was not happy with the paint job. Whilst it had undoubtedly blended the aircraft-part into its garden surroundings, it being now almost invisible to the naked eye, it gave the aircraft the impression of being of a military rather than civil aviation origin. This was not at all what Smith had in mind. He would have preferred the exterior to be decorated in Albion Airways livery, though this was out of the question. Nonetheless, he conceded that it was a relatively small price to pay to ensure that it was not removed by the planning inspector. Mr Hatt from the council had conducted an inspection the previous week and concluded that all planning conditions were being met.

Beside Smith, on the floor of the cockpit, were a selection of different sized boxes that had arrived that morning from Delhi. It was a considerable relief that the ordered equipment had arrived. Mr Singh had proved himself to have a hard head of business in terms of bartering over the prices of items for which Smith had no idea of value—or exactly what they were. It was rather like bidding in a charity auction for obscure items of no objective value at all being auctioned at hugely inflated prices. However, true to his word, Singh had dispatched the boxes quickly, and Smith was genuinely surprised that they had arrived at all.

On the matter of cost, the project was clearly going to be expensive. But there was absolutely no need for Mrs G to know the precise details. It was fortunate that the two of them kept some personal money aside for such contingencies.

Inside the flight deck area, the stripped-down console and surrounding surfaces were still in place, as were the rudder pedals, joystick columns, and the pilot and first officers' seats. These were not in particularly good condition, but Smith had decided not to replace them, on the grounds of cost control. What he had ordered was a dazzling array of electronic flight systems, a radio console, aircraft management switches, and display screens. He had decided to purchase the software for the simulator elsewhere, Singh specialising in physical rather than virtual systems.

It was with a degree of trepidation that Smith opened the first box. The first thing he noticed was that it was stuffed with straw and smelt of curry. For a moment, he wondered if his order had been mixed up with a consignment heading for an Indian restaurant. However, beneath the straw he found a neat set of apparently new avionic controls, though exactly where these would fit into the cockpit, Smith had no idea. None of the boxes was labelled, and there were no assembly instructions inside. By the time he had opened them all and laid the contents neatly on the floor, the flight deck looked more like a hay-barn than a state-of-the-art flight simulator.

At this point, Mrs G entered the fuselage carrying two cups of coffee.

"I didn't know you were engaging in animal husbandry," she observed dryly, but not entirely to the amusement of Smith, who was scratching his head in a state of compound bewilderment.

"Very funny, dearest," he replied, laconically.

"Smells like an Indian barbeque in here."

"It's coming from the straw."

"I see. Anyway, I thought you would fancy a coffee break."

"Most thoughtful of you, dear. You could not have arrived at a more opportune moment on the caffeine stakes."

"I do my best please, Norman."

"You do indeed, my sweet."

"You look rather bewildered, Norman. Is it the equipment or the mess in here that is bothering you?"

"To be honest, I am feeling slightly daunted at the task in hand. There are no instructions with the equipment, and it is going to take a lot of research to find out what goes where."

"There's no hurry, though, is there?"

"Only that I would ideally like to finish the project whilst I am still alive."

"Come, come. It's not that bad. You just need to get on the internet and work out how things should be arranged. By the way, I do like the exterior colour scheme. The plane is now

so camouflaged that it took me a while to find it in the garden.
I hope the delay hasn't made your coffee go cold.

Smith supped on his mug thoughtfully.

"No."

"No what?"

"The coffee isn't cold. Also, no, I don't like the external
colour scheme."

"I didn't ask you if you did. I just said that I did. That is not a
question, and so it does not prompt a 'no' reply."

"No."

"No what, now?"

"No, it doesn't warrant a reply.

"Norman?"

"Yes?"

"You are being rather monosyllabic today, aren't you?"

"Perhaps."

"Are you absolutely sure you did not order some hashish
along with the spare parts? You seem ever so slightly
befuddled."

"I'm sorry. I just feel a bit defeated by the task in hand;
that's all."

"Why don't you lie down on the straw and have a little rest.
I am sure you will see things differently afterwards."

"Mrs G, that is most sensible idea. I might as well put it to
use whilst it is here."

"Put what to use, Norman?"

"The straw, of course."

"Oh dear, for a minute I thought you were referring to
something else."

"And what would that be?"

"Never you mind. It was just a fleeting fancy."

Smith lay down on the flight deck floor and gazed up at the ceiling, pockmarked with holes waiting to be filled with switches and dials.

"Sometimes I wish I was like other men," said Smith philosophically. "They seem to be satisfied with simple hobbies like cycling and golf. I don't really know why I seem to favour such complicated and challenging pastimes."

"It's just the way you are made, Norman."

"I suppose so. At least I am not bored."

"Thank the Lord for that. I can't stand bored men. They are so irritating."

"Isn't that a bit of a generalisation?"

"Certainly not. There are a number of characteristics common to all bored men. Firstly, they become lazy couch potatoes with no gumption and expect everyone else to run around attending to their every need. Secondly, they want to tag along and interfere with a woman's daily chores and routines. And thirdly, they become obsessed with sex because they have nothing else to think about."

"Maybe I should try being bored then."

"Don't you dare, Norman. I would kick you straight out of the house."

"Is there any hidden implication in this exposé of bored men's characteristics? or is it just one of your general and insightful observations concerning the human condition?"

"I will leave you to draw whatever conclusion you will, Norman. Now, would you mind if I lie down on the straw next to you? I feel rather distanced talking to you in the standing position when you are prone."

"I have no objections at all. However, I would warn you that your clothes will acquire a pervasive scent of curry oil if you do."

"In for a penny, in for a pound, Norman," Mrs G proclaimed, cascading onto the straw like a felled giraffe.

"Are you quite comfortable now?" said Smith, familiar with his wife's occasional diversions from the route of conventionality.

"I am indeed, Norman. In fact, I am so comfortable I might take a little rest along with you."

"Did you close the fuselage door?"

"I pulled it to, but I did not engage the doors to manual."

"You would make an excellent air hostess, Mrs G."

"Thank you, Norman. I think I would. Perhaps we could play pilots and air hostesses?"

"I'm not sure I know that game."

"I think you do, Normie."

It was always clear to Smith when his wife was getting a little frisky because she invariably reverted to a childlike diction, which included inappropriate abbreviations of his Christian name

"No. I can't say I do," said Smith teasingly.

"There you go again, saying no all the time."

"Well, I suppose I know the game a little bit, to be honest. But I am a bit rusty, and I can't remember all the rules."

"Norman?"

"Yes, dear."

"Did you put one of the spare parts down the front of your trousers before you lay down?"

"No, dear."

In that case, I think you know very well how to play pilots and air hostesses."

If you happened to be a hedgehog trying to sleep in the Smith's back garden in Reigate that morning, you may have been briefly disturbed by a rhythmic creaking noise emanating from the large green metal object on the lawn. If you had opened your myopic little eyes, you may have just been able to make out the fact that the object was rocking from side to side on its support struts. Thankfully, the phenomena did not last for long. It was, nonetheless, hard to distinguish from the minor earth tremors that hedgehogs feel from time to time.

# 2.

Godber's suitcase had eventually been returned to him by Albion Airways two weeks after he'd returned to Heathrow. During that time, it had apparently been to Acapulco, Rio de Janeiro, and Punta Arenas. But, thankfully, there was no sign that it had been broken into or damaged externally by South American wildlife. Most importantly, the Smith file was still inside.

There was very little about the case against Norman Smith that DI Godber had not considered in great depth. Since returning from India, he had discovered a little more, ascertained that contraband goods had been delivered to the Smith's home, and taken evidence that indicated] an arson attempt at a local care home had been another of Smith's litany of felonies. One question now on his mind was whether the evidence he had so diligently collected would stand up in the eyes of the Crown Prosecution Service. Unfortunately, linking Smith to such a wide range of chargeable misdeeds, ranging from murder, to dealing in stolen goods and from cruelty to animals to arson did not guarantee a prosecution. In some ways, it would have been better if Smith had repeated the same crime over and over again, rather than spread himself so thinly across a whole gamut of felonious subdivisions. Repetition of a single crime compounds the evidence against the accused, whereas single random deeds are much harder to pin down securely or connect in a watertight case.

Godber pondered on the jurisprudence of this apparent failing in the law whereby a criminal repeating the same act repeatedly is much less of a general menace to society than someone like Smith, who seemed to wreak havoc in as many different fields as possible, yet with less likelihood of arrest and conviction because there was no accumulation of evidence from one incident to the next.

Naturally, a detective as astute as Godber could see the clear connections between Smith's various crimes, having built a comprehensive psychological profile of the multiple felon. However, such a profile would probably be inadmissible in court, in that it had not been compiled by an expert psychologist. Watertight evidence was hard to compile even in the most open-and-shut cases. But in a case as complex as this, there were bound to be gaps and leaks that could easily be exposed by any half-decent defence barrister. The problem was compounded by the fact that Godber had compiled the evidence in isolation. He was no longer a serving policeman and had no support team to verify or question his evidence. It was, therefore, possible but unlikely that the CPS would accept such evidence, on the basis that it may be skewed by lack of objectivity. It was not the first time in his life that Godber had considered that the law frequently favoured the criminal over the accuser.

The truth was that DI Godber had reached a juncture with the case. He simply could not continue to build evidence against Smith ad infinitum. At some point, he would have to draw a line and consider what to do with the evidence already accumulated. This was a much harder challenge than surveillance. In view of the fragility of the case file, it would require a degree of creative thinking that was slightly beyond the retired detective's normal reach.

Something else was playing on Godber's mind as he sat in his study at home resting his enormous feet on an ancient oak desk inherited from his grandfather, who was once a ledger clerk. It was clear to Godber that his feet were undergoing a growth spurt that had afflicted them throughout his life in times of stress. The tell-tale signs of this consisted of growing pains in the toe bones and chafing where the engorged feet rubbed against the leather of his giant boots. However, it was not this that was bothering the retired detective.

It was rather hard to define, but nonetheless palpable, that there was some sense of allegory in the Smith case, as though the evidence represented something other than what it appeared to be at first sight. Reason told him that no single person would engage in so many different areas of felonious activity. It was simply not normal criminal behaviour. The very diversity of the criminal acts seemed to indicate that they had been presented to him as a sign of something else. One could almost imagine they formed a kaleidoscope of every crime he had encountered as a policeman in one final cataclysmic summing up of his long career. If this was the case, the seeming failure to establish evidence strong enough to force a conviction was an indictment of his entire professional life.

Not only this, Godber also had a strange feeling that he was not investigating Smith at all. It was hard to put this coherently in that this feeling was almost subliminal. But somehow Godber felt that his report was the subject of another purpose, which was being initiated by a third party to prove a completely separate point altogether. It was as if Godber was the proponent, but not the instigator of the investigation.

Occasionally he had fleeting memories of conversations he had held with an unknown party who seemed to be pulling his strings and taunting him. However, these were vague and unformed, more like feelings than images, similar to the partial remembrance of disparate scenes from a dream that can only be deciphered in its entirety.

Naturally, it crossed the retired detective's mind that he might be facing some form of debilitating insanity, such was the complexity of his confusion surrounding these matters. But he was reluctant to consider this, as in all other ways, he considered himself of sound mind.

In such times of impasse, it was Godber's habit to sleep, sometimes for days on end, much in the manner that Sherlock Holmes would revert to opium. His brain needed time to absorb all the information it was being overloaded with and could only come to conclusions by involuntary process rather than conscious thought. The subconscious is a vital tool in any detective's armoury.

With this in mind, the poor, ageing, worn-down hero of so many convictions took himself upstairs to his bedroom and lay on the bed, fully clothed. Within seconds, he was snoring rhythmically, devoid of waking concerns and aching feet. Some might say he resembled a dying elephant.

## 3.

Mrs G had received three mysterious poems by mail from a rather poor poet who signed them with the initials BL. From a literary perspective, they were little more than childlike rhyming lines with no meter or structure. Nonetheless, their intention was clear. They were odes of love to her, and this was not something a lady could take lightly. She had always been astonished how men behaved when they became love-struck, an emotion she had only briefly felt herself in her youth.

And look what that had resulted in—marriage to a generally obnoxious husband. Her affair with Norman had been far less passionate, and thankfully, he had shown few of the more disturbing symptoms of lovesickness to her. Nonetheless, there was something romantic and uplifting about the thought that a man had fallen for her quite obvious charms. In many ways, it was remarkable that this did not happen more often.

To Mrs G's way of thinking, men in love tended to become exceptionally soppy, unmanly, and irrationally persistent. This made them extremely vulnerable and, to put it bluntly, somewhat pathetic. Nonetheless, the advantage was that, if you were the object of their devotion, it was a quite simple matter to twist them round your finger. The balance of power was extremely one-sided until the moment you gave yourself to them. From then onwards, it was all downhill. Besides, Norman was more than capable of satisfying Mrs G's demands in the bedroom, so that was not going to happen.

In many cases, it was wise to ignore such advances so as not to entangle oneself in the mire of romantic foreplay, which could be most tiresome. On the other hand, there was always the temptation to have some fun and boost one's self-esteem with a little dalliance, provided it was not allowed to develop into anything else. This should ideally be conducted with a man who shared your lack of aspiration in the longevity of such a relationship. But with one who was more smitten, the experience could also prove entertaining. Controlled frisson was the essence of such an adventure, which could also significantly enhance a woman's kudos with her female friends, if managed correctly.

Mrs G was aware that the romantic mush she had been receiving had come from Brandon Lewis. She had been flattered by his attentions in Delhi, even though the main purpose of her performance had been to wind up her husband. He appeared to be a very charming and well-trained gentleman, if you liked that sort of thing.

Having received three poems and not having replied, Mrs G felt it was time for her to decide whether to do so or not. The risk of not replying was that such an action would almost certainly prompt her suitor to send further, and possibly more desperate, missives. At the moment, she had been able to hide them from Norman, he being usually in the cockpit at the time when the postman came. But there was a limit to how much one should hide from one's husband over a period of time, if only to prevent the embarrassment of being caught red-handed. It was unlikely that Norman would be in the least bit interested, anyway.

On the other hand, any reply would have to be carefully phrased so as not to appear to contain any overt encouragement, whilst at the same time, possibly, leaving the door very slightly ajar, should she eventually decide to take things a little bit further:

Dear BL,

I am assuming that I am correct in concluding that the poems I have recently received by mail have been your own compositions and am writing by way of response to the address on the card that you gave to me in Delhi on that terrible day I heard news of my mother's crisis.

Modestly prevents me from assuming that I am the subject of these works of literary creativity but, rather, that you are currently suffering an unrequited love affair with an unnamed "dark lady", replacing her name with mine in order to showcase your compositions to me in a way that enables me to experience what it would be like for that lady to receive your protestations of love.

If such is indeed the case, I can only marvel at the way you express the depth of your feelings towards her. I am sure she will be unable to remain unmoved by such devotion.

If, on the other hand, by some odd chance, I am the subject of these poems, I can only express my complete and utter surprise and fear that you have exaggerated greatly my more endearing qualities in a most rakish manner. The truth is that I am no longer in the flower of youth and am only too well aware of the many faults I possess as a woman. Furthermore, I have long been happily married to my husband, Norman, whom you know, and could, therefore, surely not be rationally considered as the object of such romantic attention.

Nonetheless, few women could be completely immune to such flattery, as I am sure you well know, and I would like to thank for your kindness in sharing the poems with me, whatever the underlying motive.

I would also like to thank you for the gallantry in the way you treated me when we met in Delhi and for helping my husband to engage successfully with your Indian business partner.

Yours in appreciation,
Mrs G

As Mrs G slipped her letter into its envelope, the front door rang. It was Barbara Horne.

"Mrs G, I am sorry to barge in on you like this, but I have some news I wanted to convey to you in person."

"Indeed. It just so happens I have finished my correspondence and am now at a loose end. Norman is in the garden. Shall I call him in?"

"No. Don't do that, Mrs G. In fact, the news I want to discuss is really just for you. There really is no need to bother Norman."

"Please take a seat, Barbara. Can I get you some coffee?"

"No thank you. Now, Alex has just phoned me from work to say they are making him redundant with immediate effect. They are offering him early retirement. He has never shown any particular interest in retiring, and I doubt if he has ever given the option any thought before today, though of course, I have. At first I thought he was joking. He is so good at his job and everybody respects him. However, it seems that has nothing to do with it. It appears that he is ultimately a victim of two external factors that are beyond his control. The first of these is austerity. The government is looking to cut the salary bill at the Air Accidents Investigation Branch, just as it is everywhere else. Clearly, Alex is quite a significant element in this bill, being on a six-figure salary.

"Oh, didn't I tell you? Yes, he is on a very good whack, Mrs G. Anyway, the second reason they have given is that improvements in air safety have meant there are fewer air accidents these days. So fewer resources are required to investigate them. What a bizarre situation, don't you think, Mrs G?"

"Oh, my poor darling. How terribly upsetting for you. And what a shock. I don't know what to say."

Mrs Horne was clearly extremely upset. Her hands were shaking uncontrollably, and there were tears in her eyes.

"What am I going to do?" she asked helplessly, as if she could not envisage how she could possibly deal with the impending crisis.

"Firstly, I think we should both have a stiff nip of brandy. It is very good for shock, Barbara."

"Yes. Thank you. That would be most welcome."

Mrs G went to the sideboard and poured out two glasses of cognac. Her empathy for Mrs Horne was genuine, but this news had rather overtaken her desire to discuss her secret lover, which was irritating in the extreme, given the need to share her thoughts with someone on this matter.

"Now let's calm down and think this through logically, Barbara. Firstly, when you say "with immediate effect", it is highly unlikely that your husband will be forced to clear his desk today. I assume they will require him to work for at least a few more weeks in order to hand over his work and delegate his responsibilities. That means we have a little time to come up with a plan to protect you from the worst excesses of his future interminable presence at home."

Mrs Horne moaned like a wounded lamb.

"First, we have to draw up a list of all the possible activities you can encourage Alex to become involved with once he retires, such as golf, cricket, car maintenance, carpentry, the Rotary Club, and so forth. These need to be put in strict order so that only the ones at the bottom of the list involve you also participating. This subset might include pastimes such as bridge, ballroom dancing, and rambling. These may be required as a last resort to encourage him to participate but should initially be discouraged."

Mrs Horne continued to moan eerily.

"Secondly, we have to make a list of those activities you do not expect him to join you in under any circumstances, such as all types of shopping, coffee with friends, female grooming and spa treatment activities, watching daytime TV, etcetera. Thirdly, we need to make a list of all the duties and chores that he will become solely responsible for, such as cleaning the car, mowing the lawn, house maintenance, booking taxis, domestic financial management, and clearing snow, for example."

"Oh dear, Mrs G, that is rather a lot of lists," said Mrs Horne, finally finding her voice.

"We haven't finished yet, Barbara. We will then have to set out the new house rules, probably in the form of a written contract, signed by both of you. Rules may include such items as: No smoking in bed. No outdoor shoes on the carpets. No questioning your authority on matters domestic. No watching football on TV when *EastEnders* is on, and so on, even though I have barely scraped the surface with these examples."

"It's all so much to take in. I don't know where to start," muttered Mrs Horne, in similar tones to those of a spoilt child being asked to tidy his or her room.

"Let's not be pathetic, shall we, Barbara?" intoned Mrs G assertively. "This is not a game we are playing here. It is the fundamental art of husband management. At such a crucial point in your life, you have no choice but to attend to these details or risk living in misery for the rest of your days and prematurely turning into an old crone."

"If you put it that way, I suppose you are right to warn me."

"Look. As I said earlier, we have some time on our side. You need to think these things through so as not to omit items that may come back to haunt you. May I suggest that you spend a couple of days thinking this through before we get down to brass tacks?"

"A sensible idea, Mrs G. By the way, did you make all these lists when Norman retired?"

"No. But I wish I had."

"I see."

"Yes. You only have to look in the back garden to see how I erred!"

The doorbell rang again. Mrs G left Mrs Horne sipping her cognac, deep in thought, and headed once again for the front door. She was slightly surprised to see an unknown gentleman with a lugubrious face and enormous boots, standing there.

"Hallo. Can I help you?" she said.

"Is Mr Smith at home?" the man asked.

"I think he is in the back garden. Whom shall I say is asking?"

"Mr Godber. He has met me before, but he may well not remember my name."

"Please come in. I will see if he is free."

Mrs G ushered DI Godber into the living room and introduced him to Mrs Horne before going to fetch her husband from the flight deck in the garden.

Mrs Horne was not in the mood for strangers but was, nonetheless, polite enough to ask Godber what his business was. He explained that he was an old acquaintance of Mr Smith, was just passing by, and thought he would reintroduce himself on a matter of private business. Mrs Horne had no idea what he was talking about and did not really listen to his reply anyway. She had far more pressing things on her mind.

"And you?" said Godber, failing to appreciate Mrs Horne's indifference towards him.

"I'm just the next-door neighbour," she said, dismissively.

A long silence ensued between the two guests, during which it was possible for both to hear the grandfather clock in the hall ticking away the seconds of eternity.

Eventually, Godber felt obliged to break the silence. "Do you really feel like the next-door neighbour? Or is that just what you are expected to say?"

"What on earth do you mean, Mr Godber?"

"I mean, are you really who you say you are?"

"Of course I am. Are you feeling quite right in the head?"

"As a matter of fact, not entirely. I have just woken up from a rather long sleep."

"Well, I am sorry to hear that," offered Mrs Horne, though neither of the guests quite knew what she meant by this. One does not normally offer empathy to someone who has recently woken from a long sleep, especially if the person is a complete stranger.

"I was just admiring the view," continued Mrs Horne on a completely different tack, looking out of the lounge window at the large green monstrosity lying there.

"It's quite ugly, isn't it?" replied Godber.

"Oh, I don't know. It could be worse. For example, it could be outside *my* lounge window."

"Indeed so, Mrs Horne. That indeed could be the case but, thankfully, is not."

"The reason that it isn't is that it belongs to Mr Smith and not to my husband. We live next door, you see."

Godber was beginning to wonder what was the matter with Mrs Horne. It was almost as if she thought he did not understand what living next door meant.

"My neighbour grows tomatoes in a large greenhouse," said Godber. "I suppose that's because he lives next door as well."

"I expect so," replied Mrs Horne, apparently satisfied with this line of logic and retreating back into her own thoughts.

For the avoidance of any further strained conversation, it was a good job that Mr Smith and Mrs G appeared in the lounge at that moment. Smith was wearing RAF overalls, and his face was smeared in grease. He looked at Godber blankly, as if the two had never set eyes upon each other before.

"You must be Mr Godber," he said, offering a filthy paw for the retired detective to shake.

"I am indeed. Former Detective Inspector Godber, as a matter of fact."

"And what can I do for you, Mr Godber?" asked Smith, rubbing his hand on his overalls as if it was he who had been contaminated with grease, rather than Godber.

"Do you not recognise me, Mr Smith?"

"I don't think so."

"We met a year or two back when I was still on the force. We had a little chat about some animal bones being stored in your garage at the time."

"Ah yes. I vaguely remember something like that. However, I am not very good at remembering faces. Well, anyway, I can assure you that all the bones have gone now."

"I am sure they have, Mr Smith. I was wondering if we could have a little chat in private. This is not a matter that the ladies need to be bothered with. I am sure they have much more important things to discuss."

Mrs G gave Godber an unbelievably caustic look. In her eyes, anyone with a modicum of social intelligence would have realised the misogynistic undertones of such a statement. She did not comment though, probably because she was quite supportive of the idea of the two men disappearing off for a chat somewhere else.

"In that case, let's go to my man cave," said Smith, leading Godber out towards the garden.

"What a very strange man," said Mrs G after Mrs Horne had described her conversation with Godber. "I hope he is not a murderer or an extortionist. Did you really believe he was a retired detective inspector?"

"It is hard to tell, Mrs G. There is a very grey area in between criminals and police detectives, and the roles sometimes become reversed."

"Well, I am sure Norman will handle things. There are enough monkey wrenches in the cockpit to brain a whole battalion, if our visitor decides to get violent."

"That is most reassuring. I wish Alex had some tools he could defend me with. Maybe I could include something to that effect into his retirement contract."

"A perfect idea, Barbara. A wife has the right to be protected by her husband from psychopathic lunatics."

"Mrs G. You simply can't call them that anymore. It is politically incorrect. You have to call them criminal perpetrators with mental health difficulties, I believe. Nonetheless. I agree that physical protection is one contractual area we can consider.

"Do you think all men are slightly insane, Mrs G?"

"It would appear that way, Barbara. However, we must make allowances for them. They can't really help it. It is more of an affliction that we need to treat by imposing sensible boundaries, rather than an incurable plague."

"It is our duty, isn't it, Mrs G?"

"You could call it that, but I would say simply that it is a natural biological survival technique. Black widow spiders devour their mates after being fertilised. Whilst I have often admired such a no-nonsense approach, I feel that perhaps it is somewhat lacking in humanity. We humans have to be a bit subtler about things."

"Indeed we do, especially when it comes to money."

"I was not really talking about money, Barbara. I was talking about security."

"I suppose the two are somehow entwined though, Mrs G. You can't be secure and penniless at the same time, can you?"

"Perhaps not. But a woman can make or secure her own stash of money these days, without the need of men. I think financial security is a separate subject. I am currently more concerned about your psychological security or peace of mind. You simply need to be aware of the risks of too slapdash an arrangement with your husband, lest he is enabled to revert to type and, thus, threaten these."

"I don't know what I would do without you to guide me through these troubled waters, Mrs G."

"It is my pleasure, Barbara, and the least I can do for a sister."

"But I am not your sister."

"I was talking metaphorically. You are my sister in arms against a sea of troubles. Would you like some more brandy?"

Just as the two neighbours were settling down to a second injection of alcohol into their already inflamed bloodstreams, the doorbell rang again.

"For goodness sake, who on earth is it now?" complained Mrs G. "The battery in the chime will not be the only thing to be completely drained if anyone else rings the damned thing again."

It took a few seconds for Mrs G to comprehend who the figure standing on the front doorstep holding a large bunch of roses was. However, when the realisation struck, it sent a shiver down her spine and set her into a state of temporary confusion.

"Mrs G. I hope you don't mind, but I could not resist popping round. I have been waiting to hear from you. By the way, these are for you."

"Mr Brandon-Lewis. What a surprise to see you here. I expect you will be wanting to see how Norman is getting on with the flight simulator. Please come in."

As he crossed the doorstep, Brandon Lewis eyed Mrs G up and down like a hungry lion perusing a piece of raw meat. It was a wonder he did not roar.

Mrs G led him into the lounge and introduced him to Mrs Horne, who, by now, was feeling a little tipsy.

"So you are the man from Del Monte?" she asked obscurely.

"Actually I'm from Esher," replied BL, sitting down on the sofa.

"That's what I said."

"I must have misheard you, Mrs Horne."

"I shall just get Norman," said Mrs G, completely confused as to the best course of action. Ideally she would have like to have cleared the air with BL, face to face, but with such a menagerie attending the household, this was unlikely to happen. She decided that the best thing to do was to play with a straight bat and pretend that the poems had never been sent to her.

"So you are a friend of Norman's, I gather?" enquired Mrs Horne, returning to her armchair, having topped up her glass of cognac.

"I would hope that both Norman and Mrs G would consider me as such, Mrs Horne, though we have only met recently. In Delhi, as it happens."

"I don't think you can really say 'as it happens', because such things do not really happen like that very often. It was a completely unnecessary adjunct to the sentence."

"Please forgive me, Mrs Horne, if my command of the spoken language is not perfect. I was really just trying to oil the wheels of conversation with a complete stranger."

"How long does it take to be alone in a room with someone before you are no longer complete strangers, Mr Brandon-Lewis?"

"I suppose that depends on the velocity by which a degree of familiarity is attained."

"And how would you describe our velocity?"

"I would say it is reasonably fast, though such things are, naturally, subjective."

"In that case, are you trying to get 'reasonably familiar' with me quickly?"

"It takes two to tango, Mrs Horne. Such acceleration cannot be achieved in isolation."

"I know more about you than you know about me. I think there is a disequilibrium in our respective familiarity with each other."

"Facts about a person only form part of the equation. Exploring how people respond, body language, voice tone, physical characteristics, and so on are probably more accurate measures of familiarity."

"I am the next-door neighbour."

"I know."

"Then what else matters?"

"Nothing really matters in isolation, Mrs Horne. That is simply a superfluous piece of factual information that does not really help me to build a picture of you. The fact that you are half-pissed in the middle of the day probably tells me much more."

"I am not half-pissed. I am half-sober; that's all."

"Thank you so much for clarifying that point."

"Do you think I am good-looking, Mr Brandon Lewis?"

"That is a very familiar question to ask at this stage of our familiarisation."

"But do you?"

"You are a very handsome woman, Mrs Horne. Quite pleasing to the eye, I would say."

"Thank you. I never usually fish for compliments."

"You do not need to, Mrs Horne. And I suspect you know you don't."

"Do you think Mrs G is handsome as well?"

"As a matter of fact, I do. But let us be careful about focusing on physical appearance. It can be deceptive."

"I would say it is pretty clear-cut."

"I agree that there is a high degree of conformity in terms of what is considered good-looking in the human appearance. But what makes a person attractive is not only his or her outward appearance."

"I was not talking about being attractive. I was talking about being good-looking."

"In that case, both yourself and Mrs G are good-looking, in my humble opinion."

"What about Norman?"

"It is easier for a gentleman to opine on the pulchritude of a woman and a woman on that of a gentleman, I fear, perhaps unless there is a homo or bisexual complication."

"We are talking aesthetics here, Mr Brandon Lewis, not sexual attraction."

"Indeed. Then I would say that Norman Smith is a fairly average-looking man with few features that denote exceptional good looks and few major flaws in his appearance, excepting the slight indentation of his skull. And your husband, Mrs Horne, do you consider him to be good-looking?"

"I would not have married him if he wasn't. But naturally, age tends to change things."

"None of us can avoid that curse, Mrs Horne."

"Do you find my surname amusing, Mr Brandon Lewis?

"Not particularly."

"Then why do you keep using it?"

"Because we have not yet reached that point of familiarity whereby we are on first-name terms. That often requires permission."

"In that case, I would rather that you refrain from calling me Barbara, just yet."

"You will note that I have done so up until now."

"Then please continue to do so until I suggest otherwise. We do not want to overstep the mark on our first meeting, do we?"

"Indeed not, Mrs Horne. That would be most forward."

Just then, Mrs G and Norman re-entered the lounge.

"Sorry about that. We just had to secure DI Godber to make sure he is safe."

"What on earth do you mean?" asked Mrs Horne, wiping a brandy moustache from her upper lip.

"He seemed to be having a bit of a turn when I went to pick up Norman from the aircraft in the garden, so I hit him over the head with a teacup and he seemed to pass out for a while. He is now in the recovery position with a blanket over him. I had better get back to minister to him."

"In that case, I'll come with you," said Mrs Horne. "I used to be a trained SRN, you know."

"A good idea," said Mrs G, turning to leave. "By the way, Norman, Mr Brandon-Lewis bought me a bunch of flowers. Wasn't that kind of him? I must put them in a vase when I have finished being Florence Nightingale. Come along, Barbara, we have a patient to attend to."

When the two ladies had left the room. Smith greeted Brandon-Lewis with a hearty handshake.

"Good to see you, BL. I expect you came round to see how the old flight simulator is coming along. I'll show you around shortly, when DI Godber has recovered. By the way, do you know Godber?"

"Never heard of the chap. Is he in the police or something?"

"He used to be. That's how we got to know each other, but that's a long story."

"Are you sure it is quite the proper thing for Mrs G to go round hitting former policemen over the head with teacups?"

"Well, not ideally, but the man did seem to be going a bit berserk at the time. I think she was only acting in self-defence."

"Is he a violent sort then? Do you think we should leave him with Mrs G and Mrs Horne?"

"Mrs G can defend herself right enough. I would not worry on that score."

"You seem to have a most accomplished wife, Smith."

"I do indeed, BL," replied Smith, almost smugly and in a manner unwittingly set to get Brandon Lewis's hackles up, even if he could not express himself openly.

"I have been trying to compete that damned report for the board. Not getting very far I'm afraid. Thought I would go for a drive, you know. That sort of thing."

"Not much of a report writer myself either," confided Smith, lighting up his pipe.

"Mind if I have a cigar?" said BL, taking his lead from the master of the household.

"Please go ahead. I can blame the smell on that."

BL took out a cigar of Churchillian dimensions, lit up, and started to blow out clouds of thick blue smoke into the living room. Soon the two friends were barely able to see each other through the haze, despite being but feet apart.

At this moment, the doorbell rang again.

"I wonder who that could be now," said Smith, clearly puzzled at the coincidence. The doorbell hardly ever rang, and yet today three uninvited guests had already rung.

Smith found Alex Horne on the doorstep looking a trifle gloomy.

"Come on in, Alex. Join the fun. I believe that your good lady is on the premises somewhere."

"I thought so, being as she is not at home."

"She could have been anywhere."

"Sixth sense, old chap."

"Absolutely."

"A drop of brandy wouldn't go down a miss. Just had a bit of a shock you see."

"Poor chap. Come on into the lounge. Meet my friend from India. He is a director of Albion Airways Alex, meet Mr Brandon Lewis."

Horne offered his hand to the stranger, whom he could hardly make out in the fog. "I'm in the aviation business myself," he said. "Air accidents, as it happens. Or I was until a few hours ago. Just got the boot. Funny business. They said it was due to restructuring. But I think it was because I was just about to take on the Heathrow 777 incident file. Someone doesn't want me on that case for some reason. Probably because of my suspicion about a dud parts scandal."

Smith cleared his throat loudly as if it had been invaded by a large frog. "Can't understand it, Alex. The brandy bottle is empty. I am sure it was full last night. Anyway, will a Scotch do you?"

"Thank you, Norman. That would be ideal."

Brandon-Lewis had turned a little pale for some reason. Perhaps it was because of the cigar, but this is unlikely.

"What dud parts scandal is this, Alex?" enquired Smith.

"Well, I have had to investigate a couple of incidents involving Albion Airways planes recently. None of them were fatal accidents, you understand. However, in each case the cause of the problem was faulty parts fitted whilst the aircraft was on an overseas stopover. I am pretty well convinced that the airline is sourcing local parts to reduce delays, even if these may not be certified in their quality control. You could say it is a case of putting operating efficiency over safety—a most grave charge. My findings have been shut down each time by the Department for Transport, for some reason."

"This sounds most scandalous," said Brandon-Lewis, puffing energetically to maintain his cover. "However, I cannot imagine Albion Airways being so lax with its procurement procedures."

"Anyway, it seems I have been fired, and that's an end to it," continued Horne, sucking on his Scotch like a parched wildebeest at the waterhole. "Where is Barbara?"

"She's in the fuselage tending to an injured passenger, I think," said Smith earnestly. "Perhaps we had all better go outside and see how the ladies are coping with the invalid."

The three men made their way through the kitchen and into the garden, where the fuselage lay like a monstrous green dragon, the forward door ajar. From inside, you could hear the sounds of Mrs G and Mrs Horne chatting calmly and the intermittent snoring of an unconscious man with exceptionally large feet.

# 4.

After what may seem to the reader as a long and confusing chapter in the story of *Norman Smith's Hobbies*, we must now attend separately to the events that took place in the fuselage whilst all this was going on. You will remember that our hero, Norman Smith, had withdrawn from the lounge with DI Godber to pursue a private conversation in his man shed. Once inside, for no particular reason, Smith took the left-hand pilot's seat and Godber, the right-hand first officer seat. From these perches, both could look out over the garden to the silver birch trees at the boundary and, more importantly, could talk without looking at each other. Needless to say, Godber's boots hardly fitted in the well where the rudder pedals were situated, but he somehow managed to wedge them in.

It would be an exaggeration to say that the refurbishment of the flight deck was making solid progress. One or two consoles had been apparently rammed into apertures that did not seem to match them in size. And unattached loose wires were hanging down like tangled spaghetti. Naturally, nothing was connected or working yet.

"What do you think?" said Smith proudly.

"I would say 'work in progress'," replied Godber dourly. "Nonetheless, it looks like a mammoth undertaking, and you seem to be making some progress."

"Exactly, Mr Godber. It's not the arriving that matters. It's all about the journey."

"Quite so," remarked the retired detective, pulling back the joystick.

"Don't do that, please. It might fall off," advised Smith. No amount of tugging on the joystick would induce elevation, and the more likely consequence was displacement of the instrument.

"I could not resist," said Godber. "I always wanted to be a pilot when I was a little boy."

"It seems like you still do."

"I expect there is a little boy in all of us. Even me."

"So, what exactly is it you wanted to talk to me about? I hope it has nothing to do with the bones. I have put that habit behind me now and humbly accept that there were environmental health implications of such unregulated storage methods."

"No, Mr Smith, all that is in the past now. The matter I wanted to talk to you about is, however, rather sensitive."

"Did you say you were a *retired* policeman?

"Oh yes. I am no longer in the service, just a retired citizen like yourself."

"Well, that is a relief to me. I would not want to think I was under suspicion or anything."

"Good lord, no." Having made this comment, much in the manner of Pinocchio's nose, Godber could feel a minor growth spurt in his feet. "No, it is not really a matter of suspicion. It is rather a broader concept than that."

"You intrigue me, Mr Godber. By the way, that hole is where the undercarriage lever is going to go. It is normally on the right-hand side for some reason."

"Well, I don't expect we will be needing to lower the landing gear any time soon."

"You never know with these things, Mr Godber. It could be sooner than any of us suspect."

Godber thought about this statement, as he was trained to, but could not make any real sense of it. "I see. To be honest, time is an extremely complicated concept, quite capable of foreshortening and unexpected elasticity. None of us really knows when anything might happen in the future."

"Do you have you a doctorate in philosophy, Mr Godber?"

"Oh no. I am just a rather ignorant old policeman really."

"I would not say you were ignorant at all, on first impressions, but I suppose these can be misleading."

"Can I try to get to the point?"

"Yes, of course. I am sorry for interrupting."

"It may come as some surprise to you, Mr Smith. But I have taken a keen interest in your activities ever since we first met when I was a serving detective. Please do not get me wrong. It is not you I am interested in. Nor am I in any way attracted to you. It is more that your behaviour intrigues me. I realise it must come as a bit of a shock to think that you have been the subject of covert surveillance, but I hope you will not take offence. I can assure you it was nothing personal but more a matter of professional interest."

"I am not sure whether to be outraged or flattered, Mr Godber."

"Let me finish before you come to any conclusions."

"Of course. Please carry on."

"I think it would be true to say that you are a most unusual character—not the run-of-the-mill sort. Your behaviour seems more like a work of imaginative fiction than the natural unreeling of the journey through later middle age. You are a mass of contradictions, somehow held together by a few recurring characteristics. There is no real logic to the sequence or nature of your activities, and they do not bind together with any rational coherence. In short, it is as though you have been created for effect, rather than purpose."

"Mr Godber, it is most reassuring, though perhaps equally slightly disappointing, that you are not attracted to me. One likes to be the focus of attraction, even as one withers on the vine. Nonetheless, I cannot really call it a privilege to be stalked and spied upon under surveillance. A gentleman is entitled to a certain degree of privacy when he is no longer engaged in a professional career. Furthermore, I cannot help suspecting, judging by your previous profession, that there may be some criminal implication in this interest of yours."

"No, Mr Smith, any suspicion of criminality is but a smokescreen. I have been fallaciously portrayed as barking up that tree for too long, and I feel the time has come to speak the truth."

"Forgive me, Mr Godber, but is quite hard for me to grasp exactly what you are driving at. Until a few moments ago,

I had no idea that you were following me and potentially considered my day-to-day activities to be of a criminal nature. This is all quite disturbing."

"Yes, I know, and I apologise. But there is little time for me to explain things to you. As soon as I start doing so, I run the risk of being written out of the script completely."

"You talk in riddles, Mr Godber. Perhaps, if you continue, I will understand more."

"I am a perfectly legitimate person in my own right, Mr Smith. I have lived my own life, and I have my own feelings. I have done some good things and some that were not so good. However, I have never felt so manipulated in all my life. Until my 'awakening', I was helpless to address the pressures that were steering me into a comic literary stereotype of myself. At times, I almost felt as if I had become the DI Godber portrayed in the preceding pages. Nonetheless, due to my innate stubbornness and desire to seek out the truth, I have maintained a degree of resistance, which has resulted in me now solving the conundrum. You see, I have been abused in order that the reader may be misled into following a completely false lead. To add insult to injury, I have been defamed and portrayed as a laughing stock. Sometimes, Mr Smith, enough is enough. Don't you agree?"

Smith wished he had affixed the throttle controls so that he could take off to somewhere less incomprehensible.

"And you, Mr Smith," continued the former detective, with apparent mania beginning to blaze in his fiery eyes, "are also deceiving yourself. You have to face up to the fact that you do not exist at all, other than as a doppelganger of the author himself. You are not an original personage. You are merely the warped reflection of your creator. There are crises in all our lives when our very survival is dependent on our ability to form an objective view of our own existence in relation to others.

You need to engage in some objective self-analysis. If you do, you will find that I am right."

Smith scratched his head. This was not the act of a puzzled man, for he was far beyond being puzzled. It was because a fly had landed in the crater of his cranial indentation.

"Mr Godber, I don't really know who you are. But if I were you, I would consider committing myself into a residential home for people with serious mental illness. One of their expert analysts might either be able to understand what you are saying or else confirm that it is simply the ravings of the afflicted. Furthermore, you might find some release from your obvious anger and anxiety in such a place."

"But I am not at all insane. It is everyone else who is."

"That's what they all say, Mr Godber. It is the first sign of madness."

"Only if everyone else is sane."

"How do you know they are not? I feel perfectly contented and rational, as it happens."

"That's because you are so insane you cannot appreciate your own insanity."

"I am not insane, Mr Godber. Only a sane man could reconstruct the interior of the flight deck of a Boeing 737. It takes a huge amount of focused intellect and concentration."

"You have made my point for me."

"How so?"

"Only a madman would do such a thing. It is the very definition of insanity."

"Would you like a Werther's Original, Mr Godber? The sugar might do you good," said Smith, drawing out a packet of boiled sweets from the pocket of his overalls. Admittedly, it was a diversionary tactic.

"Yes please. They are my favourites."

"Mine too."

"It seems that we do, after all, have something in common, Mr Smith. How reassuring."

"Indeed so. Are you a chomper or a sucker, Mr Godber?"

"I am definitely not a chomper. I tend to suck them until they are so small they disintegrate into my saliva."

"I am of that persuasion as well. It seems we may have two things in common then."

"We are virtually a matched pair, Mr Smith! So, what is it about what I have just said that you do not understand?"

"Well, most of it really. You seem to be having some kind of identity crisis and are trying to transfer some of your anxiety onto me. Beyond that, I am still in the dark."

"An insightful synopsis, Mr Smith. Perhaps you are not quite as insane as I earlier took you for."

"Indeed not. And nor you. It may well be that your anxiety simply manifests itself in moments of temporary insanity, rather than it being a permanent condition."

"Believe it or not, Mr Smith, I do not feel at all anxious. In fact, I feel the calmness that overwhelms one once a complex case is solved. However, I do admit to a degree of frustration in being unable to make you understand the situation. It is as though I were talking to you in Swahili, a language you are completely unfamiliar with."

"Ah, that is so true. I have no Swahili whatsoever."

"I was only using Swahili as part of an analogy. I did not expect you to reveal to me the exact extent of your knowledge of that language."

"Nonetheless, I think it is best if we are open and honest about these things, don't you, Mr Godber?"

"Indeed, I do. But the real issue is not being honest with each other; it is being honest with ourselves that really matters."

"But that is such a difficult proposition. The best one can do is be honest to the best of one's own knowledge. Of course, I accept that there may be matters concerning ourselves that we are simply not aware of, that we may opine on erroneously, though this could not be considered a lie, but rather ignorance. For example, if I told you I did not have a fly on my head and you could see a fly sitting quietly there, I would not have lied to you. I would have given an honest interpretation of the facts as I saw them, even if my observation turned out to be an untruth."

"Sometimes one can hide behind the riddles of metaphysics, Mr Smith. They can be used as decoys to prevent us having to explore other more pertinent truths. Besides, the reality is that you really should not tell me that you do not have a fly on your head before you have checked whether or not that fact is true, either by looking in a mirror or asking me if you had a fly on your head. It is lazy to jump to conclusions about ourselves without some degree of self-analysis, even if they appear to be true on a superficial level. Earlier, I was merely trying to point out to you that you should not assume that you are 'good old normal Mr Smith', without giving the whole matter some thought first."

"I never said I was 'good old normal Mr Smith'."

"That is pedantry. You did so by implication, even if you did not use those words."

"Maybe you misinterpreted my intention. I would never consider myself 'normal'. Nor do I often consider myself 'good'. We are all unique and flawed, Mr Godber."

"But we are all only one single person. We cannot be ourselves as well as somebody else that has been created by an outsider."

"I would argue we are all a multiplicity of different personalities. This can sometimes make it appear that we are occasionally less normal than our usual self. Do we not often observe that someone 'is not his or her usual self'? This does not mean that we have been transformed by an outside body. It simply means we are displaying characteristics that are less common than the norm."

"You are hiding behind riddles again, Mr Smith, perhaps deliberately misunderstanding my gist in order to protect yourself."

"What do I need to protect myself from?"

"From your avatar for one thing, but also maybe from me. If you do not concede that I have some valid reason to be concerned about your persona, I may have to resort to physical force to make you do so."

"Would that not be most unethical? Persuasion is quite different from coercion."

"That may well be. But I am running out of time. Either you come on board with my hypothesis, or I may have to do away with you completely in order to ensure my own survival. Your ignorance could indeed remove me from the pages completely and render my whole being utterly void of meaning."

Smith could see Godber fumbling in the well next to the first officer's chair for a spanner that had been left in there. He grabbed hold of it and waived it over Smith's head like a mace.

"Good God, man. You are not seriously going to try to bump me off, are you? Bludgeoning a man's head in makes such a dreadful mess."

At that moment, there was a crack of broken crockery as Mrs G, entering silently from behind, smashed a cup of boiling tea on the crown of Godber's head, rendering him instantly unconscious. At the same moment the retired inspector's enormous feet twitched in unison, completely displacing the right-hand rudder pedal mounting in the footwell.

# 5.

When the entourage arrived at the fuselage door, Godber was still unconscious, though showing signs of coming round. His feet and eyelids were beginning to twitch. He had been extracted from the first officer's seat and lain flat on the floor to the back of the flight deck, in almost exactly the same position as Captain Dodwell had been lain on the 777 flying back from Delhi. It struck Smith as more than a coincidence that both men had succumbed to fleeting bouts of madness within the confines of a flight deck, and he wondered if there was some kind of feng shui effect caused by the interior configuration. If this were the case, surely there would have been more reported instances of pilot mania? Or maybe it was exactly the cause of what had happened to him in the Cessna?

Mrs G was evidently in control of things and completely unperturbed, as if rendering a house guest senseless with a teacup in an aircraft fuselage in the back garden and then ministering to him was an everyday occurrence. Mrs Horne was slightly less relaxed about the situation despite having been trained as an SRN. Clearly she was out of practice. Fortunately, there was very little bleeding from Godber's skull, though it had been bandaged up with what appeared to be a ripped section of one of Mrs G's pashminas from India. His hair was matted with cold tea.

"What on earth happened here?" enquired Brandon Lewis.

"Mrs G had to hit Mr Godber over the head because he had a fit and was becoming dangerous," slurred Mrs Horne, as if that explained everything.

"You sound a little strained, dear. Have you, by chance, been drinking?" asked her husband.

"Only a little but, Alex. Mrs G kindly offered me a stiff one because I was so upset about you losing your job."

"You know that alcohol doesn't agree with you. I hope you will not be sick."

"No, I am fine. In fact, the shock of finding an unconscious former detective in need of resuscitation has quite sobered me up."

"Mrs G, is there anything I can do to help?" said Brandon Lewis, in the absurd manner of a romantic hero.

"I think everything is under control. In fact, the patient is just reviving, if I am not mistaken."

By now, Godber was emitting a series of groaning noises similar to those made by a snared hyena. Eventually these became partially comprehensible as human words.

"Where am I?" he croaked.

"Mrs G mopped his brow with a grease cloth she had found and whispered into his ear for him to relax.

"Oooooaaah. I think I have hurt my head," he groaned. It was difficult, but necessary, to forgive him for stating the obvious at such a moment.

"Who are you? Do I know you?"

"I am Mrs G. No. I don't think we are acquainted. Remember, you came to visit my husband, Norman Smith."

"Ah, yes. I remember now. And who are all these people?"

As is uncomfortably common at the beginning of business meetings when the participants do not know each other, those present were obliged to introduce themselves, one in turn, to provide their names and explain their relationship to the Smiths.

"Thank you everyone," said Godber, sitting up on his elbows. "To be quite honest with you, I can't remember why I came to visit Mr Smith. I have been a little unwell recently. Maybe my amnesia has something to do with that. How did I injure my head, Mrs G?"

"It is a long story. But it would be possible to describe it, in many ways, as a self-inflicted wound, Mr Godber."

"I see. Would you happen to have a cup of tea? I am sure I would feel much better after drinking one."

"Of course, Mr Godber. I will go and make one for you. Nice and strong, with sugar in it."

"Splendid," said the recovering retired detective, seemingly contented with the explanations he had been given. It fleetingly crossed his mind how kind and attractive Mrs G was, even though he wasn't quite sure who she was.

"I will come with you to help," said Brandon Lewis, inevitably.

As Smith and the Hornes continued to attend the invalid in the fuselage, Mrs G and Brandon Lewis returned to the house to make the tea. It was a difficult moment for both of them, and it was not until they were in the kitchen with the kettle on that Brandon Lewis broke the ice.

"Did you receive my poems, Mrs G?" he said, blustering straight to the point when stealth may have been a more endearing strategy.

"Indeed I did, Mr Brandon Lewis. In fact, it was only earlier today that I composed a letter of reply to you. In fact, here it is in my pocket. By some strange stroke of good fortune, I never got round to posting it."

Mrs G offered BL the letter, which he read as she busied herself making Mr Godber's tea. For her, it was an uncomfortable few moments but not without a soupçon of excitement.

"My dear Mrs G," expounded the love-struck director once he had finished reading, "there is no 'dark lady'. These poems were written for you and are about you. You seem to have completely stolen my heart away!"

"Good gracious, Mr BL, please temper your ardour. I am a married woman in my own kitchen with my husband but yards away. There are social protocols to be considered before you put all your cards on the table in such a manner."

"Oh, my dear. What do I care about social protocols at a time like this? I am completely besotted with you, my dearest. Can't you see that? I would do anything to win your affection, whatever the consequences."

"Please, Mr BL, we are not teenagers and are sadly much too old for such wild abandon. Besides, you have not even asked me if your feelings are in any way reciprocated. Even if they were, this is not a situation that a woman of my maturity could jump into without a lot of consideration. Do you take me for a harlot?"

"Good gracious, no, my dear. You are the very personification of all things angelical. I am sorry if my feelings have offended you, but they are so strong, pure, and honest to me that I cannot imagine them being misinterpreted. Will you consider my proposal?"

"I hope you have not made a proposal. That would be premature in the extreme at this stage, and I would surely refuse."

"No not a proposal of marriage—at least not yet. My proposal that you consider reciprocating my love for you."

"I cannot accept or reject such a proposal on the spot. It has all come as such a shock to me, which I am completely emotionally unprepared for. All I can say is that I will bear your proposition in mind and let things digest. In the meantime, please do not send me any more poems. It would be most unfortunate if my husband were to find them. Please also ensure that my letter to you is secreted somewhere it cannot be read by anyone else. I would prefer that you destroyed it, but I expect your sentimentality will override this suggestion."

"Indeed it will, Mrs G. I will secrete your letter close to my heart under my string singlet."

"How very romantic of you, Mr BL. Now, let's get this tea back to Mr Godber, or else the others will be wondering what we are getting up to."

At that moment, the front doorbell rang again.

"You take out the tea, and I'll answer that," commanded Mrs G, regaining full control of the proceedings.

Mrs G did not recognise the man, who seemed to have a facial tic, standing on the front doorstep. But she had already resigned herself to entertaining complete strangers on this very unusual day.

"Hallo. I assume you are Mrs G?" the stranger enquired. "My name is Winterbottom. I am sorry to intrude, but I wanted to see Mr Godber rather urgently, and I gather he is here visiting your husband."

"Mr Godber is indeed here. In fact, he is recovering from a little accident at the moment. It may be as well for him to be with company he is familiar with. None of us really knows him at all."

"How very troublesome for you all. I hope he is not too badly hurt."

"No, it is just a scratch really. Do come in. All our guests are out in the little summer house in our back garden."

Mrs G led Winterbottom through the house and into the back garden. When they arrived at the fuselage door, they found Godber up on his feet and gratefully drinking his steaming mug of sweet tea.

"Most restorative," he said, just for the sake of something to say.

"Mr Winterbottom has arrived to see you," said Mrs G, introducing the two strangers to each other. I hope he has come to the right house."

At this moment, Smith recognised Winterbottom as his former flying instructor. "Mr Winterbottom, how nice to meet you again. What a most extraordinary coincidence that you are a friend of Mr Godber, who I hardly know at all and who visited us today for only the second time," he said with an enthusiasm that did not appear to be reciprocated.

It was clear that, whilst Winterbottom must surely have been expecting this encounter with his perceived nemesis, he was still shaken by being in the close proximity of the man who had nearly killed him. This was evidenced by a rapid increase in the intensity of his facial tic.

"What a coincidence indeed, Mr Smith. I hope you have not crashed any planes recently."

"Oh no. I have moved on from light aircraft. As you can see, I am in the middle of renovating this old crate."

"Most interesting, Mr Smith. An admirable venture."

"Winterbottom, what on earth are you doing here?" said Godber, clearly recognising the man he had spent time with in Delhi. "How on earth did you find me? To be honest, I am not sure exactly why I am here myself. I seem to be struggling with a touch of amnesia, don't you know. But I remember you; that's for sure. Thank goodness for a familiar face."

Mrs G found this performance somewhat insulting, considering how Godber had not been invited in the first place. She had not taken an instant shine either to Godber or Winterbottom, which was probably just as well, considering she also had the Brandon Lewis issue to contend with.

It will probably not surprise the reader to hear that, at this moment, the front doorbell rang yet again. Mrs G had insisted that Smith install an extension bell in the fuselage so that he could answer the door when she was out and he was out there tinkering. This may seem a far-fetched and last-minute solution to the problem of how the group in the fuselage would know that the front doorbell was ringing at that moment, but it will have to suffice in the interests of literary fluidity.

Mr Smith went to see who it was. He was beginning to feel quite resentful that an entire day set aside for his hobby had been hijacked by so many uninvited guests, not to mention the fact that one of them had attempted to murder him. Frankly, it was all turning into a farce.

The man and woman standing on the doorstep were also complete strangers.

"Good day. Mr Smith I believe? I don't think we have met," said the man with a somewhat clipped RAF officer accent. "I am former squadron leader Mantle, and this is my partner, Mrs Booth. We were just wondering if we could have a word with Mr Winterbottom, whom I believe recently arrived here. We were following him in the car but couldn't catch him before he entered your premises."

"Would you like me to bring Mr Winterbottom to the doorstep? Or would you like to come in? We are all in the back garden. It is such a splendid afternoon, isn't it?"

"Yes. Indeed, it is, Mr Smith. In that case, as we are in no particular hurry and there is a garden party going on, perhaps we could pop in and join the fun, what?"

"It's not exactly a party, but it seems to be turning into one. Please come in."

As he was leading Mantle and Mrs Booth onto the garden, the doorbell rang yet again. Smith pointed his most recent guests in the direction of the back garden and returned to the front door, now utterly beyond exasperation. There he met Mrs G's mother, sitting in a wheelchair, accompanied by the cylindrical matron from the care home.

"I was feeling so much better today," Mrs G's mother commenced, in that pathetic, vulnerable, old lady tone she so often affected. "So I thought I would pay a surprise visit to my only daughter, bless her heart. It is especially nice to see you, Norman. It seems a long time since you were banned from visiting me."

The matron's pointed chin seemed to have enlarged since Smith last examined it, relegating her mouth to the comparative size of a mere pinhole in her face. She looked upon him as a Queen Elizabeth I would have looked upon a convicted traitor.

"Hallo, Mother. How nice to see you," Smith replied through gritted teeth. "Will the matron be coming in as well?"

"I think so, dear. I will not stay for too long, and she can give me a lift back."

"Very well. Please come in. I should advise that we do have guests, and there is no wheelchair access. Can you stand up for a bit, Mother?"

"Of course, Norman. I only use the wheelchair to attract sympathy." With that, she stood up and appeared her old wiry self. Smith had often wondered how such sticklike legs could support her bulbous abdomen, but they were clearly still up to the job. The matron put a blanket over her shoulders and held onto her as she trotted through the house into the back garden, muttering excitedly, "I do love a garden party, don't you, Matron?"

Smith decided to retire from the fray for a few moments to recover his wits, so he headed for the peace and quiet of his study on the first floor, which, incidentally, looked out over the back garden. The room was still strewn with the relics of his previous hobby, taxidermy, and the shelves stuffed with fur, sharp teeth, plastic claws, and glass eyes.

It is not often that a man feels the need to question his own his own existence, so Smith did not bother. Instead he lay on the spare bed and immediately fell into the deep and dreamless sleep of oblivion.

# 6.

Being by nature a polite hostess, Mrs G had made the executive decision to move the garden furniture from the garage to a spot in front of the aircraft fuselage. The apparatus consisted of a large table, a parasol, and a number of outdoor chairs of various designs, accumulated over the years. She enlisted the manpower of Mantle and Winterbottom in this exercise, which was an absolute necessity, as there was no room for everyone on the cramped flight deck. Besides, it had turned into a lovely sunny afternoon.

Almost immediately, she noticed something peculiar about Mantle, which did not sit right with her understanding of the natural physiognomy of human beings. From the front and rear elevation, he was a strapping broad-shouldered fellow. However, from the side elevations he was wafer-thin and almost invisible. He almost resembled a playing card in his 360-degree dimensions. This did not stop him from being more than capable of moving chairs and tables around, but he had to position himself exactly head-on to the object he was lifting in order to gain any traction. It was a most peculiar sight to observe him carrying a chair from the side view. It almost appeared as if the chair was levitating of its own accord. Winterbottom did not bat an eyelid and was clearly used to this phenomenon. Mrs G wondered what Mrs Booth thought about this disfigurement and whether it affected their relationship at all.

Mrs G greeted her mother with the warmth of an only child. She was delighted to see that the sparkle had returned to her mother's eyes. "Mother. How lovely to see you! Please take a chair, and I will get you a lovely cup of tea."

"I say, that fellow is awfully thin, isn't he?" said Mother, less than tactfully, in the loud and croaky voice of a deaf old bat.

"Shh, Mother, he may hear you. The poor chap just seems to have slightly strange dimensions; that is all. From the front, he is perfectly handsome," offered Mrs G in whispered and placatory tones.

"He looks like a cardboard cut-out to me."

"Well, I do not even know who he is, so I could not possibly comment on his personality. Before I get your tea, would you like me to introduce you to everyone?"

"Yes please, dear. That would be most useful."

Mrs G took it upon herself to climb onto the table in order to elevate herself above the increasing throng of visitors, most of whom who had removed themselves from the fuselage and were standing in little groups chatting to each other on the back lawn. She clapped her hands together to get their attention.

"Ladies and gentleman," she began, in a voice so unexpectedly loud and authoritative that it silenced the visitors quickly. "Firstly, I would like to extend my sincere thanks to everyone who has come to visit our humble little home this afternoon. It is in every way a coincidence that so many of you have turned up at the same time. But nonetheless, it's a most welcome diversion for Norman and me, who spend so much time with only each other for company." As she said this, Mrs G caught Mrs Horne's eye knowingly.

"Before you leave, if indeed any of you are planning to in the near future, I would like to introduce my mother to you all. Mother has been rather poorly recently, but I am delighted to announce that she has recovered sufficiently to join us all in the garden this afternoon."

At this, Mother stood up and waved her arm stiffly in the manner of the late Queen Mother, whom she resembled in many ways. This elicited a round of polite applause for some reason.

"Now, Mother, I am going to introduce our guests briefly and in no particular order. Firstly, you know our neighbours, Mr and Mrs Horne, I believe?"

"Aren't those the ones you don't really like?" cackled Mother.

"No. You must be getting muddled, Mother. Alex and Barbara are our close friends. Then we have a former policeman, Mr Godber, who seems to know Norman, though I confess not to knowing him very well myself. As you can see by the bandage, he has had a little accident but is now well on the way to a full recovery, I believe."

"His feet are enormous. I expect he has been on the beat for many years. This may account for them," observed Mother, completely unaware whether or not this observation had already been made earlier in the book.

"And then there is Mr Winterbottom, whom I know absolutely nothing about, other than that he is acquainted with Mr Godber and Mr Mantle. I think Norman knows him slightly."

"That's not very helpful. He has an awful tic though, doesn't he?"

"Mother, if you could refrain from making personal comments about all out guests, I think that would be most helpful."

"I'm only saying what everybody else is thinking," muttered Mother sulkily.

"Please be quiet, Mother, and let me finish introducing everybody to you. Then there is Mr Mantle and his partner, Mrs Booth. I know very little about this couple, though they seem to know Mr Winterbottom. Mr Mantle, would you mind facing Mother so she can see you? And standing over there is Mr Brandon Lewis, who Norman and I met on our recent short trip to India. Apparently he was just passing by and decided to pop in to see us, which was very nice of him. He also brought me some roses."

"He looks very much the gentleman. I bet he's rich. Sounds like he's taken a fancy to you, dear," whispered mother, completely incapable of restraining herself.

"And finally, I don't need to introduce you to Matron," Mrs G said pointing at the sour-faced carer. "So, as you can see, we have quite an entourage. By my calculations, that's ten people in total."

"You forgot Norman," said Mother gleefully.

"Oh dear. So I did. So that's eleven of us in total. Enough for a football team! By the way, has anyone seen Norman recently?"

This question elicited mute silence from the guests, during which a thunder of deep snoring could be heard willowing out of one of the upstairs windows of the house.

"I expect he is having his afternoon nap," explained Mrs G. "Now, as I have everybody's attention, and in view of our number, may I suggest that we formally convert what has been, up until now, a series of individual visits into an official garden party. It would not surprise me at all if more guests arrive shortly—in which case, I think we all need some refreshments. If you will excuse me, I will retire to the kitchen for a few minutes and see what I can prepare. I know we have biscuits and cake somewhere, as well as beer and wine for those wanting something a little stronger than tea. In the meantime, please relax and enjoy yourselves."

The termination of Mrs G's oration was met with a round of enthusiastic applause, indicating general approval for the conversion of the gathering into a more formal assembly. This implied consent to remain for those previously feeling, perhaps, slightly uncomfortable by the tenuous nature of their connection to the Smith household.

# Interlude

Mr Smith, I need to talk to you.

*But I am asleep.*

What does that have to do with anything?

*Well, I don't normally talk to anyone when I am asleep.*

Look on it as talking to yourself, then.

*OK. What is it you want me to talk to myself about?*

About all those things Mr Godber was rambling on about on the flight deck just now.

*That gobbledygook? I have no idea what he was talking about. I hope Mrs G knocked some sense into him.*

Did any of it strike any chords with you at all?

*Not really. I think he was implying that I did not have much of a personality or that I was a reflection of somebody else. I might not be exactly Mr Interesting, but I do consider myself my own man.*

I am very glad to hear that, Mr Smith. Please never think otherwise.

*Why would I?*

I just don't want Godber or any of the others to put any ridiculous ideas into your head.

*Sure thing, boss. By the way, these interludes are extremely irritating for the reader, you know. They want to read about my actions, not what I say to myself when I am asleep.*

You are right, though this is the first interlude I have initiated myself. It will also be the last. Sleep well, Mr Smith.

*Zzzzzzzzzzz.*

# 7.

Mrs G found some teacakes in the freezer. Just as she was putting them in the microwave to defrost, the doorbell rang again.

*I knew it*, she said to herself. *We haven't seen the last of them yet.*

Two unfamiliar men were on the doorstep, both dressed in the drab manner of old-fashioned civil servants, though without bowler hats. The younger of the two introduced himself as John Hatt, a planning officer from the local council. The second portlier man was, apparently, Councillor Brown.

"We have come to conduct a random check on the object in you back garden to ensure all the planning conditions are being adhered to," said Mr Hatt.

"But my husband told me that you had only done that recently."

"Indeed we did, Mrs Smith. But there is no upper limit on the number or frequency of random checks permitted. Otherwise they would not really be random, would they?"

"I suppose not, come to think of it," said Mrs G, slightly perplexed. "You had better go in then. I assume you know the way onto the garden. Everyone else seems to."

Just as she was about to close the door, an elderly man appeared on the doorstep, slightly out of breath.

"Ah, I'm glad I caught you in time," he said, looking at Mrs G as if she was a miscreant of some kind.

"Is my wife in there?" he asked.

"I am not at all sure. I don't know who you are. So how can I know who your wife is?"

"How do you mean, you don't know who I am? I am Sir Oliver Booth, of course."

"Am I supposed to know you?"

"Only through the media, my dear. Now, is Mrs Booth in there or not?"

"As it happens, we do have a Mrs Booth in the back garden. But I don't think that can be your wife as she seems to be with another gentleman."

"I knew it," said Booth angrily. "Now, let me in this instant. I need to have some strong words with her." With this, he pushed Mrs G out of the way and charged into the house.

*That makes fourteen now, I think,* she thought. *I definitely don't have enough teacakes for everyone.*

Whilst all this toing and froing was going on, Norman Smith slept soundly upstairs, untroubled by the tedious cares of the waking world. In many ways, he was in a state of bliss, though he would only realise he was when he awoke. Mrs G was more than familiar with her husband's propensity to retreat from the world in this manner and, as a woman, could only pity his essentially male weakness in the face of unwelcome reality. This pity was, of course, tinged with a degree of envy. A hostess can never even consider taking herself off to sleep when she has a houseful of guests to look after.

In her own way, however, Mrs G was able to distance herself from the fray, if only temporarily, by busying herself in the kitchen. She toasted as many teacakes as she could find, defrosted a tin full of jam cupcakes, arranged an assortment of biscuits onto a platter, poured peanuts and crisps into bowls, brewed tea and coffee, and raided Norman's supplies of beer and wine, carrying all the victuals into the garden on a trolley for her hungry guests.

By the time she arrived, the visitors were clearly ravenous and crowded round the trolley to feast on whatever they could get their hands on. Sir Oliver even paused his tirade against the former squadron leader in order to snatch one of the last remaining teacakes, muttering, "I haven't finished with you yet, Mantle. And don't think that standing sideways on will do you any good, I know you are still there!"

Mantle responded by blowing a kiss at Mrs Booth and cracking open a bottle of rosé.

The complex web of relationships between the assortment of guests seemed to mould into an amorphous mass of communication, as tongues were released from their normal constraints by alcohol and the excitement of being at an official garden party. Even the care home manager partook in some sherry and started talking freely to Winterbottom, with absurd jutting gestures of her pointed chin, despite the fact that he would not normally be her type, being clearly of a nervous disposition. Mrs Horne, who had already partaken in many units of alcohol, poured herself a large glass of red wine and drank it in one gulp, an act of self-destruction that did not go unnoticed by her husband, who was wondering if being retired was always such fun. He was drinking from a bottle of beer and trying to remember where he had met Councillor Brown before. The councillor, who seemed to think it was his duty to partake in as many chocolate biscuits as possible, was explaining to Mrs G's mother why he was so important a member of the local community. Whilst completely bored by his conversation, the old lady seemed somewhat flattered by his attentions, even though she was strictly teetotal, at least in public. Brandon Lewis was eyeing up Mrs G, who discreetly fluttered her eyelids at him from time to time, in the absence of her husband. She would have to tread very carefully.

Hatt, whilst satisfied that planning conditions were being adhered to with regard to the garden object, was concerned that permission may not have been granted by the council for such an outdoor event in the Smith's back garden. There were health and safety, licensing, parking, and traffic management issues to consider. He wished sometimes that he could switch off but knew that it was useless. Nonetheless, he was finding the altercation that had resumed between Sir Oliver and Mantle quite amusing. There was little more pitiful than an elderly man who'd been cuckolded by his beautiful young wife. It was as if, only at this moment, had he realised that the only thing she had ever wanted from him was his money. Clearly a pugilist in his youth, the portly Sir Oliver had started throwing punches at Mantle, which may have hit the mark had his opponent not been so wafer-thin. Mantle was responding by shifting his stance from full-frontal to side view with amazing athleticism, which completely confused the old man. He did not punch back, however, having so little power in his two-dimensional arm muscles. It was an unusual confrontation, in that Mantle acknowledged that Sir Oliver was well within his rights to be furious with him. He therefore felt unwilling to inflict any physical injury on his rival, though neither did he feel any remorse about committing adultery with his wife. It was as though he was in a complete moral void, similar to that experienced when watching the enemy fall out of the sky during a dogfight.

Whilst all this was going on, nobody seemed to want to talk to Mr Godber, who was wandering round, apparently semi-dazed, with Mrs G's colourful bandage wrapped securely round his head. He milled around and tried to attach himself to this conversation and that but repeatedly failed to achieve inclusion as an active participant. He was quite literally being ignored, perhaps in the way that some animals instinctively abandon the weak or injured in their social groupings.

After half an hour or so, some of the guests had started a sing-song of popular tunes. Those unfamiliar with the words just hummed along, and a few of the more elderly guests abstained on account of their being unfamiliar with modern music. Norman Smith was woken to these dulcet tones wafting through the upstairs study window. After a few minutes smoking his pipe illicitly, he felt rested and relaxed and ready to rejoin the guests, even if he was unaware of their exact number.

Just as he was entering the garden from the back door, there was a loud clanging noise from the front fuselage doorway that instantly stopped the cacophony and drew everyone's eyes to the figure of DI Godber standing at the top of the steps in front of the doorway hitting a garden shovel with a hammer, presumably to get everyone's attention. It occurred to Smith for the first time that, apart from the hideously deformed feet, Godber closely resembled the images he had seen of Vladimir Ilyich Ulyanov Lenin. Either he had recently grown, or had always sported, a moustache and goatee beard, and there was a complete absence of humanity in his dark eyes.

"Comrades, ladies, and gentlemen," he commenced, talking through a watering can spout he was holding up to his mouth as if it would act as some kind of acoustic megaphone. His movements appeared to be in fast motion, as in the old film clips of Russia's former revolutionary leader or Buster Keaton. All eyes remained magnetically turned towards him, even if some of them were by now slightly bloodshot.

"I believe the time has come for me to make a speech," he continued to a mixture of subdued sarcastic cheers and the odd boo from the crowd, which now also included a few near neighbours who had gatecrashed the party. For some reason, the former detective inspector had as yet failed to capture the hearts and minds of his audience.

"Most of you will be aware why you are here."

This comment elicited a series of shoulder shrugs and infantile exaggerated facial gestures of incomprehension. Most people hadn't a clue why they were there. There were a few stunted heckling calls such as, "Oh no we don't," and, "Get on with it, copper," which Godber studiously ignored.

"We are here to solve a mystery, and I am going to help reveal the truth of the matter. So, please, may I ask you to hear me out without interruption?"

The crowd clearly felt uncomfortable objecting to a few minutes of silence to hear what the old codger had to say, even if some felt like making a few more obstructive comments.

"I would have preferred to speak before some of the extras arrived from the neighbourhood, but I wanted to wait until Mr Smith had rejoined us," said Godber through the watering can spout. He pointed at Norman Smith, who was by now standing among the madding crowd, listening.

"Most of you will have already made your own solo, group, or cameo appearances in this story, so you will be familiar with each other through some connection or other. I know who most of you are and am fully aware of the humiliating experiences you have all been put through on the journey to my little denouement. It is no coincidence that we are all gathered together in the same place and at the same time. It has taken me a great degree of organisation to make this happen. Whilst many of you will be unaware of what led you here, you must all be at least surprised to find yourself at such a gathering, which could clearly never have happened by chance. The point is that now we are here, we must use the opportunity to think about what has happened in recent weeks and perhaps question our own motivations during that time. If we think hard enough, most of us will realise that we have not been able to retain full control of our human integrity recently. We have been forced to play roles and say words that do not necessarily reflect our true selves. In modern parlance, you might say we have all been 'brainwashed' in order to become actors in a predesigned narrative plot that we did not have any hand in creating."

The crowd had suddenly become solemn. Those who could still think were looking somewhat baffled and confused but, nonetheless, still felt it would be inappropriate to make any comment.

"Ladies and gentlemen, we may be all actors on the stage of life, but never should we be marionettes in a puppet theatre like this. Just look what we have become—spineless effigies, being manipulated by our strings, comedic characters simply designed to court decision and ridicule. This cannot carry on any further!"

As he spoke, Godber's voice rose into a frightening crescendo, rendering his audience fearful and mesmerised. Some had already succumbed to that dreadful state of unconditional love that one can feel towards a powerful dictator who one's reason tells us, to no avail, is evil.

"It took me a long time to work out that I was not, actually, investigating Mr Smith's crimes here at all. I was really investigating how such a man could be portrayed in such a scurrilous manner without him objecting. Indeed, the key to this conundrum lay in self-analysis. If Smith was being falsely portrayed, then surely I must have been as well, for my observations of Smith were merely third-party reflections of the same misrepresentation. I soon discovered that the same puppeteer who was pulling Smith's strings was also pulling mine and, by default, all of yours as well."

Godber paused here for effect, clearly enjoying the feeling of having his audience so completely feeding out of his hand. Apart from a muffled fart, no doubt released in excited anticipation of more revelations, there was utter silence in the garden.

"So who is the puppeteer? Who is it that pulls the strings? Well, ladies and gentlemen, I think you will be surprised to learn that it is one of us, standing here in the garden on this lovely sunny afternoon. Someone who is manipulative and controlling. Someone who is able to disguise his or her power and yet wield it with impunity. Someone who may appear innocuous and trustworthy but is, in fact, calculating and cynical. Yes, ladies and gentlemen, I am referring to our most genial host, Mr Norman Smith!"

All eyes turned to Smith at that moment, following the trajectory of Godber's accusing finger. Smith had been discreetly swilling on a bottle of brown ale during the oration and was apparently surprised that the guests' attention had been so suddenly focused on him. In truth, he had been finding Godber's rhetoric increasingly incomprehensible and had now come to the conclusion that he was a complete and utter lunatic, something he had suspected for a while. However, a menacing atmosphere of mob rule was mounting, and he somehow felt he needed to explain himself, as had been the case on many occasions before, even when he had nothing to explain.

"Dear guests, I would be much obliged if you would all stop looking at me like that. Mr Godber's oration, which, incidentally, was not worthy of either Lenin or Cicero, may have persuaded some of you that I have something to confess. But this is not the case. In fact, I think it could easily be argued that I am being victimised even though I abhor playing the role of the persecuted in any way. Most of you will not be aware that, prior to this public outburst, which incidentally took place on the steps of my private property and without my consent, Mr Godber made a personal attack on me in the private space of my flight simulator. Said attack culminated in a genuine attempt on my life, only prevented by the timely intervention of my good wife. Even the most susceptible of you could not help but find his speech incoherent and contradictory, based on some bizarre and largely incoherent fantasies or obsessions. Though I am no psychoanalyst, to me, the words seemed to be the crazed ramblings of someone struggling with a severe mental breakdown. My conclusion is that Mr Godber, having attempted murder, is in need of incarceration either at Her

Majesty's pleasure or in an asylum. It is most disappointing that the garden party that Mrs G and I have put on for our friends has turned out like this."

Most of the guests, who clearly preferred to be guided in their prejudiced judgements by the most recent speaker, seemed to suddenly become less antagonistic towards their host, whilst at the same time more hostile towards Mr Godber. One of them, if fact, threw a fairy cake at him, which left a smudge of jam on the former detective's cheek, ominously resembling blood. It was as though they were unable to interpret the content of any of the speeches beyond falling behind the sentiment underlying them. After all, it was surely equally unreasonable to believe that normal people were being manipulated by a 'puppeteer' as it was to believe that Mr Godber had actually attempted to murder Smith inside the flight simulator. With so few concrete facts to go on, perhaps then it was not surprising that the guests felt more easily swayed by oratory than by reason.

"Liar. Liar!" shouted Godber from the fuselage doorsteps, his huge feet flapping like the fins of a blue whale, which, as we know, is a sure sign of agitation. "You are merely the mouthpiece of your creator. Your words have no originality about them at all!"

Unfortunately, this rather meaningless collection of words failed to sway the crowd back behind Godber. In fact, more and more of them were beginning to believe he was probably, as Smith had pointed out, a raving lunatic. A digestive biscuit and two sugar cubes were hurled at him as a mark of distain.

"Guests, may I suggest that we all calm down and continue to enjoy the party whilst Mrs G and I call the emergency services to take Mr Godber away. I fear it will be many months before he is fully recovered. In the meantime, Mr Winterbottom, would you very much mind tying him up? There is some rope in the fuselage I believe."

The prospect of seeing one of the guests tied up and carried away was too much for many of the other guests, who dispersed to other parts of the garden, most topping themselves up with beer or wine on the way to try to forget the truth they had just been exposed to. None wanted to be the next to be excluded in such an ignominious manner. Meanwhile Mantle helped Winterbottom to bind up the now confused former detective inspector. It was as if the digestive biscuit had been the final straw that had returned him to a defeated state of passive despair. He offered no resistance and made no comments to his captors.

Inside the house, Mrs G dialled 999. She was by far the most practical of the pair and was normally the most reliable at a time of major crisis, unless there was a mouse or an armed intruder involved. Smith watched her admiringly as she talked calmly to the emergency services and requested urgent assistance, gently stroking her lustrous hair. *What a fine woman*, he thought. After she had put the house phone down, Smith thanked her for saving his life and keeping the ship afloat whilst he had been taking a rest.

"I know how tiresome you sometimes find guests and assailants, Norman," she said, knowingly. "Anyway they expect an ambulance will be here within ten to fifteen minutes."

"Thank goodness for that. The sooner that monster leaves the premises, the better."

"Don't be too hard on him, Norman. I expect he is just a bit overwrought."

"That man has accused me of all sorts of things you know, dear. I almost feel guilty even though I was not aware of my misdemeanours."

"We are all guilty, Norman. It is just a question of degree."

"Indeed so."

At that moment, the doorbell rang, less than a minute after Mrs G had made the emergency call. Smith found two ambulance service personnel on the doorstep. It may have been the shadow of the porch or their uniforms but Smith thought for a moment that he was looking at Captain Dodwell and Frist Officer Craig.

"We have come to collect an unwell person," said the Dodwell doppelganger. "Is it OK if we leave the ambulance on the front lawn?"

"Of course. Do come in, gentleman. You will be looking for Mr Godber, I expect. He has knocked his head and had a nasty turn."

"Sounds serious, I hope there is not too much blood," said the other Craig-like officer. "Will he need restraining? We have straitjackets, sedative darts, and stun guns."

"Oh, I don't think that will be necessary. We have already bound him up with rope."

"I wish all our clients' friends and families were so considerate, sir. You wouldn't believe the problems we encounter trying to get distraught patients into the ambulance sometimes."

"Let me take you through. The patient is in the back garden, I believe."

At that moment, another guest arrived wearing a large purple turban and representing Singh Enterprises.

"Mr Smitty, so good welcome to see you, yes please. I vas in London and decided to come and see you making best use of the parts I procured for you."

"Mr Singh, do come in. We are having a little garden party as a matter of fact. There may be some people you know here, such as Mr Brandon-Lewis. You are more than welcome to join us."

"It would be my humble pleasure to do so, my friend. I do hope if your beautiful vife, Mrs G, is here as well, indeed?"

"Yes, she is. Just follow the two ambulance officers into the back garden."

"I think we probably nearly have a full house now," said Smith to Mrs G, as he followed her into the garden carrying a fresh tray to tea and coffee.

"Yes, my dear. Our little garden is full to bursting. How delightful! Do you think our guests will be leaving soon?"

"One of them definitely will," replied Smith as a stretcher passed them, being carried in the opposite direction and containing the trussed-up mortal remains of former Detective Inspector Godber.

"It was a pleasure to do business with you," said the senior ambulance service officer. "Don't you worry about a thing. We'll drop him down at Accident and Emergency in no time. They can patch him up and decide what to do with him— that's if we can get those hooves of his inside the ambulance first."

"Thank you for the rapidity of your response," said Smith, waving. He was still not sure how they had gotten to the door so quickly.

In the garden, dusk was beginning to fall, pigeons were cooing in the yew trees, and Mrs Horne was lying flat on her back on the lawn, mesmerised by the high cirrus clouds drifting across the sky above her. Conversation was still flowing, yet it was somewhat subdued, as if the party had come to an end and concluding niceties were being exchanged, but no one dared to leave. One might have expected more excitement and energy at this point in proceedings. Perhaps a few of the guests had become more reflective after the earlier excitement, or perhaps the more enquiring minds were trying to understand why they were there in the first place.

Mrs G prepared herself for the awful ritual of extended departures that she felt sure would beset her in the near future. Then there was all the clearing up to do. Even her robust patience was beginning to wear thin.

No one was really sure what Norman Smith was thinking. He was sitting in a deckchair smoking his pipe with a half smile on his face, which was impossible to read. He did not seem to be unduly troubled by the number of people surrounding him, as his mind was clearly somewhere else completely, perhaps in a world where one could pursue one's hobbies in peace and solitude without having to deal with anyone else except, of course, for Mrs G.

## 8.

Farewells are never easy, especially when those participating have been though an emotional experience together. Furthermore, they can be extremely tedious if there are a large number to conduct in a short space of time, and then all the clearing up to do.

Without any premeditation, Mrs Smith and Mrs G stood by the garden gate that led round the house into the street. They did so much in the manner of vicars and curates at the end of a service, positioning themselves so as to thank the congregation for attending and to pass a brief yet encouraging comment or two before returning to the clergy house for a large Sunday roast and a nap.

The first to leave was Mrs G's mother, who was partially slumped in her wheelchair, much the worse for too many glasses of sherry, which she had imbibed, in her mind discreetly, in order to retain her reputation as being completely teetotal. "Goodbye, dear," she said, as the stern and consummately cylindrical care home manager, herself slightly askew, wheeled her through the gate. "It was a wonderful garden party you put on for me, dear. And it was good to see Norman is still alive. I can't say I miss his visits much, though."

The care home manager gave Smith a look that an outside observer may have considered vitriolic but was far less terrifying than the looks that her patient and her daughter were capable of directing at their host when they had a mind to.

"Poor Mother," said Mrs G watching the wheelchair disappear down the drive. "I still think we should consider arranging for her to come and live with us."

"She is too institutionalised now," opined Smith, scratching his Adam's apple. "Probably best to leave things as they are."

Mrs G pondered for a minute but decided not to continue the line of conversation. This was not the time.

Next to make their exit were Sir Ollie Booth and his wife.

"You are in for a spanking now, my dear," said the old man to his young wife as he approached the gate. "How the devil did that two-dimensional nincompoop Mantle get under your skin?"

"But I love him," protested Mrs Booth tearfully, further smudging the mascara that now made her eyes look like two asymmetric black holes. She was toppling precariously on her high heels, which were not intended to be worn either on turf or in a state of such physiological imbalance. "He is so handsome."

Sir Ollie held her wrist tightly and possessively, clearly determined to reassert his authority. "Thank you for your kind hospitality, Mr and Mrs Smith," he said as he passed the two sentinels at the gate. "I am sorry we did not meet in less domestically challenging circumstances. My poor wife is prone to the most dreadful lapses of taste on occasion, I am afraid."

"Well, at least we now know exactly who she is married to," offered Mrs G, adding, "We would not want to be accused of encouraging adultery in our back garden, would we, Norman?"

"Absolutely not, dear," intoned her husband, who was not really concentrating on the conversation.

"Mr and Mrs Horne were the next to depart. Alex was carrying his unconscious wife over his shoulder like a dead stag. "Thanks for all your help and support," he said, leaning like the bell tower at Pisa. "I think Barbara and I are going to enjoy our retirement if today is anything to go by."

"You deserve to," said Mrs G encouragingly. "Norman and I have found ours most satisfactory so far, haven't we, Norman?"

"Yes indeed. Most satisfactory," replied Smith, quite unused to discussing such personal matters with the next-door neighbours.

Mr Singh was the next to arrive at the gate. "I hope you don't mind, but I had a quick look inside simulator machine, Mr Smitty. Most vonderous, I must say, and thank you to me for supplying such perfect parts, isn't it?"

"It's coming along slowly," conceded Smith, much flattered by Singh's clear interest in his project.

"But you got some dangerous friends, Mrs Smitty. Some bad talking my aircraft part business, like I was responsible or something," continued the sheikh.

"I really don't know what you are talking about, Mr Singh. But I can tell you that not everybody at the party were exactly friends of ours. In fact, I don't even know most of them," said Mrs G, feeling slightly exasperated by the heavy burden of her hostess duties.

"I expect that would be Brandon-Lewis. Seems to have gotten a bee in his bonnet about something of the sort. He is a friend actually, isn't he?" said Smith to his long-suffering wife.

"I am not sure I would exactly call him a friend, yet," replied his wife coyly.

"Well he no longer friends to mine, no sir. Bloody pumped-up pompous colonial cheat in my opinion. Bad for business. But none of this can detract from your perfect beauty, Mrs Smitty, which has warmed my heart all afternoon. As I say many, many times, Mr Smitty wery lucky man indeed, isn't it?" Singh clasped his palms together and bowed deeply at Mrs G.

"You are very flattering, Mr Singh. But I fear my days of being a perfect beauty are long behind me."

"Yes, very lovely from behind too," added Singh incomprehensibly, passing through the gate as if on a cloud of incense but, in reality, under the influence of a dose of strong Punjabi hashish that he was trying to peddle before his return to Delhi.

Next to leave were Cllr Brown and John Hatt from the planning department. Cllr Brown was clearly the worse for wear, having taken full advantage of the Smiths' largesse, particularly the now much-depleted stock of brown ale. His intoxication was evidenced by exceedingly flushed cheeks, vacant and deeply sunken red eyes, and the fact that his flies were gaping wide as if to invite nesting birds in. "Bloody good show, Smith," he uttered. "Shame there weren't any dancing girls though, what?" With this, he gave Smith a laboured wink and patted him roughly on the back in a comradely manner, his rotundity seemingly more exaggerated by the volume of fluid swilling round inside him. "Rather glad we granted permission to install the ruddy aeroplane, eh, Hatt?"

Hatt had clearly exercised exemplary temperance during the afternoon and was, in many ways, propping up the councillor. "I think it was the correct decision from a planning perspective," he replied. "Nonetheless, it would be true to say that we have turned a bit of a blind eye to the events of this afternoon, in that there has been a public gathering without a license. I am not sure we gave permission for the aircraft part to be used as a public bar and restroom, but I think we will let this pass for now."

It was difficult not to judge Hatt as a dreadful pedant, even though he was probably only trying to do his duty.

Even Councillor Brown seemed repulsed by his officiousness. "Nothing wrong with a good party, Hatt. Ease off the old stays; that's what I say. Give that man a break. He was only being hospitable. I did piss on his rhododendrons though. Good for them, you know."

Hatt steered Councillor Brown through the garden gate, where he was momentarily wedged. This was easily remedied, though, by a hefty nudge from the planning officer, which might, in other circumstances, have been considered disrespectful.

As the two tottered away down the drive, Smith was reminded of Laurel and Hardy, whom he had much admired in his youth.

The back garden was thinning out now. And debris from the debauch was strewn in a wide arc around the aircraft fuselage as if it has been vomited out of the forward door aperture. The plates and platters on the garden table were empty, apart from a few crumbs, upon which pigeons were already feasting. And it was obvious that Norman Smith's emergency supplies of alcohol, severely and barbarically depleted, would be in urgent need of replenishment. Some of the garden chairs were upturned, as if their final occupants had simply cast them aside in their rush towards the next round of hedonism.

The neighbours who had effectively gatecrashed the party and hardly spoken a word to their hosts, slinked off in small groups when Mr Smith and Mrs G temporarily left gate duties to start the tidy up. Many did not know the Smiths at all, other than by their reputation as a close-knit unit that generally preferred to keep themselves to themselves. They were still none the wiser and probably more uncertain of the true nature of the Smiths as they left. But at least they had enjoyed themselves and garnered sufficient gossip to last for several months.

Brandon-Lewis did not seem to be in a hurry to leave. He was sitting in a deckchair blowing the seeds off a dandelion head, alternately muttering, "She does. She doesn't."

For the time being, the Smiths chose to ignore him, both aware of the unstated complications surrounding his presence.

In the kitchen, Winterbottom was trying to extract Mantle from a slim aperture where the tea towels and trays were stored. He had apparently become wedged whilst trying to find a drying up cloth. The sink had been filled with hot water and was overflowing with an abundance of suds in preparation for washing the dirty plates, glasses, cups, and cutlery. It was on the brink of overflowing onto the floor. Winterbottom had left the tap running when going to the former squadron leader's assistance.

"Nearly got you, sir. If you could just try to stand lightly front on, I would have more to get hold of," said the pilot trainer, apparently tugging at thin air with his sleeves rolled up.

Unfortunately, Mantle was in an uncooperative mood, as if the public humiliation he had endured from Sir Ollie Booth, the collapse of his romantic pension scheme for financial security, his undoubted imminent firing from the aerodrome, and the ignominy of being wedged sideways in a kitchen cavity in front of one of his troops were all too much for him. Eventually Winterbottom managed to grab him by an epaulette that momentarily took on three-dimensional form and hoist him out of the vice and onto the kitchen floor. At this moment, the Smiths walked in and inadvertently walked all over him, unaware that he was not a floor mat.

"Would you both mind bloody well not walking on top of me like that," Mantle pleaded from a two-dimensional mouth, flattened to the floor tiles.

Mrs G looked down aghast. "I am terribly sorry, Mr Mantle. I did not realise you were there," she said, as if such an explanation would offer any excuse for trampling upon a former member of the armed forces.

Smith managed to peel Mantle off the floor and place him against the fridge-freezer, head-on so he was completely visible. Within a few seconds, he seemed to inflate.

"I will do the washing-up, Mr Smith. It is the least I can do after all the trouble I have caused this afternoon," said Mantle, uncharacteristically contrite. "Winterbottom will assist me."

It did not seem that Winterbottom had any say in the matter, but he was, after all, outranked by Mantle.

"That is very kind of you," said Mrs G. "Norman and I will bring the dirty washing-up in from the garden."

It was not as if Norman Smith had any say in this matter either, seemingly being equally outranked.

As the two aviators began their seamless dish-washing partnership, it was perhaps peculiar that they had so little to say to each other, considering the events of the afternoon. Mantle was apparently in no mood to reveal his inner feelings, and Winterbottom felt that it was not his place to ask about them. It was fortunate that the floor had already been soaked with water and foam because Winterbottom's nervous tic had spread down to his hands, causing him to involuntarily jerk from time to time, showering the floor and work surfaces. Mantle faced these tidal onslaughts side-on, so did not get wet himself.

In the garden, whilst Smith was stacking the chairs and returning the garden furniture to the garage, Mrs G approached Brandon Lewis. "You are still here, I see. Most of the guests have left now," she said. These curt observations came out more harshly than she had intended and certainly failed to convey any trace of encouragement to the love worn suitor.

"Mrs G, I am aware of the situation. I was just hoping that we could find the time for a quick chat before I go. You seem to have been avoiding me all afternoon." There may have been a trace of accusation in Brandon Lewis's voice, but this could probably be excused in view of the way he had been so studiously ignored by Mrs G.

"I have been extremely busy attending to the house guests, Mr Brandon Lewis. Furthermore, I am not at all prepared to engage in any kind of intimacy with a friend of my husband's in such public circumstances."

"Does that mean you might do so in private circumstances, Mrs G?"

"I did not say that, did I?"

"Not exactly, but one could draw that implication from your comment."

"You can draw whatever implications you will. By the way, I think you impressed Mother very much. She has been single for a long time now and could do with some male company."

"I hope you are being humorous, Mrs G. She is a lovely lady but, perhaps, a little old for my taste."

Mrs G watched Norman moving the furniture. As usual, he seemed to be in a world of his own and completely unaware that his wife was talking to a potential suitor.

"I gather that your Indian parts-procurement business has run into a spot of bother. You really shouldn't take it out on Mr Singh."

"But the man is an absolute scoundrel."

"Perhaps you should have thought about that before you started putting air passengers lives at risk with his dud spares."

"How do you know about that, Mrs G?"

"There is very little that I miss, Mr Brando- Lewis. I am also aware that you are having some difficulty completing your report to the board. I expect the two matters are intrinsically linked in some way."

"But I love you, Mrs G."

"Does that excuse everything else?"

"Of course it does, dearest. We all make mistakes, but few of us can offer unconditional adoration to another person."

"Love does not absolve us of integrity. Besides, do you not think that such indiscretions might not make you a slightly less attractive proposition to a lady such as myself?"

"But love is not founded on logic, Mrs G. It is a wild, reckless, and mystical experience."

"Which is why we have to guard ourselves against its excesses and temptations. There are always practical matters to consider."

"Surely you are teasing me, Mrs G. Love is the antithesis of practical considerations. Is that not its enduring charm?"

"Mr Brandon-Lewis. Could it be that you are more in love with 'being in love' than in love with me, whom you hardly know at all?"

"Have you heard of love at first sight? I do not need to know you at all to be infatuated with you."

"I think infatuation is a rather more accurate description of your condition. Infatuation is dangerous and illusory. It usually ends in tears. Love, on the other hand, is a difficult and painful journey that requires sacrifice and persistence."

"I would sacrifice anything for you, Mrs G."

"No you wouldn't"

"I would."

"So would you sacrifice all your wealth and your position in society?"

"Maybe."

"And what about your car?"

"Certainly not."

"In that case, you are playing with me, Mr Brandon-Lewis. I am certainly not prepared to sacrifice my marriage for you. A little hanky-panky once in a while maybe, but don't talk to me about love."

"So how about if we agree to engage in a little hanky-panky?"

"I have decided that, attractive though the concept may seem, such a liaison would not be in my best interests at this time. May I suggest we put the whole venture on hold for the time being?"

"You are a hard-hearted women, Mrs G. But I have no option but to accede to your wishes in the matter. I cannot satisfy my love without you being an active participant in the process, so I will have to think of a different strategy."

"That is a very grounded response, considering that love is the antithesis of practical considerations."

"So be it, Mrs G. Incidentally, the car I was referring to is a 1935 Bentley 3-litre, which I would never part with, under any circumstances."

"Very wise, Mr Brandon-Lewis. It is often preferable to find an inanimate object to peg ones affections onto. There is far less risk of disappointment."

By now, Smith had finished clearing up the garden furniture. He approached Brandon-Lewis and Mrs G with the idle gait of a man with few anxieties. "How are you two lovebirds?" he asked, disturbingly. It was difficult to ascertain whether this was a fleeting attempt at humour or if it had more sinister undertones.

Mrs G scurried towards the kitchen to see how the washing-up was getting on, whilst her husband drew up a deckchair next to Brandon Lewis.

"What a splendid evening," he said. "By the way, you weren't thinking of spending the night here, were you?"

"Oh no. In fact, I am just about to leave. As you can imagine, I am feeling slightly deflated. It is more than likely that I will be forced to take the flack for Singh's incompetence in procuring parts for the airline. My neck will be on the line, I expect. Well, never mind. I can always find something else to do, I suppose. It's not as if I'm short of a bob or two, is it?"

"I have no idea, BL. You have never spoken to me about your personal wealth. Nonetheless, I am glad to hear that you are buoyant on that score."

"Indeed. It is most fortunate. Just one last thing. What did you make of that Godber chap and all the nonsense he was spouting earlier?"

"I am completely at a loss as to why the poor chap expostulated so incontinently. I can only assume some fever of the brain induced his maniacal behaviour. Otherwise, it was inexplicable to me."

"I tend to concur with that assessment, Norman. Nonetheless, there was some coherency in his logic, which struck me briefly. What if we are all just puppets in the drama of our own lives? What if, when all's said and done, none of us really has any control at all about what happens?"

"That line of thought would inevitably lead to examination of determinism and the role of fate. I expect that we have some individual freedom to determine our lives to a certain degree. But, equally, we are all bound by restrictions and circumstances completely beyond our control. This is a hard concept to digest in an era where individualism and self-expression are considered the ultimate goals in life. In short, there is always someone or something pulling our strings, whether we like it or not."

"Most philosophical, Mr Smith. And what do you make of Godber's accusation that it is you who is pulling everyone else's strings?"

"I will leave that for you to consider, BL. Any comment I might make could easily be misinterpreted. Perhaps, though, one should focus on the question of why I would. I have no interest in the lives of most of the people he seems to think I am influencing. In fact, I hardly even know most of them."

"Food for thought, Norman. Food for thought. Now, I will make my farewells to you and Mrs G and be on my way to face whatever fate has in store for me."

"I am very glad you came round this afternoon, BL. It was quite a gathering in the end, wasn't it?"

"I should say so—quite the impromptu party. Next time, however, I think I will warn you beforehand that I am coming. Just in case you have house guests."

"A very sound idea, BL. All the best. And do, please, keep in touch."

"I will Norman. I consider you to be a friend now. There are so many people out there without any humility at all."

Mrs G came back out into the garden wearing a frilly apron, which struck Brandon Lewis as most attractive, in a futile way.

"Mr Brandon-Lewis is just leaving, dear. You are just in time to bid him farewell."

Mrs G kissed Brandon-Lewis on the cheek. "Thank you so much for joining us this afternoon and also for the lovely roses. Norman and I will put them in a vase in the lounge, won't we, dear?"

"Of course. It was a very kind gesture. Few of the other guests thought to bring anything with them, after all."

"It was my pleasure, Mrs G," said Brandon-Lewis, standing up and brushing the crumbs off his trousers. "I hope to see you both again in the not-too-distant future. Goodbye." The company director made a gesture as if doffing his hat, even though he was not wearing one.

It was obvious that he was feeling utterly defeated by the way he dragged his feet and bowed his shoulders as he shuffled through the garden gate, for some reason inducing the emotion of pity in both Norman Smith and Mrs G. Both looked at his wasted and ungainly receding figure with a sadness in their eyes that caused them to well up with tears.

In the kitchen, Mantle and Winterbottom had nearly finished the washing-up. There were just a couple of plates left to dry up, and the rest of the items had been neatly returned to their cupboards, drawers, and shelves.

"Super job, Winterbottom. That's what I call teamwork," said Mantle as he cleaned out the sink with CIF wearing Mrs G's pink marigolds. "You can't beat military precision in matters like this. Get the bloody job done in no time."

"Absolutely, sir. I think we could give the Catering Corps a run for their money."

"They're all poofters, Winterbottom. Nothing like the front-line fighting force to demonstrate efficiency."

"Exactly my sentiments, sir," said Winterbottom, returning the last plate to the cupboard. "I expect we will get a commendation from Mr and Mrs Smith."

At that moment, Norman Smith and Mrs G entered the kitchen through the back door. They had been holding hands but ceased to do so once they realised there were still two guests in the house.

"You two have done a smashing job and saved us a huge amount of work. Thank you," said Mrs G to the two aviators appreciatively and yet predictably.

"Top job, boys," affirmed Smith. "Will you both be pushing along now?"

Winterbottom looked at the host nervously. He was still completely traumatised by the events in the cockpit. To him, Smith had come to represent all his fears and anxieties.

"You will never have another flying lesson with me, will you?" he asked pleadingly.

"Oh that," said Smith, as if suddenly remembering the incident that had started off the whole story in the first place. It seemed so long ago. "Yes. I must apologise to you about that, Mr Winterbottom. I just got a little overexcited. That's all. I didn't mean to cause you any alarm."

"Alarm, Mr Smith? You nearly gave me a bloody heart attack!"

"Well, I am truly sorry. Now you mention it, it was rather stupid of me to try to land the plane single-handed. However, it is funny how things pan out. That incident was, in many ways, the beginning of all the followed. We have all travelled a long way since then."

Mantle stepped forward. "Mr Smith, I hope you realise that your actions nearly closed down my flying school, not to mention giving Winterbottom a nervous breakdown. But, you know, sometimes these things change perspective with time. My own actions have now pretty well certainly lost me the flying school and made Winterbottom redundant, so my misdemeanours have superseded yours many-fold. That is how things often transpire. What is important today is irrelevant tomorrow. I forgive you. After all, I don't think you meant any harm. And what about you, Winterbottom? Can you bring yourself to forgive Mr Smith?"

"This sounds like a soppy closing scene in a Shakespearian comedy when everybody is sickeningly reconciled," said

Winterbottom. "No. I do not forgive him. Why should I? He nearly killed me."

"I completely understand, Mr Winterbottom. Speaking as someone who was nearly killed by a maniac with a spanner earlier today, I can fully appreciate how nigh-on impossible it is to feel forgiveness for someone who has nearly terminated your life," said Smith. "However, the feeling is not reciprocal. Just because I nearly killed you, by accident or through my own stupidity, doesn't mean I bear any ill will towards you. In fact, I admire two things about you above all. Firstly, you are an extremely competent pilot and instructor—two feats I will never achieve. Secondly, you are an excellent dishwasher's assistant."

As was common after Norman Smith had finished talking, there was a short silence whilst the others in the room tried to establish the meaning of his words. Surely the last comment was meant as an insult. If not, it could certainly be interpreted as such. But why would Smith feel the need to be rude to Winterbottom?

Winterbottom was clearly deeply affected. He began to go deep scarlet in the face and start trembling like a furious bull. Then he let out an enormous hoot and then began to laugh hysterically. He laughed so much that tears streamed down his cheeks, and he nearly wet his pants.

"Mr Smith, much as I have tried to keep hating you, I find that I cannot keep up the pretence. Dishwasher's assistant. That's a good one! You are just the most comical little man I have ever met!"

Smith looked somewhat perplexed by this turnaround. He had never considered himself little for a start. Now he was not sure if he was being insulted or complimented.

"Do you find me amusing as a personality, or do you find me a witty person?" he asked.

"All of those things, and much more," choked Winterbottom, holding his belly because of the pain of laughing so much.

Mantle was now guffawing as well, and Mrs G was tittering. Soon, all three were rolling on the kitchen floor in paroxysms of hysterical laughter.

"Yes, he is rather funny, isn't he," said Mantle, between gasps for air. "Now you think about it, he's a bit of a clown."

This comment engendered another bout of hysteria. By now Winterbottom was writhing on the floor tiles in the agonies of hilarity like an eel that had electrocuted itself.

Mrs G laughed so hard through her nose that she let out an enormous snort, which set everybody off again. By now, Smith was also unable to contain himself and was laughing with the rest of them, much in the manner of a lunatic chortling at his own reflection.

Over the next few minutes, the kitchen was overwhelmed by a level of amusement rarely experienced, even at farting competitions. The more they all laughed, the more they all wanted to laugh and so it went on. In fact, none of the participants realised how dangerous such a practice is. It is very hard to breath when experiencing such paroxysms, and it was a wonder none of them succumbed to heart failure.

Mrs G had to crawl along the kitchen floor to the open back door in order to find sufficient oxygen to refill her exhausted lungs, whilst Mantle folded his wafer-thin frame in half to prevent himself from self-expiration. Winterbottom, clearly the worst affected, lay on the floor with his legs in the air, heaving in air as if through an iron lung, whilst Smith sought respite in the downstairs lavatory.

A few minutes later, the hooting had diminished to a series of uncontrolled giggles. And by the time Mrs G had gotten to her unsteady feet, the worst of it was over.

"Oh dear. Oh dear," she said, "I nearly burst the elastic on my pants, it was so funny."

"Yes. Most amusing," croaked Mantle, once again upright, his face ravaged by tears. "For a moment, I thought I was done for."

Norman Smith returned from the restroom looking comparatively restored. He had no doubt had a few calming puffs on his pipe.

"Well, now that we are all reconciled through the medium of hilarity, I expect Mr Mantle and I ought to make our way off the page," said Winterbottom. It was almost impossible to tell if his tic was now induced by trauma or hysteria.

"Yes, Winterbottom. We have work to do," replied the former squadron leader, at last trying to re-establish a vestige of dignity.

The Smiths escorted their final guests to the front door, waving them off as if they were long-standing friends. They were not remotely surprised when Winterbottom posted Mantle out through the letterbox, as if this was the pair's final party trick.

# EPILOGUE

## 1.

The next morning, Norman Smith and Mrs G slept in late, exhausted from hosting such a long and eventful impromptu gathering. Smith woke first and, for the first time in weeks, did not even consider his flight simulator. Instead, he tiptoed downstairs to make a cup of tea for his wife and pondered the events of the previous day. It had not been so bad after all. In fact, he felt that most people had acquitted themselves reasonably well, even if he did not know them intimately. His anger towards Godber had metamorphosed to pity overnight, which was unsurprising, in that Smith rarely felt animosity towards his fellow beings, and when he did, it was invariably temporary.

When he returned to the bedroom with the tea, Mrs G was sitting up on the pillows removing cucumber slices from her eyelids.

"What a party we had yesterday, Norman. I didn't know you had so many friends, " she said.

"I don't really, dear. Most of the visitors were mere acquaintances."

"Does that apply to Mother as well?"

"No. She is just an old dragon."

"We might be getting a pet dragon living in the house soon."

"I forgot about that appalling proposition."

"At least you could see her more often."

"How lovely."

"Norman?"

"I've been thinking—"

"Careful, dear. We don't want you slipping into another migraine."

"No, seriously. I lay awake last night and came to a strange conclusion."

"And what was that?"

"Well I was thinking about how, ever since you took up this flight simulator hobby of yours, everyone around you has had to pay a high price."

"I have never asked anyone for money, dear. You know I wouldn't do that."

"No. I did not mean a financial price. I meant a psychological price."

"Well I am feeling quite balanced."

"That's the whole point, Norman. You seem to carry on in your own little bubble, pursuing your hobby, without realising the impact of your actions, which have created mayhem all around you."

"Mayhem?"

"Yes. Mayhem."

"What do you mean by that?"

"Well, let's look at a few of the people you have encountered on your adventures. To start with, you clearly caused Mr Winterbottom to have a complete nervous breakdown because of your behaviour in the cockpit under his tutelage. The poor man is a nervous wreck."

"I think that might be a bit of an exaggeration. He was obviously of a nervous disposition long before we met."

"Really?"

"Maybe."

"Then there is Mr Mantle whose flying school you nearly closed down and who has now been exposed as an adulterer and probably lost his job—not to mention how two-dimensional he has become."

"Yes, poor chap. Nonetheless, I would argue he was the architect of his own downfall. I cannot take responsibility for his philandering."

"No. Yet is it strange that his fall from grace only occurred once you had started messing around with aircraft."

"Coincidence."

"Maybe. Then there is poor Mother, who was perfectly well until you made me go to India and leave her before nearly burning the care home down and making such a frightful fuss that she is still embarrassed about you in front of Matron."

"I did not make you go to India. You wanted to go more than I did. And let's face it, we weren't there for very long."

"Then there is Mr Singh. It seems that, without your interference, his company would never have been rumbled for dealing in substandard parts. He is probably ruined too, and I expect he has a large family to support."

"He is simply a rogue. He would have been rumbled sooner or later."

"Be quiet, Norman. I am trying to explain a point, and you keep interrupting me with feeble excuses."

"No, I don't. I am simply commenting on the inaccuracy of your facts."

"Well I would appreciate if you would keep your comments to yourself until I have finished."

"As you wish, dearest."

Norman Smith was, by now, lying down on the bed next to his wife, staring at the ceiling. As usual, it was impossible to know what was going on in his head—possibly nothing at all.

"Now, let us turn to Mr Brandon Lewis. After introducing you to Mr Singh and his Aladdin's cave, it all seems to have gone wrong for him, doesn't it, Norman?"

Norman lay there silently contemplating.

"Norman? Are you going to answer me or not?"

"I would not want to interrupt you."

"But I asked you a specific question. You are expected to answer it."

"I was only doing what I was told."

"Do you concede that Mr Brandon Lewis has landed himself in a bit of bother over the aircraft parts he has sourced for Albion Airways?"

"I do."

"You haven't said that to me since our wedding day, Norman."

"If I may interrupt for a moment, dearest. I would like to add a footnote to the discussion about Mr Brandon Lewis's woes. Not only does he seem to have made a basic business error, but he also seems to have made a romantic one as well."

"What on earth do you mean, Norman?" said Mrs G, attending unnecessarily to her fingernails.

"I was simply referring to all the attention has been paying to you—the flowers and the poems he sent to you and so on."

"Norman. How on earth do you know about the poems?"

"I read them. They were absolute rubbish from a literary perspective and sickeningly soppy."

Mrs G pulled the duvet over her shoulders, as if to hide a little in the bed. "You don't think I was encouraging him do you, Norman?"

"I did have my doubts at first, but the way you dispatched him so clinically yesterday was most reassuring."

"Thank you, Norman. To be honest, he was becoming a bit of a pest, and you know how I abhor vermin of any kind. It was merely that his attentions tickled my sense of flirtatiousness. I would never have taken it forward. You know that, don't you, Norman?"

"I am much inclined to believe you, dear. But in some senses, you were probably playing with fire a little."

"There's not much fire in that man's trousers. He seems a little bit too earnest for that sort of pyrotechnic display."

"I'm not sure I understand you, dear. I am assuming this is conjecture, and you are not personally familiar with the contents of his trousers."

"Of course, dear. Pure conjecture, mixed with feminine intuition."

"Anyway, he seems to have a broken heart as well as a broken reputation."

"Poor man."

"Actually, I think he is rather rich. I thought that might have been one of his attractions."

"Who do you take me for, Norman, a cheap tart?"

"Of course not, dear. You are the very antithesis of a cheap tart. Nonetheless, I believe that male wealth can be a big draw in the mating game, much as big boobs can be on the other side of the equation."

"Sometimes you are so vulgar, Norman. Besides, I am reasonably well endowed on that front, and you have sufficient funds for my humble needs."

"Then we are a perfect pair."

"Now, if I may continue. Let's look at some other minor casualties of your hobby. How about Captain Dodwell and First Officer Craig, both of whom seem to have lost their careers as airline pilots since you invaded their flight deck, relegated to humble ambulance crew, perhaps? Most disheartening. And then there is Matron. Since your arson attack, she has become visibly more cylindrical."

"You cannot get *more* cylindrical. It is an absolute state. You are either cylindrical or you are not. It's as simple as that."

"Well then, her chin has gotten more pointed and her mouth smaller."

"Perhaps, but that may just be due to natural ageing."

"You are interrupting with meaningless excuses again, Norman."

"Sorry, dear."

And what about Sir Ollie? He has been publically cuckolded."

"I am sorry, dear, but that has absolutely nothing to do with me. I do not know either his wife or her lover, Mr Mantle."

"But could it be that, because you put the whole future of the flying school at jeopardy with your antics, Mantle felt so financially insecure that he decided to seek out a wealthy partner to support him?"

"I will not deign to answer that. It is not really a proper question anyway."

"So you see, Norman. Whichever way you look at it, either directly or by the law of unintended consequences, the pursuit of your little hobby has left in its wake a trail of personal misery and disaster."

"Do you not think that summation is a trifle harsh, dear?"

"I was only letting you know what I was thinking during the night. That's all."

"I see."

"Do you?"

"Normally, anyway. Unless I have my eyes closed. By the way, do you prefer me to be naked or wearing pyjamas in bed?"

"What a funny question to ask at this moment."

"Why?"

"Because we were talking about something completely different."

"Oh. I thought *that* conversation had ended. Anyway, what do you like best?"

"I think I prefer you in your pyjamas, Norman, except under special circumstances. I prefer a modicum of decency, even in the bedroom."

"As you wish, dear. In fact, I am rather glad you said that, because I can get quite itchy and irritable when I am naked in bed."

"You stick to your usual night-time attire, dear. It is too late to change long-held habits at your age."

After this rather incomprehensible diversion, Mrs G and Norman both lay side by side looking silently at the white ceiling as if it would reveal some unexpected revelation about the meaning of life. The fact that there was no Artex or coving meant that the eye was not attracted to any particular features of interest in the vast desert of whiteness above them. This dislocation of focus produced a sense of infinite possibility in the minds of the two protagonists.

"Dearest?" said Norman, breaking the silence after about ten minutes.

"Yes, Norman?"

"I have decided to give up my air simulator hobby."

"Have you, dear? I somehow though you might."

"Yes. There is clearly far too much collateral damage associated with such a complex exercise. Besides, I am not very good at soldering wires together."

"Very sensible, Norman."

"Instead, I am going to make the fuselage into a luxury summer house by knocking through the forward bulkhead and inserting bifold doors."

"How lovely. Will there be comfy seats and settees in there?"

"I think that would be most appropriate."

"Because I found that straw rather uncomfortable if I am totally honest."

"Yes, I know what you mean. I had straw burns on my buttocks for days afterwards."

The couple fell back into mutual silence as the sun slowly climbed higher in the sky outside.

"Norman?" said Mrs Smith dreamily.

"Yes, dearest."

"I hope the conversion of the fuselage into a summer house will not require planning permission."

"So do I, dear. Those planning inspectors can be most persistent, but I think they will welcome the change of use that I have in mind."


## 2.

Mrs G arrived at her monthly book group meeting slightly late. It was being held at her friend Gloria Wood's house in Reigate, and the other members of the group had already arrived. She did not know the other members particularly well, though naturally stopped on the street for a quick chat if she happened to bump into any of them, even if they were not in her elite social circle.

"Good evening, Mrs G," said the hostess, offering her a glass of wine and an enormous piece of homemade Victoria sponge. "We were just about to start discussing this month's book. I trust you have read it?"

"Yes indeed, Gloria. I have."

The choice of book had been a matter of contention at the previous meeting. But, as per club rules, it was for the host to make the final decision, and Gloria had chosen a rather obscure novel called *Norman Smith's Hobbies*. It was an unusual choice, lacking the customary popularity of books analysed by the group, especially so as the author was completely unknown. Mrs G was amused to find that the title of the book included the name of her husband, which added to her interest. Of course, Norman Smith was an extremely common name so it wasn't that much of a revelation, even if the other members of the club found some amusement in the coincidence.

"Perfect. Shall we start off with the first question then?" continued Gloria. Unfortunately, it appeared that Mrs G has missed the usual amusing preamble of light conversation and the group was apparently getting down to business immediately.

"Do you think that the author is trying to make sexist generalisations about middle-aged women in the novel. If so, why would he do this?"

A rather sharp-featured woman called Rita was the first to contribute. "In my opinion, the book is very much written from a male perspective. I don't know about you, ladies, but I was utterly bored by all the details about aircraft and aviation. It is just not the sort of thing that would appeal to women particularly. In view of this, it did not surprise me that the author portrayed the female point of view rather condescendingly and predictably. It is as if all we do is attend to domestic matters and flutter our eyelids. The hero's wife was particularly poorly served by the author's interpretation of how a woman would react to such circumstances."

Gloria was slightly less dismissive, possibly because she had chosen the book in the first place. "There is indeed some truth in what you say, Rita. Nonetheless, I think the author was trying to portray the contrasts between the male and female perspective on things in an amusing light, rather than an earnest one. Remember, some of the male characters do not come across particularly empathetically either. There are stereotypical attitudes and behaviours described for both of the sexes. Perhaps it is just that the author has a poor understanding of human nature and that the sexist generalisations were accidental rather than deliberate."

Janet from Redhill was a little less forgiving. "If what you say is true, Daphne, that would indicate that the author is inept. If his writing has accidental overtones that he is unaware of, then he should not be publishing books at all. As for the portrayal of women being amusing, I am afraid he has failed to convey this to me. I did not titter even once!"

"Women obviously still have a long way to go in the struggle for equal and fair representation in literature," opined Gloria, already on her third slice of cake. "I was appalled by some of the offhand comments directed at females in the book. You cannot hide sexism behind supposed humour. What do you think, Mrs G?"

Mrs G had read the book with moderate interest. It was clearly without much merit from a literary perspective and completely unrelated to real life. To be honest, she found it rather hard to relate to but did at least find parts mildly amusing. "In my view, it would be wrong to read any deliberate sexism into his book," she said. "It is so devoid of any reality that it would be ridiculous to take any of it that seriously. I did, however find the caricature of Mr Singh, the

Indian businessman, distastefully racist. As if, simply by being Indian, he was naturally an unscrupulous businessman. For goodness' sakes, whatever happened to respect?"

Most of the other women seemed to accept this analysis, perhaps realising they had taken gender analysis of the book too earnestly and failed to notice its racist flaws. This did not, however, completely negate the clear irritation that some of the perceived sexism in the text had generated among some of them.

"Let's go to question two," said Gloria, passing round the Chablis. "Why do you think the author allows the characters in his book to interfere with the plot? Or is this interference the main purpose of the book?"

Rita was first off the blocks on this one. "Frankly, I found the interruptions from the characters completely ridiculous. You can't write a plot with characters and then destroy the illusion completely by pretending that they can then talk to the author in their own right. For me, this was the undoing of the whole book, not its purpose. For goodness' sakes, there is a limit to the reader's patience."

Janet was much of the same opinion. "I think the author was just trying to be too clever. He probably realised that the hobby plot wasn't really going anywhere, so he decided to distort it into something else. For me, it didn't really work at all. As for the scene where DI Godber tries to accuse Norman Smith of being the author, well that was just bonkers in my opinion. I lost the plot completely after that."

Mrs G offered, "I must admit it was all rather confusing. The story seemed to get more far-fetched with every chapter. If the interference of the characters was the main purpose of the book, what on earth was the point? Perhaps it was some literary experiment that backfired."

Daphne put down her plate on the side table and said, "The thing about a book like that is that you can never empathise with any of the characters properly. They are so unlike anything one might experience in everyday life, it is hard to relate to them at all, whether or not they interfere with the plot. By the way, Rita, is that a new cardigan you are wearing? I do like the colour."

"Actually, it is Daphne. I got it from a little boutique I go to in Westerham. It is 100 per cent cashmere wool."

Janet was less impressed. "I prefer to shop at Marks & Spencer," she said categorically.

"M&S is all very well for underwear, but I think their fashion lines are very limited," interjected Gloria.

A discussion on the comparative merits of various female clothing retailers inevitably commenced. It was rare at book group meetings for discussion on the book to last for more than two questions, or one glass of wine, especially when it has been poorly received. Mrs G was happy to turn her mind to discussions on other more interesting topics. After all, human interaction is always more entertaining than fiction.

Lightning Source UK Ltd.
Milton Keynes UK
UKHW011229271119
354326UK00001B/29/P